DEAD
WRONG

DEAD WRONG

A NOVEL

CLAIR M. POULSON

Covenant Communications, Inc.

Cover image *Violence* © Roc Canals Photography

Cover design copyrighted 2009 by Covenant Communications, Inc.

Published by Covenant Communications, Inc.
American Fork, Utah

Printed in The United States of America
First Printing: September 2009

16 15 14 13 12 11 10 09   10 9 8 7 6 5 4 3 2 1

ISBN-13: 978-1-59811-812-4
ISBN-10: 1-59811-812-9

To the men and women of law enforcement and the courts who have helped shape who I am and who have provided much of the inspiration for my stories.

PROLOGUE

"YOU DID WHAT, KAITLYN?" Kelvin demanded. "Have you lost what few brains you had?"

Kaitlyn turned away from him and from her mother and stepfather. The news that she'd joined the LDS Church apparently didn't sit well with any of them, especially her stepbrother. Of course, it didn't surprise her, but she had hoped . . . For a moment she fought back the tears that threatened to trickle down her face. Then Kelvin moved closer to her and thrust his head forward, a menacing sneer on his face. "Well?" he snarled.

She looked up and faced her stepbrother again. "I joined The Church of Jesus Christ of Latter-day Saints, Kelvin. I've been considering it for quite a few months now. I feel really good about it. I know I've done the right thing."

"You mean the Mormon Church, don't you?"

"That's just a nickname," she explained.

"You stupid girl," he said, shaking both fists and his head. "First that feeble-minded idea you had about barrel racing in rodeos and now this. It shows how immature and naive you are. You've been brainwashed, and you aren't even smart enough to know it."

"I made this decision on my own," she insisted. "And I am not immature. I'm almost nineteen. I've been to college for a year, and I have very good grades."

"You're an idiot," he said hotly. "You better renounce that cult you've joined. Or, better yet, I'll help you do it."

"It's not a cult. And I'll never denounce it. My decision makes me happy. I just wish my family could be happy for me," she said, choking on her last words. She was determined not to let the tears flow.

"You're a disgrace, Kaitlyn. You've brought shame on all of us. What will our friends think? How do we tell them what you've done this time?"

"You don't have to tell anyone. I didn't have to tell you. I only did it because I happen to love you, all of you," she said, still fighting to control her emotions. *Not that Kelvin didn't bring shame on the family,* she thought.

"They'll find out, and they'll laugh at me," he said. "And that makes me mad. As far as I'm concerned, unless you renounce your so-called new religion, I no longer have a sister. Not that you were ever really my sister."

"I'm sorry you feel that way," she said sadly. Then she faced her mother and stepfather, who so far had said nothing. "Do both of you feel the same as Kelvin?" she asked.

"You bet we do," her stepfather snapped. "You're no longer welcome in this house."

Kaitlyn looked at her mother. Her eyes were downcast and her face red. She was far from convinced that her mother shared her husband's and stepson's feelings. Ever since Kelvin was a young teenager, her mother had been intimidated by the two men. She would never have the courage to say so even if she did disagree with them. Kaitlyn turned away again, and this time she left the house.

Moments later, after she reached her pickup, the well-fought tears erupted. For several minutes she leaned forward on her steering wheel and sobbed. Finally, she pulled herself together and slipped the key into the ignition.

She had nothing to take with her. Everything she owned had been removed from the house over a year ago, following the flap that occurred when she'd announced that she was going to start barrel racing. Despite the anger shown toward her for becoming a *cowgirl,* as her stepfather and stepbrother often disparagingly called her, she'd come to visit often. It appeared that even that would have to stop now. She pulled down the visor and flipped open the little mirror there. She wiped the tears from her face, straightened her hair, studied her blue eyes, and then forced her mouth into a smile, reminding herself that she was happy about the decision she had made.

Someone tapped on the window. As Kaitlyn turned, she found herself looking straight into Kelvin's smoldering eyes. She was tempted just to drive away. She was certain he had nothing good to say to her. But that was behavior contrary to everything Kaitlyn had been taught. She had to give him the benefit of the doubt, despite his harsh words just moments ago. She lowered the window. "What do you need, Kelvin?"

"I just wanted to remind you that despite what Dad and I just said, we are all family."

"Thank you, Kelvin," she responded, surprised but suspicious. She had learned long ago that whenever he tried to act politely—to be "warm and fuzzy"—he wanted something. She'd also learned to pay more attention to his expression than to his words. His face was definitely an open book.

He went on, his smoldering eyes seeming to catch fire. "And since we are—family, that is—I thought you and I should talk about that trust fund your father left. By rights, as your brother, half of it is mine."

Kaitlyn almost exploded. Her father had been a wealthy young man. Kelvin and his dad had stepped into a lot of money when the two small families were joined together. And they had blown it on everything imaginable, leaving her mother destitute.

For many years they hadn't known about the money that had been placed in a trust for her when she turned twenty-one. The only reason they learned about it was because of how desperate her mother had become. One day she'd said to Kaitlyn, "We don't need to be so poor, especially when there's your trust. We could use some of the money from it."

"But I can't even get to it until I'm twenty-one. Don't you remember? You told me that when Dad realized he was probably going to die, he set the trust up so that it couldn't be touched until I was of age."

"That's true, but I bet a good lawyer could probably help out there. There must be a way to get around all the restrictions."

Kaitlyn was a toddler at the time the trust was established, and it had grown to be quite sizeable. Even as a young teenager she was wise enough not to agree with her mother's proposal. She knew that she and her mother would not enjoy the benefits of the money if the trust were somehow accessed early. Kelvin and her stepfather would find a way to weasel it out of her mother's hands.

Unfortunately, Kelvin had overheard the conversation between Kaitlyn and her mother, and ever since then he and his father had made plans for the money. She wasn't sure what kinds of schemes they had tried, but they soon learned that the inheritance couldn't be accessed until her twenty-first birthday. Kelvin had apparently forgotten that a few moments ago when he had so hastily disowned her. *But now he remembered.*

"You know, Kelvin, I'd thought about sharing it when the time came, but after what has happened, I don't think so. You have no right to any of it."

"I think I do, Kaitlyn, but even if I don't, your mother does."

"That isn't true, either, but I would share with her if she were to remember that I'm her daughter. However, I expect that you guys would take it all from her and spend it, just like you did the money my dad left for her. I'm sorry, but you can forget about my trust account. You want me out of your lives, and that is exactly where I'll be," she said.

"In a pig's eye," Kelvin said menacingly. "I'll get what's mine, and don't you ever think I won't. You haven't heard the last of this."

She turned her face away from him and rolled up the window. He was still pounding on it and cursing as she pulled away from the curb. She looked back one last time and caught a last glimpse of the home she'd grown up in, her stepbrother still standing in front of it, gesturing offensively with both hands. She resolutely drove away.

Kaitlyn decided against going straight to her apartment. Instead, she went to the stables on the outskirts of the city, where she kept her new horse. He'd only recently been broken, and she'd been working with him almost every evening, teaching him to barrel race.

She'd spent every penny she could save from her part-time job to buy him. She never regretted the sacrifice. She had quickly grown fond of him—a small, shiny sorrel gelding with an even temperament. She called him Tony B, short for the name that appeared on his registration papers, Antonio Blaze. He had a uniform, wide white blaze from just above his eyes all the way down his face and over his nose. The woman she'd bought him from had named him for the blaze and her late husband, Antonio.

She spent a couple of hours with Tony B that evening before driving to her apartment. Being with him helped ease the pain of parting from home. He was the best friend she had.

* * *

Two weeks later, after having waited and hoped for at least a phone call or a letter from her mother, Kaitlyn finally drove by the house early one afternoon. She hoped Kelvin and his father wouldn't be home so she could visit with her mother. If at all possible, she wanted to repair the rift in their relationship. But to her dismay, there was a Realtor's sign on the front lawn. She knocked on the door but received no answer. She tried the doorknob, but the house was locked. She peered in the living room window. *The room was bare.*

"Kaitlyn," the familiar voice of the next-door neighbor called from across the white vinyl fence that separated the two yards.

"Hi, Mrs. Jameston," she called back and walked toward the kind woman. She looked over the fence at the woman's round, friendly face. "Do you know where my folks are?"

"They just moved out yesterday," Mrs. Jameston replied.

"Do you know where they moved to? They didn't say a word to me."

"I know that, dear. It's that brother of yours. I hate to speak badly of anyone, but he's not a good man," Mrs. Jameston replied. "And I think he's destroyed what little good there was in your father—stepfather."

Kaitlyn nodded in agreement. "Did my mother happen to mention where they were going?"

"She tried, but Kelvin stopped her. He said that I might tell you and that you had no business knowing what they were doing or where they were going. Kaitlyn, your poor mother is a broken woman, thanks to that boy, but I know she still loves you, dear."

Kaitlyn knew Mrs. Jameston spoke the truth, about both her mother and her stepbrother. Kelvin had the wrong kinds of friends. She knew he'd long been into drugs, but she had no idea what else he might have done. She honestly didn't want to know. Five years her senior, Kelvin had been the one she'd looked up to from as early as she could remember. Her widowed mother had married Kelvin's father when Kaitlyn was only four. For the first few years, he'd seemed like a real brother to her. She wished those early memories were the only ones she had of him. Unfortunately, they were not.

As for her mother, she prayed they would meet again. If she could, she'd make things better for her. Kaitlyn truly loved her mother.

CHAPTER 1

Three years later

THE CROWD IN THE STANDS cheered as a young cowgirl urged her horse to greater speed after coming around the last barrel. As the rider hunched forward over the horse, working her quirt feverishly, her horse responded by giving its best. Kaitlyn Glenn was up next. She knew the time she had to beat, and it was a fast one. She also knew the capability of her horse. The sturdy sorrel gelding under her was throwing his head and stamping his feet, anxious for his turn at the barrels. Tony B loved to run.

Kaitlyn glanced nervously toward the stands. She wasn't nervous over the race she was about to run. She had confidence in her horse and in her own ability as a rider. But she was nervous over who might be in those stands casting a possessive eye on her.

She thrust her worried thoughts of Jace Landry from her mind and concentrated on the ride she was about to make. Calmness settled over her like a down comforter. Her horse sensed it, and he too settled down. Kaitlyn took a deep breath, and then they were off. After rounding the first barrel, she felt confident that she was going to have a fast time. She leaned lower in the saddle and let Tony B do the work. It was her job to ride smoothly, making it easy for him to turn rapidly. She didn't need a quirt to get him to perform. He did it for the sheer joy of running.

As she brought the horse to a stop after streaking across the finish line, she could hear the announcer calling out her time. They'd done it. She and Tony B had beaten the previous best time of the night. And there was only one more rider to go. Kaitlyn had a great chance of winning.

Her time held up. She won. It wasn't the first time. Kaitlyn, at twenty-two years old, was a seasoned barrel racer, and though she'd won many times before, each victory brought with it the same thrill and adrenaline rush as the previous one. She fondly patted Tony B's neck. She loved this sport.

The stirring in the pit of her stomach began again when the announcer asked her to come back into the arena to take a victory lap. She forced a smile and looked into the stands again. It seemed unlikely that she could actually pick out a specific face in the throng of fans that had come out for the rodeo. She hadn't spoken to Jace in days, and she hoped he hadn't figured out where she was riding tonight. But she had a sinking feeling that he was up there in the stands. She'd talked to her former roommate just a few days ago, and she'd warned Kaitlyn that Jace had sworn to find her.

Two-thirds of the way around the arena, her eyes met those of a young man in a black cowboy hat and bright blue Western shirt. He was sitting just a couple of rows back, next to a bored-looking but attractive blond. He smiled at Kaitlyn as their eyes held for a moment, and she smiled back. Then she let her eyes drift to the crowd above him. She gasped.

Jace was there! He was grinning broadly and waving a cowboy hat. She'd never known Jace to wear one before. Fear swept over her. She intentionally looked away from him. Her eyes again caught those of the young man in the black hat. He was still smiling and lifted a hand in greeting. She tried to smile at him again but found it impossible. The smile fell from his face and his hand froze in midair. Then she tore her eyes away from him and looked ahead, not even glancing at the crowd again. The seconds seemed like minutes before she reached the gate and rode through. She jumped off her horse, whipped off her hat, and wiped the sweat from her face.

He doesn't know where I'm parked, she told herself, trying desperately to calm down. *I can load Tony B and drive out of here before he finds me.* She wished she could leave that instant, but that wasn't possible, not if she wanted the money she'd won and, more importantly, if she wanted to stay in good standing with the rodeo association.

As the evening wore on, it seemed like forever before the winners of the night's events were officially announced. Fifteen long minutes later Kaitlyn collected her winnings and headed for her truck and horse trailer, feeling not only alone but vulnerable. The excitement of her victory was gone. Apprehension had taken its place.

* * *

Brock Hankins watched as the cowgirl they called Kaitlyn vanished through the far gate on her beautiful horse. Brock had an eye for horses, and Kaitlyn was riding a good one. And the horse wasn't the only capable one—Kaitlyn was an excellent rider. She'd looked right into his eyes as she rode near his seat. He'd smiled at her and she'd smiled back. It had been a smile and a young woman not easily forgotten.

After her eyes left his, she'd looked above and behind him in the stands. Then, when her eyes briefly met his again, he had been shocked. If ever he'd seen paralyzing fear in someone's eyes, it had been in hers at that moment. Something had frightened her badly in the few seconds between the times their eyes had met. Even now, as the rodeo ended, he couldn't erase her panic-stricken face from his mind. She was talented, she was appealing, *and she was terrified.*

The young woman Brock had brought as his date to the rodeo touched his arm, and he turned his attention to her. "It's finally over, isn't it?" she asked.

"Yeah, that's it, Jodi," he said, still thinking of the cowgirl and wondering what or whom she'd seen in the stands above him that had caused her to suddenly become filled with terror.

"So, can we go now?" Jodi asked, tugging at his arm.

"Oh, yeah, sure, we can go." Brock stopped himself from asking if she'd enjoyed the rodeo. It was obvious that she'd been bored all evening. He'd never dated Jodi before, and he had a feeling he might not be taking her out again, even if he asked her. It seemed they shared little common ground. At the very least, she didn't like rodeos.

"Good," she said, confirming his impressions. "Now what?"

Brock stood up, shrugging as he did. "Maybe we could go somewhere and get something to eat," he suggested. "You name the place."

"Great, I know just the restaurant," she responded with the first enthusiasm she'd shown since arriving at the rodeo grounds that evening. "But I've got to warn you—it is a bit pricey."

"That's okay. Just tell me where to go," he responded, forcing a smile as Jodi worked her arm through his and leaned close to him. She didn't seem angry with him now. *Maybe I can still salvage this date,* he thought.

Brock had met Jodi at a regional young singles dance a couple of weeks earlier. She'd seemed fun and was very attractive. She'd responded with a quick affirmative when he'd asked her out. He hadn't mentioned what they'd be doing, and she hadn't inquired. That had apparently been a mistake.

Her face had wrinkled into a cute little frown when he told her about the rodeo as they pulled away from her home earlier that evening. She'd tried to cover it over rather quickly, but he suspected then that he'd asked the wrong girl to accompany him to one of his favorite forms of entertainment. He'd tried to spark her interest, telling her that one of his former missionary companions, Dan Burke, was roping that night. Of course, Jodi had never met Dan, and when he didn't win, she wasn't all that impressed that Burke knew one of the contestants. He'd have to call Dan later, he thought, and give him a hard time. Tell him that he'd told his date about him and that it hadn't helped the evening go well at all.

In the meantime, he didn't want the night to be a total disaster for Jodi. Maybe he could still salvage the date with an expensive dinner, he thought as he guided her through the crowd. Perhaps letting her choose the place to eat would help. He didn't want the evening to be a complete washout for him either. Another date at a different venue might prove fun for both of them.

They merged with the crowd, and Brock thought again of the barrel racer, Kaitlyn Glenn. And he wished he could meet her and say or do something to erase the fear he'd seen in her eyes. It had seemed to him that she was almost pleading for help.

* * *

Kaitlyn hurried her horse along, wanting to get him loaded as quickly as possible and leave. She didn't know where she would spend the night, but it wouldn't be in Cheyenne. *Wyoming's a big state,* she thought. *I need to get away from Jace again.*

She rode up to the trailer, dismounted, opened the door, and led Tony B inside without even removing the saddle. That would have to wait until later, maybe up the road a ways. She tied him securely at the front of the trailer and stepped out.

"Were you going to leave without even saying hi?"

Kaitlyn nearly stumbled. Jace was leaning against the trailer next to hers, leering at her under the faint light of a nearby street lamp. She looked around in alarm. Others should be getting to their trailers any moment now. She'd be safe with others around. *Where is everyone?*

Jace moved lazily toward her now, looking both strange and frightening in his new felt hat. She shut the door to her horse trailer and faced him. How she wished she'd never met the man, let alone agreed to go out with him that first time. He'd seemed like a decent guy, just overly persistent. How wrong she'd been. He was frightening—and he was dangerous.

"You looked great out there tonight, Kaitlyn. You're unbelievably pretty in your cowgirl clothes," he said. "Course, you're pretty whatever you're wearing."

"Thanks, Jace, but I've got to go now," she said as she began to back alongside her trailer toward her truck. Jace followed her. "Hey, we need to talk. You can't just run away from me like this," he said in a low, menacing voice, one not intended to be overheard.

"Jace, it won't work," she said, purposefully speaking loudly, hoping someone would hear her. "We have nothing in common."

He was not the kind of man she could ever marry. The thought of living with him was repulsive. Not that he wasn't handsome and rich and well-connected—things that a lot of women would want. But she wasn't interested in that kind of man. She never had been, even before she'd joined the Church. Now, marrying someone like Jace was unthinkable. She should never have agreed to go out with him. She'd only given in to his persistent invitations for a date because her roommate had repeatedly told her she was being rude. She wished now that she had continued being rude.

"Oh, but it will work, Kaitlyn," he said with a wicked grin. "You are *my* girl. No one else is going to have you."

His words struck fear in her heart, as did the chilling look in his eyes when he uttered them.

* * *

"Why are we going this way?" Jodi asked after Brock had steered her out of the crowd that was pushing toward the parking lot. "You didn't park with all these trucks and horse trailers."

"That's true," he said. "But there aren't as many people pushing and shoving through here. It might be faster."

"There's almost nobody," she said. "These must belong to the rodeo cowboys. I don't see how going out of the way like this will make it any faster for us."

"Trust me," he told her. "I know what I'm doing."

I'm searching for Kaitlyn Glenn, that's what I'm doing, he thought. It didn't seem like the most appropriate thing to tell Jodi, however. He was quite sure she hadn't seen the look of desperation in Kaitlyn's eyes. But he had, and he needed to know that she was okay. That last terrified look she'd given him had seemed like a plea for help. The least he could do was see that she was safe from whatever or whoever had frightened her.

"Okay, then I guess we'll go this way, but I'm getting hungry," Jodi said before lapsing into a stony silence as they started down a row of parked trucks with horse trailers attached to them.

Some of the horse trailers they passed had horses in them. Some had rodeo participants unsaddling their horses beside them. Others were still empty. Some of the trucks were pulling out. It was all a familiar scene to Brock. He'd spent his life with horses, around the rodeo circuit. He loved horses, and he loved the cowboy life. That might have been part of what had attracted him in some strange way to the young woman the announcer had called "Kaitlyn Glenn from the state of California."

They came to the last row of horse trailers and, even though Brock had woven his way around them, he'd seen nothing of the girl or her sorrel horse. Although he tried to tell himself that it was ridiculous to think that he'd actually see Kaitlyn, he knew he would never feel at ease if he didn't try. Several trucks and trailers on the last row were unattended. As he started across the lane to them, he saw a man about fifty feet away, near the front of a truck three spaces to Brock's left.

Instinctively, he turned that direction. Jodi was dragging on his arm, but he pulled her along. The man he'd seen didn't move except to hunch over. It appeared that he was watching something beyond them. He wondered what the guy was doing. A moment later Brock heard something that made him stop and listen, taking his mind from the man they'd just passed.

* * *

"Kaitlyn, I'm going with you, and you are going to like it," Jace thundered. "I came by taxi because I knew you'd be able to take us home from here."

She couldn't believe what he was saying. There was no way she was taking him anyplace, least of all to his home in Des Moines, Iowa. Anger partially displaced her terror now.

"Jace," she said firmly, trying to hide the panic and fear in her voice, "I'm not taking you anywhere. Just leave me alone. I never want to see you again. You have no place in my life."

Unexpectedly, Jace struck her in the face with the open palm of his hand. It happened so quickly that Kaitlyn didn't see it coming. Her white felt hat flew off, and she stumbled back against the driver's door of her truck. She was stunned and only vaguely aware of what happened next. One moment Jace was standing there glaring at her as she struggled to stay on her feet. The next moment someone barreled into him, sending him flying through the air.

Jace landed unceremoniously with a thud on the pavement in front of Kaitlyn's truck. He lay there for a moment while she leaned helplessly against her door. Then, as her senses cleared, she realized that Jace was slowly getting to his feet. "You are going to die," he said with such venom that it was like being struck again. "I've killed before, and I'll do it again."

It was only a split second before she realized that she was not the one on the receiving end of Jace's wrath. It was someone else. And that someone, a man with his black cowboy hat now askew, was charging straight toward Jace, arms outstretched in front of him. Jace went down again, harder this time, landing on and smashing his new hat. This time he stayed down, momentarily unconscious. Her rescuer turned toward her as he straightened his hat. "Are you all right, Kaitlyn?" he asked.

"I think so—thanks to you," she said as she rubbed her face where Jace had struck her. "I've got to go now. He'll be after me again, and I can't let him find me again. And he'll be after you, too."

"I have a cell phone. I'll call the cops," Brock said.

"No! Don't. It'll only make things worse. You need to go now, both of you. He's dangerous," Kaitlyn said. "I can get away okay." She prayed that was true.

"Okay, if you're sure you'll be all right."

"I'll be fine. Thanks for helping. But be careful."

"By the way, I'm—" her benefactor began.

"Don't tell me!" Kaitlyn interrupted anxiously. "It might be dangerous for you if I know who you are. And he might wake up and hear you. It'll definitely be dangerous for you if he knows your name. We've all got to get away from him right now." Kaitlyn pulled her truck key from the front pocket of her jeans. Then she glanced at Jace just long enough to be sure he was still on the ground. Reassured, she unlocked the door with shaking hands.

The young man opened it for her and helped her get in. "Thanks again," she said as she started her engine. "But you've got to get away from here fast. You can't be here when he comes to. He'll hurt you if he can. He's an evil, dangerous man."

"Here's your hat," the young man said, reaching toward her with it.

"Thanks," she said, accepting it and dropping it on the seat beside her.

"Are you sure we can't do anything else for you?" the young man asked.

"There's nothing more you can do. We've all got to get away from here—now," she warned again.

"Okay. But be careful," he said as he shut her door.

As she pulled out of the parking area, Kaitlyn chanced one quick look back and saw the young man and the young blond woman who had picked up her hat leaning over Jace. She pushed on the brakes. She couldn't let them stay. They had to leave now or risk letting Jace see them. She had to warn them again. Then, they both straightened up and started away from Jace, leaving him lying there. She breathed a sigh of relief and pressed on the gas pedal.

* * *

"Brock, that was an incredibly brave thing you did," Jodi said as she laced her arm through his. "That girl was lucky we came along when we did. You must have been inspired to come this way."

"Yeah, I guess so," Brock said absently. He was still thinking about Kaitlyn. And he was thinking about the man who had attacked her, the man she'd called Jace. He still couldn't believe his dumb luck. He was not a fighter and might have gotten beaten badly. But the man had gone down twice, and Brock didn't have a scratch on him. He also felt lucky the man was alive. His head had struck the pavement with such force the second time Brock shoved him down that it had knocked him out. But he was breathing steadily and his heartbeat was strong.

Jace, whoever he was, was a vicious man. And Kaitlyn seemed . . . wholesome. He wondered what could have ever brought the two of them together. He also wondered if he'd ever see her again.

"I wonder why he was attacking her," Jodi said.

"Most likely because she rejected him. At least, that's my best guess," Brock said. "And we'd better move fast. I'm sure she's right, that we don't want him finding us."

"Why do you think she rejected him?" Jodi asked. "Because he's a jerk?"

"Could be. He sure is one," Brock said impatiently. "Or maybe it's because she's a Mormon and he's not."

"She's a Mormon? You mean you know her?" Jodi asked. "That is really a coincidence."

"I've never seen her before tonight," he said as he pulled Jodi along a little faster. Now was not the time to be dawdling.

"Then how do you know she's a member of the Church?" she asked.

"She was wearing a CTR ring," he told her. "I saw it when she unlocked the door."

"Choose the right," Jodi said, and she smiled and held up her right hand so Brock could see her own CTR ring.

"You're right, Jodi. Maybe by choosing the right she rejected that Jace guy. Now, we'd better get to my truck and get out of here before that guy comes after us. We'll go find something to eat. Where did you say you wanted to go?"

* * *

The episode with Kaitlyn, Jace, and Brock had been observed by a set of angry dark brown eyes. When Kaitlyn had ridden up, Norman Thatcher had barely made it out of sight behind a nearby truck after a short visit to Kaitlyn's horse trailer. He watched as she loaded her horse in the trailer without unsaddling him. A guy and a girl walked past just then, and a moment later he saw someone attack her. He chuckled to himself. Then anger surged through him as he also witnessed the man in the black hat free his arm from the slender young woman he was with and give the attacker a quick but thorough thrashing. He would have liked to see exactly what the first fellow had in mind for Kaitlyn. It wasn't good, whatever it was. That thought dispelled some of the anger, and he even smiled to himself and stepped out from his hiding spot after Kaitlyn and the young couple left.

He was sick and tired of his nineteen-year-old daughter, Jordan, always losing out to Kaitlyn Glenn. Jordan had a bright future as a barrel racer, and Norman had invested a lot of money in her horse. The bay mare was, in his opinion, the best that money could buy and well-trained. Yet it seemed that each time Kaitlyn won a competition, Jordan ended up second. And each time Kaitlyn placed somewhere lower than first, Jordan was always at least one place behind her. He'd come to hate the young woman. He also resented her horse, partly because he had to admit that it was better than the one Jordan rode.

Well, Kaitlyn wouldn't win tomorrow night in Laramie. He smiled again at the thought. He walked over to the downed man, who had just begun to stir and was slowly pushing himself to his knees. Norman offered him a hand and pulled him to his feet. "That young woman is trouble," Norman said as he picked up the man's hat, straightened it out, and handed it to him.

"Not for long," the injured man said through clenched teeth, tossing the hat back on the ground.

"Yeah, I agree," Norman said. "Do you need help or a lift anywhere?"

"I'm fine," the fellow said curtly. He strode away, leaving the slightly damaged but obviously new hat on the ground.

Norman watched him, wondering what his beef was with Kaitlyn Glenn. He didn't recognize him. He was quite certain he hadn't seen him at any of the other rodeos Jordan had competed in, which meant it wasn't likely that his anger at Kaitlyn was over barrel racing. Not that he cared. It seemed that he had unexpectedly found a confederate in the fellow. He was more confident than ever that Kaitlyn wouldn't be beating Jordan at the rodeo in Laramie, or perhaps ever again. He picked up the stranger's hat and checked the size and make.

No sense in wasting a brand-new, expensive hat, he thought as he headed for his truck.

"Where have you been, Dad?" Jordan asked him a few minutes later. She had already unsaddled her mare and stowed the saddle and bridle in the tack room of the trailer.

"I was looking for Kaitlyn Glenn," he said. "I wanted to congratulate her on her win tonight. But she was already pulling out by the time I found where she'd parked."

"That's nice of you, Dad," Jordan said as she affectionately brushed the glossy coat of her stocky mare. "It's too bad you missed her. Maybe we can talk to her in Laramie."

"Yeah, maybe so," Norman responded.

"She's sure good. I hope someday I can be as good as her," Jordan said. "I feel so lucky just placing close to her as many times as I have."

"You'll beat her soon," Norman said confidently. "You're the better rider. Take my word for it, Jordan. I'll bet you even beat her in Laramie."

"Nice hat, Dad. Where did you get it?"

"A fellow gave it to me. He said it didn't fit him. Now let's get that horse loaded and be on our way."

CHAPTER 2

THE SUN APPEARED IN HER rearview mirror in a burst of blazing red-orange. Kaitlyn glanced at the clock. It was hard to believe that she'd been able to drive all night long, pressing west on I-80. She'd stopped once for gas, a restroom break, and a candy bar, then continued on. Fear of falling asleep at the wheel had troubled her, but fatigue hadn't proven to be a big problem. She'd been wired all night, her mind busy with fragmented plans for her future and worries about what lay behind her. And, frequently, she'd envisioned the handsome face of the man in the black hat, who had come to her rescue when Jace attacked.

After driving for two or three hours, Kaitlyn realized that the young man was the same one who had smiled at her when their eyes had met just before she'd spotted Jace—and just after. She wondered if he'd seen the terror that must have been on her face. As her thoughts wandered, she speculated about whether he and his girlfriend had come looking for her, just to make sure she was okay.

That's a stupid thought, she told herself, but she couldn't get rid of it. *You'll never see him again, so you'll never know for sure.* Nevertheless, she couldn't help thinking about what might have happened to her if he hadn't come along when he did. *Where would I be right now?* That question was terrifying.

Kaitlyn felt very alone. Ever since her stepfather and mother had disowned her and moved shortly after her baptism a little over three years ago, she'd been alone. She had made friends in the places she'd lived, of course, but with none of them had she enjoyed a deep, long-term friendship that she needed to fill the emptiness in her life. Not even her roommate in Des Moines.

More than anything, Kaitlyn longed to speak with her mother. She knew, however, that the influence of her stepfather and stepbrother had severed all ties. She'd often felt that she could have patched things up with her mother, and maybe even her stepdad, had it not been for Kelvin. He'd apparently made sure that his fabrications carried enough weight that they believed the worst about the Church and her reasons for joining.

There was no one else in her life—except Tony B, of course. She enjoyed barrel racing, but more than that, she had a deep affection for her horse. At just under fifteen hands, Tony B was not large. But he was fast, surefooted, and totally dependable. Kaitlyn admitted that without him, she would not have had the success she'd enjoyed the past few years. While she'd worked in Des Moines for the winter, she'd kept him in a stable on the outskirts of the city. She rode him at least twice a week and usually more, both to keep him in shape and well-trained and to enjoy the pleasure of his company. The sturdy sorrel gelding was the closest thing to family that Kaitlyn had.

Her thoughts turned to Jace Landry and she shivered. She wished she'd never met him. She especially regretted having given in to his demands to take her out. What a dreadful choice that had been. She wanted to forget she ever knew him. But he had other ideas. Since she'd quit her job at his company, he'd been following her—or more accurately, stalking her.

Jace owned the large paint manufacturing company where Kaitlyn worked as a secretary during the rodeo off-season. Well-to-do and inclined to flaunt his wealth, he'd been persistent, even demanding, in trying to convince her to go out with him. Her roommate had finally talked her into it. "It's rude to offend your boss. That's not smart," she told Kaitlyn more than a few times. "And so what if he's a lot older than you? Age doesn't matter." Oh, how she wished she'd never given in. With hindsight she realized that she should have quit her job the first time he'd tried to flirt with her.

Earlier Kaitlyn had left I-80 at the mouth of Echo Canyon in Utah and headed toward Ogden on I-84. Now she merged onto I-15 and soon passed the city. Some distance north of Ogden she pulled off the freeway and parked her pickup and horse trailer among a group of big rigs at a truck stop. Grabbing her suitcase from the backseat, she went inside. After a shower and change of clothes, she turned toward a mirror and began to brush her hair.

She stopped mid-stroke, shocked by her reflection. Her normally thick, wavy auburn hair was limp and lifeless. Her blue eyes looked back at her, bloodshot and glazed. Her lightly tanned skin was pasty, and the skin beneath her eyes was puffy and dark. Even her typically square shoulders were stooped, visibly reducing her five-foot-five height. Her bright blue Western blouse seemed to hang on her.

Surely I haven't lost that much weight these past few days, she thought. She squared her shoulders and forced a smile. *That's better,* she told herself. *But I need to start taking better care of myself.* The smile disappeared, and she slowly lifted her brush again.

A short, stocky black woman came in and approached the mirror. Kaitlyn kept brushing her hair, trying not to feel self-conscious about the middle-aged woman's scrutiny. She was not surprised when the woman spoke to her. "Hey, are you okay?" she asked.

"Just tired," Kaitlyn said.

"Too tired to drive, I'd say. Are you sure you aren't sick, honey? You don't look like you feel so good."

"I'm fine. I've just been driving for a long time."

"If you're not sick, then you must be starved. No offense," the woman added quickly, "but you do look gaunt. Why don't you join me for breakfast?"

"Oh, sure, thanks," Kaitlyn said, grateful to see a smiling face. "But I'll need to take my suitcase to my truck first."

"Sure, you do that, and I'll meet you in the café in five minutes. By the way, my name is Celia Dulce. I drive out of Omaha."

"Kaitlyn Glenn. I'm from northern California. It's nice to meet you."

The older woman smiled again, her white teeth flashing brightly. "Five minutes," she said. "And you're gorgeous. I'd die for a face and hair and figure like you have."

"Thanks. You're kind. I'll hurry," Kaitlyn promised.

She finished brushing her hair, clipped it into a ponytail, and then took her suitcase back to the truck. As promised, Celia was waiting when she entered the café. "Counter or booth?" she asked.

"Booth, if that's okay with you," Kaitlyn responded.

After they were seated, a waitress handed them menus, promised to bring them each a glass of orange juice, and then hurried away. The two women studied the menus silently for a few moments. Then Celia looked up. "You don't look much like a truck driver, Kaitlyn. I'm surprised."

Kaitlyn couldn't help the grin that surfaced. "I'm sorry if I misled you," she said. "My truck is actually a pickup, a Ford F-250. I'm towing a horse trailer."

"There we go. You do look like a cowgirl. Are there horses in your trailer?"

"Just the gelding I do my barrel racing on."

"I see. You've been to a rodeo recently, haven't you?"

"Yes, several."

"Off to another one now?"

"I, uh—I don't know," Kaitlyn said, suddenly confused.

"You don't know?" Celia asked, leaning forward, her round face and penetrating eyes expressing concern. "There is something wrong, isn't there?"

Slowly Kaitlyn nodded. Before she realized it, she'd shared her story with Celia Dulce. It felt good just to be able to talk about her problem with someone who seemed so caring. When she finished, Celia said, "I take it that you think this Jace fellow will try to figure out where you've gone?"

"I know he will, Celia. That's why I didn't stop back in Laramie for the next rodeo I'd planned to ride in. He found me in Cheyenne, so I figured he could find me in Laramie—or anyplace else I might want to race," Kaitlyn added bitterly.

The two women visited as they ate, and it was with reluctance that Kaitlyn finally stood up. "I'd better pay for my meal and get going again," she said.

"Keep your money, Kaitlyn. Breakfast is on me," Celia said. "As for driving, I know fatigue when I see it. You need some sleep first, girl."

"Yeah, I know. I figure I'll pull off at a rest area after I've gone a little farther," Kaitlyn said.

"And sleep in your pickup? You sure won't get any rest that way," Celia said firmly. "You need a real bed. This Jace guy can't be that close behind you. I'm sure he's no genius. He can't know where you've gone yet."

"I hope he doesn't." Kaitlyn felt far from certain that Jace wasn't already closing in on her, even though she couldn't imagine how that could happen. But he'd traced her to Cheyenne. It scared her to think how furious he'd be if he found her again.

"Relax, Kaitlyn. Now, about that bed . . ."

"Oh, don't worry, Celia. I have a small living quarters in the front of my horse trailer. I can sleep there when I find a place to stop," Kaitlyn told her.

"Why don't you just stay here? You can bring your truck right over next to my rig. I plan to sleep some myself. That's why I passed on the coffee this morning. Anyway, with all of us truckers around, you wouldn't be alone, and you could get some real rest. You'll be safe here," Celia assured her.

"But won't they make me leave?" Kaitlyn asked.

"No. We truckers sleep here all the time. They won't mind you any. Go get your truck, and I'll make sure there's an empty spot near my rig for you to park."

Kaitlyn was still nervous when she crawled into her bed a few minutes later. But she was grateful that she'd found a friend, even if only a temporary one. She pulled the sheet up around her chin and, despite all that she had on her mind, was soon sound asleep.

* * *

There was a message on Myler Keegan's answering machine when he walked into his office late that Saturday morning. Myler didn't usually come into the office on a Saturday, but he'd wrapped up a case the day before and needed to write his final report and submit it to his client before the day was over.

He debated checking the message that the blinking light on his phone assured him was there. But he finally decided that it might be a prospective client, and as soon as today's report was completed, he'd be without a job again. Private investigators without clients could get very hungry. He checked the message and smiled. Jace Landry had lots of money. He'd worked for Jace a number of times in the past. He wouldn't mind working for him again. Jace was good to work for because he paid whatever the amount he was billed and never had second thoughts about ethics. Jace wanted results, and he didn't care how anyone got them.

Myler fondled his long, black mustache for a moment, and then he ran a thick hand through his greasy mop of graying black hair as he thought about Jace Landry. It was always a double-edged sword with Jace. The last case he'd worked for him had made him a lot of money, but it had also gotten the cops on his tail for a while. Eventually, all had ended well. Only one cop had died, and his death had looked so much like an accident that his colleagues never even thought twice about it. Jace had given him a handsome bonus for his troubles.

Finally, Myler picked up his phone and dialed Jace's number. On the first ring Jace answered angrily. "About time you got back to me, Keegan," he barked.

Myler smiled to himself. If there was one thing he'd learned in the ten years he'd been a PI, it was to not let clients push him around. Including the wealthy ones like Jace Landry. "I've been on an important case, Jace," he said with a slow, easy drawl. "So, what can I do for you?"

"I need you to help me hunt someone down and bring her home," Jace said.

Myler smiled smugly. This was the kind of case he liked most. He considered himself a hunter—the best in the business. When Jace explained that it was a twenty-two-year-old woman he would be looking for, Myler laughed out loud. "Piece of cake, Landry. Ain't never searched for a woman I couldn't find," he bragged.

"All you have to do is get close, and then it'll be easy. I attached a tracking device to her truck a few weeks ago. The only problem is that you have to be within a hundred miles for it to work."

"Great. Give me the rest of the details, and I'll get right on it."

"Stay put, Myler. I'll drive over to your office right now."

As soon as Jace walked through his door ten minutes later, he began filling Myler in on the case. "This is a picture of Kaitlyn," he said as he held out a glossy print.

Myler whistled. "Wow. No wonder you want to find her."

"Yeah, she's a looker all right," Jace said grimly. "Now, there's just one other thing. I'm going with you on this one."

"Oh no, you aren't. I work alone," Myler growled, shaking his heavy jowls and scratching his ruddy, pockmarked face.

"It's my money," Jace said darkly. "But I'll make it worth the inconvenience. I'll pay you half again over your normal fee to let me tag along. I won't be any trouble, but I want to be there when you find Kaitlyn. She's done me dirt, and I aim to see that she learns her lesson. And once she understands that she'll be spending her life with me, I intend to find out from her who the guy was that knocked me around. I'll have you find him next."

"Whatever you say," Myler agreed, wondering what Jace had not yet told him. He was intrigued—not only by the scanty details he'd heard, but also by the dollar bills he envisioned piling up for him. He was always game for a few extras when he could get them.

* * *

Despite the less-than-perfect date with Jodi the previous evening, tonight's date had ended on a high note. They enjoyed an excellent dinner and conversed comfortably. Brock found that there were actually many things the two of them had in common—rodeos, of course, not being one of them. As the evening went on, Brock even found himself thinking less often of the mysterious Kaitlyn Glenn. He knew that his short encounter with her had been just that—short. That was the end of it. He had decided to try to enjoy his time with Jodi. And he really had. He looked forward to seeing her again.

When he left Jodi at her door the night before, he'd asked her out again, and she had eagerly accepted. He quickly assured her that they wouldn't be going to another rodeo. She told him, however, that the rodeo wasn't as bad as she thought it would be, especially after the excitement of Brock's heroic rescue. He tried to downplay his success in defending Kaitlyn, but Jodi would have no part of it. He was her hero, and she told him so several times. He had to admit that her flattery felt good.

Brock was anticipating his next date with Jodi. It wasn't until the following Friday evening, but he had a feeling that it would be an exceptional night for both of them. And between now and then, he thought it might be nice to call her and just chat.

The ringing of his phone startled him. And what he learned in that call meant he wouldn't be going out with Jodi on Friday after all. He'd just been offered a job he had applied for a few weeks before when his current employer announced that there would be layoffs coming by midsummer and that he could be affected. The timing was good in one way because it meant he wouldn't suddenly be unemployed, something he worried about each day. On the other hand, the timing was bad for his personal life. He was reasonably sure Jodi would understand. If she didn't, then he guessed that would just have to be the way it was. He was going to Utah and would be working with horses at a small lodge on the

Colorado River. They needed him there by the middle of the next week at the latest, as one of their hands had suddenly announced his resignation. A large group of tourists was coming in on Thursday and would want to ride that day or the next.

Promising to make it to Utah by then, Brock couldn't wait to start packing. But before he did, he knew he should call Jodi. He lifted the phone and dialed her number. Too bad she couldn't relocate to Moab. After all, he was getting along in years, and he really would like to find a wife and settle down. *Twenty-four for an LDS returned missionary is almost middle-aged,* he reminded himself. And Jodi, after the negative beginning, had suddenly seemed like as promising a prospect for a long-term relationship as he'd had since Tanya, and he'd dated her only four or five times before she'd broken it off.

When Jodi answered, he said, "Hi, it's Brock. How are you doing today?"

"I'm fine. But is something wrong?" she asked suspiciously.

"Well, yes and no. There's something I need to tell you."

"Okay," she said, sounding crestfallen before she even heard what he had to say.

Then inspiration struck him. "I'd rather tell you in person," he said. "Are you by any chance free for dinner tonight?"

"Well, I did have plans, but I can change them. What time would you like me to be ready?" she asked. The excitement in her voice made him wonder if he'd made a mistake. He should have just told her his news and been done with it. This way he would only draw out what was already going to be a bit of a difficult separation. Then again, even though they'd be a few hundred miles apart, it wasn't like with Kaitlyn who—

Brock sharply severed the thought. *I don't even know Kaitlyn.*

He barely knew Jodi, but he really would like to see her again. It wasn't as if he would never have time off from his new job. He could come to Cheyenne if she wanted him to. And maybe she'd even come to Moab sometime. He found himself smiling at the possibilities.

* * *

The big airliner touched down with only a couple of bumps, and then the engine brakes came on and rapidly slowed the plane. Young Nina

Schiller was so excited she felt like she might explode. This, next to the takeoff, was the most exciting part of the whole ride. She always looked forward to it. But she looked forward even more to the vacation that she and her parents had planned in Utah. It was very different from London, they'd told her, as different as any place could be. They would be spending a month visiting the sights in and around Utah. And from pictures she'd seen, she could hardly wait.

She was out of her seat and into the aisle before the plane had come to a complete stop at the gate. "Nina, sit down," her mother said sternly. "They haven't told us we can get out of our seats yet."

Nina did as she was told. She usually did. Even though she was an only child and had the possessions to prove it, she was still obedient. She would be nine before this trip was over. Last year she had turned eight in India, and the year before that she had turned seven in Africa. In fact, every birthday she could remember had been spent in some exciting part of the world. But this was the first time her family had been to Utah in the United States, and for some reason she had looked forward to this trip more than any other.

Nina had fair skin, light red hair, a few freckles on her face, and what her nanny often said were the prettiest blue eyes in the whole world. Of average height for her age, she was not at all overweight, unlike many of her friends. She had good eating habits and stayed physically active. Because her parents owned their own tennis court, and because it was something her nanny was especially good at, Nina played tennis almost every day. She also swam frequently in their private indoor pool, and she spent time at the beach with her nanny when the weather permitted, which wasn't as often as she liked.

Nina enjoyed life. In fact, she enjoyed it so much that she was unaware that she saw far less of her parents than did the average girl her age. They were busy, but she didn't know that other parents weren't equally busy. Her parents were gone a lot, but she didn't notice. Her nanny was always there when she needed an adult. And every summer, just before her birthday, she was allowed to travel with her parents.

CHAPTER 3

AFTER A GOOD REST, KAITLYN bid her new friend, Celia Dulce, good-bye.

"Hey," Celia said, "keep in touch. If there's ever any way I can help you, just give me a call."

Kaitlyn couldn't imagine how that could ever happen, but at Celia's insistence, they exchanged cell phone numbers. Then Kaitlyn pulled her pickup and horse trailer next to a gas pump. She filled the tank and went inside to pay. She grabbed a couple bottles of water and a few snacks, and then paid for everything with her Visa card.

Shortly afterward, she was on her way north again. It was purely on impulse that she exited I-15 at Brigham City and headed for Logan. She'd once ridden in a rodeo near Logan, and the thought occurred to her that it might be possible to find someone there who would stable Tony B and keep her horse trailer for her until this nightmare with Jace was over. She'd miss the horse terribly, of course, but it would be much easier and faster to travel without the burden of pulling the trailer and feeding, watering, and exercising her gelding.

Her instincts were good, and before nightfall she'd found a ranch a few miles north of Logan where she could board the horse and park her trailer. The helpful rancher, who introduced himself as Jim Perrett, appeared to be near sixty. His wife, Nancy, who joined them as Kaitlyn opened the door of the horse trailer, was an attractive lady slightly younger than Jim.

As Kaitlyn led Tony B from the trailer a minute later, she felt a twist in her gut. Something was wrong with the horse. He was sluggish and his eyes were rheumy.

The rancher noticed it too. "It's good you're not planning to compete on him for a while," he said. "I have no idea what it is, but there's something wrong with your horse."

"He was fine earlier. I won the barrels on him last night in Cheyenne. What could be wrong?" she asked as she ran her hands down his front feet, almost expecting to feel some heat. There was none.

"Have you changed his feed?" Jim asked. "Maybe he has a touch of colic."

That frightened Kaitlyn. She knew colic could be fatal to a horse if it was severe enough, and it could come on very fast. "Well, yes," she said nervously. "I bought some new hay when I got to Cheyenne, but it was certified and looked similar to the mix of grass and alfalfa I'd been feeding him," she said.

"I suppose that could be the problem. But I'm sure he'll be fine." The rancher, as he spoke, was also running his hands down the gelding's legs. Then he put his face close to Tony B's. Next he circled around him and pressed on his stomach. Tony B flinched. Jim looked up. "Something with his feed, I'd say. He seems uncomfortable when I poke his belly."

"Oh, the poor thing," Nancy said. "He's such a beautiful animal."

"What should I do? I . . . I can't stay here," Kaitlyn said after a moment of worried silence.

"Actually, you'd be welcome at our home," Nancy said. "The kids are all grown and gone. We have lots of room."

"Thank you, but I don't know if I should," Kaitlyn said as she felt a wave of panic.

"You mentioned an emergency a few minutes ago, Kaitlyn. Is that why you can't stay?" Jim asked.

"Yes, I've got to be on my way."

"Then you go. Nancy and I will see to your horse. If you'd like, I could have my vet come by and take a look at him if he doesn't seem to be feeling better in a few hours," he volunteered.

"You don't mind doing that?" she asked.

"Of course not."

"That would be great. I'll pay whatever it takes. I do have money," she said as she thought of her large trust—the one her stepbrother would like to tap into, the one she'd only been able to access herself on her twenty-first birthday. She'd bought the horse trailer and her new truck with some of that money, but she hadn't used much other than that. She tried to live on her winnings and various temporary jobs. That reminded her of Jace. She had to get going. Who knew where he might be right now.

"Do you have a cellular phone?" Jim asked.

Kaitlyn nodded.

"That's good. Why don't you give me the number, and I'll let you know how he's doing. What's his name, by the way?"

"Tony B," she said. "I would like to hear from you. I could call, though." She hesitated to give out her phone number. She'd bought the phone and changed her number when she left Jace's employment. The only person who knew it besides her was Celia.

"That would be fine, but I would like to be able to call you if I need to." He'd pulled a small notebook out of his shirt pocket and was ready to write down the number.

"Okay, but make sure you don't let anyone else have it. I'm kind of stingy with my phone number," she said with a forced smile.

"No problem. You've got my word," he said. "Nobody else gets your number."

After leaving Tony B, Kaitlyn was confident that she'd left him in good hands and hoped it wouldn't be too long before she could pick him up again. She knew she would still worry over him. She couldn't understand why he was sick. It didn't make sense. She was always careful about his feed.

* * *

Without even her gelding to keep her company, Kaitlyn was really alone now. Because she wasn't sleepy, she left Logan and headed toward Tremonton, where she again got on the freeway. This time it was I-84 that would take her into Idaho and then on to Oregon. There was no particular reason for traveling that direction as she didn't know where she was going. Maybe it was because her new friend Celia had mentioned that she was taking her load up I-84. Perhaps it was comforting just knowing there was someone she knew, a friend of sorts, traveling the same freeway.

Or maybe it was because her childhood home was not that far south of the Oregon border. Not that it mattered. She had no family there now, just memories.

Kaitlyn had never known her grandparents—her mother's parents—Benjamin and Kathryn Jensen, but she knew about them, and she liked to think she was named for them. Grandpa Ben had owned a prosperous vineyard in Napa Valley, California. His highly resistant rootstock was unaffected in 1983 when a high percentage of the vineyards in the valley were destroyed by infection from a root louse. When many other owners decided to sell their vineyards after the pest outbreak took them by surprise, Grandpa Ben bought their land and replanted, using the same rootstock he had planted on his place.

Kaitlyn knew that her mother, Carolyn, who was Ben and Kathryn's only child, had married her high school sweetheart the next year. Ben was so impressed with his new son-in-law, Cliff Ellsworth, that he took him under his wing and ultimately made him a partner in the business. Because of the size of their holdings, good decisions, and uncommon insight into the grape-growing industry, the two continued to prosper.

Even now it was hard to think of Cliff as her father because she had never known him. But he was a good man and became sole owner of the business upon Ben's death. Well schooled by his father-in-law not only as a vintner but also as an employer, Cliff paid his seasonal workers generously and provided good housing for them. In turn, his employees respected him and returned each year, ready to work again in the vineyards for which they too felt ownership.

Kaitlyn was Carolyn and Cliff's only child. The young couple had planned on having a much larger family, but Cliff developed cancer and died just before Kaitlyn turned two years old. Carolyn was left a wealthy widow, and Kaitlyn had a trust that would easily take care of her needs when she reached adulthood.

Two years after Cliff's death, Carolyn married Richard Glenn, who had courted her nonstop for eight months. Perhaps the flowers, candlelight dinners, and weekly gifts finally overwhelmed her. Before she knew it, Carolyn had remarried; she had a stepson as well as a daughter, and she had agreed to sell the vineyards.

Everything went downhill after the last candlelight dinner. The huge sum she received from the sale of her property and equipment disappeared like snowflakes on a sun-warmed sidewalk. Soon Carolyn and Richard were limping from one paycheck to the next, trying to make ends meet on Richard's meager salary as an appliance salesman. Fortunately,

Carolyn resisted selling the house she and Cliff had bought in Redding, and the family had a home during their hard times.

A bumpy patch of highway roused Kaitlyn from her reverie. *It's just as well,* she thought. *The memories after that aren't worth remembering.* Fully into the present now, she realized that all she wanted to do was get as far away from Jace as she possibly could.

Fortunately, she had plenty of money in the bank, thanks to the foresight of her late father and a hefty line of credit available on her Visa card. At least money wasn't a worry. Not that she would spend too much anyway; she was a careful spender. Money aside, Kaitlyn knew she had to keep moving. She didn't know how he could find her again, but Jace possessed both wealth and connections. He would search for her until he ran her down, which he would do unless she kept moving until he finally gave up.

Although it was fully dark long before she reached the Idaho border, she continued driving. With no schedule to keep, she knew that when she got tired again, she could find a place to rest. That was when she'd miss the trailer. She might have to sleep in the truck, but at this point she was determined to do whatever she had to. The last thing Kaitlyn ever wanted to see again was the evil, leering face of Jace Landry.

* * *

Jordan Thatcher couldn't figure out why Kaitlyn hadn't shown up at the rodeo in Laramie that evening. She knew she'd signed up for it. Besides really liking Kaitlyn, she appreciated the helpful tips the older girl gave her from time to time. She considered Kaitlyn a good friend.

Jordan was back at the truck with her horse, brushing the mare carefully. She'd had another good showing in her event. At least, she considered it good. Once again she placed second, just as she had the previous night in Cheyenne.

Well, not just like last night, she reminded herself. *The girl who beat me wasn't Kaitlyn.* But her dad seemed pleased. When he joined her at the truck a few minutes later, he was nursing a bottle of beer and wearing his new Stetson hat, the one someone had given him in Cheyenne. "You almost did it, Jordan," he said with a chuckle.

"I got second, same as last night," Jordan agreed. She was happy with the finish she'd achieved.

"At least it wasn't Kaitlyn Glenn that beat you," he said with a note of satisfaction. "This other gal just got lucky tonight. You'll win next week."

"Unless Kaitlyn's there. I wish she'd been here tonight. She really is a good rider, Dad. And she's been giving me a lot of helpful tips. With her help I'll improve."

"You'll improve without her help, Jordan. I'm sure Kaitlyn won't be there next week either," Norman said.

Jordan looked up quickly. The note of finality surprised her. "Why do you say that, Dad?" she asked.

Her father had neither a quick nor glib answer. He didn't meet her inquiring glance. "Just a feeling I have," he finally said. "She's not here tonight. And there would be no good reason for her not to be unless she's decided she's tired of riding."

"She's not, Dad," Jordan said with conviction. "She loves this life."

"Maybe not as much as you think," he said. "People don't always tell the truth, you know. Sometimes they say what they think you want to hear rather than what they really think."

Somewhere deep in Jordan's stomach she felt a pang of fear. The strong dislike she sensed in her father's tone stunned her.

The discomfort in her stomach intensified as the thought occurred to her that maybe her father hadn't really been looking for Kaitlyn last night. Someone just giving him an expensive new hat didn't make sense. *What was he really doing? And why did someone give him the hat? Surely he wouldn't lie to me or do something to make sure Kaitlyn didn't win . . . would he?*

Jordan suddenly felt guilty. She loved her dad. She had no right to think like this. She thrust the negative thoughts from her mind and busied herself with her horse. *Kaitlyn will be there next week,* she repeated to herself again and again.

* * *

Myler Keegan's bushy black mustache always twitched when he grinned. It was twitching now. He looked over at his client.

"Did your friend find something for you?" Jace asked.

"Good thing you had Kaitlyn's Visa card number. She's used it several times, and that makes tracing her a piece of cake," Myler said smugly.

"Most people wouldn't ever think about that. Not unless they'd just seen it on a TV show. Okay, so maybe she's not too smart. But she's good-looking, and that's what matters to me. And there's nothing I don't know about that girl," Jace said darkly. "Remember, she works for me. And she is my fiancée. I can tell you anything you want to know about her—what kind of clothes she wears, what she likes to eat, what her favorite color is, even what she carries in her purse. Yes, Myler, I know all about her."

"That's good. Now, would you like to know where she's been?" Myler asked as he placed the telephone receiver down.

"I assumed you were about to tell me."

Myler's mustache twitched again as a crooked grin spread across his pockmarked face. "Of course. She gassed up her truck this afternoon in Logan, Utah."

"That's good to know. Is there anything after that?" Jace asked.

"Some before but none after. But there will be. She'll use her card again, and when she does, my buddy can let us know when and where. For now, I suggest we fly to Utah in your jet and then rent a car in Logan. That little tracking device you put on her pickup will find her if she still happens to be in that area. And I suppose that's possible. So, let's fly out there. Your pilot's license is current, isn't it?"

"Not that you care," Jace said with a chuckle. "You'd fly with me anyway. But yes, it is. I'll call the hangar and have them get the Lear ready. We can be in the air in an hour. At the speed that jet goes, we'll be in Logan well before midnight." He was suddenly feeling better about the world. Kaitlyn would be with him before long.

* * *

After spending an hour with Jodi that evening, Brock was finding it harder than ever to tell her that his plans had changed, that he'd be leaving his job in Cheyenne and driving to Utah on Wednesday to start a new one. Finally, the time had come.

"Jodi, I've got good news and I've got bad news," he began. He knew that was a corny way to begin, but once the words were out, it was too late to recall them. So he simply went on. "The good news is that I was offered a new job today. It's one I've really wanted but didn't expect to get."

"Great, what will you be doing?" Jodi asked innocently.

"I'll be taking care of a herd of horses and making sure the people who ride them don't get hurt," he said.

"Sounds like fun for you since you like horses. Now, tell me the bad news," she said. "I hope it's not very bad."

"Well, uh, my new job is in Utah," he said. "And I have to be there by Thursday morning."

"Utah! I guess that changes our plans for Friday night. Oh, Brock. That's a big change. Do you have to go?" she asked, clearly saddened by the news.

"No, I guess I don't have to, but it's something I've always wanted to do, and I applied for the job months ago. I'm lucky there's even an opening. And anyway, Jodi, I can always come back here and see you. After all, I'm from this area, so it's not like I would be abandoning the place. I promise I'll come back the first chance I get, if you'll go out with me when I get here."

"Of course I will," she said. "But I'll miss you. I was looking forward to getting to know you a lot better."

"Same here," he admitted. "Will you write?"

"Definitely," she assured him.

And Brock began to think that maybe there could be a future with this beautiful young woman.

* * *

The small tracking device apparently wasn't in range. Jace was unable to pick up a signal. He was disappointed. He'd hoped Kaitlyn would still be in Logan. But he wasn't worried. He knew they'd catch up with her. All they had to do was get close, and then it would be easy. And he was confident that Myler would get them close.

They rented a car and drove into town. Jace was impressed with the way Myler did his job. A cashier at the station where Kaitlyn had gassed up recognized her from the photos Myler showed her. She'd been in the station that afternoon.

"Did she say where she was going?" Myler asked. "We're her cousins. Her father has had a heart attack. He's in very serious condition, but we can't seem to get in touch with her. Either her cell phone isn't working or she might have lost it. We simply have to find her before her father passes on. She'd feel terrible if she didn't get the chance to say good-bye to him."

"The poor girl. Let me think. I'd barely come on shift when she was here," she said, looking at her watch. "And I'm due to get off in ten minutes."

"I see," Myler said patiently. "Please think. Did she say anything that might help us find her?"

"Well, I remember her because she was pulling a horse trailer with her pickup," the woman said. "She was really attractive—beautiful hair. But she looked tired."

"She may have been. We really need to find her," Myler said, his patience wearing thin.

The cashier squinted as if she were rerunning a movie in her mind. Suddenly she brightened up. "Oh, yeah, I just remembered what we talked about. She said she had her horse in the trailer when I asked her if she was going to a rodeo. She was dressed like a cowgirl. You know, boots, Western blouse, tight Western jeans, and a fancy white cowboy hat."

Myler nodded and Jace said, "That's our cousin Kaitlyn. She's a rodeo girl all the way."

"Yeah, well, anyway, I asked her if she had a rodeo tonight, and she said she didn't. In fact, she said she needed to board her horse somewhere and leave her trailer for a few days. She asked if I knew of a place she could leave them, but I couldn't help her with that. And I'm afraid there's nothing more we talked about."

"You've been a big help. Thank you so much for speaking with us," Myler said politely. After they were back in their rented car, Myler turned to Jace. "There can't be that many places in the area that board horses. Let's ask around."

It was after midnight before they discovered where Kaitlyn had left her horse and trailer. Myler turned to Jace. "Do you want to wait until morning to ask these folks what they know?" he asked. "We could get some sleep now and be ready to continue the hunt then."

"Good grief, man," Jace said. "Wake them up. Who knows, Kaitlyn might still be reasonably close by, and if she is, I don't want her getting farther away while we sleep."

"People are more inclined to cooperate if their sleep isn't disturbed," Myler said, drawing out his response. "I think morning would be best."

"I think tonight would," Jace insisted angrily. "And it's my money that's paying for this little *hunt,* as you call it."

"Whatever you say," Myler said with exasperation. "But they may not be cooperative when we wake them up."

"There are ways to make people talk," Jace growled. "You do it all the time."

"This may not be a good time, though. This seems like a peaceful community. We would attract too much attention," Myler argued, then exhaled. "All right, we'll knock and see what we can learn. But we won't risk making them angry and getting the cops on our tails."

"That didn't bother you the last time you worked a case for me. Have you forgotten already?" Jace sneered. "You didn't even seem to mind wasting a cop then. What's so different now?"

Myler's expression changed as he turned to Jace. "I told you never to mention that again! I did what had to be done, as you well know. You would do well to forget. Never mention that again!"

Jace looked at his hired detective for a moment, started to say something, and then slowly closed his mouth. For a moment the two stared at each other. Finally, Myler said, "Enough of this. Do you still want to knock on that door tonight?"

Jace nodded. "Yeah, let's at least ask them about her. Turn on your charm, and they'll probably tell us whatever they know," Jace suggested. "There won't be a need for a scene."

The wait on the front porch seemed interminable. After the door was finally opened, Myler introduced them as cousins of Kaitlyn Glenn and repeated the lie about her father's illness.

"Are you sure she doesn't already know? That could be the emergency she mentioned. She didn't tell me what it was, just that she needed to hurry," the pajama-clad rancher said. "She told me she hoped it wouldn't be long before she would be back to get her horse. She didn't say anything about her father being ill."

"Well, he is, and it's serious," Myler said. "But I can assure you that she doesn't know about it yet. That's why we've got to find her. Thanks for your help."

"Sure thing," the rancher said. "I hope the girl's father will be okay. She sure seemed like a sweet young lady."

"The best," Jace said. "Thanks again." As he began to walk away he turned back quickly. "Oh, by the way, Kaitlyn got a new cell phone and

I've lost her number. I didn't get it stored in my own phone. I was busy when she gave it to me. I'm sure she left it with you. If you would get that for us it would help a lot. We could call her and save her some valuable time."

After what seemed to Jace like a slight hesitation, the rancher said, "Sorry. I can't help you there. She just said she'd call in occasionally to check on Tony B."

"Who?" Jace asked without thinking. "Oh, you mean her horse," he said as his mind raced. She'd never mentioned what she called her horse, but that had to be it.

"Yeah, Tony B," the rancher said. "Sorry I can't help you any more."

When the men were back in the rental car, Myler, thinking aloud, said, "Where could she be headed? Do you know of any connections she has out here? Where her family is?"

Myler had never seen such a blank look on Jace's face. "She must have lived in California at some point, but I don't know what part of the state," he admitted. "And come to think of it, I don't remember her talking about her family."

Myler shook his head. "I thought you said you knew everything about her."

"I guess I missed this one thing, but we can figure it out. You'll know what to do. That's why I hired you," Jace said angrily.

"That's right, and I will figure it out, but it might take a little time. First we'll need to find out where she was born. That might tell us a lot about where she's from. We'll start with California, if you're sure she's from there."

"I'm sure. The announcer at the rodeo in Cheyenne even said she was from California," Jace said.

"Okay, so California it is. But there's no sense in starting 'til morning. So we'd better find rooms for tonight and get some sleep."

"Will it be a problem finding what we need since tomorrow is Sunday?" Jace asked.

"Yeah, it probably will." Myler was thoughtful for a moment. "I'll call my contacts in Iowa tomorrow morning. I suspect that Kaitlyn's still leaving a credit card trail, and even on a Sunday my friends can help me with that. They got us this far on a Saturday without too much effort. But figuring out where she was born will have to wait until Monday."

* * *

"Something is very strange," Jim Perrett said to his wife as they slipped into bed again. "Kaitlyn specifically told me not to give her phone number to anyone. And I remember wondering what kind of emergency she was worried about. I'm pretty sure it wasn't her father, or I think she'd have said so. Anyway, since those two cousins of hers said she didn't know about him yet, her concern must have been about something else."

"Hmm," Nancy murmured. It was her standard response when she was mulling over an idea. "Something about those two seemed a little off. I can't put my finger on it, but my gut feeling tells me something's not right," Nancy commented. "I wonder if Kaitlyn's in some kind of trouble."

"I hope not. If it wasn't so late, I'd call and tell her about their visit. But I guess I'd better leave that until morning," he said.

"Yes, she's probably in a motel somewhere by now," Nancy agreed.

"Tony B," Jim mused as he pulled the sheet up to his chin. "Why didn't her cousin know her horse's name if they're so close? I'm sure he didn't."

"I wonder if they're really her cousins," his wife said. "I hope the poor girl is okay."

* * *

Sunday morning found Kaitlyn in Twin Falls, Idaho. She'd spent the early morning hours asleep in a motel room. She'd made that concession only because she wanted to attend church, and she could never make herself presentable if she spent the night in the truck. Her cell phone rang only minutes after she stepped out of the shower.

She looked at the display on her phone, suddenly chilled. She hoped Jim Perrett didn't have bad news about Tony B. "The vet came early this morning and looked at your horse," he said a moment later. "He seems to be doing better. The vet ruled out colic, but he took some blood, said he wants to run some tests on it."

"Why would he want to do that?" she asked, her worries over her horse not diminishing.

"I don't want to alarm you, but he wonders if Tony B might have eaten something harmful," the rancher said.

"I can't imagine how that could have happened," she said.

"He took a sample of your hay and grain, and that supplement you had in the trailer as well," he informed her. "He'll test all that, too."

"Thanks, Mr. Perrett. I sure appreciate what you're doing for me," she said.

"It's not a problem," he responded. "And I'll keep you informed."

"Well, thanks again," Kaitlyn said and prepared to hang up.

Suddenly Jim said, "Oh, by the way, a couple of fellows were here last night, quite late—after we had gone to bed actually—asking about you."

Kaitlyn's stomach churned. "Oh," she murmured.

"They said they were your cousins. They wanted your cell phone number, but I did like you asked and pretended I didn't have it."

"Thank you," she said, hardly able to speak.

"They said they needed to find you to tell you that your father is very ill. Were you aware of that? Have you talked to your family?"

Kaitlyn was dizzy. She sat down on the motel bed and pressed one hand to her face. "My father died when I was a baby," she said softly.

"Kaitlyn, are you in danger?" Jim suddenly asked.

"Yes," she mumbled weakly. "Thanks for not giving them my number."

"I take it they aren't your cousins," he said.

"That's right," she agreed, wondering how Jace and whoever was with him had traced her to Logan.

"Kaitlyn, how can I help?" Jim asked, concern evident in his voice.

"I'm afraid there's not much anyone can do. It would help, though, if you could describe these men to me."

His description of one of the men meant nothing to her, but the other one could only be Jace. It was unbelievable. *How does he do it?* "Thanks for calling," she said to Jim. "I better go now."

After hanging up, Kaitlyn considered going out to her truck right then and driving on. As she reached for her purse, she thought, *How can I expect the Lord to help me if I don't do what I know I should?* Taking a deep breath instead, she located the phone book in a drawer in the credenza and found a ward that started at eleven o'clock that morning.

It turned out to be a good choice. The people there were friendly. Even the bishop introduced himself and immediately asked, "Are you going to be living here?"

That was a familiar question when she was on the road following the rodeo circuit. "No, just passing through," she said.

"What are your plans for dinner?" the Relief Society president asked after the final meeting was over.

"Oh, I'm traveling, and I'll stop at a café after a few hours," Kaitlyn said.

"A café? You'll do nothing of the sort. Come home with me and you can eat with my family. We'd love to have you."

That had also happened before, and usually Kaitlyn declined. However, today, alone and afraid, she rather liked the idea of spending an hour or two with a friendly, generous LDS family. "If it's not too much trouble, I'd like that a lot," she finally responded.

"Of course it's not too much trouble. I put a roast in the oven this morning, and I made salad and rolls last night. All we have to do is mash some potatoes, heat up some vegetables, and presto, dinner will be ready," the president said. "You can just follow us home."

The afternoon proved to be enjoyable. Sister Stevenson's simple meal was melt-in-your-mouth delicious. When the last plate had been emptied, Kaitlyn helped clean up the dishes. Then she played with the children for a few minutes. She'd never known the kind of happiness this family enjoyed. It was a feeling that filled every corner of the home as well as Kaitlyn's heart. *Peace. That's what it is,* she told herself.

Her greatest dream was to someday find a worthy young man and have a family of her own—a real family, not the kind she was raised in. The face of the young man in Cheyenne came unbidden to her mind. Immediately she thrust it out. Instead, she concentrated on enjoying her last few minutes with the Stevenson children.

Kaitlyn realized she needed to get going again. Who knew where Jace might be by now? He'd certainly traced her to Logan in record time. She still couldn't imagine how he'd done it. And he wasn't alone. Who could possibly be with him?

She thanked Sister Stevenson for dinner and attempted to excuse herself a little after four that afternoon.

"Are you in a big hurry?" Sister Stevenson suddenly asked. "I mean, do you have to be somewhere soon? If not, we'd be honored if you'd stay here with us for the night."

Kaitlyn attempted to decline, but she found it difficult. Sister Stevenson was persuasive. Finally, figuring that she would be safe in the

Relief Society president's home, she accepted. *It will be nice to be with a real family for a few more hours, to feel like I belong,* Kaitlyn rationalized.

That night, despite a comfortable bed in a safe place, Kaitlyn spent more time awake than asleep. When she finally did fall asleep, she dreamed of a young man in a black cowboy hat. When she woke the next morning, he was still on her mind. There was something about that man, a man whose name she didn't even know, that impressed her. And it wasn't just the fact that he'd rescued her from Jace.

He has a girlfriend, she reminded herself firmly. *Or a wife.* But she didn't think that was the case. Neither he nor the young woman wore wedding rings. And the young woman also didn't have an engagement ring. Strange that she'd noticed those little details with all that had been going on in their brief meeting. She'd seen his bare fingers when he'd opened the door for her with his left hand. And she'd noticed the same thing about the blond. She'd used her left hand to return her hat. He was so . . . *Quit thinking about him,* she scolded herself again.

* * *

The phone rang, and Brock picked it up. "Hi, I miss you." It was Jodi's voice.

They'd spent the morning and part of the afternoon together. She'd attended his ward with him. Then he'd gone home with her and she'd fixed him dinner. He met her folks and younger brothers and sisters. The atmosphere in Jodi's home was comfortable, and he was feeling more at ease around her all the time. Leaving for Utah on Wednesday was going to be more difficult than he'd expected.

"It's only been a few hours," he said with a chuckle. "And I'll be seeing you tomorrow night." They were having dinner together again, an idea that appealed to both of them.

"When are you going to pack your stuff?" she asked.

"It won't take long. I don't have all that much to pack. I'll have time if I start as soon as I get off work tomorrow afternoon," he said.

"What time will that be?"

"Four, unless they fire me for giving such short notice. I wouldn't blame them."

"They won't fire you," Jodi said. Then she asked, "Could you use some help packing? I'll be off at four, too."

"If you have time, that would be great." He actually didn't need help, but he certainly wouldn't object to her company.

"I have your address. I'll come there straight from work."

* * *

"She finally used her credit card again. She gassed up in Twin Falls, Idaho, early this morning," Myler said. "Let's go and see what we can find there. While you're piloting this bird, I'll be using my laptop and phone to see what I can learn about where your girl was born, in case we need that information."

"It's about time we got moving again," Jace grumbled as he started the sleek jet's engines. "We've lost a whole day."

"We aren't far behind her now, so there's no need to be testy. We'll catch up with her before you know it," Myler said with a grin. "This is the fun part. It's the hunt that I love. Catching the quarry is almost a letdown."

"It won't be for me," Jace said grimly. "Finding her is what I look forward to—that and what will follow."

* * *

It was Kaitlyn's third day on the run. She wondered where Jace was now. She hoped he wasn't anywhere near Twin Falls. She couldn't imagine how he could be, but she also knew that she couldn't afford to underestimate him. He'd somehow tracked her to Cheyenne and then discovered that she'd been in Logan. She found herself watching her rearview mirror, hoping she wouldn't spot him and his black Cadillac Escalade.

She was near Boise when her cell phone rang. "Are you doing okay?" Celia asked.

"Yeah, I'm all right," Kaitlyn responded.

"Do you mind if I ask where you are?"

"Of course not. I'm almost to Boise."

"You're kidding. I just passed through Baker, Oregon, coming back toward you. Looks like I've put a lot more miles on than you have. You must have stopped somewhere." Celia laughed.

"Yeah, I did. I spent yesterday with a family I met in Twin Falls. I just left this morning," Kaitlyn said.

"What advice did they have for you?" Celia asked.

"I didn't tell them what was happening."

"Oh, I see. Hey, we could meet somewhere if you like. I'll buy you lunch. We should both be in Ontario about the same time. That's a town on the border of Oregon and Idaho."

"That would be great," Kaitlyn said. "Call me when you get close."

"I'll do that. You take care. I'll see you in a little bit."

Kaitlyn put the phone back in the little case on her belt. Then she opened her purse, which was on the seat beside her, and pulled out a stick of gum. *Only one more piece,* she noted as she shut her purse again.

A few minutes later the traffic slowed. Soon it was a bumper-to-bumper crawl. Then it came to a move-nowhere, absolutely dead stop. *There must be a wreck up ahead,* Kaitlyn thought. *Or maybe some construction.* It seemed like she always ran into construction when she traveled during the summer. She knew the roads needed maintenance, but the constant disruption of her schedule was a little irritating. She didn't remember seeing any construction signs and became convinced that an accident was causing the delay. *Celia will be in Ontario long before I am,* she realized, *and she might not have time to wait if this slowdown goes on for too long.*

She finally turned off the engine after remaining in one spot for over ten minutes. Taking a deep breath, she leaned back against the headrest. *Time for a little relaxation,* Kaitlyn told herself. For her that meant visualization. Visualizing Tony B, his sleek coat, and the barrels they needed to avoid.

A knock on her passenger-side window jump-started Kaitlyn's heart. A woman was standing there, apparently under a lot of stress. Kaitlyn rolled down the window. "Are you having trouble?" she asked, relief settling over her like a bag full of feathers tossed into the wind. It wasn't Jace!

"Yes, miss, terrible trouble. Please help me. My car broke down and I had to leave it beside the road. It's just up ahead. I've got to get to Boise. I've asked a dozen people for a ride, but they all said no. Please, will you take me? You can let me off right on the freeway when we reach Boise. I won't be any trouble," she pleaded.

The woman was about the same size as Kaitlyn and perhaps two or three years older. Kaitlyn hesitated. The woman's long, black hair swirled wildly around her, emphasizing her shabby, unkempt clothing. She'd heard stories of drivers who stopped to help people and ended up getting robbed or even killed. "I don't know. We might be in this traffic for a long time. There must be a wreck up ahead. I'm sure the cops there can help you. It can't be much farther."

"Okay, you're right, I'm sure. But will you at least give me a ride that far? Then I'll get out," the stranger said.

"Well, I guess," Kaitlyn answered reluctantly, looking around at the huge traffic snarl. *After all, what could happen with this many people so close?*

The woman clutched a purse with her grimy hands. She was already reaching through the open window and unlocking the door. A moment later she was in the truck. "I really appreciate this," she said.

The traffic began to move, and soon Kaitlyn's pickup had reached ten miles an hour. The woman was silent. Fidgety and nervous, she frequently finger-combed her long, unruly hair. Kaitlyn had second thoughts. It might have been a mistake letting the woman in her car.

Relax, she told herself. *Just be grateful it wasn't Jace who knocked on the window.*

Her speedometer registered fifteen and then twenty miles per hour. Soon she was moving along at thirty miles per hour. Then she saw the flashing lights of police cars a short distance ahead. The mangled remains of two vehicles were hunkered down on wreckers just off the road to the north.

"It must have been a bad wreck," she said to her passenger, who mumbled an unintelligible response. Cops were all over the place, but at least the traffic lanes appeared to be cleared. She slowed down when she reached the first police car.

"Keep going," the woman beside her said. She spit out the words as if they were offensive gnats lodged in her mouth.

"But you were going to—" Kaitlyn began as she looked over at her passenger. A small handgun, held just a few inches above the seat, was pointed upward at Kaitlyn's chest.

"That's right. This is a gun," the woman said. "And I'll use it if I have to. Keep going. You're going to give me a ride to wherever I need to go."

Kaitlyn carefully swallowed the bile that threatened to rise in her throat.

CHAPTER 4

THINGS HAD NOT BEEN THE same on this trip. Nina had never missed her nanny during vacations in previous years. She'd thought about her but had not been lonesome for her. But this time she wished Ruby was here. She felt all alone. In the past her parents had made sure she saw everything and did everything. They had doted on her, buying her little souvenirs and taking her picture with dozens of other tourists. They even asked others to snap photos of the three of them together. None of that had happened on this trip.

Something was different on this vacation, and it was getting worse. Nina wished Ruby was with them so she could talk to her about it. Ruby would help her understand what was happening. She always seemed to have answers when Nina had questions. And Nina certainly had questions right now.

She silently watched her father and mother, trying to figure out on her own what was going on. They'd always been happy, but neither of them smiled very much now, and they were uncharacteristically distant. They were even late to breakfast this morning. She'd lounged in their room at Ruby's Inn—Nina loved the idea that they were staying at a place with her nanny's name—watched cartoons, and been terribly bored before they finally went to breakfast. Then, while they were waiting for the food to come, neither her father nor mother seemed to have anything to say.

Shortly after their steaming plates arrived, her mother leaned over and whispered something to her father that Nina couldn't hear. Then she rose and left the table, her eggs and hotcakes untouched. A minute or two later, her father also left, having eaten only half of his breakfast.

Neither of them had spoken a single word to her. She suddenly found herself alone at the table, the only one who seemed to be hungry.

She ate everything on her plate, asked the waitress to charge the meals to the room like she had seen her dad do so many times, and then she too left the restaurant, embarrassed because she had no money to leave as a tip for the waitress. Back at the room, she found her mother sitting on the side of one of the beds. Her eyes were red, as if she'd been crying, and she was slumped over. Her father, pacing back and forth, folded his arms across his chest, his head bent. Neither of them acknowledged Nina.

Since the morning was wasting away, she asked, "Are we going to see the sights today? You told me that Bryce Canyon was one of the most awesome places in the world." She waited for a response.

Finally, her mother spoke, but not to her. She said, "Why don't you take her out there, Maurice. I'll wait here."

Nina, who had been watching her mother, turned expectantly to her father. He finally stopped his pacing. Her bright blue eyes watched him expectantly. He said, "If that's what you wish, Maggie, then that's what we'll do. Come on, Nina. Get a hat and your sunscreen. We'll go for a little while."

"But I don't want to go without Mum," Nina said stubbornly. "She'll miss the awesome sights."

"That's true, but it can't be helped," her dad said briskly. "Now run out to the car. I'll be there shortly."

Shortly turned out to be about ten minutes, and when her father came, he was brooding. She was both puzzled and saddened. Something terrible was going on, and she had no idea what it was.

"Get in the car and we'll go," Maurice said to her. He didn't smile. He didn't open the door for her. And he got in rather slowly himself.

Big tears welled up in Nina's eyes and overflowed down her lightly freckled face. "We don't have to go if you don't want to, Father," she said meekly.

"We are going. It's all right," Maurice said, not even turning his head as he spoke.

It was awful, but Nina decided that she'd try to have fun anyway. Surely whatever was wrong with her parents would be over soon, and then they could all have a good time together again, the way they used to.

* * *

"We'll be landing in a little while in Boise. I've already arranged for a car there," Jace said as Myler looked at the receiver he held in his hand. With a little luck, it would soon pick up a signal from the tracking device Jace had attached to the frame of Kaitlyn's pickup truck.

"I have a feeling this will do the rest for us," Myler said. "My guess is that she'll be within a hundred miles of Boise—one way or the other."

Jace chuckled. "She probably thinks she's gotten away, the beautiful little fool. I can't wait to get my hands on her."

"Probably won't be long. When we do get her, will we be flying her back to Des Moines?" Myler asked.

"I will be. But I won't need your services then. I'll buy you a ticket on a commercial airline," Jace said.

"I'd rather fly back with you. It would be quicker, and I'm a busy man. You're not my only client, you know," Myler said as he flashed an ugly frown at his wealthy client.

"I'm afraid that won't be possible. She and I need time alone," Jace insisted.

"You'll have plenty once you get her to that mansion of yours," Myler argued.

"Look, I'm the boss here," Jace reminded Myler with an expression that suggested he should drop the subject immediately.

Just then the small receiver started beeping. "Hey, I've got a signal! She's going west still."

"Great!" Jace said with a laugh. "We've got her now, Myler. I need to get this baby on the ground. We can't let her get away." He chuckled for a moment and then added, "She's in for a lovely surprise."

"We'll land as soon as we reach the airport. You pay attention to your flying. I'll keep an eye on this device. No sense losing her now that we're this close," Myler said as his huge mustache began to twitch. He stroked it gently with one hand.

* * *

The woman with the gun was scaring Kaitlyn. When they'd passed through Boise, Kaitlyn had asked her if they'd missed their exit, but the woman had just waved the gun. "Keep going. I'll tell you when to stop," she said.

She wouldn't say where she wanted to go, although Kaitlyn assured her that she would take her wherever that might be. As the miles passed, the woman became more distraught, fidgeting and waving the pistol around while frequently looking out the windows as if she expected to see someone or something suddenly appear alongside the freeway. Even though it was scorching hot outside and the air-conditioning was working fine, the woman lowered her window. The heat surged in, but the woman seemed a little calmer, so Kaitlyn said nothing. Anything that would calm her down was an improvement at this point.

Kaitlyn cast cursory glances at her dashboard clock. It was already past twelve. The traffic jam had really held her up. Not that it mattered now. She was sure this crazy woman wouldn't let her meet Celia in Ontario, even if she dared to bring up the subject.

Suddenly, her cell phone began to ring. "Don't answer it!" the woman shouted. "Give it to me."

She held the gun in Kaitlyn's face as Kaitlyn struggled with her left hand to ease the phone from her carrying case while trying to steer with her right hand. It could be Celia, calling to see how close Kaitlyn was to Ontario. It could be Jim Perrett calling from Logan to report on Tony B's condition. Her shaking hands fumbled with the case, and it took her longer than normal to remove the phone. The longer it rang, the more frenzied the woman became. The hand holding the little gun jerked so violently that Kaitlyn prayed she wouldn't accidentally pull the trigger.

"Shut it off!" the woman ordered, and her eyes met Kaitlyn's for a brief moment.

Kaitlyn noticed that they were glazed, unfocused. She wondered if she might be on some kind of drugs. That would explain a lot of the strange behavior. But it also heightened Kaitlyn's fear. *This woman is dangerous.*

She finally got the phone out, turned it off, and handed it to her abductor. The woman took it, glanced at it, and then tossed it out the window into the flow of traffic. Kaitlyn felt like her lifeline had just disappeared.

They traveled for several more miles before the woman suddenly said, "Pull to the edge of the freeway and stop."

It was a fairly remote area. Bushes and grass lined the side of the freeway, and small trees grew a little farther back. Kaitlyn wondered hopefully if the woman was going to get out now, although it seemed like a strange place to do that. But she didn't care. She would be glad to get rid of her.

Once she was stopped and had put the transmission in park, Kaitlyn looked expectantly at the woman, willing her to leave. She didn't move. Instead, she said, "Leave the truck running. You'll be getting out now. I'll be going on alone. And don't try anything, or this is the last place you'll ever see."

Their eyes met again, and the dull emptiness in those eyes convinced Kaitlyn that obeying was the lesser of two evils. Losing her truck was better than losing her life.

"Leave the purse," the woman ordered when Kaitlyn grabbed her bag and opened the door.

"But it has my—" she began.

The woman cut her off with a fanatical wave of the gun. "Leave it or I'll shoot you right now."

Kaitlyn hastily dropped her purse and jumped out of the truck. She hurried around to the back of the vehicle and stepped off the shoulder of the road as the woman slid beneath the steering wheel. "Hey, you, keep going. Down there," she said, waving the gun barrel toward the trees. "Don't try stopping nobody on the freeway if you know what's good for you."

Kaitlyn hurried off the pavement, glancing over her shoulder just as the woman put the pickup in gear and stepped on the gas. Instantly, Kaitlyn saw a large semi coming at full speed toward the distracted thief. She screamed and watched in horror as the truck hurtled into her pickup. The next few seconds crept by in slow motion as the semi smashed and twisted the pickup—tires, glass, plastic, and metal flew through the air like pellets from a shotgun. The sound was deafening as the semi bulldozed the crushed truck along the highway. The pitiful pickup then began to roll over, sliding on its side before finally coming to rest in a huge cloud of dust.

Kaitlyn's mind and body suffered a momentary paralysis. The woman who had stolen her truck at gunpoint was dead. It would have been impossible to live through that disaster. But then she thought about the driver of the semi, and the possibility that he or she had been injured spurred her rigid limbs into action. She scrambled back to the pavement and then along the shoulder toward the truck. She was aware of vehicles on both sides of the freeway as they stopped. People leaped out of them and rushed toward the tragic scene. Others reached the truck before she did and began trying to get to the driver.

Kaitlyn slowed to a walk. Then she stopped. She thought about Jace, and panic swept over her. *What if he's here somewhere? Among all these cars, these people?* That thought almost smothered her. She was on foot now and totally helpless without her truck. If she had her phone, she could at least call Celia, but that too was gone.

Then she realized that the police or highway patrol would be coming. Certainly, someone would have dialed 911 by now. Slowly she backed away from the wreck, carefully stepping off the road. Maybe she should hide in the bushes or trees until the police came. Then she could ask them for help. But could they protect her from Jace and his friend, whoever he was? She had serious doubts.

She kept watching for Jace's black Escalade. Then a terrible thought occurred to her. He had a plane, a jet. She'd forgotten that. Maybe it was because she'd never seen it, only heard him speak of it. At any rate, he could fly and rent a vehicle from anywhere. He could be in any kind of car. She needed to flee. But how could she do that without her truck? Suddenly, Kaitlyn wasn't sure she wanted to be here when the cops showed up. She didn't want to be anywhere that Jace might see her.

Quit it! she scolded herself. *There's no way he can find me so quickly.* But then she had no idea how he'd found her in Cheyenne, which was a long way from Des Moines, and then followed her to Logan. But somehow he had!

Watching the wreckage of the semi, Kaitlyn backed into the brush and grass, hoping to make it to the concealment of the nearby trees. Her foot caught on something and she stumbled and fell hard on her back. Momentarily stunned, she finally cleared her head and pulled herself into a sitting position. When she looked around to see what had tripped her, she spotted a purse—not her purse, but one that did look familiar. After studying it for a moment, it struck her. It was the woman's purse—the kidnapper's, the thief's. She had pulled the pistol from it.

Kaitlyn picked up the purse. It was open and weighed very little. She assumed most of the contents were strewn throughout the bushes along with bits and pieces of her destroyed truck. Still sitting on the ground, she looked inside. There was a large wad of bills held together with a heavy elastic band. With instinct borne of desperation, she shoved the bills into the front pocket of her jeans, knowing she would need money. Her own money, like everything else she carried in her truck—credit card, driver's license, and other forms of ID—was in the wrecked truck, probably destroyed.

Kaitlyn looked into the purse again, hoping to discover the identity of the woman who had stolen her truck. There was nothing else in the purse but some lipstick, a set of keys, and a wad of tissues.

She dropped the purse and looked up as she heard sirens wailing in the distance. Struggling to her feet, Kaitlyn again headed for the trees. She had to get out of sight. Suddenly, someone shouted, "Get back people! It might explode. There's gas here, and there's a flame by the engine."

She looked back. People were stampeding away from the wreckage. An explosion suddenly rocked the ground. Flames shot skyward. Her mangled truck levitated, flipped over at least once, and then plummeted, a searing ball of flames. Kaitlyn's legs were barely working now as she tried to move away from the burning wreckage. Her breathing shallow and rapid, her eyes wide but unseeing, she sank to the ground, sobbing softly.

She sat immovable until a hand gripped her shoulder and a voice spoke. "Kaitlyn. I'm so glad I found you. I was afraid you'd been killed."

Kaitlyn yelped and tried to get to her feet, but strong dark arms restrained her.

"Hey, hey, calm down, girl. It's only me. It's Celia Dulce. I didn't mean to startle you."

"Oh, it's you. I'm sorry, Celia. I've been so afraid that Jace would find me. My truck's demolished. I have no way to get out of here. I don't know what I'll do now." She fired off her thoughts in machine-gun fashion.

"I'm here, girl. You can come with me," Celia said.

"How did you find me? I'm sorry I didn't make it for lunch." Her rapid-fire statements now spilled out in an emotional rush. "I got stuck in traffic on the other side of Boise, and then this woman pulled a gun on me. She was trying to steal my truck just now. But she . . ." Kaitlyn couldn't go on. It was all a terrible nightmare.

Celia's strong arms surrounded her friend's shoulders. Kaitlyn could feel Celia's arms shaking as she said softly, "I thought it was you in the truck. I saw it start to pull out just before it got hit. I knew it was your truck. I was one of the first people at the wreck after the dust died down, and when I saw what was left of the driver, I just knew it was you."

"I guess I'm lucky," Kaitlyn said.

"Yes, you are," Celia agreed. "Somebody found your purse in the truck before the explosion. A man read off your name from the driver's license. And you can't tell by looking that it's not you except that the hair didn't look right. Her face was pretty much gone. Now, of course, she's burned, which will make it difficult for anyone to identify the body."

"I feel terrible. I hate to see anyone killed. It's so awful. But I've got to go and let them know it's not me in there . . . unless . . ." Kaitlyn's mind began to function again.

"Unless what, dear?" Celia pressed.

"Unless I let them think I'm dead. Then maybe Jace will think that, too, and stop hunting for me," she said, suddenly hopeful that she'd stumbled onto a way of eluding him permanently.

"Good idea, girl!" Celia said, giving her a squeeze. "There's no reason for them to believe anything else. I can't think they'd suspect that it might not be you . . . unless . . ." She hesitated now.

It was Kaitlyn's turn to ask, "Unless what?"

"Unless they found her purse in the truck, too. You know, before it started to burn. She did have a purse, didn't she?" Celia asked.

"Yes, but it's right over there," Kaitlyn said, pointing. "It somehow got thrown out when the semi hit my truck. There wasn't any identification in it, but they could probably still find that if they look hard enough."

"Not if we find it first. Let me think for a minute, Kaitlyn. The most important thing we can do right now is keep you alive, and if that means deceiving the police—well, at least temporarily—then that's what we'll do. Let me think," Celia repeated.

She was silent for a moment, her hand over her eyes. Kaitlyn looked toward the wreckage again. The police had arrived, and other people were milling around. The police seemed to be attempting to restore some sort of order, trying to move people back. No one was paying any attention to her and Celia, who also began looking toward the wreckage. After a moment, she said, "Show me the purse, Kaitlyn."

"It's right over there," Kaitlyn said, and she started moving toward where she'd left it. "Here it is." She bent and picked it up.

"Good, now let's see if we can figure out where the contents were strewn," Celia suggested. But the grass and brush were too thick, and after a few moments of futile searching, they gave up. "We can't take more time. Someone will begin to wonder what we're doing over here. Anyway, if we can't find her billfold or whatever—if there even was one— it's not likely that anyone else will. Come on. Let's get into my rig."

"Are you sure?" Kaitlyn asked hesitantly.

"Of course I am. If this Jace guy is as dangerous and persistent as you say he is, then it would be best if he thinks you're dead," she said.

"But what if he doesn't hear about the wreck?" Kaitlyn asked.

"Then it will mean he couldn't trace you this far, and that would also be good. But do you dare take that chance?" Celia asked.

"No," Kaitlyn answered softly. "I don't."

"Then away we go."

A few minutes later they were several miles from the scene of the accident. Kaitlyn felt strangely removed from the tragedy. It was as if she no longer existed. She was no one.

But she was alive. She closed her eyes and poured out her gratitude in silent prayer.

* * *

"We're closing in on her," Jace said exuberantly. "She's just a few miles ahead. She must have stopped for something."

Myler just grinned and stroked his mustache. This was the part he loved, closing in on his quarry. He drove a little faster. A few minutes passed. "Kaitlyn's stopped. Her truck's not moving," Jace announced. "There must be a motel or a restaurant not too far ahead."

The instrument in his hands began beeping more rapidly just as they came to a traffic slowdown. Before long, the traffic was at a crawl, then a standstill. "What's going on?" Jace demanded. "We don't have time for this."

"We have no choice, man. We're in a traffic jam, a big one."

"We do have a choice," Jace said. "Drive up the shoulder."

"You've got to be kidding. The other drivers won't like that," Myler replied.

"I don't care what they like," Jace yelled. "Just do it. Do it now!"

Myler was right. Drivers honked and shouted angrily as they passed. The beeping from the locator unit grew steadily stronger and faster. Soon, they could see smoke curling into the air. "There must be a wreck ahead," Myler said.

Even by driving on the shoulder, it took nearly ten minutes before they were close to the wreck. The instrument in Jace's hands was beeping madly. "It's right near here," Jace said. "She's probably stalled in the traffic near the wreck."

"Looks pretty bad up there," Myler said. "We can't go any farther unless we rejoin the traffic. I'll see if I can squeeze my way in."

"No, stop the car right here. We'll walk from here. The locator is close. It's very close. My girl is close. She's probably frustrated with the stalled traffic, too."

Neither of them could see Kaitlyn's pickup in the mass of cars and trucks. The police stopped them just before they arrived at the actual crash site. All they could see was the jackknifed, overturned trailer of a big rig. Beyond it was the fire. "Is there another car involved?" Myler asked an officer.

"Yes, and it's burning. You've got to stay back. Go to your car, please. It's a mess up there."

"What is the other vehicle?" Jace asked.

"I think it was a pickup, but I can't be sure," the officer said. "It's all crunched up and burning. As soon as they can get the fire suppressed, they'll try to get the body of the driver out, or at least what's left of her, which won't be much, I'm afraid. Now, please, you've got to stay back."

"No!" Jace suddenly cried, his face pale. He rushed headlong past the officer.

"Hey!" the officer yelled. "Get back here right now." He ran after Jace, grabbed him by the collar, and jerked him back. "Don't go up there. They're trying to work."

As Jace fought to free himself of the officer's grip, Myler walked past both of them, his mustache twitching. But the grin on his face faded when he saw the wreckage. The fire was almost out now. Myler caught a glimpse of what was left of the driver, burned beyond recognition. Then Jace, who had finally freed himself from the officer, rushed up.

One look at his face told Myler that Jace had figured it out. To Myler's disgust, Jace grabbed his face and began to sob, calling Kaitlyn's name over and over again.

CHAPTER 5

"AM I DOING THE RIGHT thing?" Kaitlyn asked her friend as the semi rolled east through Boise.

"Are you afraid of Jace?" Celia asked, her face expressionless.

"I'm terrified of him."

"Then you're doing the right thing. Kaitlyn, you said yourself that you haven't known Jace all that long. What makes you think he's such a terrible person?" Celia asked. "I mean, I know he's obsessed with you, but that doesn't necessarily make him a killer, does it?"

"Maybe not, but he is a killer," Kaitlyn responded. "I haven't told you everything. When that guy at the rodeo knocked him down the first time, as Jace was getting back up, he threatened to kill the guy. If you'd heard him you'd know what I mean. It wasn't an idle threat. He meant it. You see, even though I was stunned after Jace hit me, I also heard him tell the guy who saved me that he'd killed before. That's why I wouldn't even let the guy or the girl with him tell me their names. I was afraid that Jace might regain consciousness, and I didn't want him to hear who they were. I know that if Jace ever catches me, he'll try to find out who the guy in the black hat was. If I don't know, he can never make me tell him."

"I understand what you're saying," Celia told her, "but Jace was angry. He'd just been knocked down in front of his girlfriend."

"I'm not his girlfriend," Kaitlyn said sharply.

"I know that, Kaitlyn, but that's obviously not what *he* thinks. Anyway, he was probably embarrassed, and that makes anger even worse. And he might have said all that even if it wasn't true. Isn't that a possibility?"

Kaitlyn nodded. "I suppose so, but I don't dare take that chance. I mean, if you could have seen his eyes when I told him I wouldn't go out with him again, I think you'd understand."

"Okay, Kaitlyn, I'm with you on this. But we've got to decide what you're going to do now," Celia said. "You're without transportation. Of course, you're welcome to ride with me for as long as you'd like to, but I know that will soon bore you."

"Celia, I'm so lucky to have met you, but you don't have to do this for me. I'll be such a burden," Kaitlyn said.

"You won't be any such thing. But I have an idea," Celia said brightly.

"Really?" Kaitlyn asked, cheered by the inflection in Celia's voice.

"Yeah, really. We still haven't had lunch. Let's stop somewhere before we get out of Boise and eat. Then we'll talk about it."

Kaitlyn couldn't help but smile. Celia was trying to cheer her up, and it was working.

* * *

Jace was a basket case, his behavior totally repulsive. Kaitlyn's death had hit him hard. Myler had never expected that. The Jace he'd worked for before was cold, merciless. He cared nothing for the life of anyone who got in his way. That was why the two had always hit it off. They were cut from the same mold.

Or so Myler had thought. This reaction to some woman's death wasn't what he had anticipated. He'd thought Jace wanted Kaitlyn as a toy, a possession that he could discard when he got tired of her, just like the others before her. But now he wondered if Jace actually had some feelings for the woman.

She must have been quite a girl, Myler thought as he pulled off the freeway in Boise in search of a place to eat. He was hungry. Jace said he didn't want to eat, but Myler wasn't going to let that stop him. Anyway, they had time. It might be a while before Jace could pull himself together enough to fly the jet, which was waiting for them at the airport. He really hoped they wouldn't have to spend the night here. Of course, if they did, he'd bill Jace for every second.

He pulled into a café that looked acceptable. There were a few trucks parked near it, and a number of other vehicles. It wasn't fancy, but it would do. "I'm going to get something to eat, Jace. You coming?" he asked as he opened the door to the rental car.

"No. You go. I can't eat. I'll just wait here," Jace said glumly.

"Whatever suits you," Myler said. He wasn't in any mood to try to cheer up his companion. This hunt had ended on a low note, a real downer. He preferred to find the prey alive. And even though it didn't make any difference to him that the girl was dead, he did care that his hunt had ended so poorly.

* * *

After double-checking the number Kaitlyn had given him, Jim Perrett tried again. He knew he was punching it in correctly. Once again, however, he received a message that said the number he was calling was not available. He disconnected and turned to Nancy. "Either her phone is off or she can't get a signal," he said.

"Cell phones. They're not very reliable," Nancy responded.

"But it rang when I called earlier. She just didn't answer. I'm sure she'd want to know what the vet said about her horse's condition."

"Possibly, or maybe it'll frighten her. The girl's in some kind of trouble. I'm sure of it," Nancy said.

"I'm afraid you're right, but she should know about the sedative that the vet found in Tony B's blood. Someone intentionally put it in his feed bin. Whoever it was, according to the vet, knew what he was doing. It wasn't enough to kill a horse, just enough to make it ill, to keep it from racing well."

"Are you suggesting that someone was trying to keep Kaitlyn from winning?" Nancy asked.

"That's exactly what I'm suggesting. And unless I miss my guess, it has something to do with those two men who were here asking about her," Jim concluded.

"You may be right, and that's frightening. Surely they can't have found her and done something to her," Nancy said with a shiver.

"I hope not, but I'm afraid it's a possibility. I think that if she doesn't contact us in the next day or two, we need to let the police know," Jim said decisively.

* * *

"Here you are, ladies," the waitress said as she placed their meals in front of them.

"Thank you," Kaitlyn and Celia replied in unison.

"You're welcome. If I can get you anything else, please let me know."

After the waitress walked away, Kaitlyn said, "I feel so strange. It's like I don't even know who I am."

Celia chuckled. "Then maybe we'd better figure that out. This is what I wanted to speak with you about earlier. You need a new identity. Maybe we could start by giving you a name, something you can go by until it's safe to let it be known that you're not really dead."

"But what name could I use?" Kaitlyn asked. "Anything will sound strange, I'm afraid."

"Of course it will, but you can get used to it. I think something common and easy to remember would be good." Celia suggested.

"You mean like Jane or Lucy or something like that?" Kaitlyn asked.

"Something like that, but neither of those will do. How about Kathy? You could be Kathy Green. Would that work? It's even close to your real name," Celia said with a grin.

Kaitlyn sat there for a minute. Finally she said, "Sure, Kathy will be fine. Kathy Green. Yeah, that'll work I guess."

"Good, then Kathy it is. Now let's eat. Time's passing, and I've got a load to move down the freeway."

* * *

Myler picked a seat at a table in the center of the room, sat down, and looked around. The place appeared to be full of truckers. *Well, mostly full of truckers,* he corrected himself. The two women in one of the booths by the window couldn't be truckers. Nor was the old couple directly across the room from him. And the three teenagers at the table a short distance from him were too young to drive the big rigs. And, of course, he was not a trucker. But he was hungry and ready to eat, regardless of the company.

A waitress placed a glass of water at his table. "Would you like a menu, sir?" she asked.

"Of course I'd like a menu. What do you think I came in for, to sit and drink water? I'm a hungry man," Myler said. "So get my menu right now." Stupid questions made him testy. Especially when he was on edge, and he had certainly been edgy since his hunt had ended so badly.

The waitress hurried away and returned momentarily with the menu. "Do you need a minute or two to decide?" she asked.

Myler looked up, annoyed at her again. That was another stupid question. "I haven't even glanced at it yet. You be back in three minutes," he said testily. "I'll order then."

"Yes, sir, I'll do that," the waitress said, a catch in her voice.

By the time she returned, Myler was ready to order. "I'll have the meatloaf," he said.

"I'm sorry, sir, but we're out of meatloaf. Is there something—" she began.

Myler cut her off angrily. "If you're out, you have no business having it on the menu," he protested loudly. "What kind of place do you run here, anyway?"

"I'm sorry, sir," the waitress said. "We usually have it. We just ran out a few minutes ago. There is more almost ready to go in the oven, but it will be an hour before it's done."

"You want me to go and then come back later, is that it? Like I have nothing better to do?" he complained, still loudly.

"No, sir. If you'd like something else, I'd be happy to get it for you," she said, fighting to maintain a semblance of composure.

For a moment Myler hesitated as he looked again at the menu. Finally he said, "Roast beef on toast. And you better not be out of that."

"No, sir, we aren't," she said. Then she took the rest of his order and hurried toward the kitchen.

* * *

Only a few yards away, Celia and Kaitlyn had witnessed the embarrassing exchange, as had the rest of the customers. As the waitress rushed past them, she was wiping her eyes.

"The poor girl," Celia said. "I despise people like that guy. If this were my café, I'd refuse to serve him after such offensive behavior."

Kaitlyn nodded, then spoke very quietly so she couldn't be overheard. "Jace acted like that one time when we were having dinner. This guy acts just like him."

"There are a lot of people like that," Celia said. "It's just too bad, Kathy." She winked, and a tiny smile formed at the corners of her mouth at the use of the newly assumed name.

That cheered Kaitlyn up a little, and she began eating again. A couple of times she glanced in the direction of the overweight man with the long mustache, sagging jowls, and badly pockmarked face who had been so rude. The second time, he happened to look up at the same moment she did, and their eyes met briefly before she looked away. The look in the man's eyes made her uneasy. For several minutes she made an effort not to glance in his direction. But finally, she couldn't help herself and cast a glimpse his way again.

He was wolfing down his lunch. Her unease grew. Celia, watching her, said very softly, "You've had a rough day, honey. Don't let every creep you see remind you of . . . well, you know who. Your life begins now. Let's finish eating and hit the road."

After a few minutes the loud fellow with the mustache got up, his chair scraping noisily on the floor. "I need my check," he shouted at the waitress, who was helping a customer at the booth next to his.

The young woman cringed but spoke politely. "I'll be right with you, sir." Then she leaned over to talk with the tall, broad-shouldered trucker at the booth she was serving near Kaitlyn and Celia. "I'm sorry, sir," she said. "I need to go help that guy. But I'll be right back."

The big trucker smiled. "It's okay. The sooner you give him his check, the sooner he leaves. I'll enjoy my lunch a lot more when he's gone."

A minute or so later, Kaitlyn looked up and saw the man paying his bill at the cash register. Her eyes didn't linger that time, however. He appeared to be studying her while holding some cash in his hand. She whispered to Celia. "That horrid man is watching me. He's spooking me really badly. Something about that awful face of his seems familiar somehow."

"Don't look at him again, *Kathy,*" Celia said, with emphasis and extra volume on her new name. She reached across the table and put her hand on Kaitlyn's. "You'll feel better about things soon," she added in a barely discernible whisper.

* * *

Jace appeared not to have moved since Myler left to go eat. Myler got into the car, slipped the key into the ignition, and then hesitated before starting the engine. Something about that young woman in the restaurant was bothering him. She seemed so familiar to him. Then suddenly it hit him. She looked a lot like the girl he'd been hunting. "Jace, give me that picture of Kaitlyn you have in your pocket," he demanded.

Jace sat statue-like, but Myler held out his large, open palm. Slowly Jace turned his head. His face was contorted into a hideous, hateful frown. "How dare you ask for her picture?" he asked bitterly. "She's dead. You didn't find her in time. You're finished. You don't need her picture."

Myler took a deep breath. "We don't know she's dead," he said.

"We do!" Jace shouted, spraying spittle into Myler's face. "You saw that wreck, Myler. No one could have survived it."

Myler struggled to control his temper. Jace could be a real pain at times, but he was also the source of a lot of money. Taking his time, Myler found his handkerchief and wiped his face without a word. He then folded the cloth neatly and put it back into his pocket. Nodding toward the restaurant, he said, "Jace, I think she's in there. The woman with her called her Kathy, but she reminds me of the pictures you showed me of Kaitlyn. If I could see one now, I'd know for sure."

Jace's face went pasty white. "You'd better not be lying," he said, threatening the one person who might be able to help him. "Or so help me, I'll—"

"Give me the picture. I'm going back in," Myler said, cutting off the impending threat.

Jace slowly reached into his shirt pocket and pulled out the small photo of Kaitlyn he'd carried ever since the hunt began. He held it out to Myler, who studied it carefully for a minute before handing it back to Jace. "I don't know who was killed in her truck, but Kaitlyn's alive, Jace," he said. "She's in that restaurant. Let's go get her!"

The two men jumped out of the car and raced to the restaurant. "I'll be the one to grab her," Jace reminded Myler as they hurried along. "If you're right, that is."

* * *

"Celia!" Kaitlyn said urgently, suddenly feeling faint and ducking down in the cab of Celia's semi.

"What's the matter?" Celia demanded.

"It's him. It's Jace! He's with that hideous man from the restaurant."

"Where?"

"They just ran past us, headed inside."

"Yes, I see them. Are you sure that's Jace?" Celia asked.

"I'm sure. I could never mistake Jace. That man with him, he must have recognized me in there. He must have seen pictures of me. I knew he was staring at me for some reason. And now I know why he seems familiar. Jim Perrett described him to me with amazingly accurate detail."

"Calm down, girl," Celia said as she started the truck. "We'll be on our way in a moment. They have no way of knowing what we're driving. You'll be safe."

Celia put the big rig in gear and pulled away.

* * *

"They're gone. They were right there eating when I left, and now they're gone," Myler said, pointing toward the booth by the window.

"Then let's find them. They can't be far," Jace said eagerly.

Myler spotted the young waitress who had been so incompetent. "Hey, you, miss," he said as he lunged across the room toward her.

"Me?" she asked, turning pale.

"Yes, you. I didn't stutter," he said rudely. "The two women who were in the booth there by the window—when did they leave?"

"I guess just after you did," she said.

"Did they go out the front door?" he said, pointing. "Or did they go out the back door?"

She looked flustered. "I don't know. I didn't notice."

"You," he said, turning to a burly man in the booth next to the one the women had been seated in. "That good-looking girl in that booth. I know you saw her. No red-blooded man could have missed her. Which door did she and that black woman with her leave through?"

The man looked up and smiled, but he said nothing. "Hey, jerk!" Jace shouted, shaking his finger in the customer's face. "My friend asked you a question."

"Yes, he did," the fellow answered. "But that don't mean I got an answer."

"So help me . . ." Myler said, his face flushing as he pointed a fat finger in the trucker's face. "So help me, you will tell me. Jace, show him her picture."

Jace took out the photograph. "Was this her?" he asked. "Was she one of the women who was eating there?"

The big trucker nodded. "Could be," he said.

"Which way did she go?"

"Why do you want to know?" the trucker asked.

"Ain't none of your business," Jace said hotly. "I'm only asking one more time."

The fellow smiled again. Then he pushed back his chair and got to his feet. He towered over both men. "Follow me. I'll show you," he said.

The room was still. Everyone was watching the drama unfold. Jace and Myler followed the trucker to the back exit, where they stepped outside with him. "They came this way, did they?" Jace demanded.

"I didn't say that," the burly man said as he suddenly grabbed both men by the backs of their shirts and slammed their heads together with tremendous force. Then he dropped them to the sidewalk and reentered the restaurant.

It took a moment for Myler to shake the cobwebs from his head. He rose unsteadily to his feet, looking at Jace, who was still on the ground groaning. "I'll kill him," Myler said, "right this minute."

Jace got to his knees before he spoke. "Not before we find Kaitlyn," he said weakly. "She can't be far."

Ten minutes of frantic searching through a parking lot full of trucks revealed no sign of the women. Myler was angry. Jace was strangely calm. "It was her, wasn't it?" he asked Myler.

"Oh, yeah, she's alive, Jace. I don't know what her game is, but so help me we'll find her."

CHAPTER 6

BROCK'S BOSS WASN'T SURPRISED BY the news that Brock's last day at work would be Tuesday. He'd already planned to make some cutbacks in personnel in a few days. He asked that Brock plan to put in a long day on Tuesday to wrap up a project he'd been working on. He also kept Brock a little late that Monday afternoon. Brock called Jodi's cell phone as soon as he was finally able to leave, but he was afraid she might already be at his apartment, wondering why he wasn't there.

She confirmed that a moment later, and he apologized, explaining that his boss needed his added help since he was leaving so soon. "I'll hurry," he said. "I hope you don't mind waiting a few minutes for me to get there."

"When it comes to you, I think I'll have a lot of waiting to do, but I'll try getting used to it," she teased.

Relieved that she wasn't angry, Brock promised to hurry. It was almost five before he got home, but Jodi greeted him with a smile and a hug. "Let's get to work," she said lightly.

Brock unlocked his apartment door and ushered Jodi in ahead of him. She really was a nice girl, he thought. Being so far away in just a couple of days wasn't going to be easy. He could envision a terrific future with Jodi.

"I ordered pizza," he told her a moment later. "It should be delivered about six."

"Sounds good," she said.

* * *

Nina had tried to enjoy the day, but her dad was distracted. "Let's go see how your mother's doing," he said that evening after they trudged back up a steep trail they had gone down earlier. "Anyway, it's time for dinner pretty soon. I'll bet you'd like to eat."

Nina nodded. She was hungry. It was several hours ago that she and her father had eaten lunch. She looked around her at the towering red rock spires. They were magnificent, like nothing Nina had ever seen before. But her mother's absence took much of the enchantment out of the hike and the gorgeous surroundings. She was ready to go back to Ruby's Inn. And yet she wasn't. Her mother's mysterious behavior was a worry to her. She wished she knew what was going on, but it didn't seem that either parent was going to talk to her about it.

When Nina and her father returned to the motel, her mother was asleep on the bed. Her father put a finger to his lips and whispered, "We'll have to eat a little later."

Nina didn't argue. She simply picked up a coloring book and silently went to work with her crayons. Her father sat down with a book and began to read. Nina noticed how he frequently looked up and gazed at her mother's sleeping face.

Something was definitely wrong.

* * *

Kelvin Glenn was badly in need of money. It never occurred to him that he could relieve some of the pressure by getting a steady job. Work was too much trouble. Regular jobs were for other people, not for him. He did have a solution in mind, however. Kaitlyn had her trust account. If he could find a way to tap into it, he'd be on easy street and wouldn't even have to take the odd jobs he did now. It hadn't been hard to find the information on the bank that held Kaitlyn's money. He had even located her account number when, with the help of a friend, he'd picked the lock of her apartment over a year ago. But getting into the account was not as easy as he had assumed it would be. He'd tried several times to access it under various guises but failed each time. He'd even resorted to having an acquaintance who was good at hacking into computers make an attempt for him. That too was unsuccessful.

It made Kelvin livid to think that his stepsister had access to all that money while he struggled to make ends meet. The more he'd thought about it over the past few months, the angrier he had become. He went back to her apartment, determined to force her to give him some money. That's when he discovered she no longer lived there. The woman who answered the door had never heard of Kaitlyn Glenn. He'd been searching for Kaitlyn ever since.

Finally, he was having some success. At least he'd learned that she had a horse named Tony B that she was running in barrel races at rodeos across the country. With what money he could raise by selling a few drugs on the street and by begging and borrowing from his dad, he'd gone in search of her. He was closing in now. The Internet provided his most recent information. He found that Kaitlyn had won a race in Cheyenne just a few days earlier.

As he sat in a sleazy bar that Monday evening in a suburb of Cheyenne, he sipped a beer and considered his next move. He already knew where rodeos were scheduled in the area for the next few weeks. But he didn't want to have to show up at all of them if he didn't have to. Why spend all that effort if he could avoid it?

That's when he had an idea. All Kelvin needed was to find someone else who was involved directly in professional rodeo, someone who could feed him information. He might even get lucky and find someone who knew Kaitlyn or had at least met her. If he could do that, he was sure he could also find out where she was likely to be at a future date, and that's where he would show up.

Kelvin smiled. This couldn't be too hard now. He just needed to find out which bars the rodeo cowboys frequented in the area. *Easy street, here I come.* His smile turned into a lopsided smirk.

* * *

That same night Kaitlyn was pondering her future as she rode in the cab of Celia's dark blue semi while her new friend drove east. Celia was heading for Columbus, Ohio, where the load of furniture she was hauling was to be delivered. She kept assuring Kaitlyn that she could ride with her for as long as she liked. In fact, she could even stay with her when she took a few days off the next week. Her home, Celia explained, was in Alabama. That was where she spent some of her days off, which, frankly, were not many. She preferred to work as much as she could.

They talked as they traveled. Celia seemed excited about helping Kaitlyn find a new life as Kathy Green, and even though they had seen Jace and the man who seemed to be helping him pursue Kaitlyn, Celia assured her there was no way they could find her now.

Kaitlyn wasn't so sure. She continued to worry about Jace and how close behind them he might be at that moment. She also worried about Tony B. She couldn't just abandon him. She loved her horse. She wanted to make sure he was okay, that he was over the sickness he'd been suffering from when she'd left him in Logan.

"You're worrying about your horse, aren't you?" Celia asked suddenly.

Kaitlyn looked over at her. "Yes," she said. "You don't understand what he means to me. He's more than a pet, he's a . . ." She hesitated, embarrassed to share the feelings she had for her horse.

Celia's white teeth suddenly shone in her dark face as she grinned. "It's okay," she said. "I think I understand. Tony B is like a close friend."

"Yeah, that's right," Kaitlyn agreed.

"And he should be. I'm sure the two of you have spent a lot of hours together," Celia said.

"Yeah, hundreds."

"Would you like to check on him?"

That question stunned Kaitlyn. It wasn't that she didn't want to, but that Celia would suggest it was surprising, considering the fact that they had to pretend she was dead—that Kaitlyn Glenn had perished in the accident. It took her a moment to answer as she thought about the dangers that checking on Tony B might present to herself and to Jim and Nancy Perrett. Jace knew they had her horse, and if he now suspected that she'd survived the crash, he might go there and harass them.

Finally, she said, "You know, I would like to check on him, Celia, but I don't want to put the Perretts in danger."

"Because Jace thinks you might not actually be dead," Celia reasoned.

"Exactly," Kaitlyn agreed.

"Well, there should be a way to find out and still convince this Jim Perrett guy that you really did die."

"Like what?"

"Well, let me think."

Silence reigned in the cab for the next few minutes. Finally, Celia spoke. "Perhaps you could fake a will. Leave the horse to me in that will. Then I could present myself at the ranch and make arrangements to pay for his keep and discuss moving him away from there. They wouldn't need to know where I was taking him," Celia said thoughtfully.

Kaitlyn mulled that over for a moment. Then she asked, "Okay, suppose that worked, how would we move him? Even if we rented a pickup to pull my horse trailer, it would be risky. Jace knows what my trailer looks like. Who knows, he might have even written down the license number."

"I guess we could use a different trailer as well as a different truck," Celia suggested. "Perhaps we could pretend that the trailer is now mine as well, and Jim could see about disposing of it for us." She grinned at Kaitlyn again. But the grin faded. "Actually, that probably wouldn't work," she said. "Without a court order or something, it might not be possible to transfer the title."

"The same is true of Tony B," Kaitlyn suggested. "He's a registered horse, and there would need to be a transfer made."

"Oh," Celia said, crestfallen. "Even with a will? Actually, that's a bad idea. Wills have to be probated, and that takes a lot of time. There must be a way, but whatever we come up with, it could be complicated. I really don't understand all that kind of stuff. Maybe we just need to forget it."

"Or maybe I just need to be me," Kaitlyn said. "That way I could buy a new truck, go get him, and take him somewhere else."

"And have Jace chasing you again," Celia reminded her.

"Yes, and that," Kaitlyn agreed hopelessly. She was silent for a moment and then said, "I've got to do something. I've got to know that Tony B's okay."

"We'll think about it for a while, Kaitlyn. Then, when we get closer to Logan, maybe we'll have a better plan," Celia suggested. "I'm a little ahead of schedule on delivering this load, so if we needed to we could swing over that way. If nothing else, I could somehow at least check on him. Don't worry. We'll think of something."

Kaitlyn was not comforted. She felt an obligation to Tony B as well as to Jim Perrett. She worried that Jace and that horrid man with him might do something to the horse out of sheer meanness. For that matter, they might even harm Jim and his wife if they thought they knew more than they were saying. She didn't feel right about protecting herself if it put someone else at risk. She closed her eyes and offered a short prayer. She needed help knowing what to do.

* * *

An Idaho state trooper examined the purse of the dead woman. He could still smell and feel the horror of the accident that had claimed her life. Phillip Franson had been a trooper for only five years, but he was dedicated to the job. This accident had certainly not been the first he had worked on, nor was it the worst, but it was nonetheless a bad one.

He carefully upended the purse on the table in front of him. He counted the modest amount of cash and wrote down the amount, although he knew that had been done earlier. He was just being thorough. He also counted the change. Then he studied each item he'd laid out. There was a small key ring. It contained only three keys, and he wondered what they might open. He laid them down and ran his eyes over the comb, the hairbrush, a tube of lipstick, some makeup, a checkbook, and a variety of other items.

He picked up the driver's license that had been secured in a small compartment in a zippered pocket of the purse. He stared sadly at the picture of the victim for a moment. She had been a beautiful woman, and in the picture she was smiling broadly. She didn't appear to be much younger than his wife, Jennifer, and it made him shudder to think of a woman dying in such a tragedy when her whole life was still ahead of her.

Witnesses had clearly established that she had pulled onto the freeway from the shoulder directly into the path of the semi. How she could have failed to see the huge vehicle was beyond him. Apparently, she had not looked. That oversight had cost Kaitlyn Glenn her life. He looked once more at the picture and then at the license itself—an Iowa driver's license with an Iowa address on it and a recent issue date. He jotted down the address.

After putting aside the license, Officer Franson picked up the checkbook. The checks had the same Iowa address on them, but a phone number was also imprinted. Someone would need to contact that address, but not by phone, he decided. One of the things he'd been assigned to do was discover who her next of kin were so they could be located and advised of her death. So far, that address was the most likely lead.

He returned the checkbook and then examined the single credit card she had carried in the same zipped pocket of the purse where he'd found the license and checkbook. It was a Visa, issued by a bank in Des

Moines, Iowa. He looked at it for a moment, wondering if would be of any value in his investigation. He decided it could be and placed it next to the checkbook

Next he picked up the address book he'd originally arranged on the table beside the money. This was where he was most likely to find names of people that had to be notified. Surprisingly, it contained only a few names and addresses, and none of them matched her last name. Perhaps the address on her checkbook would be the only place that family could be located. Only her name appeared on the checks, but he still wondered if a husband was waiting somewhere, pacing the floor and worrying about why he hadn't heard from his beautiful wife.

He scrutinized the address book again and then wrote down each of the dozen or so names, addresses, and phone numbers listed there. Because they were mostly addresses in California, he began to wonder if that might be where she was from. Her truck had carried Iowa license plates, but that didn't necessarily mean she'd been in Iowa all of her life any more than the address on her license and checks did. And if she was married, it could explain why none of the names in the book matched her last name. It was very likely that some of the people whose names he'd written down were relatives.

After a few more minutes, his sergeant came in. "Making any progress, Phillip?" he asked.

Phillip explained what he'd found.

"Well, looks like you'd better start calling some phone numbers," the sergeant said. "That's not many. Shouldn't take you long."

"But what if one is a husband, or a brother, a sister, or parent or something? Wouldn't a visit by someone be more compassionate?" he asked.

"Yeah, I suppose it would, but I'm not sure it's compassion we're after right now," the sergeant snapped. "We don't have a lot of time to waste. The woman's dead, and we have what remains of her body at the morgue. It needs to be disposed of. Someone will be broken up, but that can't be helped. Start calling those numbers, Phillip. Start with the one on her checks."

"Maybe the ones from the address book would be better," Phillip suggested. "What if I could find out that her husband lives at the address in Des Moines? I could call and have an officer there make a personal contact for us," Phillip suggested.

"Whatever makes you feel good, trooper, just get it done soon," the sergeant brusquely ordered and left the room.

Phillip picked up his notebook and moved to the end of the table by the phone. Then he looked over the list. He decided to start at the top and work his way down through the names until he found the information he needed. He picked up the receiver and punched in the first number, Judy Adams, with an address in San Jose, California. The phone rang once before a message informed him that the number was no longer in service. As he worked his way through the list, he got similar results each time he dialed. Some numbers were no longer in use, and others were not answered. One had an answering machine, but he didn't feel it would be appropriate to leave a message. He could call that number again later.

The eighth name was Jim Perrett in Logan, Utah. He punched the number in and waited as the phone rang. It was answered on the third ring.

* * *

"Jim, it's for you," Nancy said as she extended the phone to him. "It's a police officer in Idaho."

"Jim Perrett speaking," he said, wondering what the police from Idaho would want to talk to him about.

"Hello, Mr. Perrett. My name is Trooper Phillip Franson. I'm with the Idaho Highway Patrol."

"What can I do for you, trooper?" Jim asked.

"I need to know in what way you know a young woman by the name of Kaitlyn Glenn," the trooper said.

Jim caught his breath. "Kaitlyn?" he said. "Is something wrong?"

"Is she a relative?" the trooper asked.

It seemed to Jim that he was avoiding answering his question. He felt an uncomfortable rolling in his stomach.

"No, she's just someone I did a favor for," Jim said. "Please, tell me, is something wrong?"

"What kind of favor did you do?" the trooper asked.

Jim was nervous. How could he be sure this was a trooper? For all he knew it could be one of those men who'd been here looking for her in the middle of the night. "Just a moment," he said, and he cupped his hand over the phone and spoke to his wife, who was still standing nearby, her face white with worry. "Did you look at the caller ID before you answered?" he asked.

"Yes, it's a legitimate call," she said. "Has something happened to Kaitlyn?"

"I don't know. He won't tell me," Jim said, and he again lifted the phone. "Trooper, I have some property that belongs to Kaitlyn. I've been keeping it for her. That's my only acquaintance with her."

"What kind of property?" he asked.

"A horse and a horse trailer," Jim said. "Now you've got to tell me what's going on. Is she in some kind of trouble?"

"Why do you ask that?" Trooper Franson asked.

"Because when she left the horse, she was frightened of something or someone. And the horse was ill. Turns out, my vet tells me, it had been intentionally fed some kind of substance that made it ill. And when Kaitlyn left, she asked me not to tell anyone that I knew her. I'm afraid I'm breaking that confidence now, but I don't know what else to do. I was thinking about calling the police anyway because I haven't been able to get an answer on her cell phone."

"You're doing the right thing, Mr. Perrett. I'm sorry to have to tell you this, but Kaitlyn has been killed. She was—"

"They murdered her!" Jim blurted. "Those two men murdered her!" He was addressing his wife more than the trooper. "They found her and they killed her."

"Hey, Mr. Perrett, calm down, please," Phillip said. "She is dead, but she was not murdered."

"Maybe they made it look that way," Jim said, sounding very upset. "But I'm here to tell you, those two men who were here looking for her are behind it."

"No, Kaitlyn was in a traffic accident," Phillip revealed. "Her pickup was struck by a semi. It all happened very fast, and she died instantly. But I would like you to tell me about those men."

In response, Jim related the brief story.

Then the trooper asked, "Do you know anything about her family? We need to notify them, and so far we haven't found out who they are. From what you've told me, it appears that she was single."

"Oh, yes, she was that," Jim agreed. "And she didn't mention any family except to tell me that her father wasn't dying the way those men had told me since he had passed away when she was very young."

"I see. Did she mention her mother?"

"No. Trooper, what would you suggest I do about the horse and trailer?"

"I don't know. If we can find her next of kin, I'll let you know how to contact them, and maybe you can work out a resolution then," Trooper Franson suggested. "I'll call you when I learn anything. In the meantime, we'll look into those two men you mentioned. Maybe someone saw them at the scene of the crash."

After he'd hung the phone up, Jim turned to Nancy. "We hardly even know the girl, and yet I feel like we've lost a close friend."

Nancy was wiping her eyes. "We did, Jim. She was a dear friend."

CHAPTER 7

PHILLIP ABSENTLY HELD THE RECEIVER in his hand for a long time after Jim Perrett disconnected, and he stared at the far wall. The conversation with the Utah rancher had disturbed him, leaving him with more questions than answers. He still didn't know who he should notify regarding the dead woman's accident. And he wondered if in fact the men who had claimed to be cousins of Kaitlyn's were in some mysterious way involved with the accident. Jim Perrett had certainly felt strongly about that.

He had a list of names of witnesses, some of whom might have seen something more than was related in the brief statements they had given at the accident scene. He had a feeling they should be questioned again, and yet he also knew that his sergeant would not like the idea. He wanted this accident investigation wrapped up, the reports completed, and next-of-kin notified. And he wanted it done immediately. *But is that fair to the dead girl?* Phillip asked himself. He knew the answer to the question even as he asked it.

There were still four names left from the address book and the phone number from the victim's checkbook. Before he did anything else, he knew he should finish those calls. One of the four from the address book netted him some information. The woman who answered said she'd been a friend of Kaitlyn's at college but that they hadn't talked for months. She wondered why Phillip was asking.

When he told her, she broke down. It took several minutes before she could finally speak. "I met her brother one time," she said. "Actually, he was a stepbrother and several years older than Kaitlyn."

"What's his name and how can I reach him?" Phillip asked.

"His name's Kelvin Glenn. But I don't know how you can contact him. Kaitlyn's mother, her stepfather, and Kelvin disowned her when she joined The Church of Jesus Christ of Latter-day Saints. It made them furious. I don't know why. I went with her once to a meeting on Sunday, and it seemed like a nice church. She tried to get me to go back, but I never did. Now I wish I had, for her sake."

Phillip felt a jolt. He and his family were active members of the Church, and his current calling was ward missionary. Between his work now and his full-time mission a few years ago, he could relate to the rejection that some converts felt. It made him all the more determined to get to the bottom of Kaitlyn Glenn's untimely death.

"Do you know where any of them live?" he asked.

"No, they moved shortly after that, and Kaitlyn was unable to find them. I don't know of any other family," she said through her sniffles. "I can't believe this has happened. She loved her new church. She loved life. She loved her horse."

"You know about her horse?" Phillip asked.

"Sure. The last time I talked to her was just before she left to barrel race last summer. I talked to her several times in the first part of the summer, but then things changed in my life, and she said she wasn't going to be coming back here, and we sort of lost touch. Now I feel terrible," the young woman said. "Kaitlyn is . . . was . . . a really good person. It's just too bad her family didn't know that. Her stepbrother is awful." She paused for a moment, and when she spoke again, there was a touch of anger and suspicion in her voice. "Are you sure it was an accident? I wouldn't put it past Kelvin to hurt her. She had some money in a trust account left by her real father. Kelvin wanted that money. He's into drugs, never had a job to speak of, and he told her that the money was as much his as hers and that he really needed some of it. He might have decided to find her to try to get it."

"How much money?" Phillip asked suspiciously.

"I don't know. She never said. But I think it was a lot. I know she paid cash for her new pickup and horse trailer before she left, and from something she said I remember thinking that it must not have put a dent in her account."

Phillip took a deep breath, considering the unknown men who had contacted Jim Perrett. Then he said, "If you think of anything else that might be helpful, please give me a call." He gave her his cell number and then disconnected.

The last call was to the number in Iowa. It was answered by a young woman named Rachel Young. She too was broken up by the news of

Kaitlyn's fatal accident. "She was being stalked after she left here," Rachel told him.

"Stalked?" Phillip asked, his blood turning cold. This was the third call that had given him a similar result—*there had been enemies in Kaitlyn's life.*

"Yes, I'd say that was what you'd call it," Rachel confirmed. "Kaitlyn and I were roommates. It's my fault about the guy."

"Who is the guy?" Phillip asked. "And what do you mean by it being your fault about him?"

"She worked for the company he owns. His name is Jace Landry," Rachel said. "Kaitlyn worked for Jace's company as a secretary. He was always asking her out, and she kept refusing. I told her that was not polite, so finally she gave in and accepted. That was a mistake. Turns out he's a real jerk. He thought he owned her after one date. She got really scared of him, took her horse, and left the state. She bought a new cell phone just before she left, and she never did give me the number. She said it might be best if I didn't have it. She was right. Jace tried to get it from me. He didn't leave me alone until I let him look at my cell phone, my address book, and even the drawers of my desk. I guess I finally convinced him I didn't know where she went. I never heard from her after she left here that last morning." She sobbed for a moment. "Now I never will."

Phillip stared at the picture on the dead girl's driver's license for a long time after hanging up. He'd never had an accident case that so thoroughly saddened him. He was still holding the license when his sergeant walked into the squad room.

"Hey, Phillip, some guy just called and said he had some information about the accident, and he thought we might be interested. I told him to come in and talk to you. He'll be here in about thirty minutes."

"Okay," Phillip said. "Maybe he can help me. It seems like this girl's life had more than the normal amount of twists and turns. She may even have been in danger. I spoke with three people who knew her. All three of them indicated that they wouldn't be surprised if she was murdered. One guy has her horse down in Logan, Utah. She was in some kind of trouble but didn't tell him what it was. Later, two men showed up claiming to be her cousins. He said they were not decent guys, and he was sure they were lying to him. Her former roommate said that her former boss was stalking her, and a friend of hers from college told me that she has a stepbrother who wants some money she has in a trust account. She said he too might go so far as to hurt or kill her if he thought he could somehow get the money."

"All that might be true," the sergeant said, "but you and I both saw the wreckage. It was her fault. That girl pulled out in front of the semi. End of story."

"But why did she do that?" Phillip pressed.

"Because she forgot to look, trooper. People do that all the time. Now forget all this nonsense about murder and get this thing wrapped up. You're wasting time."

* * *

Celia and Kaitlyn were drawing closer to Utah. Celia looked over at her young friend. "Look, let me just call this Jim Perrett guy and see what happens. I don't have to give him my name, and maybe he'll say something about Tony B when I tell him you got killed and that I knew you'd be worried about the horse. Let's just see what he says," she suggested. "At least it might put your mind at rest. I could even tell him you told me about Jace and the other guy before you died and ask him if he's heard from them. And I could warn him that they could be dangerous and that he might want to call the cops."

"Okay," Kaitlyn said. "But let's use a pay phone, not your cell. I don't want Jace to find out anything about you. I refuse to put you in more danger."

"Hey, girl, I can handle myself," Celia said. As she spoke, she reached over and dropped open her glove compartment. "Look under all that paper in there," she instructed.

Kaitlyn sifted through the contents. Beneath the things she moved was a shiny silver pistol. "I have a permit for it in several states," Celia said. "And I know how to use it. It's not always safe for a girl who travels alone all the time." She chuckled. "If we need it, it's there. Now let's get off the freeway at the next exit and make that call."

* * *

Jim's phone rang again. The number on his caller ID indicated that the caller's number was not available. His heart began to pound fiercely. He looked at Nancy. "Could it be those men?" he asked fearfully.

"Maybe you better not answer it," Nancy said.

"That won't help. Whoever's calling has our number. And, of course, those two who were after Kaitlyn have been here. They know where we live. Anyway, it could be anybody." He picked up the phone, held it to his ear for a moment, and then said, "Hello."

"Is this Jim Perrett?" a woman with a deep voice and Southern drawl asked.

"Who's asking?" he responded.

"You don't know me, but I'm a friend of a young woman you helped. I tried to help her, too. Her name is Kaitlyn Glenn," the voice said.

"I . . . I . . . uh, I don't know what you're talking about," Jim said, remembering the charge Kaitlyn had given him that night.

"Please, let me explain. Kaitlyn told me about you. She said she left her horse, Tony B, and her horse trailer with you. The last time I talked to her, she was very worried about the horse. She said he was sick."

"Ma'am, like you said, I don't know who you are, so I don't have anything to say to you," Jim said uncomfortably.

"Please, listen to me for a minute. I have some really bad news about Kaitlyn. She was in a terrible wreck in Idaho. She was going to meet me for lunch and didn't show up, and then I drove up on the wreck. She was killed. I was just hoping that you would tell me how her horse is. She was so worried about him, and I'm so upset. She was such a good girl. I would just feel better if I knew that her horse was okay and in good hands. She loved that horse. He was the only thing she had in the world that she was close to."

The woman quit speaking. Jim was trying to sort out his thoughts. The woman must have actually known Kaitlyn or she wouldn't know so many details about the horse. Finally, he decided to say something. After all, the poor girl was gone. No one could hurt her now. "I know about her death. A trooper from Idaho called me. He was looking through her address book, trying to locate next-of-kin."

"It's so horrible," the woman said.

"It sure is. She was a sweet girl. For what it's worth, Tony B is fine. Someone had put something in his feed that made him sick. But my vet took good care of him, and he's as good as new now. I just don't know what to do about him," he said.

"Would you do me a favor? Keep him there for a while. Feed him and provide whatever else horses need. I'll send you some money. Maybe later we can figure out what to do about him. Will you do that?" she asked.

"Yes, of course I will. It's the least I can do, but I don't need any money."

"I'll send some anyway. When you get it, you won't know who it came from. It will just be cash. I'd just feel so much better knowing that Kaitlyn's horse is receiving good care. Oh, and one more thing," she said. "If two men come there looking for her, don't tell them anything. But you might want to call the police, let them know what's happening. The guys are dangerous. And I know Kaitlyn would not have wanted you to get hurt."

Before Jim could respond, the call was terminated. His hands were trembling. As he looked over at his wife, who had listened to most of the call on another handset, he saw that she too was shaking.

"I guess we better call the police," he said.

* * *

The witness identified himself to Trooper Franson as Craig Stern from Boise. He'd been returning from a business trip to Portland when the accident occurred. "I didn't actually see the wreck happen," he said. "But I saw the pickup that was hit just before the accident occurred. It was maroon in color and was pulled off the road to the north. I didn't think anything of it until I heard the report on the radio about the accident and a woman being killed. I guess what disturbed me was that there was no mention—"

"Trooper, I'm sorry to interrupt," the sergeant said as he burst into the room, clearly not the least bit sorry. "I just spoke on the phone with the lieutenant. We have decided to release the name of the victim. The press is hounding us, and it sounds like there are no more notifications that can reasonably be made."

"That's fine. I'm afraid you're right," Phillip said.

The sergeant was gone as quickly as he had appeared. Phillip turned back to his witness. "I'm sorry about the interruption, Mr. Stern. Now, you were saying that something disturbed you when you heard the report on the radio."

"Yeah, well, I'm more disturbed than ever now. I don't know how you can release a victim's name at this point," Craig said, sounding agitated.

Phillip responded quickly in an attempt to soothe him. "We can't find any next of kin, and the public does have the right to know. Someone might be out there wondering if it's a loved one of theirs and worrying for no cause."

"But what if you've got the wrong lady? You surely haven't had time for an autopsy or anything," Mr. Stern objected.

Patiently, Phillip told him that the purse had been found in the truck with the dead woman just before it exploded and burned.

"But what about the other woman?" Craig asked.

"What other woman?" Phillip was puzzled.

"That's what I was just about to tell you. I saw the truck just before the accident. There were two women in it. One of them, the driver, was just getting out. The other one was sliding over under the wheel. I assumed the first one got back in on the other side," he said. "I thought there should have been two fatalities, not one. That's why I came in to talk to you. Maybe the other girl didn't get back in the truck before it was hit. But she must have been right there when it happened. I'd have thought she'd have been injured, at the very least."

Now Phillip was stunned. "Are you sure about this?" he asked.

"Of course I'm sure. The woman that got out was very attractive. I could tell that even from my side of the freeway. She had long auburn hair and a really nice figure. She was wearing tight blue jeans and a light blue blouse—the kind of woman a guy couldn't miss," Craig said.

"And the other one?" Phillip asked.

"I couldn't see her as well because she was in the truck. She did have long hair, but I'd say it was very dark, possibly even black. Like I said, she was sliding under the steering wheel. She was the one that must have been killed."

"Did the woman who got out have her purse?"

"Well, not as far as I could tell. Seems like both hands were empty. The last I saw her she was stepping around the back of the truck. Then a semi on that side of the freeway blocked my view in the mirror. That's all I saw. I didn't realize there had been an accident until about an hour ago. But I know there were two women. Didn't anyone else mention the other woman?"

"No," Phillip said as he got to his feet, thinking of calls that would have to be made to all the other witnesses on his list. He stepped down to the other end of the table to the phone and called his sergeant on the intercom. "Sergeant, have you released that name yet?"

"I did it as soon as I spoke to you. I told you I was going to do that."

"I think you'd better come in here. This case just got really complicated," Phillip said.

Sergeant Ritter stomped into the squad room a moment later, clearly annoyed. But Phillip ignored his mood. "Sergeant Ritter, this is Craig Stern," he simply said. "He lives here in Boise. There's something he just told me that changes everything."

"How could it change everything?" the sergeant demanded impatiently. "The girl was in the pickup. The pickup pulled onto the road in front a semi. The semi hit the pickup. The girl died. It's that simple."

"I'm afraid it's not that simple, sergeant," Craig Stern said, rising to his feet and squaring himself toward the officer. "You see, I saw the truck just before it was hit. There were two women in it."

"There was one woman," the sergeant countered, glowering.

"No, there were two. One had just gotten out of the truck on the driver's side. The other one was sliding beneath the wheel," he said. "I saw them very clearly."

Sergeant Ritter, although impatient and impulsive, was also a seasoned officer. Phillip could tell by the look on his face that he was as stunned as Phillip had been. "Sit down, Mr. Stern. I guess you better tell me everything you saw."

Twenty minutes later, Lieutenant Rick Alger joined the men in the squad room. He too listened to the eyewitness account of Craig Stern. For ten minutes the men discussed the possible ramifications of this new information. Finally, Lieutenant Alger said decisively, "None of this goes to the press yet. Please, Mr. Stern, don't say anything to anyone else until we call you. Sergeant, round up as many officers as you can. We're going back out to the scene."

"To do what?" Sergeant Ritter asked.

"Search the surrounding area."

"But it's getting dark."

"I realize that. We'll use flashlights if we have to."

"What are we looking for?" the sergeant asked stubbornly.

"Evidence that another person was there. Get busy finding more officers and get out there as soon as you have some more help coming. Phillip and I will be going out right now."

* * *

Jace Landry and Myler Keegan continued to argue. Not about whether or not Kaitlyn had actually been at the restaurant a few hours earlier, but about how to continue with the search. Myler, the professional hunter, had the cooler head of the two. He insisted that it would do no good to go running around the country like wild men. They needed to wait and let things cool down. "We have no idea which direction to go from here," he argued. "I'm afraid her credit card won't help us anymore, nor will your tracking device."

Jace, on the other hand, simply wanted to get on the freeway and drive. Beyond that, he had no plans. The radio in their rental car was on, and they were sitting outside another café in Boise.

Suddenly, Myler said, "Shut up, Jace. Listen."

Both men turned their attention to the radio, where a newswoman was talking about the accident. "The police have now released the name of the woman killed in the accident," she said. "She has been identified as Kaitlyn Glenn, age twenty-two, of Des Moines, Iowa. She died instantly in the crash. It's unknown if drugs or alcohol were involved, but the badly burned remains of the victim have been taken to the medical examiner's office for an autopsy, and further information will be available at a later date. The investigation is still ongoing at this hour."

"Well, I guess that takes care of that," Myler said. "I must have been mistaken. We might as well go home. That girl in the café sure did look like your Kaitlyn, though."

"Maybe, maybe not. Let's go find out," Jace said coolly.

"What are you talking about?" Myler asked, looking at Jace as if he had lost his senses.

"Let's go to the morgue. We can tell them we're her cousins and demand to see the body," Jace said.

"That won't do any good. You saw her at the scene. She was burned badly. You'd never be able to recognize her," Myler argued. "And I don't think you'd want to anyway. You haven't exactly been calm and collected about this whole thing."

"I'm under control now. Let's go to the morgue. If I see her hands, I'll know if it's her or not," Jace said stubbornly.

"Her hands? Why would that help?" Myler asked. "Her hands are probably burned badly, maybe even gone."

"The ring won't be," Jace said.

"What ring?"

"The one on her right ring finger."

"Anybody could have a ring on their right ring finger."

"Not like this one, Myler. It was different. She called it her CTR ring. Never did tell me what CTR stood for, but she seemed proud of it. It was made of sterling silver, and those initials were on the ring where a stone would be on a lot of other rings."

"Jace, you're a blooming genius," Myler said with a grin as he slapped Jace on the leg. "By golly, let's go. You're right. The ring should be there. Let's find out where the morgue is in this city. They'll have to let us have a look."

* * *

Celia and Kaitlyn were also listening to the radio, and they too heard a report confirming the identity of the dead woman. "Looks like they bought it," Celia said after the report was concluded. "Now let's just hope Jace and that creep with him hear it, too."

Kaitlyn nodded in agreement. "It's strange, sitting here in your truck and listening to someone talk about me as if I were dead."

"You are, Kathy. You're a new woman now. As hard as it is, we both know you need to put your past behind you and begin a new life. It'll work out, you'll see."

But in Kaitlyn's mind, it was not that simple. There were so many things that she couldn't just give up—like her membership in the Church. That was the most important thing in the world to her. And she needed the money she had in her name—in her real name—in the bank. There was also Tony B. She couldn't just let go of him.

She didn't mention any of those things to Celia. For now, at least, she would have to play along. She would be Kathy Green. Kathy Green from nowhere.

* * *

"We've both got to get some rest tonight so we can work tomorrow," Brock said. "We better knock off. It won't take me long to pack up the rest of my stuff. You've sure been a lot of help."

"It's been fun, Brock," Jodi said wistfully. "I'm going to miss you. I wonder if they need a waitress or something down there in Moab for the rest of the summer."

"I could ask," Brock said with a grin, "if you're serious."

"I'm serious," she said with a nod of her head. "I'm really going to miss you."

"Likewise," he said. "But for now, you better get home. Your folks won't be happy if you're too late, and I don't want them mad at me."

The two stood facing one another. As they slowly moved closer, Brock leaned down. Jodi reached up. Their faces were just a few inches apart when the phone shattered the electricity of the moment.

"Darn," Brock said as he stepped away from Jodi and grabbed his phone.

"Brock, Dan here," he heard.

"Dan Burke! What are you up to?" Brock said, surprised to be hearing from his friend and former missionary companion. Dan, who had roped in Cheyenne the night he and Jodi had gone to the rodeo, was actually from Idaho Falls, Idaho. The two had remained friends since their missions. Dan had married a girl from Utah and had, at her insistence, given up riding broncos. In his earlier years he'd been pretty good. But he hadn't given up rodeos altogether. He was an excellent roper. That was what he was spending the summer doing.

"I'm just sitting here with my wife watching the news," Dan said. "We just heard some really bad news. Do you remember the barrel racer from the other night, the one who won, I mean?"

Brock felt a jolt. He hadn't thought of Kaitlyn, the pretty cowgirl, all evening. "Yeah, we watched her race on Friday night. She's pretty good."

"Exceptionally good is more like it. I didn't see you after the rodeo," Dan said. "But I did see you in the stands. Was the pretty blond with you?"

"She was," he said, thinking about the man who had threatened Kaitlyn and wondering if the bad news he was about to hear had anything to do with him. To Dan, he added, "You did pretty well yourself."

"Yeah, I guess, but I didn't win much. I've got to do better or my wife will make me quit the rodeo scene altogether. But anyway, the barrel racer, Kaitlyn Glenn, she was supposed to race in Laramie Friday night. I roped there and did better. They mentioned Kaitlyn. She was a no-show. Nobody seemed to have any idea why she didn't come," Dan said. "She'd paid her entry fee and everything."

"I might know," Brock said.

"But you don't even know her," Dan protested.

"Actually, I did meet her. She was threatened by some guy. I sort of got involved in it after the rodeo. She was afraid of the guy. She wouldn't even let me tell her my name. She said it might be dangerous for me." Brock's eyes met Jodi's as he spoke. They were wide with questions.

"Really?" Dan said. "Well, anyway, we were just sitting here watching the news. They said she was killed today in a traffic accident on the interstate west of Boise."

Brock felt like he'd been kicked in the back by an angry horse. He hadn't thought of her all evening as he and Jodi worked in his apartment, but he'd dreamed about her last night. She had really affected him. He couldn't believe what he was hearing. "What happened?" he managed to ask Dan.

"They said she had pulled over on the shoulder of the road and then, when she pulled back on, she drove in front of a semi—she died instantly."

"What about her horse?" Brock asked as shock continued to settle over him.

"Don't know," Dan said. "She didn't have the horse trailer with her. Don't have any idea where she left the horse or trailer. It's a terrible thing. She was LDS. I talked to her a few times. She was a convert."

"Yeah," Brock said. "I noticed her CTR ring that night." Even the near presence of the pretty girl he was looking at didn't temper the deep hurt that slashed through him. It was ridiculous, he told himself. He didn't really even know Kaitlyn.

"Well, what are you up to these days?" Dan asked. "Find a girl yet? That blond, maybe? You're getting old, you know."

"Yeah, I know," Brock acknowledged. For some reason, he didn't feel like discussing Jodi with Dan. But he did tell him about his new job in Moab.

"Hey, that's great. I envy you," Dan said. The two talked for another minute, and then the call was over.

Brock slowly replaced the receiver.

"Brock, what is it?" Jodi asked. "Who was that? Did something happen to that barrel racer you saved? You look like you've seen a ghost."

"That was Dan, a former mission companion. He ropes in rodeos. Remember, I pointed him out to you Friday night. He knew the girl we helped that night after the rodeo," he said. "I need a drink of water."

Jodi followed him into the kitchen. "You mean the girl you saved from that dreadful guy?"

"Yeah, her."

"What about her?" Jodi asked. "Did something happen to her?"

"She's been in a wreck. She was killed."

"Oh no," Jodi moaned. "That's terrible, Brock."

* * *

"There were two women," Lieutenant Alger said as he lifted a purse from the brush. "We'd better fingerprint this. And we'd better search more closely. The contents have to be somewhere around here."

Phillip had never doubted the witness, Craig Stern. Now there was evidence. He wondered who was really killed in the crash. Just then Lieutenant Alger's cell phone rang. He spoke on it for a minute and then shut it. "There are a couple of men at the morgue. They claim to be Kaitlyn Glenn's cousins. They want to look at the body."

CHAPTER 8

THE LIEUTENANT ASKED PHILLIP TO follow him back to the station. "We'll go to the state medical examiner's office together. The sergeant can run the search here. As badly as the dead woman was burned, I can't imagine what these two cousins of hers can tell us, but I guess we'd better find out."

"Lieutenant, I'm betting they're not her cousins. This seems to be too much of a coincidence," Phillip said. "The rancher who has the woman's horse said two men came there looking for her. He thinks—no, he *insists*—that they were intent on doing her harm. He even said that we need to look closer at the accident. He says they had to have had something to do with it."

"I don't see how that could be, but at this point, I suppose we shouldn't rule anything out," Lieutenant Alger said.

* * *

Myler didn't like the way the two patrolmen hovered near them as the medical examiner, clad in white, pulled the body from a cooler. But he knew he and Jace had to keep their cool. He'd warned Jace adamantly to act as if they really were Kaitlyn's cousins and to control his unruly temper no matter what happened. Of course, if the body was that of Kaitlyn Glenn and Jace broke down, that couldn't hurt anything. In fact, it would add credence to their claim.

When the sheet was pulled back, Jace slapped his hand over his mouth and gagged. Myler had seen some ugly things in his life, but this was the worst. He too was sickened by the combination of the horrible smell and the grisly sight. The woman's hair was gone, and there was no face left to examine.

"I'm sorry, men," the medical examiner said. "I warned you that it wouldn't be pretty."

He started to pull up the sheet, but Jace, in a voice that was barely under control, said, "No, pull it down lower."

With a puzzled look, he did as Jace requested, pulling the sheet down to about the victim's waist. That was all that was needed. What was left of the woman's right hand was folded across the charred body. With both hands over his mouth and nose, Jace leaned in closer. Myler saw what his client saw.

"That's enough," Jace said as he stumbled back, gagging worse than ever.

A moment later, he looked Myler in the eye, and Myler gave a slight nod of his head.

"It's her. That's Kaitlyn," Jace said to the medical examiner.

"Are you sure?" the patrol lieutenant asked. "I don't see how you can be sure as badly as the body is disfigured."

"See that ring on her finger?" Jace asked.

"Yes, I see a ring."

"That's how I can tell it's her. Yes, it's our cousin, I'm afraid."

Myler said, "He's right. There's no doubt about it. That's Kaitlyn."

They attempted to leave right then, but the officers insisted on getting some identification. The two were prepared with false names they had agreed on earlier. Myler always had several sets of false ID available, and he produced one with his picture and an address in Arizona. The officers seemed to accept Jace's account of the wallet he'd recently lost.

"He's who he says he is," Myler said. "This is so hard. We loved the girl. She was such a good gal. She was like a sister to both of us. This is unbelievable."

"Are you from Arizona, too?" Lieutenant Alger asked Jace.

"No. I live in New York," Jace said.

"How is it that you both happened to be so close by when she was in the accident?"

"We were trying to locate her, and we knew she was coming this way. My father is really sick, and we wanted to tell her," Myler said. "She was real close to him."

"Why don't you fellows come on down to our office and we'll talk some more," Lieutenant Alger said. "We need a few more facts about the victim to close out our investigation."

"I'm sorry, but we don't have time." Myler was worried. Jace was heading for a meltdown.

"It won't take long," the lieutenant insisted.

"There's nothing more we can tell you. We'll call with funeral arrangements after you've had time to examine the poor girl's body," he said. "You've got to understand. She was like a little sister to us. This is just so hard for both of us."

With that, he nodded at Jace and began to walk away. The officers let them go. Myler knew they had no legal reason to detain them. Neither man spoke until they were back in the rental car and driving away.

"It wasn't her, was it?" Myler asked.

"The ring wasn't even close," Jace acknowledged. "It's someone else, that's for sure."

"Lucky the dead gal had one on that finger at all, or at least what was left of it," Myler agreed. "Made it easier to fake a positive ID. Now all we've got to do is find out where Kaitlyn's gone. She's very much alive, but she wants you to believe she's not."

"Then where do we go now?" Jace asked.

"Back to Logan, Utah. If Kaitlyn's as stuck on that horse of hers as you say she is, she'll make contact with that rancher who has him. He'll tell us what he knows, or we'll make him wish he had," Myler said darkly, his big mustache twitching as he spoke. When his hand was forced, he'd do what he had to do, and Kaitlyn Glenn had forced his hand. Frankly, he didn't mind at all.

* * *

The two men who claimed to be cousins of the dead woman had just left.

"I'd swear those guys are lying," Phillip said to Lieutenant Alger. "They're not who they claim to be."

"Maybe not, but they seemed sure about the ring on the woman's finger," the lieutenant said.

The medical examiner shook his head. "I hate to create more work for myself, but I'm like you, Trooper Franson. I don't trust those men. I'd feel better if I had some DNA from the girl to compare or some dental records," he said. "But if we can't find any family other than those two, who are suspect at best, then I don't know how we can go about finding what we need for me to make comparisons."

Phillip brightened. "I did talk to a former roommate. She's in Des Moines, Iowa. Maybe Kaitlyn left something at her old apartment that would have DNA on it."

"Great idea, Trooper. Kaitlyn might even have a dentist in Des Moines as well."

"Yes, that's possible," Lieutenant Alger agreed.

"I think I'll assign an investigator to this case and have him head for Iowa first thing in the morning," the medical examiner said. "I'll let you both know what I find out."

"That'll be great," Lieutenant Alger said. "But what do we tell the press about who the victim is?"

"Haven't you already told them that it's a young woman by the name of Kaitlyn Glenn?" he asked.

"Yes, but now we don't seem to be sure," the lieutenant said. "We probably need to let that be known."

"I disagree," the medical examiner said firmly. "We are only speculating here. I'd say that the best thing at this point is to go with the status quo. If we learn something different, then we can release further information. For now, all we have are two men who claim to be family and who have also made a supposedly positive identification—two men who we aren't sure we want to believe. Let's wait and see what I can learn."

With that decided, Philip and the lieutenant headed for their office again. Back in the car, Lieutenant Alger said, "I'd like you to stall a little before completing the accident report. I want to be sure before you file it that we have accurate information."

* * *

Celia and Kaitlyn talked late that night in their shared motel room at a large truck stop. "They'll give up now," Celia assured her. "If they haven't already heard that the cops have confirmed your death, they soon will. All we need to do now is figure out a way to get you a new identity and a way for you to make some money."

"I have money," Kaitlyn said.

"That wad from the dead woman's purse won't last long," Celia said.

"I know, but I have a lot of money in an account that was set up by my father when I was little."

"But how do you get into that without giving away that you're not dead?" Celia asked.

"I suppose that's just a risk I'll have to take. I have all the account numbers and the passwords needed to access it from about anywhere," she said. "I memorized them, and it's a good thing I did. But I think that if I don't get it moved to another bank pretty soon, it might disappear."

"How can that happen?" Celia asked.

"My stepbrother; he's not a nice guy. He and his father blew all the money that my father left to my mother. And it was a lot. Then they found out about mine and wanted that, too. They still do. And I think Kelvin—that's my stepbrother—has my account numbers. He doesn't have the passwords, but there are enough crooks out there who might be able to help him hack his way past them."

"How did he get your account numbers?" Celia asked.

"One night, not long before I left California, I'm pretty sure someone was in my apartment. I don't know where my family moved to. They didn't want me to know. But I don't think they went all that far away. Anyway, my guess is that Kelvin was the one who got in." Kaitlyn paused. "None of the windows or doors were broken, and I know that I had them locked. In fact, they were still locked when I came home that night, but I could sort of feel that someone had been in there. I'm guessing Kelvin must have taken one of my keys when I was visiting home before my family moved and had a copy made. Or maybe one of his pals picked the lock. Anyway, someone was in there and went through my belongings. Nothing was taken, but I'm sure my papers were messed with. I'm very neat in how I keep my things, and I could tell they'd been moved. Some of the papers had my account numbers on them. I have a feeling that's what Kelvin was after and that he wrote the numbers down."

"I won't insult you by asking how much money you have, because it's none of my business, but I understand your concern. Also, if Kelvin hears that you're dead, he might be able to hire a sleazy enough lawyer who could make some type of claim for transferring the money," Celia said.

"I hadn't thought of that," Kaitlyn said. "And he could claim Tony B, too. I can't take that chance. What can I do?"

"Here's an idea concerning your money. Could you move it to a different bank and have it put in the name we've given you?" Celia asked.

"Possibly. I can sure try. But what about my horse?"

"Maybe another call to Jim Perrett is in order," Celia said. "I could suggest that he have someone else keep the horse or something like that."

"That's a good idea," Kaitlyn agreed.

"We'll call first thing in the morning, when we're ready to roll again," her friend suggested sleepily.

* * *

The bed squeaked every time Brock rolled over, and he rolled over a lot. No matter how hard he tried, he couldn't quit thinking of Kaitlyn Glenn. His brief encounter with her had left deep feelings that surfaced after he'd learned of her death. It was almost like he had lost a loved one. He eventually got up and paced the floor. When that didn't help, he pulled on his sweats and went out for a run. He ran several miles before returning to his apartment. He was exhausted, but the pretty face, the frightened eyes, and the desperate voice of Kaitlyn were still on his mind. He couldn't shake the images. He showered and then went back to bed. But the insomnia continued. It was a long night.

Brock tried to think of Jodi instead of the dead girl, but it didn't work. Jodi was great. He liked her a lot, and maybe in time he'd shake the terrible sadness he was experiencing and his relationship with Jodi would be back on track. But for right now, he was feeling as empty, as sad, and as deflated as he had ever been.

The boss had asked him to be to work early, and it was with monumental effort that he forced himself out the door at six that morning. He hoped his work would take his mind off the death of a girl he barely knew.

* * *

It was only five in Logan, Utah, but Jim and Nancy Perrett were both up. They too had experienced an interminable night. Jim had talked to a deputy sheriff the night before. The deputy simply told him that if the men came back, he should call 911. That was not particularly comforting.

Nancy finally suggested that it might not be safe to keep Tony B or the horse trailer at their ranch any longer. Their oldest son had a small place where he kept a couple of horses in Randolph, in Rich County. "Let's take the horse and trailer to Jimmy," Nancy suggested as Jim was preparing to leave the house to begin his chores.

"Sounds like a good idea," Jim said. "I'll throw some more hay in Kaitlyn's trailer and get the horse loaded. We can leave right after breakfast if I hurry."

It was during breakfast, shortly after seven, that the next phone call came in. Arrangements had already been made with their son to move Tony B that morning. Both Jim and Nancy were anxious to leave. Jim looked at the caller ID. Just like the night before, the call was coming from an unidentified source. He hesitated, unsure what to do. "I think we should ignore it," Nancy said with a trembling voice.

"That won't help," Jim said, shaking his head. But he still couldn't get himself to answer the phone. He slowly put the handset back down and took a small bite of sausage.

The phone rang several more times before it finally grew silent again. "Let's clean up here and get on our way," Nancy suggested. They had both lost their appetites. In five minutes the table was cleared, their plates were in the dishwasher, and they were out the door.

Jim had barely started to pull out of the driveway, the horse trailer in tow behind them, when his cell phone rang. He looked at Nancy. She shook her head. But he flipped the phone open and again discovered that the call was coming from an unknown source. "I suppose I might as well just answer it," he said, angry that he couldn't control the trembling of his hand.

"I guess, if you think it's best, dear," Nancy said.

Jim lifted the phone, pushed the talk button, and said, "Hello."

"I'm sorry to call so early." It was the deep voice of the woman with the drawl from the night before. He heaved a sigh of relief.

"It's not early. We've been up for hours," Jim said.

"I tried to call you at your house. When you didn't answer, I remembered that Kaitlyn had given me your cell number. This is the friend of Kaitlyn's who called you last night."

"I recognize your voice," Jim said.

"I've been worrying," she said. "Kaitlyn had a brother, a stepbrother actually. Even though they were estranged, when he finds out that

Kaitlyn is dead, he might claim the horse, and that would be awful for Tony B. She told me that he is a terrible man."

"He won't find the horse," Jim said. "He's not at my ranch anymore."

"That's good," the woman responded. The relief he heard in her voice sounded genuine enough. She continued talking. "You and your wife need to be really careful. Kaitlyn had some dangerous enemies, including her brother. I think she said his name is Kelvin. It would be Kelvin Glenn, I think. Kaitlyn assumed the last name after her mother married Kelvin's father."

"Thanks for calling," Jim broke in. "Now don't you worry about the horse anymore."

"Where is Tony B?" the woman asked.

Jim shut his phone and looked over at his wife. "Nancy, something's not right here. I don't think Kaitlyn would have given my number to anyone. And the woman wanted to know where Tony B was being kept. That's why I just quit talking to her. I wonder if people trace these phones, these cellular things?" he said. "I think I'll shut it off just in case."

* * *

"He's a good man, this Jim Perrett fellow," Celia said. "When I asked where Tony B was, he hung up on me. I don't blame him for not trusting me." She smiled, and then added, "Your horse is in good hands."

* * *

Only Nina and her father went to breakfast on Tuesday morning. Her mother had spent much of the morning in the bathroom. Then she'd crawled back into bed. After their breakfast had been served, Nina nibbled for a few minutes. She was worried, but she was also getting angry. She thought her folks should let her know what was going on with her mother. Finally, she made up her mind that if they wouldn't break the silence on the matter, she would. "Daddy," she said after laying her fork on her plate and looking directly at him, "I have a question. Will you answer it for me?"

"Of course, Nina. What do you want to know?" he asked.

"Daddy, what's wrong with Mommy?"

Her father flinched, maintaining silence for a moment, taking time to put another bite of bacon in his mouth and slowly chewing. Nina didn't take her eyes from his face, and as she waited, she folded her arms across her chest.

"Daddy, you said you'd answer my question," she finally said as firmly as she could.

Her father put his fork down. "Yes, I did," he admitted. "The problem is, I don't know. All I know is that she's sick."

"Then why don't we take her to a doctor?" Nina asked, thinking that was the most logical thing to do.

"Actually, that's exactly what I've been thinking. And I talked with your mother about it this morning," Maurice Schiller told his daughter. "I hope you don't mind. I know how much you've looked forward to this vacation."

"It's okay," Nina said. "I just want Mommy to be better and for both of you to be happy again."

"We'll look for a doctor in a few minutes," Maurice promised. "I'm sure your mother will be okay soon and we can continue our vacation as planned."

* * *

"There's no one around the place," Myler said that afternoon as he and Jace walked back to the house from the barn and corrals of the Perrett ranch near Logan, where they'd thoroughly searched for one sorrel gelding.

"The only trailer here has Utah plates on it," Jace said. "I'm sure it belongs to the rancher."

"I don't know enough about horses to know if Kaitlyn's horse is here or not," Myler said. "But I intend to find out."

"How?" Jace asked. "There's no one here to ask."

"Not at the moment, but I'm sure they'll be back. We'll come back, too. We'll wait until we know they're home."

"I say we wait here for them," Jace said.

"I don't think that would be wise," Myler argued. "Anyway, it's hot out here."

"I'll bet it's not hot in the house," Jace retorted. "We can wait in there. I know you can pick the lock."

"That's right, but I don't know if I like the idea."

"Hey, we can watch through the window for them," Jace suggested. "When we see them coming, we'll slip out the back and act like we were looking around the yard for them. They won't know the difference."

"I still think we should come back. But you're the man with the money. We'll try it your way, at least for a while." Myler pulled out a couple of pairs of latex gloves from a bag in the backseat as he spoke. He handed one pair to Jace. "Put these on," he said. "We don't want to leave any fingerprints."

CHAPTER 9

NINA HAD NO CHOICE BUT to sit in the waiting room of the doctor who had agreed to see her mother. There were other patients there, but they were all absorbed with their own problems and thoughts.

No one paid any particular attention to the little girl except for casting an occasional smile in her direction. She looked at magazines that were of little interest to her and watched the TV that was set on a boring soap opera. But most of the time, she just sat with her arms on her lap and quietly watched the people as they traipsed in and out of the waiting room. And she worried, fearing that something was terribly wrong with her mother.

* * *

The doctor had left Maggie and Maurice Schiller sitting in a small examination room. They discussed the possibilities that the doctor had raised during his short exam. Maggie was scared, and she admitted as much to her husband. "I'm too young to die," she said tearfully.

"You're not going to die," Maurice said firmly. "I'm sure you just have something a simple antibiotic will clear up in no time."

Just then the door opened, and the doctor stepped in. Maurice was instantly on his feet. "What did you find out?" he asked, hoping they wouldn't be told that innumerable tests and weeks or months would be necessary to diagnose Maggie's illness.

Dr. Gregorson didn't beat around the bush with them. In one very short sentence he told them what he'd learned. They both went pale. *It wasn't a condition that an antibiotic would clear up.* Maurice, stunned into silence for a moment, finally said, "This can't be true, doctor. We have plans. As soon as we get back to England we have to leave on a business trip to Australia. How much time is left?"

The doctor told them, then he added, "There's no reason you can't travel. And I have some suggestions to make you feel better so you won't be so miserable."

Maggie took the news quietly, but Maurice was clearly upset. "This is a disaster," he told his wife after the doctor had left the room. "All our plans are ruined. And what will we tell Nina?"

"We'll tell her the truth," Maggie said firmly as they too left the exam room and started up the long hallway. "And we'll make the best of our situation. There's nothing else we can do."

"Actually, there is something else," Maurice said angrily. "And you know it. We won't tell Nina a thing, and as soon as we get home, we'll see our own doctor."

"No, Maurice, I know what you're thinking, and I won't go through that. I refuse," she said as they pushed their way through the door to the waiting room.

"We'll talk about that later, but for now, we tell Nina nothing."

His wife nodded meekly and swiped at a tear.

* * *

Nina could see the emotion in her parents' faces the second they came into the room. Her father was upset. In fact, he looked angry. Her mother looked sad. Nina concluded that whatever sickness her mother had was very bad. She wished her nanny had come with them on this trip. She missed Ruby more than ever. Ruby could always soothe her worries.

She looked at her mother with questioning eyes as Maggie reached for her hand. But Maggie just shook her head sadly. "Let's go, Nina."

Nina waited until they were outside to ask the question that was burning in her mind. "What's wrong, Mum? Did the doctor tell you what was making you sick?"

"It's nothing," Maurice said, failing to look Nina in the eye as he spoke. "You don't need to worry. We're going to pick up some medicine in a few minutes that will make your mother feel better."

Nina knew that she wasn't being told everything. It was not *nothing*, or they wouldn't be getting medicine to help her. But she knew her father well enough to realize that for the time being no amount of coaxing would elicit any more information. And she knew that her mother wouldn't say anything either, not as long as her father didn't want her to know.

"I wish Ruby was here," she said out of sheer frustration.

That only made her father angrier. "If you want us to end our vacation right now, then fine. We'll fly back to England tomorrow."

"Maurice, that isn't necessary," Maggie said. "We can finish our vacation. Nina will understand if I can't do everything we planned, but we'll still have a good vacation, won't we Nina?"

"Yes," Nina said, fighting back tears that she'd been keeping in check for hours. She swept a lock of red hair out of her face and pulled free from her mother's hand. Oh, how she missed Ruby. Suddenly her parents seemed like complete strangers, and the rest of her vacation was beginning to lose its appeal.

* * *

As they neared the short lane to their home, Jim and Nancy Perrett both noticed a car parked in front of the house. Jim slowed down. "Are we expecting company?" he asked Nancy.

"Not that I know of," she said. "Jim, what if it's those men again? I think we'd better drive on by. And let's call the sheriff's department."

"I think you're right," he said and accelerated again, passing the lane and continuing on toward Logan. His cell phone had been off since they left with Tony B for Rich County that morning. He handed the phone to his wife, who turned it on and called the sheriff's office.

* * *

Myler Keegan was unethical and dishonest, a real boon to his profession, but he was also cautious. After a couple of hours waiting in the ranch house, his nerves got the better of him. "Okay, Jace, we've tried it your way, but we better not press our luck. We can come back later like I said before, maybe after dark."

Jace was impatient. "Let's wait a while longer. Every minute we lose lets Kaitlyn get farther away. I say we stay. And you are working for me. So sit down."

"No, it's too risky. We'll just have to be patient," Myler insisted.

Jace's face turned dark, and his eyes narrowed. "You aren't listening," he said. "We are waiting right here."

Myler was at the back door. "Wait if you want, but I'm going now. I'm the professional, and even though you are my client, we do things my way from here on out."

Jace glared at him. "I could fire you, you know," he said hotly.

"Go ahead, if you think you need to. I'll be on my way, and I'll send you a bill," Myler responded flippantly. He opened the door and stepped out. As he expected, Jace followed him. His client had no further words for him as they got into the rental car, but Myler could tell he was in a foul mood.

Ten miles down the highway, two police cars passed them, going north. "I'll bet they're headed for the Perrett ranch," Myler said.

"You're just getting jumpy," Jace said snidely. "They could be going anywhere. It's the Perretts who'd be going to the ranch. They may even be there now for all we know."

"Maybe. I'm just being cautious," Myler countered. He slowed down and watched in his mirror until the cars had disappeared. Then he made a quick turn and headed back in the direction they had just come.

"What are you doing, you idiot?" Jace demanded.

"I want to see where those cops are headed, that's all," Myler said.

Jace glared at him but said nothing. As Myler had suspected, when they passed the lane to the ranch, they saw the two patrol cars in front of the Perretts' house.

"From now on," Myler said firmly as they passed by, "I'm in charge, and you keep your mouth shut. No more arguments from you. We'd have been in a jam if we'd stayed there like you wanted."

Jace never liked to admit he was wrong, and he rarely did. This time was no exception. He simply refused to respond to Myler. But Myler believed he'd made his point. It was difficult working a case with the client present, and he seldom did. But, he reminded himself, at the end of this case he'd get a big paycheck for putting up with Jace. And money spoke very loudly to Myler Keegan.

* * *

Jim Perrett and his wife were at the sheriff's office in Logan when one of the deputies came in. "There's a Trooper Phillip Franson on the phone who's been trying to reach you for several hours," he said. "He says no one answers at your house and that your cell phone must not be working."

"Oh, yeah, I've had it turned off. We're afraid that those two men, whoever they are, might be able to trace our location through the cell phone's signals if it's on," Jim explained. "I wonder what the trooper wants."

"He didn't say, but I think it would be okay if you kept your cell phone turned on. I really don't think those men would have the means to trace your phone," the deputy said. "That's not as easy as they might make it look in the movies."

"Really?" Jim said.

"That's right. I'll transfer the call to that phone right there," the deputy said, pointing to a phone on a nearby desk. "You can talk to Trooper Franson from there."

Jim took the call. It was a short conversation. His wife, who had been watching intently, asked, "What did he want? Your face is white. Is it something even worse than we've already heard?"

"No," Jim said, his voice shaky at the news he'd just received. "It seems that the highway patrol in Boise thinks that Kaitlyn might be alive."

"What! But that's not possible," she protested. "Is that what you meant when you asked him how he knew?"

"Yeah. He said two men claiming to be Kaitlyn's cousins asked to view the body. When he described the men, I knew they were the ones who visited us. They claimed it was Kaitlyn, even though the body was badly burned. But when they were asked how they knew, they said it was because of a ring she was wearing."

"That could be pretty conclusive, couldn't it?" Nancy asked.

"Well, sure it could be. But from the way the men looked at each other, the officers figured they were lying. If anything, they think the ring might have told them just the opposite."

"Why have the officers waited until now to tell us?" she asked. "It seems like we should have been told earlier."

"Trooper Franson said that they were keeping it from the press for now, and so they thought they'd tell no one but us until they could be sure."

"And they're still not sure?"

"No. However, they think they will be in the morning. They've sent an investigator to where Kaitlyn was living in Des Moines. They found a dentist who had worked on Kaitlyn's teeth. He gave them X-rays. They also got some hair samples and something else that might have her DNA on it from her former roommate. Trooper Franson said the lab there will be examining it all as soon as the investigator gets back from Iowa. They expect him back on an overnight flight. And they hope to have conclusive proof sometime in the morning," Jim explained.

"I don't understand. What makes them think there could even be someone else who might have been killed?" Nancy asked.

"That's the other thing he just told me. It seems that a witness contacted them, claiming that he saw a girl who fit Kaitlyn's description get out of the truck when another woman slid over into the driver's seat just before pulling out in front of the semi. They went back to do a search and found another purse several yards from the highway. It was almost empty, but they did find some of its contents spread through the brush alongside the highway. They also found a small handgun in the wreckage of the truck. They think the dead woman must be that other person."

"If that's true, then where's Kaitlyn?"

"Good question," he said.

"Will they contact us when they know for sure if Kaitlyn's alive?" Nancy asked.

"Trooper Franson said that if we would keep our cell phone on, they'd call us as soon as they know more. He also said for us to be really careful. He suggests that we might not want to stay at home tonight."

"I still wish they'd have let us know sooner, Jim. Those guys could be really dangerous."

"They called when they did because they'd been worrying about the same thing. But they don't want the press to learn about it yet. He asked us not to say anything about the situation, except to the sheriff's officers here and to one more person." He then explained to his wife who that one person was.

"I see. It makes sense, the phone calls and all. Oh, Jim, we can't stay at home tonight," Nancy said. "I'm really frightened of those men now."

* * *

The time had passed slowly as Celia's large blue semi rolled east on I-80 with the load of furniture bound for Columbus, Ohio. Her plan was to take I-25 south from Cheyenne to Denver. There they would take I-70 across the Midwest and into Columbus.

Kaitlyn was restless. She enjoyed Celia's company, but the hours of riding in the truck with no clear plan for her future were wearing her down. Her life, which had been so full during the beginning of the rodeo season, had become a nightmare. It didn't even seem like *her life* anymore. It was as though Jace had deprived her of everything that was precious to her.

She'd been dozing, and she awoke as the truck slowed down. "Where are we?" she asked Celia.

"We're almost to Cheyenne—not your favorite place at the moment, I know. But I need to take a break. There are laws about how long I can drive at a time," Celia told her with a smile.

"There's nothing wrong with Cheyenne," Kaitlyn said, trying to convince herself as much as her friend. "I'm sure this isn't someplace Jace would expect me to be."

"I'm sure he wouldn't either, especially considering the fact that he must believe you're dead by now."

"I wish I could be sure of that," Kaitlyn said. "And I wish I could be sure that he can't somehow figure out where I am now. He and that guy with him must have a way of tracing me. I can't figure out what it could be, but how else would they know to go to Logan and then follow me on I-84 the way they did? It makes me really jumpy to think about it. I feel like I'm not safe no matter where I go."

"Hey, Kathy, they aren't magic. They don't have special powers of some kind. The answer has to be simple," Celia said.

"Like what?" Kaitlyn asked. She really didn't like being called Kathy. She wished Celia wouldn't do that when they were alone. But since her new friend seemed to think it was a good idea, Kaitlyn didn't feel like hurting her feelings.

"Well, let's see," Celia mused as she steered the truck onto an off-ramp on the outskirts of Cheyenne. "Hey, I wonder . . ." She let her thoughts trail off.

"Wonder what?" Kaitlyn asked.

"Well, were you paying for everything with cash as you traveled? You know, gas for your truck, food, that kind of thing?" Celia asked.

"Some, but I mostly used my credit card, which I don't have anymore. The cops in Boise must have it," Kaitlyn said.

"That's it!" Celia said.

"What's it?"

"The credit card. I know the cops can trace people by following the path of where their credit cards are used. And if they can do it, so can a man like Jace. Who knows, he might have cops that he pays off for their help," she said brightly.

"It never occurred to me!" Kaitlyn said. "But that's it. I used my Visa card in Logan. And I used it in Twin Falls."

"Yep, that could be it. In fact, it almost certainly is. But you don't need to worry now. I guess it's good you can't use your card. Without it, there's no way they can trace you, even if they don't believe you're dead, which is a stretch," Celia told her.

"Okay, you're probably right," Kaitlyn said thoughtfully. "But just to sort of make sure, would you mind calling Jim Perrett again? If Jace and his freaky friend think I'm dead, they would have no reason to contact him. If they haven't tried to talk to him, that would make me feel a lot better, and maybe I'd be less of a grouch about things. I'm sure you're getting tired of my whining."

"You are not whining," Celia said. "In fact, I think you're a very brave young woman. Now, let me pull in here at this truck stop, and then I'll see if I can reach Mr. Perrett."

* * *

The Perretts were back in Randolph at their son's home. They'd decided to spend the night with their son and his family after the deputies had reported that whoever had been at their house early that afternoon was gone, and after the call they received from Trooper Franson. The police went with them to the ranch while Jim finished a few chores, and then they drove back to Rich County. Because of the officers' suggestion and reassurance, they were keeping their cell phone turned on.

They were cautious, though, and didn't make any calls from the phone. Jim had a feeling that the woman with the deep voice would call again. And, of course, both Trooper Franson and the deputies in Logan had promised to call if there was anything new that the Perretts needed to know. At seven that evening, when his cell phone began to ring, Jim was prepared to answer it.

They were sitting in the living room of their son's home, their three-year-old granddaughter, Kayla, on Jim's lap. He'd been reading her a book. He pulled the phone from the case on his belt, flipped it open, and looked at the caller ID. In response to questioning looks from his family, he nodded. "Unknown number," he said. Then he pressed the talk button.

It was the same woman again, and he mouthed to his wife, "It's her," as he listened to the deep, friendly voice.

"Mr. Perrett. I'm sorry to bother you again, but I'm still worried about Tony B," she said.

"You have no cause to be. He's safe for now, but I'm worried about you," Jim told her.

"About me?" the woman asked.

"Yes, about you. And about the young woman who's with you. Why don't you just let me talk to Kaitlyn, and I'll assure her personally that her horse is okay."

That was the one person Trooper Franson had authorized him to tell. They suspected that if Kaitlyn was alive, she must be with the woman who was so worried about Kaitlyn's horse. "But she's dead," the woman said. "You know that."

"Actually, I've learned that someone else died in her truck. She wasn't in it when it was struck by the semi. There was another woman driving it," Jim said. "Now, please, let me talk to Kaitlyn."

* * *

"Take the phone," Celia said. "It's Jim Perrett. He knows you're alive."

"What!" Kaitlyn exclaimed. "How does he know that?"

"Just talk to him," Celia said as she held the phone out to her. "He'll explain."

"Hello, Mr. Perrett," she said a moment later.

"Hi, Kaitlyn. You can't believe how relieved Nancy and I are to know you're alive. It was such a shock when we were told that you'd been killed in an accident. It was also a shock when we were told you were actually still alive, that another woman had died. But it was a great relief."

"How do they know?" Kaitlyn asked.

Jim explained.

Then she said, "So Jace and that other guy know about me. And they are still coming after me."

"I'm afraid so," Jim said. "You and the woman you are with must be extremely careful."

"We are trying to be, but Jace and that horrid man he's with—they won't stop looking until they find me," she said as what little was left of her world came crashing down around her.

"The cops are looking for them now," Jim said.

"And what will they do if they find them?" she asked. "They probably haven't broken any laws. I'm sure they can't be arrested."

"I don't know about that, but Trooper Phillip Franson of the Idaho Highway Patrol wants you to call him. If you can't reach him, then call Lieutenant Rick Alger," he said. "Do you have something to write on? I can give you their numbers."

Celia handed her a pen and tore part of a page from the phonebook in the booth they were calling from. Kaitlyn wrote the numbers down. "Thanks for your help, Mr. Perrett," she said. "I'm sorry I dragged you and your wife into this. It's so awful."

"I'll agree it is that," Jim said. "But at least you don't need to worry about Tony B. We're taking good care of your horse. Now, you call those officers in Idaho. They have your purse and identification and so on. And they need your help in determining who the other woman is. And, Kaitlyn, I'd appreciate it if you'd keep in touch with me. Oh, and tell that woman you're with thanks for helping you. She seems like a good friend."

"Yes, she is," Kaitlyn answered softly, and a moment later she hung up the pay phone. "I need to call an officer in Idaho," she said to Celia. "I guess I'm Kaitlyn Glenn again."

"We'll keep you safe, girl," Celia said, but tears glistened in her eyes as she said it. "It's going to be harder since Jace knows you're still alive." She tried to grin, but it was only a halfhearted effort. Kaitlyn could see only the tips of her very white teeth.

CHAPTER 10

JACE AND MYLER EXCHANGED HEATED WORDS that night. In Myler's opinion, Jace was a nuisance, and he wanted him out of the way so he could do his job without an amateur intruding or interrupting. Besides that, Jace could become a potential witness if, for some as yet unexpected reason, Myler had to step outside the law to solve the case. It was bad enough that Jace knew he'd killed a cop.

In the back of Myler's mind an idea was forming. He didn't want Jace around if he had to turn that idea into a plan in order to find Kaitlyn. And there was something else that was eating away at him. Although he desperately wanted Jace's money, from the moment he had actually seen Kaitlyn in the café in Boise, he'd become obsessed with her. He couldn't suppress the idea of having her for himself. If Jace were to get wind of that, Myler could kiss the money and the girl good-bye, and maybe even his life.

He had finally demanded that Jace get on his plane and fly back to Des Moines. He'd tried unsuccessfully to reason with him at first. They'd argued, with Jace claiming that he had the right to be present on this search since he was forking over the money. Finally, exasperated and ready to walk away from Jace and take up the hunt for his own purposes, Myler made one last proposal.

"Look, Jace, you leave now and I'll take a cut from what you originally offered me. It will cost you less for two reasons," Myler said. "First, if I'm working alone, it will take me less time to find her. And second, you'll be paying at a lower hourly rate if I'm alone, and that will save you money. So go on home and let me get my job done. I'll find the girl."

Jace nodded. "I guess maybe you've got a point."

"You bet I do. This search is going to take some time, possibly a lot of time," Myler said. "We have no way of knowing where she's gone, and I'm going to have to work hard to find out how she got away from Boise and where she went from there, or if she's still somewhere in the Boise area."

Continued arguing seemed pointless. Jace conceded that finding Kaitlyn did look like it could be a long-term project at this point. And spending one-on-one time with Myler was beginning to irk him. "I guess I do need to get back to my company before too much longer," he admitted to Myler. "I need to be there to make sure things are going okay."

Myler could see that the anger had drained from Jace's face. It was time to get him back to his jet and on his way home. "I'll take you back to the airport, Jace. And I'll get to work on finding Kaitlyn. I *will* find her."

"Okay," Jace agreed. "As soon as we have something to eat, I'll be on my way."

As they ate dinner that night in Logan, Myler didn't lay out his plans for Jace. He didn't tell him that he already had some leads to follow up on. He kept hidden the fact that he'd first memorized and then later written down the license numbers of several big rigs that had been parked outside that café in Boise, the one where he was convinced he had seen Kaitlyn Glenn. It would take some time to prove, but he had a gut feeling that the girl had disappeared with the aid of the driver in one of those trucks. Myler had learned over the years to follow his gut feelings. They often led to success.

It made sense to Myler that the truck he was looking for would be one of those that had been parked fairly close to the café, one of those whose license numbers he'd memorized. Then there was another idea, too, one that had been developing for the past few hours.

However, it held a far greater risk, and he determined that it could wait until after he'd tried tracking down the trucks. The other plan would be used only as a last resort. For now, he felt fairly certain that Kaitlyn was in fact traveling in a semi driven by the middle-aged black woman she'd been with in that café. In theory, Myler only had to discover which company the woman drove for in order to find the woman. Then, with a little luck and a little *firm persuasion,* if needed, he'd also locate Kaitlyn Glenn. When that happened, he would decide what to tell Jace. He definitely wanted the man's money, but with every passing hour, having Kaitlyn Glenn became even more enticing. He'd gone a long time without the companionship of a woman. And he'd never had the companionship of a beautiful one. It was about time that changed.

With a promise to report his activities to Jace at least daily, more often if he achieved success, Myler left Jace at his jet and watched until his client was airborne. Then he drove into the gathering darkness in his rented car. The hunt was on, and Myler, the hunter, was in his element.

He rolled the tip of his mustache between his thumb and forefinger as he thought about Kaitlyn Glenn. Yes, he wanted to find that girl very much. And he would do whatever it took to find her, but he would do it cautiously. The last thing he needed was to have the law on his tail.

* * *

It was Brock and Jodi's last evening together before Brock left for Utah. He had to be up and on the road early Wednesday morning for the long drive ahead of him. Jodi had been unavoidably delayed and hadn't even arrived until after eight that night, only minutes after he got home. She brought takeout for them to eat while they finished the last of his packing. By ten thirty, everything was ready. Most of his belongings— the big things—had been taken to his parents' house just thirty miles away. He'd loaded several more things that he would drop off there when he went to tell them good-bye in the morning. Only a few things, including three large suitcases and his saddle, needed to be loaded into his truck before he left the apartment for the last time the next morning. He planned to sleep on his bed that night in his sleeping bag, as all his bedding—what little he owned—was packed.

Jodi's long face communicated her feelings. Brock had mixed emotions. He'd grown quite fond of Jodi over the past few days, but the news of Kaitlyn Glenn's death had left him rattled. He could tell Jodi sensed that he was distracted. "Aren't you going to miss me?" she asked.

"Of course I'm going to miss you," he said, even as he thought about how much he missed Kaitlyn, a girl he hadn't even known.

"Will you e-mail me every day?" Jodi pressed.

"I'll try," he hedged. "I'm going to be really busy at first, learning what my duties are and getting to know the horses, the people, and the area."

Jodi grinned. "I'll make it easy for you," she said. "I'll e-mail you every day, and all you'll have to do is hit reply, type a few lines, and send it. It won't take you any time at all."

"Yeah, that would be great." Brock looked at his watch, hoping Jodi would catch the hint. It was getting late, and he had to get some sleep tonight. Jodi, however, showed no signs of wanting to leave. He looked at her and suddenly felt ashamed as tears filled her eyes. He liked her, but he had a feeling she liked him a lot more. "Hey," he said impulsively, "would you like to go for a walk? I figure I've got thirty minutes before I need to get to bed so I can be rested enough to drive safely tomorrow."

Jodi grinned. "Yeah, sure, let's go," she said as she reached for his hand.

Holding hands, they strolled in the light of a half-moon and occasional street lights. They talked, mostly about trivial things, neither of them wanting to dwell on Brock's departure the next morning. An ice cream shop caught their attention, and they bought two large cones. They ate their treats slowly as they sauntered back to Brock's apartment.

"I better not go in," Jodi said as they stopped on Brock's doorstep. "Your sleeping bag is waiting for you."

"Yeah, and so are my heavy eyelids," he said with a grin. Then he took her in his arms. The kiss they shared was soft and sweet, and they embraced tightly. Then Brock walked Jodi to her car.

As he opened her door, Jodi said, "Oh, Brock, I don't know what I'm going to do."

"You'll stay busy, you'll write e-mails, and you'll miss me," he said, trying to mask his own heavy-hearted feelings.

"And you'll be busy with your horses, with answering my e-mails, and with missing me," Jodi said. She just barely managed a little grin.

Brock nodded and helped her into the car. As she finally drove away, she looked back one last time and gave a little wave. He watched until her car was out of sight, and then he walked slowly back to his apartment. But his thoughts were focused on the beautiful girl who had entered his life such a short time ago, been there so briefly, and then disappeared in a tragic accident. No matter how he tried to shift his thoughts, they returned to Kaitlyn. He grieved her death, and he also grieved the fact that he'd never had the chance to get to know her.

* * *

Kelvin had just arrived in Denver, where there was to be a big two-day rodeo on both Friday and Saturday night. He had succeeded in finding a bronco rider who claimed to know Kaitlyn. He said she was the best barrel racer he knew. He also said that she'd told him she would be competing in Denver. "And she will probably win again, just like she did in Cheyenne," the fellow had told him. "If you're trying to find your sister, that's where you'll want to go."

The same young man told Kelvin that many of the rodeo contestants were probably either in Denver or on their way there. That particular bronco rider was going to be driving down on Thursday.

Kelvin hoped to locate Kaitlyn either Wednesday or Thursday. He wanted to get to her before the rodeo began on Friday night. He was itching to get his hands on the money that she was so selfishly keeping from him. Thanks to the directions he'd received from the bronco rider, he was able to drive directly to the rodeo grounds. He drove around for a few minutes, finding it mostly deserted, before he located a motel nearby and went to bed. He'd begin looking for Kaitlyn in earnest first thing in the morning.

Will she ever be surprised to see me, he thought as he drifted to sleep.

* * *

Before leaving Cheyenne Wednesday morning, Kaitlyn bought a new cell phone with some of the cash she'd found in the purse of the woman who had died in her truck. She also bought some clothes. She'd spent far too much time in the ones she'd been wearing when her truck was destroyed. Believing that she'd soon be able to access her money again, she wasn't quite as concerned about conserving what she'd found as she had been before her conversation with Jim Perrett. She and Celia had left Cheyenne at about ten that morning, expecting to be in Denver for lunch.

After they were on their way, Kaitlyn placed a call from her new phone to Trooper Phillip Franson in Boise. Expecting the trooper to be an older man, she was surprised when the voice that answered sounded like someone in his twenties.

She didn't identify herself at first, simply asking, "Are you the trooper who is investigating the wreck that killed Kaitlyn Glenn?"

"That's me, I'm afraid," the young trooper said. "Do you have some information about the accident?"

"I do," she said. "A friend of mine said you wanted me to call you."

"Ah, actually, yes. I want to hear from anyone who can tell me more about the accident. You know, witnesses who can shed more light on what happened. Did you witness the accident?"

"I did," she said.

"Before you give me more information on the wreck itself, I'll need your name, address, and telephone number," Phillip said.

"Yes. Well, like I said, a friend said you asked him to have me call you, and that if I couldn't reach you I was to call your lieutenant." Kaitlyn was feeling very awkward. She wanted to make sure she didn't say the wrong thing in case the trooper wasn't who he claimed to be. He did sound awfully young. The number Jim had given her—the one she'd called—was a cell phone, and it could be anybody's phone, she realized now, even Jace's or his friend's.

"You mean Lieutenant Alger. He is one of my supervisors, and in case I'm not available, he's collecting information for me. But I'm the investigating officer on the accident," the trooper told her. "Who was the friend who told you to call us?"

"He's from Utah," she said, hoping that he would say Jim's name as he had the lieutenant's. Then she would feel like she could talk freely to him.

"Logan?" he asked after a rather long pause, one that made her nervous.

"Yes, sir," she said.

"Jim Perrett?" he asked.

"Yes," she answered with some relief.

"Miss, are you by any chance Kaitlyn Glenn?" he asked after another pause.

Satisfied that she had the right person, she relaxed a little. "Yes, I am."

"All right!" he exclaimed. "I thought you were alive."

That response caught Kaitlyn off guard. "But Mr. Perrett told me you told him that I was," she said.

"I might have given him that impression, but what I meant to tell him was that I was pretty sure you were, but that we hadn't done all the tests yet to get final confirmation. The lab is working on that right now.

We sent an officer to Des Moines, and he got a set of X-rays of your teeth from your dentist and some hair from your old apartment there. The lab is testing to see if the corpse is you or not," he said. "But you've saved us some trouble by calling. Where are you now?"

"I . . . I'd rather not say," she told him.

"Why not?" he asked. "Do you think you might be in trouble?"

"Actually, I know I'm in trouble. Two pretty unsavory characters are after me, and if they catch me, I can't even imagine what will happen. I can't take a chance that they might find me," she said with an earnestness she hoped he detected in her voice.

"Can you describe the men?" he asked.

Kaitlyn described Jace and his friend.

"That sounds like the same men I spoke with," the officer said. "But, Miss Glenn, those two men claim to be your cousins," he told her.

"They're not," she said angrily. "They are my enemies. That's why I left the accident scene and let everyone believe I was dead. It seemed like I'd be safer if they thought I'd been killed."

"Miss Glenn," the trooper said, "it really is important that we arrange a meeting. For one thing, I have your purse, and I'm sure you'd like to have that back."

"Yes, of course," she agreed.

"And if what another witness told us is true, we need your statement about why you left your pickup and why the dead woman took over as driver and apparently left you standing on the side of the freeway," he said.

"I see," Kaitlyn said, but she was contemplating what the trooper had asked earlier about her being in trouble. She immediately addressed that concern. "Trooper, am I in some kind of trouble with the Idaho Highway Patrol?" she asked.

"Not at the moment," he said, "although I suppose you could be. It's illegal not to report an accident you were involved in and to leave the scene."

"But I wasn't in an accident. The woman stole my truck. I had nothing to do with the wreck," she protested.

"In that case, I suppose you're not in trouble."

"That's good," she answered, but she was still not totally convinced. She hadn't mentioned the money she'd taken from the dead woman's purse. She and Celia, while discussing the matter earlier, had both thought it best that she not mention it because of the potential trouble she could be in. And she didn't need any more trouble. Right now, her life was as full of problems as she could endure.

"Miss Glenn, I'm so sorry for what's happened to you. But I need a complete statement from you. I appreciate your calling me, but I can't complete my report without all the information you have. Nor can you collect from your insurance company on your truck, and I know you will want to be doing that," he said.

"That's true," she agreed.

"Listen," he said, "I'll meet you wherever you like. But we've got to get together, and it would be best if we do it in the next few minutes if possible. I can arrange to protect you as well."

"No, I don't think so," she said sadly. "You don't know Jace."

"Jace?" he asked. "Is he one of the men you're afraid of?"

"Yes, he is. And anyway, you must think I'm still around Boise. But I'm not. I'm a long way from there. Isn't there some way you can send my things to me?" she asked.

"I suppose there is, but I really need your help now. For starters, can you tell me who the woman was who took your truck and was killed?" Trooper Franson asked.

"I can't. I don't know her. I'd never seen her before."

"Okay, let me suggest this," Trooper Franson said. "With your permission, I'd like to record the rest of this call. You can simply tell me the whole story about the accident, and then we'll go from there."

Kaitlyn agreed, and in a few minutes she began to recite her story, starting with why she'd given the woman a ride. She concluded by simply telling the trooper that she'd caught a ride with a trucker and left the accident scene, believing that Jace was probably close by.

"Mr. Perrett told us that he thought the men who were claiming to be your cousins might have had something to do with the wreck," Trooper Franson said. "Is that true?"

"No," she answered. "But I'm sure they're still after me."

"I'm afraid you're right," he told her. Then he explained how they had falsely identified the dead woman as being her, and how he and the other authorities involved didn't believe them. "Kaitlyn, why don't you tell me about Jace and who he really is and why he's after you," he finally requested.

She thought about that for a moment and decided it was time she told the police. She couldn't see how it could make matters any worse than they already were. With a sigh, she told him all about Jace, including his attempt to take her by force in Cheyenne after the rodeo. And she told him how the young man whose name she didn't know had helped her.

"Who is the second man, the one with the heavy jowls, big mustache, and badly marked face?" the trooper asked.

"I don't have any idea," she answered. "I just know that he looks and talks like a really horrible person."

The trooper asked a few more questions, which Kaitlyn answered as truthfully as she could. Finally, he said, "Can I call you back on the phone you're calling from?"

She agreed and gave him the number of her new cell phone. "But please, don't give this number to anyone else," she said. "I don't want to take any chance that Jace will get it."

"Of course," he agreed. "Now, about your purse. How can I get it to you?"

"I don't know," she said honestly. That really was a problem.

"There's got to be someone you trust that we can send it to and you can get it from them."

"I don't know. And anyway, what if it gets lost in the mail?" she asked. "Maybe I can just have someone pick it up for me sometime, and I can get it from them. In the meantime, I'll just have to get along without it."

"Okay, if that's what you want," the trooper said. "But I really do wish you'd make arrangements to come back here from wherever you are. I promise we'll do all we can to help you and keep you safe if you'll come."

"Thanks, but I don't think so. I've got to have some time to think. I know that Jace and that other guy are still after me, and if they ever catch me, I . . . it . . . I just can't let that happen," she stammered.

"I'll be in touch, Miss Glenn," Trooper Franson said. "In the meantime, if you think of anything you haven't told me, please call me, and I'll write it down," he said.

"Okay," she agreed.

"And I promise, if you'll trust me, I'll do whatever I can to help you," he repeated.

After she'd shut her phone, Kaitlyn sighed and turned to Celia. "I think I was better off being Kathy Green," she said. "What am I going to do?"

"We'll take it one step at a time," Celia told her. "The first step will be some lunch when we get to Denver in an hour."

* * *

Jace hadn't heard from Myler since leaving Logan the night before, and it frustrated him. He'd gone into his office that morning, made sure things were running smoothly, then told his senior people that he was going to have to leave town again on some additional private business.

No one had asked where he was going. They'd given that up long ago. But Jace knew where he was going. While Myler did whatever it was he was doing to try to find Kaitlyn, Jace would do some searching on his own. He'd already been on the Internet again. He knew there was a big rodeo in Denver that weekend. And he figured he could learn something about Kaitlyn from some of her rodeo cronies if he went about it carefully.

He taxied onto the runway in his jet, was cleared for takeoff, and in a few minutes had reached his authorized flying altitude. He looked at his watch. He would be in Denver in a short time at the speed this plane of his flew.

* * *

Myler had also been busy that morning. And he was almost certain that he had the name of the truck driver he was looking for. Celia Dulce was a middle-aged black woman who drove for a company called A to Z Transport out of Birmingham, Alabama. And according to company officials, she was currently en route from Portland, Oregon, to Columbus, Ohio. The man he spoke with even told him when she was due to unload there.

They wouldn't tell him the exact location of where her load was to go or the route she was taking, but he had an almanac in his luggage. It hadn't taken him long to decide that the most likely route would be through Denver. He'd caught a flight from Salt Lake City a few minutes earlier. He would be landing in Denver shortly.

CHAPTER 11

BROCK COULDN'T BELIEVE HIS LOUSY luck. He'd been later getting away that morning than he'd planned because he'd slept in. And he'd slept in because he'd been awake much of the night, as he had the night before, with thoughts of Kaitlyn Glenn's death haunting him. Although his acquaintance with her had been brief, it had also been dramatic, and she'd affected him in a way that no other girl had before. Not even Jodi.

Guilt had also kept him awake. The tender kiss and embrace he'd shared with Jodi had been terrific, and yet as he thought about it now, he felt something was lacking. Could that something, he wondered over and over again, have anything to do with Kaitlyn? Guilt had turned to anger—anger at himself for letting someone who could never be part of his life interfere with someone who not only could but apparently wanted to.

When sheer exhaustion overtook him and he finally did sleep, there was one more problem. It seemed that he'd messed up when setting his small travel alarm after finishing his evening prayers. He'd somehow left the little handle in the wrong spot, turning the alarm to the off position instead of on.

When he finally awoke and realized what he'd done, he'd hurried to shower, shave, and dress, and to load his suitcases, sleeping bag, and other items into his truck. His father had already left with Brock's older brother to get a load of grain when he arrived at his folks' place. Brock's dad and brother farmed their place together now. There simply wasn't enough income to include Brock, or he'd have been with them. Brock's mother was worrying about why he was so late. She hugged him and gave him a peck on the cheek as he hurried away only minutes after arriving, telling him to call when he got to Moab.

She followed him to his truck, and as he was getting in, she said lovingly, "I hope things go well with that sweet girl who helped you bring your things out last night. What did you say her name is?"

"Jodi," he said. And he hurriedly drove off, embarrassed that he'd experienced a brain freeze. Jodi's last name had slipped his mind.

But Kaitlyn's hadn't. Kaitlyn Glenn was a name that was going to be hard to forget. *This whole fixation with her is unreasonable,* he told himself. *Sure, it's sad that she was killed. But her life never really had much to do with yours. Come on, Brock, forget her. Don't let that one meeting interfere with your happiness, or with Jodi's.*

Now he was in Denver, still many hours from Moab. And he was sitting in a repair shop while a mechanic tried to figure out what was wrong with his Chevy pickup. It had suddenly died just after he'd left I-25 and started west on I-76. A tow truck had taken him to the nearest Chevrolet dealership, and he was now waiting to hear what the diagnosis would be. *Just fix it quickly so I can be on my way again,* he thought.

* * *

Jordan Thatcher's horse was sweating from the workout she'd just given him in the rodeo arena. He was running very well and responding to her equally as well. Her father was beaming as she came through the gate. "Great job, Jordan," he praised her. Then he turned to a small gathering of people and said, "This girl of mine is going to win Friday night. Even Kaitlyn Glenn couldn't beat her if she were coming."

"Isn't she coming? I know she missed Laramie, but I also know she's signed up for this rodeo," another barrel racer commented. "It'll be hard for any of us to beat her and that horse of hers if she comes."

"Does anyone know why she missed the rodeo in Laramie?" a stranger asked.

Jordan, who was patting her horse's head, looked more closely at the man who'd just spoken. He looked like he might be around thirty. His flowered shirt and long, greasy hair identified him as someone she would not have expected to see at a rodeo arena or to be asking about Kaitlyn.

"We don't know for sure," her father answered, "but I have a feeling she won't be here."

"Why do you say that, Dad?" Jordan asked.

"I don't know. Like I said, it's just a feeling. Maybe it's because she doesn't want to lose to you and she knows that's about to happen."

"Dad, I can't beat her, not unless her horse slips or something. Kaitlyn is really good."

"Yes, she is," the other barrel-racing cowgirl agreed. "We can all learn from her."

"Do all of you know Kaitlyn?" the man in the baggy pants inquired.

"Sure," a young cowboy answered. "She's hard not to know. She's not only a good rider, but she's also a really nice girl."

Jordan noticed the look of disgust that crossed her father's face at that last comment. She couldn't understand why he disliked Kaitlyn so much. She was a great person. His frown deepened when she spoke. "I really admire Kaitlyn. I hope she's here Friday. I've learned so much from her."

"Yeah, and she never makes me feel like I'm not as good as she is," the other girl said. "Kaitlyn does like to win, and it gets old losing to her so often, but I'm like Jordan. I learn a lot from her."

The fellow in the flowered shirt lit a cigarette and blew out a mouthful of smoke. "Then the gist of the matter is that she should be here?"

"Yeah, I'm sure," the young cowboy said. "It's not like her to miss. I'm sure there was a reason she wasn't in Laramie, but I'm betting she'll be here this weekend."

Jordan glanced at the stranger. She didn't feel comfortable around him; he just looked downright nasty. But her father sidled up to him in a friendly manner. "What did you say your name was?"

"I didn't say. But I'm Kelvin." He thrust out the hand that wasn't holding a cigarette. Norman shook his hand, and the fellow added, "Kelvin Glenn."

Jordan took a double take. *He can't be related to Kaitlyn,* she thought. *They don't look anything alike.* Her father then asked the question she didn't want to hear the answer to. "Are you related to Kaitlyn Glenn?"

"Sure am. She's my kid sister," he said. "I came here hoping to get a chance to talk to her."

Jordan's head was swimming. Kaitlyn couldn't have a brother like this guy. "If you're her brother," she began, making no attempt to disguise the doubt in her voice, "then why are you asking us about her? You must know why she wasn't at the rodeo in Laramie."

"No, I actually don't. You see, I've been out of touch with her for a while. It seems that she must have a different cell phone, because the number she last gave me isn't working. I've been worried about her. And like you guys, I knew she was planning to be here in Denver this weekend. That's why I came—so that I could see her and catch up on things."

Jordan instinctively felt that Kelvin was being less than truthful. Not wanting to talk to the guy anymore, she began to lead her horse away from the small group.

"Go rub him down, Jordan," her father called after her. "You need to take good care of him if you expect to win on Friday or Saturday. I'll be along in a minute."

She bristled. He didn't need to tell her what to do. She always gave her horse the best treatment she could. That was one of the things she'd learned from Kaitlyn. Kaitlyn always took really good care of Tony B. Jordan refused to respond, but she looked back a moment later. Her dad was walking away from the rest of the group with Kelvin Glenn. She hated what she was thinking. *Why would he possibly want to talk to that creep?*

* * *

"My name's Norman Thatcher. Tell me about your sister," Norman said after the two of them were out of earshot of the other people.

"Not much to tell," Kelvin replied. "She's just a badly spoiled little brat. The youngest, you know."

"Kind of stuck on herself, isn't she?" Norman asked. His body language told Kelvin that the man didn't like Kaitlyn, and Kelvin instantly realized he'd found an ally.

Kelvin knew Norman's statement wasn't true, but he wasn't about to contradict the man. He did have some questions, though. "Does she make a lot of money doing what she does at rodeos?" he asked.

"More than her share," Norman said bitterly. "Sorry if that bothers you, but she's deprived my daughter of some pretty good earnings."

"Really?" Kelvin said. "Sounds like we're in the same boat."

"How do you mean?"

"She sort of stole a chunk of money from me." Kelvin let bitterness creep into his voice. "She's put it in some accounts that I can't get into. I know the account numbers, but I don't have the access I need to get my money out. That's what I'm here to see her about. She's going to have to square things with me."

"A bunch of money, you say?" Norman asked.

"Yeah, a lot. It's family money. Most of it was supposed to be mine, but she's managed to keep it from me. But that's about to change."

"Can't blame you for being upset," Norman said. "I've wondered how she could afford the expensive horse trailer and truck she has. And that horse she rides—he's a good one. He must have cost a bundle. Some of these barrel racers pay up to fifty grand for their horses. She can't have earned that much in the rodeo business yet."

That news unnerved Kelvin. He honestly didn't have any idea how much money Kaitlyn's father had left her. He wondered how much of the money Kaitlyn had already blown. Money that could have been—should have been—his. He had to get his hands on it before it was all gone.

"Yeah, the horse, the trailer, and even the truck are actually mostly mine. You can see why I need to find her," Kelvin complained.

"You ought to take the horse as part of the deal," Norman suggested. "He'll bring in a lot of money. I'd even be interested in buying him from you if you can work it out with her."

Kelvin smiled. "I'll bet that girl of yours would like to ride him."

"She'd win every time if she had that horse," Norman confided. "That's the only advantage Kaitlyn has over Jordan. Jordan's a much better rider."

"Well, maybe we can work something out. In the meantime, would you do me a favor?"

"Sure thing, Kelvin. What can I do for you?"

"It's simple, really. Just let me know if you see her. I'll be watching, but you might run into her sooner than me."

"Sounds good to me. How do I get in touch with you?"

The two men exchanged cell phone numbers. Then Kelvin asked, "You mentioned to those other people that you didn't think Kaitlyn was going to be here. Have you changed your mind?"

"No, I was just trying to help my daughter worry less. I would actually be surprised if she doesn't show up. And when she does, I'll sure let you know. I'd really rather she didn't race."

"I understand completely," Kelvin told him. "That girl has a way of getting under a person's skin."

"That's for sure. Well, listen, I'll be seeing you around then," Norman said.

"Yeah, but hey, I don't really know anyone around here. Want to have a drink with me tonight? Maybe we could talk about this a little more. I might be able to use some help in persuading Kaitlyn to give me what's mine, and I'd rather not have to go to the cops to do it. She's a rotten little brat, but she is my sister. I don't want to see her go to jail," Kelvin lied. She could rot in jail or six feet under for all he cared. He just wanted her father's money.

"Sure thing. Let me get my kid situated and I'll give you a call later," Norman said. "Maybe by working together, we can both get what we . . . uh . . . have coming."

Thatcher's conspiratorial smile was as phony as Monopoly money, but Kelvin didn't care.

* * *

The new cell phone rang, and Kaitlyn pulled it from her pocket. The only person it could be was Trooper Franson. She wondered what he wanted. She hadn't thought of anything else to tell him. "Hello," she said, her stomach fluttering. It did that a lot lately.

"Hi, Miss Glenn," he said. "This is Phillip Franson. I'm sorry to bother you again so soon. I just thought you might be interested in knowing that we have a lead on the identity of the woman who stole your truck."

"How did you do that?" Kaitlyn asked, surprised. She and Celia were in a diner at a truck stop near I-70, waiting for their lunch. They'd driven through most of the state and were near Aurora, Colorado, when they'd decided to eat.

"The description you gave us matches that of a missing woman from up in Coeur d'Alene. Her husband reported her missing after seeing her with a couple of skinheads one day. She'd left that morning to go in to the café where she worked in as a waitress. But her boss called and said that she never showed up. That's when the husband left work and started toward their home. She was riding in an old blue pickup with these two guys when they passed him, coming from the direction of their house. He was less than a mile from there. He hurried home, wondering if she might have left him a note or something. But there was nothing."

"Had she been kidnapped?" Kaitlyn asked, caught up in the story.

"No one knows. And she didn't take much except a stash of cash the two of them kept beneath their mattress; her purse, which he'd given her for her birthday just a few days earlier; and the clothes she'd been wearing when he left for his job that morning," Trooper Franson explained. "Oh, and she had their pistol, a little .38 caliber revolver. We found one in the wreckage of your truck. That could be the one she used when she stole the truck from you."

"Probably," Kaitlyn said, feeling guilty about the money. She knew she needed to tell him what she'd found and how much, because that might help them prove the dead woman was the one who was missing. "Trooper, I think I might know something that will help."

"I was hoping you would," he said. "But we do think we're on the right track. The purse—the one her husband gave her—fits the description of one we found near the accident. It was out in the bushes a few yards from where your truck was hit. Of course, the money was gone, but that's to be expected. Those skinheads probably got off with that."

Kaitlyn looked around. Other than Celia, she didn't think anyone else would overhear her, and Celia already knew about the money. She decided it was time to confess. "The money that she took from her house, did her husband say how much it was?"

"Yes, why do you ask?"

Kaitlyn ignored his question. "How much was there?"

"He said there should have been about fifteen hundred dollars. That was a lot of cash for her to be carrying when she left home, but he's sure the skinheads have it now."

"Actually, I don't think so," Kaitlyn said. "I hope I'm not in trouble, but I have a confession to make."

"Does it have something to do with the money?" the trooper asked.

Celia was shaking her head, but Kaitlyn forged ahead. Deceit wasn't really part of her nature. That was why the whole Kathy Green thing had made her so uncomfortable. "Well, you see, trooper," she said slowly, trying to choose her words carefully, "I tripped over her purse. I actually fell down when I did. Anyway, some of the stuff was still in it, even though it was open. I took the money. I thought that if I had to be on my own without my own money, maybe I could survive for a while with hers. But there wasn't fifteen hundred dollars there. There was still a lot, though. It was a little under eleven hundred."

"That's interesting," the trooper said, and she could tell from his voice that he was a little shocked. But he went on quickly, as if to reassure her that she was still the victim. "She owed you a lot more than that after taking your truck," he said. "I'm sure you don't need to worry about anyone here pressing charges against you for taking the money."

"I've spent some of it, but I'll give the full amount back when I can. It should be her husband's," Kaitlyn said.

"Actually, the cops up north believe it was drug money. Apparently, both the husband and the missing woman had been busted for drugs several times, and they think both she and the husband had also been dealing. So, when you do give the money back, at least the original unspent part, it will probably be seized as evidence by the officers in Coeur d'Alene," he told her. "They have an open investigation on the husband now."

"I'll make sure I don't spend any of the rest of this. In fact, if you'll give me an address, I'll ship it to you as soon as I can," Kaitlyn volunteered.

"But what will you do for money in the meantime?" Trooper Franson asked. "We have your purse, your cash, and your credit card up here, not to mention your ID."

"Oh, yeah," Kaitlyn said as it all struck her. She had been quite certain that she could walk into any bank in Denver or some other city and find a way to transfer her money and then withdraw some of it. Now she wasn't so sure.

"Listen, Kaitlyn, I think we need to make arrangements for you to come back here and meet us. I promise we'll protect you, and you can begin to get things straightened out on the loss of your truck. Plus you can get your personal ID and money back," he said.

Kaitlyn waffled. She feared going back to Boise, although Jace and his friend had probably moved on by now. But she also knew the trooper was right. "I don't know," she said. "Can I think about it for a few minutes?" What she really wanted to do was talk it over with Celia. She was the only person Kaitlyn could turn to for advice, and she needed advice now.

"Let me call you back in about ten minutes," Trooper Franson said. "I'll be checking on what arrangements we might be able to make to get you back here. Of course, it would help if you'd tell me where you are right now. Will you do that?"

"Not yet," she said. "I'm just so scared."

"Of course," he said. "I'll call in a few minutes."

"Girl, what are you doing?" Celia demanded sternly the moment Kaitlyn shut her new phone. "Why did you tell them about the money?"

"You don't understand, Celia," Kaitlyn said. "I'm not a dishonest person. At least, I try not to be."

Celia's stern face softened. "I'm sorry. I know you're not. Why don't you tell me about that call? I take it that they want you to go back to Boise."

"Yes, and I think they're right," Kaitlyn said. "I want to be me again, and I need to be able to get my money, and without ID, I don't think I can do it."

Celia nodded. "I understand that. Now I'm listening, so tell me about the woman who was killed."

Kaitlyn told her what she'd just learned. "Trooper Franson will be calling me in a few minutes," she added. "I need to decide what to tell him."

"I think I can keep you safe, and I'll lend you money," Celia said. "I fully understand why you can't spend any more of the money you found in that woman's purse. But I would worry if you were to try to fly back to Boise, and I don't know how else you could get back there. I can't take you, even though I would if I could."

"I can fly," Kaitlyn said, "but I don't know what I'll do about buying a ticket."

"I can lend you some money if you insist on going back. I know you're good for it. I trust you, and if you can't repay me, then you can just have it." Celia looked sad. "But I can't help it if I worry about you."

"You don't have to worry about me, Celia. You've done more than I ever could have asked of anybody. And I'm so very grateful."

Their lunch came just as Kaitlyn's phone rang again. Phillip Franson minced no words. "Wherever you are, if you can get to a major airport, we'll see that arrangements are made for you to fly here. And we'll meet you at the gate when you get off the plane. We'll put you in a safe house while you work things out. And we'll do whatever else we need to in order to protect you."

"Okay," she said. "I guess I'd better do that. But will they let me on the airplane without ID?"

"As soon as we know where you are, we'll contact the police there, and we'll work it out," he promised. "Can you get to an airport?"

"I can," she said.

Celia whispered, "I'll go with you to the airport. We'll get a taxi from here."

She nodded her thanks to Celia. "I'm in Denver," she finally told Trooper Franson.

"Just a second," he said, and she could hear him talking to another officer. However, the words were indistinct, as if he had his hand over the phone. A moment later, he came back on the phone. "Okay, we're starting the arrangements. However, there is one other thing. We've been on the phone with an officer in Cheyenne. He wants to talk to you, and after he does, he has assured us that he'll see if he can get assault and attempted kidnapping charges filed against Jace Landry. As soon as there's a warrant, we'll put it out nationwide. If we can get him picked up, it should give you some relief."

"Except that I'd have to testify against him," she said. "I'm not sure I dare do that."

"Let's at least get the warrant. Can I have the officer call you?"

"I guess so," Kaitlyn said. "But have him wait a few minutes. My lunch is getting cold."

As she again closed her phone, she thought about the handsome young man in the black cowboy hat who had saved her from Jace's attack. Who was he? Where was he? His testimony could help put Jace behind bars.

It would also put him in serious danger.

* * *

Myler took a double take. He was just making arrangements to pick up a rental car when he spotted Jace. He appeared to be doing the same thing at a counter a short distance away. *What is he doing in Denver?* he asked himself. *I wonder if he knows something I don't.*

CHAPTER 12

MYLER WAS STILL DEBATING WHETHER to approach Jace when Jace looked up and saw him. Jace stepped out of the short line he was in and hurried over to Myler. "Well, well, if *you're* in Denver," he barked, "it must mean you've learned something that you haven't bothered to report to me."

"I have nothing conclusive to report," Myler shot back. "I thought you were going to go check on your business."

"I did. Everything's okay. I thought I'd fly down here since there's going to be a rodeo in a couple of days and I figured it might not hurt to see if Kaitlyn happens to show up for it," Jace explained. "And now that I see you in the same place, it appears that we must be thinking the same thing. I suppose we might as well team up again. We can't both be wrong."

"Actually, I've got something else to do first," Myler said, surprised to hear about the rodeo and not so sure it wouldn't be a good idea to check things out there.

In any case, first he wanted to find Celia Dulce and her truck, if it happened to be in one of the truck stops along the freeway. And he didn't have time to waste if she was anywhere close by, since she would not likely be staying long. His next stop would be Colorado Springs or somewhere in Kansas if he didn't find her here. He might even fly to Topeka and then wait for her truck to come down I-70 on the outskirts of that city. But now, knowing that the rodeo was coming, he wondered if Celia might not stop by and let Kaitlyn see some of her rodeo friends, possibly even leave her with them before she left Denver. He even wondered if one of them might be bringing her horse to the rodeo and if Kaitlyn might be planning to get together with her four-footed friend.

"We can do it together," Jace insisted.

That wasn't what Myler wanted to hear, although he expected it. He didn't want Jace around when he found Kaitlyn. His own plans for the girl excluded his employer. He was in a bit of a spot, though, and he'd tip his hand if he made too much fuss. He'd just have to think of a way to get rid of Jace again later.

"Let's go get the car," Myler grudgingly agreed.

Myler had already decided that Jace didn't need to know about his plans to ride through every truck stop he could find along the freeway to look for a semi with the name of Celia's company on it. A to Z Transport was a relatively small company, and it would be easy to spot. If he found such a truck, it could very possibly be the one he was looking for, the one Celia Dulce was driving.

* * *

The service advisor finally entered the waiting room. "Mr. Hankins?"

"That's me," Brock said, rising to his feet. "What have you learned? I hope it's not going to take too long to fix my truck."

"It depends on what you mean by *too long*," the advisor said. "It will take three or four hours at best." He looked at his watch. "I'd say that we can have you out of here by four this afternoon, five at the latest."

"Oh, no," Brock said. "There's no way to speed it up?"

"This *is* speeding it up," the manager informed him. "We know you're from out of town and that you need to be on your way as soon as possible. But four or five this afternoon is as soon as we can have your truck ready to go."

Brock took a deep breath. It wasn't this man's fault, and even though he felt like lashing out and saying something angry, he knew it wasn't right and certainly wouldn't change matters. After he let out the breath, he said simply, "Okay. Thanks. I guess I'll see if I can find someplace to eat."

"If you'd like to borrow a vehicle, I'm sure that can be arranged," the man offered. "We don't do that very often, but since no one else is in this room to overhear me, I can make the offer. That way you can take a little spin around the city if you want to. It might help pass the time."

"Thanks, I think I'll take you up on it," Brock said. The thought of sitting in the waiting room for three or four hours with nothing to do but watch insipid TV shows or read outdated magazines with nothing to eat but what the vending machines could spew out was not a rosy prospect.

"Come with me," he was told. "I'll see what I can find for you to use."

The vehicle they lent him was one of their old shop trucks. Its heyday had probably been twenty years earlier. But it had tires and an engine that ran. Brock gratefully got into it and took off. He'd spent enough time in Denver over the years to know his way around the city. He thought about driving to a museum and spending some time there, but his first order of business was to find some food—real food. As he pulled onto the street from the dealership, his cell phone rang.

"Hey, Brock, I just thought I'd see how you're doing," his friend Dan Burke said. "I was just thinking about you. I flew into Denver a few minutes ago and remembered that you were going to be driving through here today on your way to Moab. Just thought I'd call and see how you're doing."

"Thanks for calling, Dan. Other than a little problem with my truck, I'm doing okay. How about you?"

"I'm fine," Dan said.

"What have you got going on in Denver?" Brock asked, thinking that it had to be a rodeo. That's what he did this time of year.

"There's a big rodeo here this weekend," Dan confirmed. "One of my bronco-riding buddies brought my truck and trailer down with my roping horse from Laramie. I needed to get home to my family, and he and his brother share a truck. When I told him I missed Sharon and my little boy, he said, 'Hey, why don't you go see them. I'll drive your rig down to Denver.'"

"How are you getting from the airport to wherever you're staying?" Brock asked.

"I'm going to take a taxi. I could have my buddy come get me, but he and his brother needed to run down to Colorado Springs for something, so I told him I'd find a way. He has my horse stabled, and my truck and trailer are at the rodeo grounds," Dan said.

"Why don't I come out there and pick you up? I could give you a lift to the arena," Brock said. "I'm looking for something to do for a little while, anyway."

"You're not in Denver, are you?" Dan asked. "I thought you'd be way beyond here by now."

Brock laughed. "I thought so too. But it looks like I'm going to be getting into Moab very late tonight. My truck broke down. I've got an old rattletrap they let me borrow to go find a decent place to eat. But if you'd like, I can come get you."

"Great, I'd like that, Brock," Dan said. "I'm hungry, too. We could both get some lunch. And then, if you have time, I could let you take a look at my roping horse, see what you think of him."

"Sounds like a deal. I'm on my way. Where do I find you?" Brock asked. A minute later he was headed for the airport.

* * *

As the taxi shuttled Celia and Kaitlyn toward the airport, Kaitlyn spoke on her phone with a detective in Cheyenne. "I'd like to interview you in person before I try to convince the district attorney to authorize charges and issue a warrant against Jace Landry."

"I'm going to Boise today. They'll be trying to keep me safe there. There's no way I can go to Cheyenne," Kaitlyn protested.

The officer said, "In that case, let me make some calls up here, and then I'll call you back. Maybe we can work something out."

"I hope so," Kaitlyn moaned. "I'm so afraid of Jace. The sooner he's arrested, the better I'll feel."

The cab was rolling east on I-70 just a few miles from the freeway that would take them into the airport when her phone rang. She put it to her ear as an old pickup truck pulled alongside the taxi and then proceeded to pass. Kaitlyn paid no attention to it or the man in the black cowboy hat. She was too busy listening to the officer from Cheyenne who was telling her that if she would let him tape a statement over the phone, it might be enough to get a warrant issued. And he could then meet with her at a later date, possibly even after they had Jace in custody.

A minute later the cab approached the back of the older pickup that had slowed down as the traffic in that lane became mired. The driver looked to his left for a moment, and Kaitlyn drew a sharp breath. In the fleeting glimpse she got from the back of the cab, the man driving the old pickup looked like the rodeo spectator who had saved her from Jace. Of course it couldn't be, but the reminder made her heart race. She thought not only about his bravery but also about the heart-stopping smile he'd given her from the stands as she'd ridden by.

The taxi was soon several lanes over from the pickup and moving ahead of it, and Kaitlyn concentrated on the taped interview that was about to begin with the detective in Cheyenne.

* * *

Brock wondered how many girls would remind him of Kaitlyn before her memory faded. He quickly turned around the second time he overtook and passed a taxi on the freeway. There were two women in the back, the one on the far side middle-aged and black. But the closer one reminded him a lot of Kaitlyn. Except for the lack of a hat, the long auburn hair and attractive profile were strikingly similar.

He looked in his mirror, wishing the cab would draw up alongside him again. When it did catch up, it was two lanes over, and he couldn't see its occupants. Then it moved out ahead of him. Not that it would make any sense for him to try to get another look at the girl. After all, he had Jodi to think about, and Kaitlyn was dead. He shook his head and concentrated on getting to the airport. He didn't want Dan to have to wait too long.

* * *

Frustration was quickly getting the better of Myler. The rental company had taken forever to get him his car. His trip to Denver was a long shot at best, and he needed every minute he could get. He didn't want to have to go to Columbus if it wasn't necessary. And he was getting angrier by the minute that Jace was tagging along with him again.

After leaving the airport, he caught the freeway and then took I-70, watching for major truck stops as he drove west. He knew that Jace would start asking questions when he exited the freeway and began driving around the parking area of the first truck stop he came to. There was nothing to do now but tell him the basic plan.

"What are you doing?" Jace asked predictably before Myler began his explanation.

"I'm looking for a truck," Myler said.

"Why are you doing that?" Jace asked. "We should be looking for my girl."

"I'm doing that, too, because I believe that Kaitlyn left Boise in a semi, and I have a good lead regarding the truck she was riding in and where it was headed," Myler said. "I'm looking for that truck now."

"How did you figure all that out?" Jace asked.

"I investigated," Myler said sharply. "That's what investigators do. I know you can't quite believe it, but I really am very good at my job. We'll check out the area around the rodeo grounds later, but first I just want to follow up on the work I've been doing since you left me in Logan last night."

"Whatever you say," Jace said with a satisfied smile. "I do believe we're going to find my girl again."

* * *

With the interview completed, Kaitlyn closed her phone. "Are you okay, girl?" Celia asked.

"Yes, I'm fine. I just wish they had Jace in custody. He'll be easy to find if he goes back to Des Moines, but I don't know if he'll do that. I'm afraid he'll keep looking for me," Kaitlyn said. "I just wish I could have my life back."

As they were nearing the airport, Trooper Franson called to tell Kaitlyn that arrangements had been made for her flight. "A security officer will meet you at the ticket counter and escort you from there," he said. "I gave him your description, what you told me you're wearing, and so on." He then told her the color of the officer's uniform and his name. "Call me if you have any trouble. Otherwise, I'll see you at the airport in Boise."

Celia and Kaitlyn exited the taxi at the terminal several minutes later. "I'll stay with you until we get inside. Then I'll stay back and keep an eye on you. I won't leave until you are with the security guard. But even then, Kaitlyn, you keep a close eye out. You can't be too careful."

Kaitlyn didn't need to be reminded of that. She was already edgy, fearing she'd see Jace at any moment. When they approached the ticket counter, Celia said a tearful good-bye to Kaitlyn and then stepped back and kept watch as Kaitlyn searched for the man she was to meet. Both women had agreed it might be best if the two of them were not seen together by the officer in order to preserve Celia's anonymity. Kaitlyn had promised to call her from Boise and to keep in touch after that.

It was only a moment before Kaitlyn met the security guard. "Hi," he said, "I'm Don Appleton. And you must be Kaitlyn Glenn."

"Yes," she agreed as she caught Celia's eye and gave her a brief smile and a nod. "I appreciate your help, sir."

"Not a problem," he said. "I already have a boarding pass for you. Is that all you have?" He was pointing to her small bag and her purse.

"I'm afraid so," she said.

"All right, then. At least we won't need to check any luggage. We'll just get you through the security area, and then I'll take you directly to your gate. I'll wait with you there until you're on the plane."

"That'll make me feel much safer," Kaitlyn said as she fell in step beside him and began walking away from the throng of people gathered around the huge ticket counter and baggage check area. She caught another glimpse of Celia, who gave her a tiny wave and an encouraging smile, and then she turned back. Suddenly, she felt very alone. Celia had been a great comfort and friend to her since the accident. She hoped to see her again someday and be able to repay her for her kindness.

* * *

Dan threw his luggage in the back of the old truck and hopped in with Brock. "Nice wheels," he said with a grin.

"At least it runs," Brock shot back. "That's better than my own truck."

They caught up on old times as Brock negotiated the traffic leading away from the airport.

"The rodeos this weekend are not going to be a lot of fun for those of us who knew Kaitlyn Glenn," Dan suddenly said. "I imagine the news of her being killed will be all over the place before long. She's going to be missed. I still can't believe she's gone."

"I can't either," Brock agreed, and then hastened to add, "although I can't really say I knew her."

"You'd have liked her," Dan said. "She was a great girl."

Brock couldn't argue with that. The two sleepless nights he'd just spent evidenced the effect she'd already had on him.

"You know, Brock, the strangest thing happened while I was waiting for you," Dan said. "A girl that reminded me a lot of Kaitlyn walked into the terminal through one of the doors a ways down the sidewalk from me. She was with an older black woman. Of course, they were a fair ways off. I imagine that if I'd been up closer, I wouldn't have seen a resemblance at all. It was the long auburn hair that first caught my eye. Anyway, it's weird. Maybe it's because I'm feeling so bad over her death."

Brock felt a strange chill pass over him. "Did you say she was with a black woman?"

"Yeah, why?" Dan asked.

"This might seem weirder than ever, but there was a taxi headed the same way I was out on I-70 a few minutes ago. There was a black woman in the back, and the girl seated next to her reminded me of Kaitlyn. Must be the same women you saw," Brock said.

"Gee, that's some coincidence. It must have been her hair. I didn't see her face for more than a second, and then it was just her profile."

"I didn't get a good look either, but she really caught my eye. I'm sure it was the same women."

Dan nodded in agreement. "Let's get on a happier subject," he said. "You'll like this new horse of mine. It's the first year I've roped on him, and he's coming along really well. By next year, I should be winning some pretty good purses with him."

"I hope you do, and I look forward to seeing him up close, but I think I'll like him better after we get some lunch. I'm starving," Brock said. "And there are plenty of places we can go as soon as we hit I-70."

* * *

"Bingo," Myler said softly, and his mustache began to twitch.

"Is this the truck?" Jace asked.

"This is it, but I don't see anybody near it," Myler told him. "Why don't you wait out here and keep an eye on it while I run inside and have a look around. Stay out of sight over past that row of trucks," he said, pointing. "I don't want you to be seen, but I also don't want this woman coming out and driving off without me knowing about it."

"What if Kaitlyn's with her?" Jace asked.

That was exactly what Myler had been wondering, and it was also why he was so agitated that Jace had shown up. "Then we'll rescue her, I suppose. But don't you do it on your own. Wait for me. I just want to see if they happen to be inside somewhere."

Myler looked through the businesses that made up the huge truck stop. There was no sign of either Kaitlyn or the truck driver. Ten minutes had passed before he rejoined Jace, who was, to his surprise, actually waiting where he'd told him to.

"They aren't in there?" Jace asked.

"Not that I could see."

"So now what do we do?"

"We wait."

"Out here? It's hot."

"Yeah, it is, and yeah, we wait out here," Myler growled.

"Why don't we run down to the rodeo arena?" Jace said impatiently. "That's probably where they are. They probably got a cab and went down there."

"No, we wait here," Myler insisted.

"I could go down there while you wait here," Jace suggested.

"No, we'll wait together. Anyway, if you'll remember, we only have one car." Myler certainly didn't want Jace finding Kaitlyn without him present. Jace would just grab her and head for his jet, and Myler's newly hatched plans would go up in smoke.

"If the truck driver comes alone, what do we do?" Jace asked.

"We'll decide that when the time comes. For now, we wait, that's all," Myler said, unable, unwilling even, to keep the impatience from his voice. He knew he was close to finding Kaitlyn, and it really angered him that Jace was here. But he'd have to deal with that problem later. He did agree with Jace that the truck driver and Kaitlyn could be at the rodeo grounds, but if so, they'd be back. At least the older woman would, he thought to himself. And Celia Dulce, the truck driver, would help him locate Kaitlyn, whether she wanted to or not.

* * *

The cab pulled up next to the rows of diesel pumps, and Celia jumped out. She grabbed some cash from her purse, paid the fare, and shoved the change back in. As she did, her hand bumped the little Smith and Wesson nestled in the bottom of her purse. She almost felt foolish now, but she knew that Kaitlyn had felt better when she'd put it in there before they'd left for the airport. She'd known she had to be very careful that no one had any reason to look in her purse—not at the airport. And no one had. That was one of the reasons she'd stayed back when Kaitlyn went to meet the security officer inside the terminal.

She was anxious now to be on her way. She was glad she'd topped off her diesel tanks before she and Kaitlyn had lunch. All she needed to do now was perform a quick safety check, get in her truck, and drive away. Hopefully, she'd hear from Kaitlyn before too many hours passed. She was anxious and worried about her. It was hard to believe how much she cared about the girl. A few days ago she hadn't even known she existed, and now she cared for Kaitlyn as if she were her own child.

Celia walked directly to her truck and threw her purse into the cab. Then she climbed down and began to circle her rig, checking the tires and the other items on her routine safety checklist. She intended to drive as long as she could before she stopped to sleep for the night. As she completed her circle, she suddenly stopped. Something was bothering her. She tried to think of what it might be. She had seen movement a few trucks down the row, but that wasn't unusual. There were bound to be other drivers who were getting ready to roll again.

It's just nerves, she told herself, and she started for the cab of her truck. It was time to be on her way.

CHAPTER 13

"IF THAT'S HER, SHE'S ALONE. We need to get down to the rodeo arena and find Kaitlyn now," Jace whispered urgently.

"No, first we need to talk to Celia."

"Who?"

"The truck driver we've been watching."

"Then what are we waiting for?" Jace screamed, his face purplish red.

"This isn't the place to make a scene, Jace. She might not want to tell us what we need to know. You can bet that Kaitlyn, if she came this far with her, will have told her all about you. And so she is not too likely to cooperate."

"Okay, okay. But she's going to get away. You're letting her get in her truck!"

"That's right, and then we'll follow her out of the city. I'd rather talk to her at some rest area along the way, out along the open road," Myler said.

"But Kaitlyn's probably right here in Denver," Jace insisted.

"Maybe, but we don't know that, do we? Calm down, man. For all we know, she's with her horse and trailer and that Perrett guy from Logan. Or she could have met someone anywhere between here and Boise," Myler said.

"But she's pulling out now!" Jace said. "We need to get to the car."

"We need to make sure she doesn't see us," Myler said, grabbing Jace by the arm and dragging him out of sight. "We can catch up with that truck easily enough. And we'll know it when we see it."

"But we don't know where she's going," Jace protested.

"*You* don't know where she's going," Myler corrected. "Remember, I know my job and I do it well. I do know where she's going."

"But Kaitlyn is in Denver," Jace insisted.

"Maybe, and if she is, we'll know for sure in a little while," Myler said firmly. "We don't want to lose track of that Dulce woman now that we've found her. Anyway, we don't have any idea what the area around the rodeo arena is like. Kaitlyn could be in a motel; she could also be with other rodeo people. She might not be all that easy to find without help, even if she is there. But Celia Dulce can direct us. And that's what she's going to do after we get away from the city. Now we can go get our car."

* * *

The uneasiness persisted even after Celia was safely away from the truck stop. She had the prickly-necked feeling that someone had been watching her. She'd sensed danger then, and she sensed it still. She began to watch every car that passed her or that even drew up behind her. Suddenly, she knew how Kaitlyn must feel. She pulled her purse with the pistol in it closer to her on the seat. She'd use it if she had to.

An hour later she began to relax. *I'm just getting paranoid,* she told herself. *There's no way anyone is after me.* But the nervousness caused her bladder to fill more quickly than normal, and she needed to pull off at the next rest area. *I'm safe,* she told herself. *I'm just being foolish, just over-reacting.*

* * *

As Dan and Brock left the restaurant, Dan's phone began to ring. It was his wife. "Dan, you aren't going to believe this. Kaitlyn is alive!"

"What are you talking about?" Dan asked in disbelief. "She was killed in her truck."

"I'm serious, Dan," she said. "I just saw it on TV. There was a bulletin and it said a man from Coeur d'Alene had reported that his wife was the person that was killed, not Kaitlyn. The police say that the identity of the woman who died is not yet confirmed. But they have confirmed that it was not Kaitlyn Glenn."

"This is really strange," Dan said. "The truck wasn't Kaitlyn's then?"

"I didn't say that. The truck was hers, but this other woman, the one who was killed, had stolen it."

Brock's head was spinning. What he'd just heard from Dan's half of the conversation on his cell phone seemed to imply that Kaitlyn Glenn was alive.

Dan said, "Just a sec, honey, I'm with Brock. Let me tell him." Then he turned to his friend. "It's my wife on the phone. Kaitlyn was not killed in the wreck. It was some woman who had stolen her truck."

"Wow! That's amazing. Where is she now?" Brock asked.

"Just a minute," Dan said, and he lifted the phone and asked his wife the same question.

"They haven't said," she quickly responded. "All the highway patrol is saying is that she is definitely alive. I'll call and let you know when I hear more."

"I wonder if you and I weren't so off base after all," Brock said after Dan had shut his phone. "Could she have been the young woman we both saw?"

"I don't know," Dan said. "It sure looked like her. Let's hoof it out to the rodeo arena and see if anyone else has heard anything."

* * *

Norman Thatcher came running to the truck. "Jordan," he called out.

She peeked out of the living quarters in the front of the horse trailer and asked, "What's the matter, Dad?"

"Kaitlyn won't be racing anymore," he said.

"Why not?" she asked. "Has she quit?"

"I guess you could say that," he said casually.

"What do you mean?"

"Well, you see, she was careless and pulled in front of a semi and got herself killed," Norman said.

Jordan was stunned. "Dad, are you sure?" she asked.

"Yes. I was talking to a couple of cowboys over at the arena. They say it's been all over the news up in Idaho. She was on the other side of Boise when it happened," he said.

"Dad, this is terrible," Jordan said as tears began to course down her face. "You don't even seem to care."

"I care that she's dead." Norman backtracked quickly. "In fact, I think it's a terribly tragic thing. But it also means that you will not have to compete against her."

"I like to compete against her!" Jordan shouted angrily. "I can't believe you, Dad."

"Hey, calm down, Jordan. These things happen."

"Was her horse killed, too?" Jordan asked.

"No, she didn't have her horse or trailer with her," Norman said.

"I wonder where he is," she said sadly. "Tony B will feel so bad."

"Horses don't have feelings," her father said coldly.

"Yes they do!" Jordan protested.

"Don't be silly, Jordan. But I've also been thinking about Kaitlyn's horse. Kaitlyn's brother, Kelvin, is part owner of Tony B. I guess he's sole owner now. I need to call him. I'll make an offer to buy the horse. Then you'll really be a winner, Jordan."

"I don't want Kaitlyn's horse," Jordan cried, and she retreated into the trailer, slamming the door behind her.

I can't believe Kaitlyn's dead, she thought. *And how can Dad be so calloused? What kind of man is he?* she asked herself as she flopped onto her bed and let her sorrow pour out. Her dad came in a moment later and spoke to her. But the last thing she wanted to do was talk to him right then.

Jordan rolled off the bed, pushed past him, and hurried outside, walking toward the arena. She knew that other competitors would feel much the same as she did about the terrible news. They tried hard to beat each other week after week, but they also had respect for one another, and some of them were good friends. Except for her father, she'd never heard anyone speak badly of Kaitlyn before.

* * *

Kelvin answered his phone. "Hello?"

"Hey, this is Norman Thatcher. I have news, my friend."

"About Kaitlyn? Is she in Denver?" Kelvin asked.

"She won't be coming," Norman said.

"Oh, great," Kelvin said. "I was hoping to take care of this little problem this week. Do you have any idea where she is?"

"Sure do. Your bratty little sister's gone and got herself killed."

Kelvin was stunned. "She's dead?"

"Yep, that's a fact. Killed in a traffic accident up near Boise."

Kelvin wasn't sure what to say. He was so close to finding her, he'd thought. Now this. "How will I ever get my money now?" he asked, as much to himself as to Norman.

"Hey, cheer up, kid. If she's dead, doesn't that mean you should be able to get not only the money but the horse, too?"

That cheered Kelvin up a little, although he needed the money now, not later.

"You're right. But it could take a while. I'll have to get an attorney to help me free up the money now, but no one else has a claim on her part of it. Most of it, of course, is already mine."

"About the horse," Norman said. "I'd be willing to buy it from you."

"That won't be a problem. But first, I've got to find it. Do you think any of the people who follow the rodeo like you do might know what she did with it? Boise is a long way from here," Kelvin said. "Maybe her horse was killed in the accident."

"No, it was just her and her truck. She didn't have the horse trailer with her from what I hear. She must have left them somewhere. I'll ask around," Norman promised. "And I'll let you know what I hear."

"Good. Then I guess I'll head for Boise," Kelvin said. "I suppose that's where I'll need to start. They'll probably need me to claim the body or at least tell them where to bury her."

"Well, good luck," Norman said.

Kelvin couldn't believe his luck. Yes, he would get the money—definitely. He had no intention of telling anyone—not a judge, not one single person—that Kaitlyn's mother was still alive. He wasn't about to split that money with someone else. But he was desperate for some now. He'd be broke by the time he got to Boise.

The decision was easy to make. He was going to be leaving Denver anyway, and with Kaitlyn dead, there was no reason for him to return. He pulled his ski mask and pistol from his glove compartment and checked the gun thoroughly. He'd done it before, and although it was risky, he had no choice but to do it again. He'd take what he could get at the first convenience store he came to. Then he'd leave town and head for Idaho.

* * *

The tired old shop truck was belching smoke as Brock pulled into a large parking area adjacent to the arena. "I hope this truck doesn't leave me stranded like my own did," he said with a chuckle. It really wasn't running any worse than it had when he left the dealership, and he wasn't worried.

"It's a pretty classy truck, all right," Dan agreed. "But I'm sure glad you picked me up."

Brock was feeling lighthearted despite the series of delays he'd had that day. The news that Kaitlyn was alive had revived his spirits tremendously. He just wondered where she was now. He and Dan had talked about what she might have been doing up by Boise—without her horse and trailer. Brock was sure it had something to do with the man who'd attacked her at the rodeo in Cheyenne. He prayed that since the miracle of her being alive had come to light, she wouldn't be in further danger from that guy.

"Hey, there are some of the gals that barrel race over by that group of horse trailers," Dan said. "Let's see if they know any more about Kaitlyn than we do."

But when the two of them approached the young women, they witnessed less-than-happy faces. Dan immediately walked up to them. "Hey, why all the tears, ladies? Is it about Kaitlyn Glenn?"

One short, stocky girl with a pretty face said, "She's been killed. She was beating us a lot, but we liked her. She was a good friend."

"Jordan is your name, isn't it?" Dan asked.

"Yes. Jordan Thatcher."

"Well, cheer up, Jordan. I just got a call from my wife. She's at our home in Idaho. Anyway, she was watching TV when a bulletin came on. Kaitlyn is alive. Some other woman died. It was a case of mistaken identity," Dan said.

"Really?" Jordan cried. "Are you sure?"

Dan first introduced Brock and then continued to explain what he had learned from his wife. The group of young women turned from sad to ecstatic. "My dad will be mad," Jordan said a minute later. "He doesn't like Kaitlyn. He says she wins too much. And I think her so-called brother will be mad too."

"Who?" Dan asked. "I didn't know she had a brother."

Jordan told them all about the man who called himself Kelvin Glenn and who claimed to be Kaitlyn's brother. She also made sure they knew how she felt about him. "My dad hit it off with him, but he looked like a real creep to me," she said.

Brock was disturbed by her story, and later, as he and Dan were looking at Dan's new roping horse, Brock said, "I wonder if this guy could have any connection with the one who attacked her in Cheyenne."

"That's a thought. Nobody seems to have ever heard her mention a brother before, and I don't think she ever had any relatives come to a rodeo when she was competing. She may still be alive, but I have a feeling that she's not okay," Dan said.

Although Brock shared that feeling, he realized he could do nothing. He had to get back to the dealership soon and then drive to Moab. He hoped he wouldn't be too late getting to the apartment that was waiting for him. He had to be at his new job first thing the next morning, and he'd like to get a few hours of sleep before then.

* * *

Kelvin left his cell phone in the car when he entered the store he'd selected. With his ski mask pulled over his face, he was in and out within three minutes.

Back in his car with a bagful of cash, his adrenaline running, his hands sweating, and the ski mask back in a pocket of his baggy pants, he forced himself to obey all the traffic laws.

Won't be a good idea to attract the attention of any cops, he reminded himself.

In just a few minutes, he'd entered the freeway and was on his way out of the city. He had no idea how much he'd stolen, but he hoped it was enough to last him until he could get his hands on the money Kaitlyn had left him. Robbery was risky business, and he'd rather not do it if he didn't have to. He preferred pushing drugs, but that wasn't an option right now. *Sometimes a guy's gotta do what a guy's gotta do,* he told himself.

A cop car appeared in his mirrors, lights flashing, gaining rapidly on him as the freeway traffic parted to let it through. He grabbed his gun in his right hand, tried to keep his speed steady, and forced his eyes to remain staring straight ahead. He was too close to getting the money he'd dreamed of for so many years to let a cop step in and mess it up for him.

Kelvin moved to the side of the freeway with the other traffic and gripped the pistol tightly. But the cop sped on past him. He heaved a great sigh of relief. He couldn't believe what that selfish sister of his was putting him through. She'd just about caused him to have a heart attack. He was glad Kaitlyn was dead. She wouldn't be missed, that was for sure.

He eased back into the flow of traffic, his heart still pounding. His hatred of his dead stepsister had just quadrupled. He laid the gun on the seat beside his cell phone and reached under the seat for a small package he had concealed there. He needed something to calm him down, even if he was driving. He hadn't had anything stronger than beer for a couple of days. It was time for the good stuff.

His cell phone rang. He ignored it. It was probably that fool Thatcher, and he didn't want to talk to him right now. Even if he had found out where the horse was, there was nothing he could do about it until later. In fact, he wasn't sure it was worth the bother. He had no idea how much the horse was worth, and he suspected that Thatcher had no intention of giving him that much anyway.

* * *

Norman closed his phone and spit out a few choice words. He couldn't believe Kelvin wasn't answering. He had to let him know that his sister was still alive. Jordan had just told him. She hadn't elaborated other than to say it seemed that it had been a case of mistaken identity. She was in one of her moods again, and he'd just have to wait until she wasn't upset with him anymore. Then he'd press her for details. But he would like to let Kelvin know. He wanted that horse for his girl, and Kelvin was the only one who could help him with that.

* * *

Myler was having a hard time keeping Jace calm. Jace wanted to confront Celia now. They'd already missed one opportunity. It had been purely bad luck that a pair of troopers had stopped at the same rest area. It would have been foolish to try anything with them so close. He'd told Jace that they'd just have to bide their time. They were eastbound now, driving out ahead of Celia. "We'll wait for her at the next rest stop," he assured Jace for at least the tenth time since they'd left her and her truck behind.

"And what if she doesn't stop there?" he demanded.

"Then we go to the next one. We'll get our chance."

"And what if she decides to turn around and go west?"

"She has a load to deliver, Jace. She won't be turning around."

"What about Kaitlyn?"

"We'll get her."

"We should have gone to the arena."

"If she plans to ride, it won't be until Friday night. That's two days. Now either shut up or I'll pull over and let you out," Myler threatened. He was angry and getting more riled by the minute because Jace was harassing him and because he knew that Kaitlyn really could be in Denver. But he had to be sure before he took any action. Celia Dulce was almost certain to know where she was. And a little delay wouldn't hurt. In fact, if it took long enough, maybe Jace would decide to go after her on his own again. And the farther they were from Denver when that happened, the better it would be. Myler's long-term plans for Kaitlyn did not include his client.

CHAPTER 14

THE FLIGHT TO BOISE WAS SMOOTH and uneventful. True to his word, Trooper Franson and another officer met Kaitlyn at the airport. They immediately helped her get some cash at a local bank. She then gave them the money that was left from the purse of the dead woman and made up the difference with her own money.

She also made contact with her insurance company about the truck and was assured that an adjuster would be contacting her shortly. She answered what questions she could for the highway patrol, helping to fill in the blanks on their investigation of the wreck that destroyed her truck and killed the woman who had stolen it.

It was with both relief and dread that Kaitlyn heard about the warrant that had been issued for Jace's arrest, based on his assault on her in Cheyenne. Bail had been set fairly high, and the authorities promised to get word out across the country, especially to airports, to watch for him and his jet. But Kaitlyn couldn't help wondering how much more dangerous he might become if he found out about the warrant without getting arrested, or if he was arrested and then made bail and was released. She knew that with his finances, even a high bail was not a serious obstacle for Jace.

Finally, as the afternoon wore on, Kaitlyn contacted Jim Perrett about Tony B. She was assured that the horse was fine and that Jim would look out for Tony as long as she needed him to. She looked forward to a safe bed in a secure place that night. But that was hours away. In the meantime, she would be kept safe while she was allowed to get more personal business done, arranging, in particular, to move her money to new accounts so that Kelvin would be unable to locate her inheritance should he try.

Kaitlyn worried about Celia. She hoped she hadn't put her in danger. But she couldn't clear her mind of the image of the obnoxious man who had created the embarrassing scene with the waitress in the café in Boise. Even worse, Kaitlyn could still visualize his face and leering eyes as he'd kept looking at her. And then, after seeing the man with Jace, it was almost too much. *Where are they now and what are they doing?* she wondered.

Often, during the late afternoon and early evening, she thought about the young man with the black cowboy hat who had rescued her from Jace. She wished she knew who he was but suspected she never would. In a way, she knew that was best. At least he wouldn't be in any danger from Jace.

* * *

Celia was in no hurry to stop again until it was absolutely necessary. The farther she was from Denver, the safer she felt. She didn't pull off the freeway again until she was entering Kansas. There she produced the paperwork she needed at the port of entry, and then she drove back onto the freeway and kept going for about two more hours before stopping at the edge of a small town to fuel up and eat. As she left her truck to go to a nearby café, she took her purse, which still contained her pistol.

Choosing a table near a window where she could see her truck, she glanced that way from time to time. She ate slowly and was almost finished when her phone began to ring. She was relieved to hear from Kaitlyn, who said things were going fine and that an arrest warrant had been issued for Jace.

"Are they keeping you safe?" she asked Kaitlyn.

"I'm fine for now," Kaitlyn assured her. "But I'm worried about you."

"Don't worry," Celia told her jovially. "No one has any reason to be after me. Now, if I was as gorgeous as you are, I'd be worried. But other truckers don't even give me a second glance."

"It's not other truckers I'm worried about," Kaitlyn said. "It's Jace and that horrible man he was with in Boise."

"But they wouldn't have any reason to look for me," Celia assured her young friend, feeling anything but assured and knowing that she'd been seen with Kaitlyn at the café.

"That man—that friend of Jace's—saw us together," Kaitlyn said. "What if they figured out what company you were driving for?"

Celia wished Kaitlyn hadn't thought about that. She didn't want the girl to be worrying about her. "I don't think we need to worry about them," she said, knowing that was not the truth. "Now you just take care of yourself, and I'll keep on truckin'."

"Please promise me you'll be careful," Kaitlyn begged.

"I will. I have my purse with me, and you know what I have in there."

"Good, I just hope you don't have to use it."

Celia glanced toward her truck as she finished her meal. Then she paid, took a short detour to the ladies room, and headed for the truck again. She was anxious to drive a little farther up the freeway before she stopped to rest. When she got back to her truck, she again felt the prickly sensation and looked about her as she stood beside the cab. Then she walked all the way around her truck, checking the tires and inspecting as she always did. But she was also searching the area around her.

Finally, nervous but anxious to be on her way, she climbed up into the cab, put her purse beside her, and inserted the key into the ignition. As she did so, she felt a chill pass down her spine. Something felt different. At that moment her eye caught movement in a light blue car, a newer model that was parked about two hundred feet away. She looked closely, and for a moment her eyes met those of the man sitting in the passenger side of the car. Her heart sank. She was almost positive it was Jace Landry.

But where's that other heathen? she wondered. *The man with the heavy jowls, the pockmarked face, and the oversized mustache?* A tremor shook her body.

* * *

Jace had watched as the woman climbed into the cab of the A to Z Transport semi. He continued to watch as she settled in behind the wheel. He flinched as their eyes met across the parking lot. Then he waited breathlessly for Myler to make his move.

But Myler remained motionless. The truck pulled out of its parking spot, drove past him, and moved onto the road. What was going on?

Myler wasn't supposed to let that happen. Not this time. They had agreed.

He slid over beneath the steering wheel and reached for the key so he could start the car and follow the truck. But the key was not in the ignition. Myler had taken it with him. He'd left the car the moment Celia had disappeared from her table by the window inside. "Wait right here" had been his instructions. "Don't do anything foolish. I'm going to have a talk with that woman when she comes back to her truck."

"Why are you taking your bag?" Jace had asked. "You don't need your clothes and shaving kit to talk to her."

"That's not all I carry in here," Myler had said, patting the bag. "I may need some 'persuasion' to help her talk." Without further explanation, he'd headed for Celia's truck.

But the truck was leaving now, and Jace was powerless to stop it. Angry and confused, he burst from the car and ran after the truck, waving his arms and shouting for the truck to stop.

* * *

Celia watched in amazement as Jace raced on foot behind her up the road, his arms waving in the air. *Is he crazy?* she asked herself. But when he ran back to the car, she worried that he was going to come after her.

Where is the other guy? she wondered.

And then she knew. A small breeze blew across the back of her neck as the curtain that separated the cab from the cramped sleeping area behind it was opened.

"Just keep driving and don't be alarmed, ma'am," a frighteningly familiar voice from the sleeper compartment calmly said. "And don't turn around. You and I need to talk."

She knew that voice. It was the voice of the vile man who had been so rude to the waitress in Boise. Jace's friend. She felt a shiver and had to stifle the impulse to reach for her purse. She wasn't a foolish woman, and she knew that until the opportunity presented itself, she'd have to obey.

"Who are you and what do you want?" she asked.

"Now, ma'am, no reason to get upset. You just do what I tell you and you'll be fine. I want you to take me back to Denver and show me where you left Kaitlyn," he said coldly.

She started to turn her head, but a bit of cool steel pressed into her neck. "I didn't say to turn around, Celia. There's no reason for you to see me. It would only force me to do something neither of us wants."

Celia knew a threat when she heard it. She wouldn't attempt that again. Anyway, she already knew what he looked like. "How do you know my name?" she asked.

"I know a lot of things about you," he said. "It's my business to know."

"What's your business?" she asked.

"I'll ask the questions," he said, pushing the gun tighter against her neck. "You just do as you're told. We're going back to Denver, and you're going to show me where you left Kaitlyn Glenn."

"We don't need to go back to Denver. I can tell you where I left her," Celia said, trying to think of a way out of the mess her carelessness had gotten her into.

"Head for Denver," he said. "We'll talk on the way."

She turned west as she entered the road and then took the first freeway entrance in that same direction. It wasn't until they were on the freeway and up to speed that she felt the barrel of the man's gun leave her neck. When it did, he spoke again. "Don't relax, Celia. I know how to drive one of these rigs, if you force me to."

Though indirect, the threat was still very real, and she knew better than to underestimate him. She had the sinking feeling that he had no intention of letting her live, no matter what she told him. Surely he knew she could give his description to the cops if she ever got a chance. He wasn't likely to allow her that chance. If she was going to survive, she would have to make the chance herself. When that reality finally sank in, she kept her eyes on the road as she considered her dilemma. She wasn't finished yet.

Celia had never had it easy; she'd had to fight for things before. As the middle child of thirteen, she hadn't made it to adulthood without some serious struggles. Her bigger and stronger older brothers and sisters, and all the babies younger than her, had seen to that. Even having a father in the home hadn't made life easy. Her brothers seemed to always be out finding trouble and costing them more money. No matter what kind of work he did besides his farming, her father never brought in enough. And her mother was always busy with the babies. Celia finally dropped out of school early to help the struggling Dulce family.

None of that seemed important to her now—none of it, that is, except for the lessons she'd learned. And she'd use every bit of ingenuity and every ounce of strength to save her life. And while she was at it, she'd do everything she could to avoid betraying the young woman she'd befriended and come to care about.

"Why don't you tell me where she is," the man behind her said casually a few minutes later. "I'm listening."

"I didn't say I knew where she was. I only said that I could tell you where I took her. And I can do that. But where she's gone from there, I have no idea," she lied. She had no intention of telling him that Kaitlyn was in Boise.

"Where did you take her?"

"Actually, I didn't exactly take her anywhere. I accompanied her in a taxi to the airport. I left her there at a ticket counter. She was going to catch a plane, but I didn't make it my business to ask her where she was going. She just wanted to get away from Jace," she said. "And speaking of Jace, I suppose he'll be behind us in your rental car."

The man behind her laughed. It was an ugly sound. "He's just a rich fool who thinks that money will buy him whatever he wants. I have the keys to the rental car. And since I'm pretty sure he has no idea how to hotwire it, I guess he'll be looking for alternate transportation right about now."

"And he'll be after you. I'm sure it's not part of his plan for you to leave him stranded," Celia guessed.

"Probably not," the man agreed. "But back to Kaitlyn. You don't seriously think that I'm going to buy a story that you left her at the airport and that you don't know where she was going, do you?"

"It's the truth. I can't help what you believe and what you don't," she said. "All I did was give the girl a ride. She told me a little about her troubles, but not much. And she didn't want me to risk myself for her anymore, so when we stopped in Denver for fuel and lunch, she told me that she should leave me."

"That's a great story, but I happen to know that the cops in Idaho found her purse. Her money and ID, her credit cards, and everything else—they were all in there," the man said. "She couldn't even afford to buy a ticket."

"Unless I let her borrow some money," Celia said.

"And if you did, you'd know where she was bound to, now wouldn't you? She'll be in touch with you if you're telling the truth, but I don't think you are. I think she's in Denver, and I intend for you to show me exactly where."

"I can show you what terminal she went to at the airport, if that will help," Celia said.

"You intend to stick to that story, don't you?" he said. "You might rethink that. I suggest that you do. We have plenty of time. It's what, four or five hours back to Denver?"

"If I don't get too tired and fall asleep at the wheel," Celia said. She was getting angry at the smugness of the man. She hadn't liked him from the moment he'd begun to belittle the waitress in Boise. And she liked him less with each passing minute.

"You won't do that," he said. "Knowing my gun is pointed at the back of your head should give you plenty of reason not to get drowsy."

"What do you want with Kaitlyn?" Celia asked a few minutes later.

"That's not any of your business," he said, "and I would advise you not to ask again."

She took him at his word. The tone of his voice had changed. She had hit a nerve. She didn't ask him again, although she did try to stir up conversation from time to time. He seemed disinclined to talk except to remind her that she was going to tell him where Kaitlyn was in Denver and that he would make her take him there if he had to.

Finally, after another half hour, she gave up and just stared at the road ahead, trying to come up with a plan to retrieve her gun from her purse. Unfortunately, it didn't seem likely that she'd be able to do that anytime soon.

Then her cell phone began to ring. "Answer it," the voice behind her said. "And don't even consider giving any hints about what's going on."

The phone was in her purse. Hope surged. Maybe, just maybe, she could get her gun instead of the phone.

"Don't try anything foolish. Just get the phone and hand it to me," he said. "You never know what a woman might have in her purse." He laughed as if he had told an outrageously funny joke, and she opened her purse just enough to slide her hand in. As she did, he grabbed her arm. "Slowly now."

She did the only thing she could and pulled the phone out. He took it and a moment passed. She figured he must have been looking at it, and then he thrust it in front of her face. "Take the call. Say nothing that will get you killed."

Celia looked at the phone and saw that there was no number displayed on the screen. Kaitlyn had been firm about that issue when she'd bought the phone that morning in Cheyenne. Celia was positive it was Kaitlyn calling her. She knew she had to be careful about what she said. She lifted her phone. "Hi, Mama," she said.

* * *

Hi, Mama?

Kaitlyn's heart sank. She was sure she hadn't dialed the wrong number. This could mean only one thing. Celia was in serious trouble and she was trying to warn Kaitlyn. Her mind raced as she tried to think of how she should handle the situation. She started by putting the Kleenex she'd been wiping tears with only moments before over the little speaker on her phone. She also thought it might not hurt to disguise her voice by dropping it down a few notches and adding her best attempt at a Southern accent.

With a racing heart, she lifted the phone and spoke into it. "Hello, Celia," she said. "You haven't called yer mammy today. Y'always call before now. Have ya had trouble with your truck?" She hoped Celia would be able to respond appropriately.

"My truck's fine. And I'm just driving down the highway like I do every day," Celia said. "I've just been tired today and forgot to call. I would have called in a few minutes."

"I miss ya, honey. You know I'm just a lonely old lady with nothin' to do but wait to hear from her daughter," Kaitlyn said. "Ya promised ya'd come home soon. When will ya be here?"

"Not for a couple of weeks," Celia responded. "I've got more loads to haul before I get a break. And heaven only knows I need a break. I just wish my boss knew that."

For another couple of moments, Kaitlyn tried to keep up a stream of meaningless chitchat, but it wasn't easy. Finally, Celia said, "Mama, it's good of you to call. I promise I'll call tomorrow at noon. I'm sorry I worried you."

"Okay, honey," Kaitlyn said. "I love ya and miss ya. It's so lonely around this ole house."

"I love you, too, Mama," Celia said. "I'll get home for a visit as soon as I can. Bye for now."

As Kaitlyn closed her phone, her hands were sweating, and drops of perspiration dripped from her forehead. She had to help Celia. It was obvious her friend was in serious trouble. She took a minute to wipe her hands and head and calm her racing heart. Then she called Trooper Franson's home number.

"Call my lieutenant at home," he said after listening to her concern. "You have his number. In the meantime, I'm on my way over to the safe house to meet you. We'll see what we can do."

When Kaitlyn called Lieutenant Alger, he was as concerned as Phillip had been. "I'll be on my way over. I'll call you on my cell phone in just a moment, and then you can give me all the information on Celia and about where she should be now. We'll call whoever we need to in order to get help moving in her direction."

Kaitlyn was grateful that neither officer had questioned her judgment about Celia's plight. She just hoped they could find her in time.

* * *

Celia shut her phone and shoved it back into her purse. *That's my girl,* she mentally congratulated Kaitlyn. She definitely was an intelligent girl. With any luck at all she would have fooled this horrible man.

"Shut it off," he said. She did. "Put it back in the purse," he ordered next.

Now was her chance. *Can I do it?* she asked herself. *If I can get the gun out, will it help?* she wondered. Slowly, she lowered her hand into her purse.

CHAPTER 15

MONEY COULD GET A MAN *whatever he wanted.* That had always been Jace's philosophy. Most of his life it had worked well for him. And thanks to what his father had left him, he'd always had all he needed and a lot more. With Kaitlyn, however, his money had failed him. She'd been unimpressed with his wealth. But his money would eventually get her back—one way or another.

Once he cooled down after the semi had driven away without him, he began to scheme. He was quite certain that Celia and Myler had headed back to Denver. Without a car he was stranded and couldn't pursue them. His cell phone was practically useless because Myler had never given him his number. That was an oversight he intended to correct as soon as he found the man again. He also intended to get some things straight with him, starting with who was boss.

But first he needed his money to speak for him. He looked around for a likely candidate. A young man pulled into the parking area near the café a few minutes later. He was driving an old gray Chevy Malibu with a temporary sticker in the window. Jace approached the young fellow as he got out of his car. He looked to be perhaps sixteen or seventeen. He could use some money, Jace was sure.

"Hey, kid," he said. "I have a little problem. I wondered if you could help me."

"Doubt it." The boy scowled.

"You look like you could use a little cash. And I need a ride west to Denver. My rental car, that blue one over there, just broke down," Jace said, pointing. "And I don't have time for anyone to bring me a replacement."

"Still don't see how I can help," the young man mumbled.

"Like I said, I bet you could use some money," Jace repeated.

"Why? 'Cause I don't have fancy clothes like you?" the kid said, and he turned and started toward the café.

"Whoa, I'm not trying to offend you. I remember being a teenager. I could always use some extra cash. And if you'd like to make some money, I'd be glad to help you out." As he spoke, Jace pulled a wad of bills from his pocket, quickly caught up with the boy, and shoved the money in his face.

The young man's eyes grew wide, and he stopped. "What do you need me to do? I don't do illegal," he said as he eyed the large bundle of high-denomination bills.

"That car of yours. How much did you pay for it?" Jace asked.

"Thousand bucks, why?" the kid asked. His eyes didn't stray from the wad of money.

Slowly Jace began to peel off bills. The top five were hundred-dollar bills. Beneath them were several five-hundred–dollar ones. The young man started to squirm as he looked at the money. "I'll give you fifteen hundred if you'll let me borrow it. I'll see that it's returned right here to this café by this time tomorrow."

The young man's eyes narrowed. He shook his head slowly, his mouth zipped into a tight line. "Two thousand," he said.

The kid's greed made Jace angry, but he didn't have time to argue. He peeled off two thousand dollars and handed it to him. "The keys," he said, holding out his hands.

The exchange was made, and Jace hurried back to the rental car without another word. He grabbed his overnight bag from the backseat, threw it in the Malibu a minute later, and then got in. The young man was standing by the café, watching him, the money Jace had just given him still in his hand. The kid had just doubled his money. If he didn't get his car back at all, he'd be better off than he was before. And Jace had no plans to return the kid's car to him. He had more important things to do.

* * *

Celia still had her head because she'd used it. There was no way she could pull the gun from her purse and gain an advantage over the man behind her as long as he had his weapon aimed at her. She simply let go of the phone, pulled her empty hand out, and concentrated on the road and traffic. She knew she had to think of some way to distract him if she could.

"Where does your mama live?" her captor asked.

"In the South," she said. "She likes me to call her every day, and I do usually call her about noon. But I forgot today."

"Because you were busy helping Kaitlyn hide somewhere in Denver. And you are going to have to show me where."

"And if I don't?" Celia asked.

"I think you know."

"I don't think you would really do anything to me," she said, trying to sound confident.

"Maybe you're tired of living," he said. "Maybe you aren't afraid to die. But there are things worse than dying." He paused as if to let the impact of his words sink in. "You will tell me where that girl is, Celia Dulce. Believe me, you will," he said with finality.

Celia was suddenly very afraid of the man. It was the tone of his voice, the coldness and lack of humanity in it, that scared her. There was no doubt in her mind that he was capable of doing whatever he put his mind to.

But Celia was a strong woman. She'd been in danger many times in her life, and she'd had to learn to deal with things on her own. And one of the assets she'd gained over the years was the ability to be calm in the face of danger. She didn't lose her cool very often. It was that way now. She felt fear, almost mind-numbing fear, but she was also calm, and with the calm came resolve. She would not let him harm Kaitlyn if she could help it. She knew that she had to force his hand a little further before she tried to get her gun from her purse. But when she did, there was no doubt in her mind that she would use it.

She looked in her mirror and was surprised to see an old gray car speeding up behind her. Then it slowed down and made no attempt to pass her. It hugged her tail so closely that at times she could barely see it in her mirrors. Occasionally, it swung out, and one of those times she got a good look at the driver's face in the mirror. She was certain that it was Jace looking through the windshield of the old car, the anger on his face almost palpable.

An idea flashed into her mind. There was bad blood between Jace and this other man. She was reasonably certain of that, or the two would not have separated. Perhaps she could use that bad blood to her advantage.

"Looks like your friend Jace has found you," Celia said, surprised at how level she was able to keep her voice.

"What are you talking about?"

"There's someone in an old gray car following me. I haven't got a real good look, but I'd say it might be Jace," she explained. "At least, he looks like the guy Kaitlyn described to me."

"Can't be. You're wrong," the abductor said. "Anyway, you can't possibly see him very well in your mirror."

"I can see his face quite well in the mirror. Whoever it is, he looks angry and determined, and he doesn't seem to want to pass us," Celia told him.

She could tell that she'd hit a nerve, that he was nervous or upset by what she'd said. For a minute or two he said nothing. In the meantime, she let up on the gas pedal, and the truck began to slow down. The gray car continued to follow closely.

"What are you doing?" the guy suddenly demanded.

"I'm slowing down so he'll pass us," she said reasonably. "I don't like being tailgated."

"And I don't like a client who thinks he needs to tell me how to do my job," the man growled.

That shocked Celia. Could this man possibly be a private detective? Not likely, she decided. He was a kidnapper, and unless she somehow managed to turn the tables on him, he might be a murderer—with her as the corpse.

It was time to take a risk, Celia decided. "Why don't you look in the mirror and see for yourself?" she asked. "I'll move my truck over a lane, and you can look from over there." She pointed to the passenger side mirror.

He hesitated. Then he said, "I'd rather stay right where I am."

"Suit yourself. I just thought you might like to know for sure who it is," she said.

"Don't look back here," he said. She could hear him scuffling around behind her, and for a moment, she thought about her gun. Unfortunately, because she couldn't be sure what he was doing, she didn't dare reach for her purse. A moment later he said, "Guess I'll move up there beside you. Try something, and I'll shoot you."

"And cause the truck to crash," she said unnecessarily. She shouldn't be provoking him, but she couldn't help it. It just slipped out.

He was a big man, and it was not easy for him to crawl from the sleeper into the cab beside her. She glanced at him and was surprised to see that his face was covered with a nylon stocking. He must have just put it on. That would explain the recent noises behind her.

While he was struggling to get into the seat, Celia changed lanes, removing the gun from her purse while he was distracted and stuffing it under her leg. He pointed his gun at her and threatened her again after he got settled. She made no reaction. She didn't even mention the nylon pulled over his homely face. She couldn't help but think that it was an improvement. Finally, he looked toward the mirror and swore viciously.

Celia had already decided that she didn't want a standoff with the man when she actually displayed her pistol. There was always the possibility that he would shoot before she did. Knowing the time had come, she simply raised her gun and, hoping her employers would understand, fired a well-aimed shot. Not that she had far to aim. The gun he was holding was only a foot or so from her side. But she blew it out of his left hand, injuring his hand at the same time. She was pretty sure that the gun had landed on the floorboard. She wasn't sure where the bullet had ended up, but there was not any broken glass, so it hadn't hit a window.

He began screaming, holding his left hand with his right.

Waving the little pistol toward him, Celia said, "Shut up or the next one will be in that fat gut of yours."

She was still slowing down and judged, without looking at her speedometer, that she was going only about thirty miles per hour. She suddenly slammed on her brakes, sending the semi into a skid. The big man smashed forward into the dash of her truck. At the same time there was a thump from the rear, and she was sure that Jace had hit her from behind. Then she touched the gas again, switched back to the outside lane, and continued forward at a slower pace, not more than ten miles an hour.

"Open the door," she said as her former abductor tried to straighten up.

"What are you doing?" he demanded, his uninjured hand feeling his face, which was bleeding through the nylon. She was sure the blood was coming from his nose. The blood-soaked stocking made him look like a grotesque Halloween monster.

"I'm giving you a way to get out of my truck alive," she said. "But the longer it takes you, the faster I'll be moving." The truck was already beginning to gain speed. "And don't ever come around me again, nylon stocking or not," she added.

Celia continued to accelerate as the big man jumped and hit the ground. A moment later she spotted him in the rearview mirror. He was already getting to his feet, so he wasn't too badly hurt. Not that she cared. He deserved it. The gray car, with the front end smashed in, was pulling to the side of the road a short distance behind where he'd fallen.

As Celia continued to gather speed, her right door began swinging wildly. But she didn't want to stop to shut it while Jace and his companion were still close, especially since she didn't know what condition the gray car was in. She had to assume they could still pursue her. She put her gun back in the purse and retrieved her cell phone. She thought about calling 911 but decided not to. Calling the police would only complicate things for her and slow her down even more. She'd learned to be not only independent but responsible, and she didn't want anything to jeopardize her job with the trucking company. She was fairly certain that others who were on the freeway in the vicinity at the time the gray car struck her would probably make the call anyway. Besides, Kaitlyn was already working closely with the cops. They would take care of Myler and his friend, she tried to reassure herself. A few minutes later a police cruiser flew by on the eastbound side of the freeway, its lights flashing and its siren wailing. She hoped they'd go after Jace and her abductor and not come after her.

Seeing the patrol car, however, did give her enough confidence to bring her truck to a stop at the side of the freeway long enough for her to scramble over and shut the passenger door. There was a jagged hole in the door where the bullet had gone after striking the gun and injuring her abductor's hand. And there was a small amount of blood spattered about. She must not have done a lot of damage to the guy's hand, she concluded.

More sirens sounded in the distance as she slid back to her seat beneath the steering wheel. She noticed the man's gun on the floor of the truck in front of where he'd been sitting, but she left it there and put the big rig in gear. Now what she needed to do was change directions. At the nearest exit she left the freeway and then entered again, driving east, knowing she'd be passing the scene of the accident and hoping she wouldn't have to stop and talk to the cops. She just wanted to drive past Kaitlyn's enemies and put as much distance between her and them as she could. She felt fortunate to be alive, and she had every intention of staying that way.

* * *

Jace and Myler were teamed up again. Myler didn't like it, but that's the way it was. He'd lost his overnight bag with his spare pistol in it, along with money, clothes, several sets of ID, and other things he needed. The other pistol, to his dismay, was in Celia's truck. The only one who was armed now was Jace, which added to his irritation. And Jace wasn't in the mood to spend another second doing things Myler's way.

The gray car, after hitting Celia's big rig, was useless. The crash had done nothing more than bruise Jace in the chest when he hit the steering wheel and cause him some minor whiplash, but the radiator had been punctured. Although he had managed to drive a little farther after stopping to pick up Myler, the engine soon seized up. The borrowed car was disabled.

Myler was still wiping blood from his face with his handkerchief while trying to nurse his injured hand when a Good Samaritan in a minivan consented to give the men a ride to the next town. They took it, and when they saw the first of the police cars a few miles later, they were quite relieved to have dodged the cops. Neither had anything they wished to disclose to law enforcement. And both were in sour moods.

The driver of the minivan exited the freeway and drove into Burlington, Colorado, not far from the Kansas border. Both men were glad to have made it across the state line. They felt more insulated from the police by entering another state. Jace wanted to keep heading for Denver right then, even if he had to spend more money on another car. He was certain they'd find Kaitlyn there.

But although Jace had the only gun, Myler prevailed. They rented a room in Burlington where they could clean up, try to rest their pain-riddled bodies, and then find a way to get to Denver the next day. There they'd look for Kaitlyn among the rodeo crowd that was gathering for the weekend rodeo.

Both of them vowed to make Celia Dulce pay, but she would have to wait to reap the rewards of her stupidity, they agreed. Finding Kaitlyn came first.

* * *

Celia waited to call Kaitlyn back until she'd passed the point where the gray car was abandoned alongside the freeway, surrounded by police cars. She knew the young woman must be worried about her. And she had enough to worry about without adding Celia to the list.

Kaitlyn answered on the first ring. "Celia, are you all right?" she cried.

"I'm just fine, girl. You sure are quick to catch on," Celia praised. "Thanks for reacting the way you did when I called you Mama."

"I knew you were in trouble when you did that," Kaitlyn said. "And I have been worried sick since then. What happened? Was it Jace and that friend of his?"

"It was," Celia said. "But thanks to you, I was able to buy a little time, and then, with the help of my little .38 revolver, I got rid of them."

"I'm sure it wasn't as simple as you make it sound," Kaitlyn said sternly. "Tell me exactly what happened."

Celia related the events, scoffing each time Kaitlyn grew alarmed.

"My friends in the Idaho Highway Patrol have contacted the authorities down there. They're watching for you," Kaitlyn said.

Celia was alarmed about that. "Tell your friends to call the authorities here and let them know I'm fine."

Kaitlyn was somber. "I'll do it. But Jace and that ugly guy will come after you again, you know," she said.

"Maybe, but they also know I'm not afraid to use my gun. Actually, I have two guns now, although the one is slightly damaged. It'll probably still shoot, though," Celia said with a chuckle.

"What do you think they'll do next?" Kaitlyn asked.

"Probably go to Denver and look for you. They're convinced I left you there with some of your rodeo friends. But when they don't find you there, I have no idea what they'll do."

"Maybe I should report what they did instead of telling the police to ignore it," Kaitlyn said.

"No, don't do that. I'm not exactly sure what to do. I know what the law says, but these aren't exactly normal circumstances. The guy thinks I don't know who he is. He apparently doesn't realize that I remember what he looks like from the café in Boise or he wouldn't have bothered pulling that nylon over his head," Celia said. "Please call the cops off. I'll be okay now. I just need to drive as far away as I can."

Kaitlyn reluctantly agreed. Then the two chatted for a few more minutes. "I'd better let you go. You need a good night's rest," Celia said.

"As if I can sleep. I'm going to worry about you all night."

"Don't," Celia commanded. "I've steered those two in a different direction for now. I'm sure of that. I'll sleep with my gun in my hand anyway, no matter where I decide to stop tonight."

* * *

Kelvin was feeling smug as he found a room for the night in Salt Lake City. He'd pulled off several mini robberies without a hitch. By now he had the procedure down to a science. His take had been surprisingly large—over twenty thousand dollars. But that was just a drop in the bucket compared to what was waiting for him when he figured out how to get the money his dead sister had kept from him for so long.

He didn't bother to turn on his cell phone. There was no one he wanted to talk to—not even that Thatcher guy. All Thatcher wanted was the horse. Kelvin decided that if he ever got around to locating Tony B, he could get a lot more money for him from someone other than Norman Thatcher.

* * *

Jim Perrett answered his cell phone. "Kaitlyn," he said with delight as he heard her voice. "How are you?"

"I'm okay, I guess," she said.

Jim didn't think she sounded okay. "Maybe I should ask, are you safe?"

"Yes, I'm in a safe house right now," she said. "I'm sorry I dragged you into this mess. I'll try to come get Tony B in a day or two, as soon as I can get a new truck. You shouldn't have to worry about him."

"He's safe and he's just fine," he said. "You take care of yourself, and I'll take care of your horse."

"I'll be careful," she promised.

Jim could hear the doubt in the girl's voice, and it worried him. "Have you heard anything about Jace or that other man?" he asked.

"Oh, yes," she said, her voice betraying her concern.

"Kaitlyn! What's the matter? Are you sure you're safe? Where are you? Should I call the cops?" He fired off the questions rapidly and with real concern. His wife, son, and daughter-in-law were all watching him, worry etched on their faces.

"I'm fine. It's Celia I'm worried about."

"The truck driver?" he asked.

"Yes. They . . . they . . ." Kaitlyn's voice faded.

"They what? Did they do something to her?"

"Yes, they did," she said. With a catch in her voice, she related to Jim what had happened to Celia. "She says she's okay now, but I don't know if she really is. I feel so helpless."

"Don't you come out of that safe house as long as those two are running around," Jim cautioned.

"I have to. I can't stay here while everyone who has tried to help me is in danger," she said. "There is a warrant out for Jace, but I don't know if the police can catch him. And even if they do, I'm sure he'll just make bail and be free again. Seems like he has all the money in the world and he can do whatever he wants."

"What about the other guy?" Jim asked. "Surely there'll be a warrant out for him after what he did to your friend."

"Nobody knows who he is," she said. "Celia's sure it was one of the guys you saw at your house the night I left my horse, but he was wearing a nylon stocking on his face, so it would be hard for her to identify him for sure. Anyway, Celia didn't talk to the cops. She says she doesn't dare. She's just driving, trying to get her load delivered. I'm so frightened for her. And I'm frightened for you. Please be careful."

"You stay put, Kaitlyn. We'll be okay."

"I'll call you later," she promised. "And I am going to come get Tony B. Thank you for all you're doing for me."

* * *

It had been a slightly better day. Nina's mother had followed the procedures the doctor prescribed for her, and she seemed to feel stronger. They had driven to Zion Canyon and had enjoyed a reasonably good day there. Maybe the vacation would be okay after all.

And maybe it wouldn't.

Though her mother seemed to feel better, her father was in a dreadful mood. Whatever was wrong with her mother was making her father worried or angry or something. Nina still wished she had her nanny with her, or at least someone who could make her feel better and worry less.

"Get your pajamas on," her father ordered. "We're going to drive up to Canyonlands National Park tomorrow, and you need to get some sleep. They say it's a really beautiful place. We may spend a couple of days there."

Obediently, she kissed her parents good night and climbed into her bed. Late that night, or at least she guessed it was late, she woke up. She could hear her parents talking to each other in soft but strained voices. She listened, trying to hear what they were saying.

It seemed like they were arguing. Her mother had said, "There is no way I'm doing that."

Doing what? Nina wondered.

"There is no other choice," her father whispered.

"I don't want to talk about it anymore," her mother insisted. "We need to go to sleep. We don't want to wake Nina. She mustn't know what you are suggesting. She would just die if she had any idea."

Nina thought the heaviness in her chest would stop her heart from beating. Why would she die? she wondered. What were her folks talking about? Frightened, she curled up in a ball. Something was terribly wrong. She wished they could just go home. She didn't want to have this vacation anymore.

CHAPTER 16

ALTHOUGH HE'D ARRIVED LATE THE night before and hadn't slept well again, Brock was excited this morning. Already his new employers and the man he was replacing had shown him around. The corrals and outbuildings were in good order. The horses looked okay, too. And the setting was breathtaking.

The Red Cliff Lodge was a series of buildings. The guest rooms were in long buildings that resembled bunkhouses, some of which lay along the bank of the Colorado River. Others bordered a small stream that came from a canyon to the north and flowed right past the corrals. The main lodge contained offices, meeting rooms, and a restaurant with a long deck that overlooked a large bend in the Colorado River. Towering red cliffs rose above the river on the far side to the north. Beyond those cliffs was the area known as Arches National Park. Even though he'd never been there, he knew it to be a rugged and beautiful place. He planned to visit the park when he had a day off.

The ranch itself spread between the river and the road that came out of the beautiful canyon. A well-manicured vineyard lay between the lodge and sleeping rooms and the road. A riding trail wandered up the canyon to the south, leading toward the small town of Castle Valley. It was a beautiful place, and Brock couldn't wait to get started.

"We have guests who would like to ride today," Ray, the man he was replacing, told him. "This is my last day, but I'll show you around and help you get a dozen or so horses ready. And, of course, I'll ride with you so you'll learn the lay of the land."

"Great," Brock said with excitement.

"The big buckskin you see over there," Ray said, pointing at a gelding, "is the one you'll probably want to ride. He's way too full of energy for the guests. He's been my pick from the first day I came here."

Brock looked toward the animal. He'd noticed the buckskin earlier, and he liked the idea of riding him.

"Pick out whatever saddle you'd like to use for yourself. There's plenty to choose from," Ray said.

"I brought my own, if that's okay," Brock said.

"Even better," Ray said with a smile. "I did the same thing. Do you have any questions?"

"Don't think so," Brock said.

"Good. Then let's get to it."

A moment later Brock's cell phone rang. "Hi, Brock, it's Jodi. Did you make it to Moab okay?" she asked cheerfully.

"Sure did. And what a great place this is," he said.

"I hope to see it soon," she told him.

"Hey, thanks for calling, Jodi. I don't have time to talk right now, but I'll call you back later. I'm just getting ready to start saddling horses," he said.

As he hung up, he wondered where Kaitlyn Glenn was right then. He had a feeling she'd love this place. He wasn't so sure that Jodi would. He scolded himself. Why couldn't he quit thinking of Kaitlyn? He didn't even know her, nor would he ever. He was glad she was still alive, but he had to quit thinking of her. It wasn't fair to Jodi. He dragged his forearm across his brow. It was going to be a very hot day.

* * *

The two men had gotten a fairly early start. At least they'd gotten out of bed early. Myler was angry about not having a change of clothes. Jace had his small suitcase with him and was able to change into something different. Myler's ankle, sprained when he jumped from the truck, was a little better, and he'd bought some bandages for his injured left hand. His nose was swollen and noticeably purple.

The two of them had barely spoken to each other as they raced west in a car that Jace had bought at about eight thirty that morning. It had been owned previously by a woman who had left it in front of the convenience store across from the motel with a sign and a phone number in the window. Jace had talked her down quite a bit before he'd finally shelled out two thousand more dollars. It was an old Buick with an abundance of rust spots, but it ran well. Anyway, they wouldn't need it for long. When they got back to Denver, they'd ditch the rust bucket and try to get another rental car under one of Myler's false IDs.

Jace was driving. And he kept the car steadily above the speed limit, but not so far that he was likely to get pulled over. Neither man wanted a run-in with the law. Although Myler was confident that Celia Dulce couldn't identify him, he still worried just in case she made an attempt. Myler hoped to be back in Denver and searching the rodeo arena for Kaitlyn shortly after noon.

* * *

Norman Thatcher was not a happy man. He'd repeatedly tried to call Kelvin Glenn. But Kelvin had apparently turned his phone off. He was afraid that Kelvin, not knowing that Kaitlyn was alive, might mess up the whole thing with the horse. And he really wanted to get his hands on Tony B. He decided to try again that morning while Jordan was at the arena working with her horse. But once again the call did not go through. He would try again that afternoon. If that didn't work, he'd probably have to write Kaitlyn's brother off as a lost cause. It rankled him.

* * *

Celia was also on the road again. When she'd prepared to go to sleep the night before, she'd found the bag her abductor had left in the sleeper compartment of her truck. In it she found a number of business cards, each with a different name and a different line of business. But there was nothing with a picture of his dreadful face on it. She assumed that he could make himself out to be any number of people with any number of professions. And he could be from whichever state suited him at the time. But he also had several cards in a small silver box that identified him as Myler Keegan, private detective, from Des Moines, Iowa. Among the cards were a couple that advertised him as an expert in several facets of private investigation work, one of which was searching for missing persons. *Or persons who didn't want to be found,* Celia thought, thinking of her friend Kaitlyn.

Myler Keegan. The name seemed to fit the face she'd come to despise. She wondered if those cards might be the only real ones of the bunch. There was no way of knowing for sure, but for now she chose to think of him as Myler Keegan.

As she dug deeper into the bag, she found another handgun, the same caliber as the one he'd threatened her with, a 9 millimeter semi-automatic. And with it was a box of ammo that fit both guns.

While driving through Kansas, she smiled as she thought of the big man, the possible PI. He was probably unarmed, at least for a while. But she had three guns. And if he ever accosted her again, she vowed she'd use one of them. She also smiled at another significant discovery from his bag. A cell phone. She had put it in her large purse. It might come in handy someday. If nothing else, it might save her some minutes on her own phone. After all, she reasoned, the guy owed her.

Finally, she frowned as she thought of one other item she'd found. It was an envelope that contained a picture of Kaitlyn Glenn. She was almost positive that Myler Keegan was a ruthless, rogue PI who had been hired by Jace Landry to find and kidnap Kaitlyn Glenn. Even if he wasn't, he was clearly helping Jace find her.

Thinking of Kaitlyn made her pull out her cell phone. She wanted to make sure the girl was safe and assure her that she was safe as well.

* * *

Kaitlyn answered her cell phone. She was glad it was Celia. She'd worried about her all night along. "How are you doing?" she asked.

"I'm fine. I slept fairly well last night. And I haven't seen hide nor hair of Jace or Myler."

"Who?"

"I don't know for sure what that other guy's name is, but I prefer to think of him as Myler Keegan. I think there's a possibility that the *ugly man,* as you call him, is a private investigator from Des Moines," Celia said. "He left his overnight bag in my truck when I booted him out the door. He had a bunch of business cards with several different names, vocations, and addresses on them. Some of the cards advertised him as a PI who specializes in finding missing persons."

"You think that maybe Jace hired a crooked PI to look for me," Kaitlyn said. "That explains why he was able to track me so well. That's frightening, Celia, especially since we know it doesn't bother him to break the law to do what his clients want."

"Well, there is one bright side," Celia said. "I have his guns."

"Guns?"

"Yep, he had two. One was in his bag."

"He'll get another one," Kaitlyn said.

"I'm sure, so we just keep being cautious," Celia said. "What are you doing right now?"

"I'm with a highway patrolman, and he's helping me buy a new truck."

"A new truck!" Celia exclaimed. "Don't tell me you're planning to go somewhere by yourself."

"I'm going to go get Tony B."

"Kaitlyn, not until these guys are stopped!"

Kaitlyn couldn't miss the panic in her friend's voice. But she was tired of others taking risks for her. She couldn't just sit around waiting for something to happen. "Don't worry so much, Celia," she said, smiling at how much the two of them kept telling each other that very thing. "I'm going to get a different color truck. I'm looking at Fords right now. That's what I had before, but I liked it. And I'm also going to stay away from rodeos for a while. I'll go somewhere else and be careful about using a credit card. And I'll change cell phones every so often. What I can't do is sit around Boise for very long. Jace and that other guy—what did you say his name might be?"

"Myler Keegan," Celia responded. "Of course, I could be wrong. It could be any of the names on the cards, but for now, I guess I prefer that he has a name, and that's what I'm thinking it is."

"Sounds good enough to me. I can't sit around and wait for them to come here again. And I'm sure they will," she said.

"Well, I'll let you get back to truck shopping," Celia said, "but please keep in touch."

For several minutes, Kaitlyn and Lieutenant Alger, who had taken a personal interest in her safety while she was in Boise, wandered around the Ford dealership looking at trucks. The lieutenant's phone began to ring. He answered it and stepped back while Kaitlyn and a salesman discussed a black Ford pickup. "It will have to have a fifth wheel installed," she said after making up her mind that this was the truck she wanted.

"That'll be fine, but it will take until tomorrow to get that done," the salesman said.

"I'll need it by tomorrow morning for sure," she said. Kaitlyn wanted to leave Boise no later than Friday morning. She hoped to have her horse loaded and away from Logan by Saturday. She was looking forward to going to church on Sunday. The meetings she'd attended in Twin Falls and the family she'd stayed with Sunday night seemed like distant memories. She felt the need to partake of the sacrament and listen to the gospel being taught after so many days of turmoil in her life.

She wasn't sure where she would go after leaving Logan with Tony B. She just knew that she needed to drive somewhere and that she needed to find another place for Tony B to stay until she could get back to the rodeo circuit. She supposed she'd start by driving south through Utah.

"Let's go inside and get some paperwork started," the salesman suggested.

"Oh, yes, that's great," she agreed, bringing her mind back to the present.

"Kaitlyn," Lieutenant Alger said.

She turned toward him and her heart began pounding. She didn't like the look of concern on his face. "Is something wrong?" she said.

"I don't know. I just got a strange call from the medical examiner."

"What about?" she asked.

"He said a man called him a few minutes ago. He wants to come and identify your body and collect your things," Lieutenant Alger said. "He even said he'd arrange for your burial. The medical examiner didn't tell the fellow that you are very much alive and that you have already claimed everything. Anyway, it's someone who doesn't know you're alive but also claims to be your brother."

Kaitlyn's heart nearly stopped. Kelvin! *What's he doing in Boise and how did he find out about me?*

"Do you have a brother?" Lieutenant Alger asked.

"Not really. I have a stepbrother, but I haven't heard from him for a long time," she said. "In fact, the last time I knew anything about him was when he broke into my apartment in California and went through my things. I know what he wants. Kelvin wants my money."

"Kelvin—that was the name he gave the medical examiner," Lieutenant Alger said. "He's not a good man, I take it, this stepbrother of yours?"

"He's into pushing drugs, theft, whatever he can do to keep from having to work for a living," she said. "He even managed to turn my mother against me when I joined the LDS Church when I was nineteen. I haven't heard from her or Kelvin's father since then."

"So he's up to no good?" the lieutenant asked.

"That's for sure. I can't believe he heard about my death, but apparently he hasn't heard the latest news. I'm sure he figures that he can get my money now. He'll be shocked when he finds out he can't. Is he in Boise?"

"No, but he's on his way here. He expects to arrive this afternoon and wanted to make arrangements to meet the medical examiner. He even asked what he had to do to get a death certificate," the lieutenant explained.

"What did the medical examiner tell him?" Kaitlyn asked.

"Very little. He told him to be there at three this afternoon. Then he called me," Lieutenant Alger explained. "He wants to know what to tell him when he shows up."

"The truth, I guess," Kaitlyn said. "And he'll be mad, I'm sure."

"Did you want to meet him down there?" the lieutenant asked.

"Absolutely not! I have nothing to talk to Kelvin about. He'll just start in on me again about how the money my father left me should really be his. No; in fact, he doesn't need to know I'm here. By tomorrow at this time I won't be."

"Where are you going?" he asked.

"I don't know for sure, at least not until I get my horse and trailer. I do plan to go to Utah and get them. I'll figure something out after that," she said.

"He'll know you've been here when he finds out you have your purse back," Lieutenant Alger pointed out.

"That can't be helped, I guess," she said.

"Kaitlyn, would he hurt you?" he asked.

"I don't know. If he was high on meth he probably would. I just need to stay away from him. I wish I could get the fifth wheel installed in my new truck today, then I'd leave this afternoon or evening."

"Maybe we can get that sped up for you," the lieutenant suggested. "I'll talk to the folks in here while you do your paperwork."

* * *

It was as Nina had feared. Her parents were no fun at all on Thursday. They went through the motions, and it was a pretty drive, but they barely spoke to each other. She was so frustrated she felt like screaming. Whenever she wanted to take a walk to some scenic point, they would protest. Then she'd insist, and her father would walk with her, saying practically nothing to her the whole time. Her mother always stayed in the car.

Finally, as they were driving through Canyonlands National Park that afternoon, she leaned forward from her place in the backseat. "I want to go home. This is not any fun."

"We have a vacation planned and we'll finish it," her father growled.

"Why?" she asked. "You and Mum aren't having any fun, and now I'm not either. I'd rather be home with Ruby."

"That's not possible," her father said. "Ruby is also taking a vacation. If we went home now there would be no one to take care of you."

That set Nina back. It had never occurred to her that Ruby might not be there if they went back early. Without another word, she sat back in her seat and crossed her arms.

"You see what I mean, Maggie?" Maurice said. "You better rethink what we discussed."

More of their mysterious grown-up talk, Nina was thinking. Whatever was wrong with her mother and whatever was bothering her father would just have to be their secret. She would try to have fun whenever she could. Maybe they'd stay somewhere in the next few nights where there were kids she could make friends with.

* * *

Jordan Thatcher kept stepping out of her trailer and looking about for Kaitlyn. She missed the older girl, and she hoped she would come and ride in the rodeo. She thought about the man who had claimed to be her brother. *What if he really is?* she wondered. Her father was convinced of it. But she still couldn't imagine how someone as nice as Kaitlyn could have such a loser of a brother. She also failed to see any resemblance between the two of them.

Her dad was acting strangely, and that worried her. She'd never seen the side of him she was seeing now. And she didn't like it. He acted nice around her most of the time, but he couldn't seem to stop badmouthing Kaitlyn. Something was upsetting him, and she was sure it had to do with Kaitlyn. Jordan loved her father. He'd given up so much to help her find her dream. But now he wanted more for her than she wanted for herself, and it was driving her crazy. She was content just to ride well, and if she made a little money along the way, that was great. But her whole life didn't revolve around winning. She simply loved competing. But to her father, winning was everything.

She left the trailer once more and looked around. Then she went back in and grabbed her hat. She decided to go for a walk. "Where are you going, sis?" Norman asked. He'd been sitting in their cramped quarters studying some kind of business book, but now he put it down.

"I'm just going for a walk," she said.

"Could you use some company? I think it would do me good to move around a little bit."

"Sure, Dad, that would be great," she said, and she meant it. *As long as we don't talk about Kaitlyn,* she mentally added.

They wandered to the arena, then into the stands. After that they took a look at the livestock that would be used in the rodeo the next evening. More cowboys and cowgirls were milling about as well. Like Jordan, others were anxious for the action that would begin the next evening and were out walking off the boredom of waiting.

Jordan spotted Dan Burke. Like Kaitlyn, he was always friendly to her. He waved and walked their way. "How are you, Jordan?" Dan asked.

"I'm good," she said.

"And you, Mr. Thatcher?" he asked her father.

"Just anxious to get underway. I see you've been looking at the roping calves. What do you think?" Norman asked.

"Looks like some good ones," Dan responded, and he fell into step beside them as they walked away from the corrals.

They walked toward a group of cowboys who were talking to a couple of men who looked almost as out of place as the man who claimed to be Kelvin Glenn. The one man, a good-looking guy of probably thirty-five or so, wore expensive-looking clothes. He was slightly taller but much leaner than the second man. The other man was . . . Jordan didn't like thinking such thoughts, but *ugly* was the word that came to mind. His face was pockmarked, his heavy jowls hung down, and his mustache, which he kept stroking with one hand, was way too big. His other hand was bandaged. He was a huge man. It was hard to guess his age, but he was almost certainly older than the first guy.

Jordan tried to steer her father and Dan away from the group. But one of the cowboys, Billy Jones, a young bull rider Jordan liked, spotted her. "Hey, Jordan, come over here," he called out. "These guys are cousins of Kaitlyn's. Maybe you can answer their questions. They're trying to find her."

The smile that Billy gave her made Jordan's heart beat a little faster. He was really cute. She couldn't say no to *him*, so she, along with Dan Burke and her father, joined the little group.

Billy pointed to the two strangers. "I thought that since you're a barrel racer like Kaitlyn, maybe you could help them."

"Yes, it's nice to meet you, Jordan," the big man said. "We thought surely she would be here by now. She told us several days ago to meet her here. I can't imagine that she's changed her plans."

Jordan was uneasy, and by the look on Dan Burke's face, she knew that he was as well. Her dad, on the other hand, seemed pleased to meet the guys. The big man was not only unattractive, but his eyes were, well, downright scary, she thought. She didn't like the looks of him. Her father was watching her, expecting her to say something. Jordan said simply, "She missed the last rodeo. I haven't heard from her, and I don't know if she's coming here or not."

"Surely she is," the big man with the bandaged hand said.

"I was hoping so. She's a nice girl," Jordan said.

"Actually, I was sort of hoping not," her father said, and she cringed at the tone in his voice. "When your cousin doesn't come, my girl rides better." The two men looked at her father with interest. She hated it.

"Sorry, I can't help you," Jordan said before either of the men chose to say anything else to her. Then she flashed a smile at Billy. "See you around," she said. Leaving her dad standing there, she walked off.

But she hadn't gone more than five or six steps before she heard her father. "Funny how family keeps showing up looking for Kaitlyn. Today it's you guys. Yesterday it was her brother."

She walked faster. She didn't want to hear whatever else her father had to say. She was surprised when she realized that Dan Burke was only a half step behind her.

"Hey, wait up, Jordan. I need to talk to you," he called to her.

She slowed down, and Dan stepped up beside her. "Those guys troubled you, didn't they?" he said.

"Only a lot. I don't think that guy yesterday was her brother, and I don't believe these guys are her cousins," she said flatly. "They didn't even say what their names are, and that seems spooky to me. I wish my dad wouldn't talk to them. I don't know why he hates Kaitlyn so much."

Jordan looked back. Her father was still talking to the men. The others in the group had walked away. "Dan, do you think Kaitlyn is in some kind of trouble?" she asked.

"Can you keep something to yourself?" Dan asked.

"Of course I can," Jordan responded quickly. "Especially if it's about Kaitlyn."

"Okay, I'm going to trust you. Kaitlyn is in danger, a lot of danger, and I think these guys are behind it," he said. "You might be able to help. The better-dressed guy—the not-so-ugly one—I think I know who he is. Give me a minute while I make a quick phone call, then I'll tell you about him if I'm right. But whatever you do, don't repeat it to anyone, Jordan. Don't tell any of your friends. Don't even tell your dad."

"I especially won't tell him," Jordan promised. "Like I said a minute ago, he doesn't like Kaitlyn. I guess it's because she's such a good rider and he's jealous for me."

Dan was already making a call. "Brock," he said a moment later, "you won't believe what's going on here. Tell me what that guy you punched out in Cheyenne looks like."

Dan listened for a moment. "It's got to be him, Brock," he said. "Your description fits. He's here right now—over by the rodeo arena— and some big man with a huge mustache is with him. And they're claiming to be Kaitlyn's cousins."

Dan listened again to whatever the other guy was saying. Then he asked, "You don't think she ever told the cops what he did to her in Cheyenne?"

Dan listened once more. "I sure wish I knew more," he said. "And I wish I knew how to contact Kaitlyn."

"Was that Brock you were just talking to the same Brock I met yesterday?" Jordan asked.

"It was," Dan said. "And if it wasn't for him, that slick-looking guy might have kidnapped Kaitlyn and worse after the rodeo last week. In fact, Brock probably saved her life. He knocked the guy out cold when he caught him throwing her around by her truck and horse trailer. She's scared of that guy. I'm certain now that he's the reason Kaitlyn didn't show up in Laramie. And I hope she doesn't come here now. If she does, let me know right away, Jordan. Also, if you see her, let her know that those guys are here. If they see her first, we could have a real nightmare."

Jordan was alarmed. It was the most frightening thing she'd ever heard. "What's that man's name?" she asked.

"I wish I knew. Brock never heard her say it, and she wouldn't tell him anything. She wouldn't even let Brock tell her his name because she was afraid the guy would go after Brock. But now I need to know, and I'm going to try to find out."

"How will you do that?"

"She was in Idaho when they thought she was killed in the wreck. I'm from Idaho, too. I'm going to call the highway patrol in Boise to see if anyone there will tell me anything. Maybe by now they know who this guy is. And maybe they don't. But I intend to try to find out," Dan said firmly. "If nothing else, maybe they know how to reach Kaitlyn. Whatever happens, we can't let those guys get to her."

CHAPTER 17

LIEUTENANT ALGER WAS IN HIS office when the call was transferred to him. "Hello, Lieutenant Alger," he said. "How can I help you?"

"My name is Dan Burke," the voice on the other end of the line said. "I'm a friend of Kaitlyn Glenn's. I need to speak with her or at least get a message to her. She's in terrible danger."

First a brother, now a friend, he thought to himself. And yet this one sounded genuinely concerned. Well, he could check him out soon enough. Kaitlyn was waiting in the squad room. "Thanks for calling, Mr. Burke," Lieutenant Alger said. "Give me just a minute. I've got someone with me. As soon as I can get clear, I'll come back on the line."

"Thanks," Dan said.

After he'd put Dan on hold, Lieutenant Alger hurried to the squad room. Kaitlyn looked up from the book she'd been reading to pass the time. "Do they have my truck done already?" she asked.

Lieutenant Alger had managed to move up the installation of the fifth wheel in the back of Kaitlyn's new Ford pickup. He'd helped her get her few things from the safe house, and then he'd brought her here to wait while the installation was completed.

"No, not yet, but I got another phone call," he told her. "It's from someone who claims to be a friend of yours."

He felt bad when she once more looked stricken. "What did he say his name was?" she asked.

"He says he's Dan Burke."

The stricken look faded, and Kaitlyn's eyes lit up. "Oh, it's Dan? He's a great guy. Like me, he's a Mormon. He ropes calves in the rodeos, and he's really good at it. May I talk to him?"

"Certainly, if you want to."

* * *

Kaitlyn was worried that the caller might be an imposter, but she was so anxious to speak with someone she knew and respected that she was willing to take the chance. She picked up the phone Lieutenant Alger indicated and waited for just a moment as he picked up another line so he could listen in.

"Hello."

"Kaitlyn?" It sounded like Dan's voice. She was sure it was. What a relief.

"Yeah, it's me. Thanks for calling, Dan. How is everyone?"

"Everyone is fine, but we're all worried about you. As I'm sure you know, a lot of us are in Denver for the rodeo this weekend," Dan said.

"I wish I could be there, but it's too dangerous for me."

"I realize that; that's actually why I'm calling," Dan said. "There are a couple of characters down here asking about you."

"Oh, no," Kaitlyn moaned. "It never ends. Who are they?"

"They claim to be cousins of yours," Dan informed her. "They never did say what their names were."

"Cousins," she said. "I don't have any cousins, at least not any that I've ever known about. But there are some guys who are stalking me who claim to be my cousins. They are dangerous men."

"I gathered that. Let's just make sure we're talking about the same guys," he suggested. He then described the two men.

Not surprised that it was who she thought, Kaitlyn said, "That will be Jace Landry—he's the well-dressed one. And Myler Keegan might be the name of the other one. I'm not sure of that, though. I just learned about him a short while ago. I think he might be a crooked private investigator from Des Moines who was hired by Jace to help find me."

"Jace Landry and Myler Keegan," Dan repeated.

"Jace Landry for sure. The other name I'm not sure about. But whatever his name is, if he and Jace ever catch up with me, I'm toast," she said.

"It sounds like you're with the cops right now," Dan said. "You need to let them keep you safe. In the meantime, a former missionary companion of mine says that he witnessed this one you call Jace assaulting you. He should be charged and put in jail for that, you know."

"A missionary companion said that?" she asked as her heart began to race unexpectedly, and she pictured the face of the man in the black hat. He was a Mormon. She couldn't believe it. What a coincidence.

"That's right. His name is—"

"Don't tell me!" Kaitlyn interrupted. "If these guys ever catch me, I don't want them to be able to force me to tell them who it was that knocked Jace down. Jace said he'd kill him, and if he finds out who he is, he'll do just that, or at least have someone else do it. For your friend's sake, don't tell me his name."

"Okay, okay," Dan said. "I understand. Anyway, he says he thinks Jace should be charged with assault."

"That's been done already," Kaitlyn said.

"Is there a warrant out for him?"

"There is."

"Great. Then I need to call the cops here in Denver, because I know where he is," Dan told her.

On the extension Lieutenant Alger said, "Dan, I'm sorry to be eavesdropping, but this is Lieutenant Alger. If you'll tell me where he is, I'll get on the phone right now with the police in Denver and have him arrested."

"Thanks, that would be great. As of just a few minutes ago, he was in a parking lot on the west side of the rodeo arena." Dan gave him an approximate address. "He and the man with him were talking to a guy by the name of Norman Thatcher. Norman's daughter, Jordan, is a barrel racer like Kaitlyn, and she's with me right now."

"Good, stay on the line with Kaitlyn while I try to get someone moving down there," Lieutenant Alger said.

Kaitlyn watched as he hung up the extension. "Tell Jordan hi for me," Kaitlyn said, "and ask her how she did in Laramie."

"I know that already," Dan said. "She placed second again."

"Great!" Kaitlyn said. "Hey, why don't you let me talk to her for just a moment."

"Sure, here she is."

"Kaitlyn, you had us all awfully scared. I'm so glad you're alive," Jordan said.

"I'm glad too, but I've had a miserable few days. The men that Dan was just asking me about are determined to find me. It's so frightening, but that's not what I wanted to talk to you about. I'm so glad you did well again in Laramie. Congratulations."

"Thanks. It was fun. I just wish my dad wasn't so down on you."

"Your dad? He's down on me?"

"Yeah, he's convinced that I'll never be a champion as long as you're racing. I love my father, Kaitlyn, but he's scaring me lately," Jordan confided.

"What do you mean?" Kaitlyn asked in despair. Could it have been Jordan Thatcher's father who'd put something in Tony B's feed? she wondered. That's what the vet in Logan told Jim Perrett had happened to her horse—that he'd been intentionally poisoned.

"He can't say anything good about you," Jordan said. "And then when that creep came around claiming to be your brother, Dad acted like they were best buddies."

"Was the guy's name Kelvin?"

"Yeah, he said he was Kelvin Glenn," she said. "But he couldn't be your brother, could he?"

"He's my stepbrother, Jordan. My mother married his dad after my dad died when I was very young. Kelvin and his dad are real creeps. Kelvin wants whatever money he thinks he can get from me."

"I didn't think he seemed like someone who was actually related to you," Jordan said.

"You said your dad made friends with him?" Kaitlyn asked.

"I guess that's what you'd call it."

"If your dad hears from him again, will you let me know?"

"Sure, but how do I do that? I don't have your cell phone number."

"Yeah, that's a problem, and for your safety, especially where your dad is talking to all these guys who are out to get me, it would probably be best if you don't have it. I'll tell you what. How about if I call you occasionally? That is, if you'd be willing to give me your number."

"That would be great," Jordan said. "But then your number would be on my phone and Dad might find it and give it to them."

"My number is blocked, but just to be on the safe side, I'll call from pay phones," Kaitlyn said. "Believe me, I'm learning to be careful. Thanks, Jordan. Can I talk to Dan again?"

Can Norman Thatcher be the person who tampered with Tony B's feed? she again wondered as she waited for Dan to come back on the phone. The thought frightened her, as much for Jordan as for herself.

* * *

"Is Kaitlyn going to be okay?" Jordan asked as soon as Dan ended his conversation with Kaitlyn.

"I hope so. But she's in a lot of danger," he said. "I think I'll walk back and see if the cops show up to arrest Jace Landry."

"I'll go with you, if it's okay," Jordan said. "I'd like to see Dad's face when the cops put handcuffs on that creep."

But before they arrived back at the arena, they met Norman Thatcher. "Hi Jordan, Dan," he said cheerfully.

"Dad, did those two men leave?" Jordan asked in alarm.

"You mean Kaitlyn's cousins?" he asked. "Yeah, they are really concerned about finding her. I can't imagine why she's being so difficult. All they want to do is help her."

"That's not true," Dan said angrily. "First, they are not her cousins, and second, they intend to harm her."

"Now that's just plain crazy," Norman retorted. "They are nice men, and they *are* her cousins."

"Dad, the guy that was dressed nicely, the slim one, his name is Jace Landry, and he's wanted by the police. The other one is Myler Keegan, a crooked private eye," Jordan said. "Do you know where they are now?"

"It *might* be Myler Keegan," Dan corrected her, "but we don't know that." He turned to Norman. "Did they ever tell you their names?"

"No, but they drove off after we'd visited for a minute. That's all I know, but you two are obviously mistaken," Norman insisted. "They have nothing against Kaitlyn."

"I'm afraid that's not the case, Norman," Dan said. "I just talked to an officer. They're looking for the men right now. Which way did they drive when they left?" As he asked the question, two Denver police squad cars raced past. "I need to talk to them," Dan said, and he left at a run toward the arena.

"What's with Dan Burke?" Norman asked. "I though he was a decent guy."

"He is, Dad," Jordan said. "But those guys you were talking with aren't. Can't you see that?"

"Hey, if Dan Burke is going to get you all worked up, then you better not be talking to him," Norman said. "Anyway, I think he's married. I don't want you flirting with married men."

Jordan couldn't believe what her father was saying. "Dad, I'll talk to whoever I want to. I'm not a child, you know. And I know Dan's married. All I was doing was talking to him about Kaitlyn."

"You better forget about Kaitlyn, Jordan," he said. "If what you say is true—and I don't believe it for a minute, but if it happens to be—then Kaitlyn has created a lot of trouble for herself. She's not someone you want to be friends with."

Jordan had heard all she wanted, and she abruptly swung around and walked off in the direction of the arena. She ignored her dad when he called after her, and started to run. She hoped he wouldn't try to follow her because she was angry with him. He was being so stubborn and so blind, all because he was jealous of Kaitlyn Glenn.

The police were talking to Dan when Jordan ran up to them. "Jordan," Dan said, "you saw the car those two men were in. Can you describe it for these officers?"

"Yeah, it was a blue Chevrolet Lumina," she said. "Looked like a rental car to me. It had an Avis sticker on the bumper."

"I didn't notice the sticker," Dan said. "Thanks." Then he turned to the officers. "Will that help?"

"Sure will," one of them answered. Jordan noticed he was wearing sergeant stripes. "We'll contact Avis right away. We'll also alert other officers to be looking for the blue car."

The police soon pulled away in their squad cars. "I can't believe this," Jordan moaned. "If they'd been a little quicker getting here, Jace would have been arrested and Kaitlyn would be safe."

"You're right. It's too bad they didn't catch him here," Dan agreed. "But they still might get him. However, even if they do catch him, from what Kaitlyn told me, he's got a lot of money. He'll bail out of jail in no time. It will take a prison sentence for him before it will be safe for Kaitlyn, and that might never happen."

"Why do you say that?" Jordan asked.

"Because it will be his word against hers, and who knows who a judge or jury might believe," Dan told her.

"But your friend Brock could help," she suggested.

"Yes, he could, but Kaitlyn doesn't want him involved, because she's afraid Jace will go after Brock. She wouldn't even let me tell her his name in case they catch her and try to force her to tell them who he is."

"Maybe he should decide if he wants to help her," Jordan said. "He helped her once before, and I'll bet he will again, whether she asks him to or not."

"That's a good point, Jordan. If they get Jace in custody, I'll call Brock. It'll need to be his decision what he does from that point," Dan said. "But I'm pretty sure I know what he'll decide."

* * *

Kaitlyn was disappointed but not surprised when she learned that Jace and Myler had left the rodeo grounds before they could be apprehended. She'd hoped to hear that Jace was in jail, but she knew that he would never stay there long, even if he was arrested. Lieutenant Alger tried to persuade her to go back to the safe house for a few days after he delivered her some more bad news. It appeared that the man with Jace *was* a very shady private investigator by the name of Myler Keegan. Celia had been right.

"I can't live this way," Kaitlyn told him, despite what she'd just learned. "I've got to go on with my life, messed up as it is. I can't just sit around and wait."

"Surely you don't still intend to go to Logan to get your horse," Lieutenant Alger said.

"I have to," Kaitlyn replied, trying to make him understand. "I can't let those good people continue to be in danger because of what they're doing to help me. I'll leave tonight, but I'll be careful."

"I wish I could talk you out of it," he said.

"You can't," Kaitlyn said with a smile.

"About your stepbrother . . . He'll be showing up at the medical examiner's office anytime now. And when he does, they clearly can't turn any of your property over to him since you have it all. What do you think they should do?" he asked.

"They might as well let him know I'm alive so he won't be trying to pry into my financial affairs thinking that he has some kind of legal right," Kaitlyn said. "I just don't want him to know when I was here or when I left."

"We won't tell him anything," Lieutenant Alger promised.

There were still a few hours of daylight left when Kaitlyn entered the freeway and started east in her new black pickup. Although fearful, she was calm and determined. She at least had an idea where Jace and Myler had been recently. That gave her, she believed, a few hours of driving time in which she had nothing to worry about. She called Jim Perrett and told him she was coming for her horse. "I'll be there early in the morning," she promised.

"Kaitlyn, you are worrying about us needlessly," Jim said. "We can keep the horse for as long as you need."

"I know that, and I appreciate it," she said. "But I want to see him, and I think I need to take him somewhere else, because I have a bad feeling about leaving him with you. Not because I don't trust you to take care of Tony B, but because of the danger it puts you in. I've put you through too much already."

"You're worrying too much about us," Jim said. "But if you are determined, then I guess I can't tell you what to do. Are you really sure about this?"

"Yes, I'm sure, and I have the money to pay whatever I owe you when I see you," she said.

"Okay. I'll load him and meet you at the sheriff's office in Logan," Jim agreed. "Then you can take him and your trailer right from there."

Despite the past few tense days, the thought of seeing her horse again gave Kaitlyn comfort, and she looked forward to picking him up the next day.

* * *

"Let me see the body!" Kelvin demanded.

"There is no need for that," he was told. "The victim was not your sister. We have positive ID, including DNA and dental X-rays. We know who the dead woman is."

"Then why did you tell the world that it was Kaitlyn?" Kelvin asked angrily. "You've caused me a lot of needless suffering and pain. You made me think I'd lost my only sister."

"We thought at first that it was Kaitlyn, and we're sorry for any inconvenience it caused you, but your sister is alive and well."

"Then where is she?" Kelvin shouted.

"I can't tell you that because I don't know," the medical examiner replied evenly.

"You're lying," Kelvin accused him.

"I'm sorry you feel that way. I'm sure that if you and your sister are so close, she'll be attempting to contact you. You'll need to leave now."

Kelvin left. He left angry. And he left determined to find Kaitlyn, and when he did . . .

* * *

Anger was making the rounds. Jace and Myler also had a bad case of it. They'd decided to fly back to Des Moines so that Myler could pick up some additional forms of identification—new names, of course—and a few other things, like another gun, to replace the items that had been in the overnight bag Celia Dulce now had. Myler dropped Jace near where he'd left his jet and went to return the rental car to Avis. There he was confronted by a police officer.

"Are you Myler Keegan?"

"No," Myler said, glad that he always carried at least one alternate set of identification. It was under the name of Joseph Brown of Los Angeles that he'd rented the car. He showed the ID and then, when asked if he knew Jace Landry, he said, "Never heard of anyone by that name. Why?"

"There's a felony warrant out for him, and you match the description of the man some witnesses saw near the rodeo grounds with him a short while ago."

"Your witnesses are mistaken. I'm not that man, and I haven't been near any rodeo grounds. Do I look like a cowboy?" he asked with a chuckle.

The officer agreed that he didn't, and Myler left, wondering if any of the authorities had seen Jace yet. When Myler called him on his newly acquired cell phone, Jace answered in a panic. "There are cops standing over by my plane," he said. "I'm walking away from there as fast as I dare. I don't want to attract attention."

"That's smart," Myler said. Then he filled Jace in about the warrant that had been issued in Cheyenne. He called a taxi and picked Jace up a few minutes later. They rode to a small airport outside the city, rented a small, single-engine Cessna, and headed for Iowa. Their plan was to be back in Denver before the rodeo began the next evening.

Jace was the more furious of the two. "I can't believe she went to the cops," he said.

"They'll never make it stick," Myler assured him. "It's your word against hers, and who is she? She's a—"

"She's nobody compared to me," Jace broke in. "But she's a beautiful nobody, and I'm going to have her."

Myler had no reply. He still had his own plans regarding Kaitlyn, but they would have to wait. "Didn't you tell me that some cowboy butted in and caught you off guard in Cheyenne?" he asked, drawing the conversation away from Kaitlyn.

"Yeah, and I'll . . ." Jace paused for a moment. "I bet that's who turned me in— that guy in the black hat. He had some blond with him. He's the reason there are charges against me."

"You may be right," Myler assented.

"I bet I am. Well, when we find Kaitlyn, she'll tell me who he is, and I'll see that he never testifies," Jace said darkly.

"What about the blond who was with him?" Myler prodded. "Did she get a good look at you, too, or do you know?"

"I don't know for sure, but she might have. Anyway, there's no way I'm taking any chances. Same goes for her. Oh, yeah," Jace said. "They'll both pay for interfering."

"Why do you have to wait until we find Kaitlyn?" Myler asked.

"What are you suggesting?"

"I hunt people down. That's what I'm good at," Myler bragged. "For a little more money, I could find out from some of the rodeo crowd who the guy in the black hat is. That won't be hard. That fellow we talked to earlier, Norman Thatcher, will help me. In fact, odds are that he knows the guy you're after."

"Whatever it takes," Jace said. "You know I'm good for the money. Find him, find the blond, and I'll take it from there."

"I'll get on it as soon as we get back to Denver. But you're going to have to let me work alone for a while, you know," Myler said, thinking that the warrant for Jace was just what he needed to keep Jace out of his way. "That warrant is out there, Jace," Myler added, trying to hide his smugness. "You can't let the cops see you."

"Maybe they're looking for you, too," Jace said. "That truck driver gal probably turned you in."

"Maybe. The cops did know my name, but she could have gotten that from the things in my bag she stole. But she didn't see my face. There's no way she could tell them positively who I am, so I'm safe. It's you that's not."

"Myler, she saw you in that café in Boise," Jace reminded him.

"Oh, yeah, I guess you're right. But still, there's no warrant out for me. I'm safe, Jace. But I need to work on my own again for a while," Myler stressed.

"Well, while you're looking, maybe you should also see what you can find out about that other guy that Thatcher mentioned," Jace suggested.

"You mean her brother?"

"Yeah, the guy who says he's Kelvin Glenn," Jace agreed. "I don't know what he wants, but if Kaitlyn has money, it will be mine, not his. I'd like to know where he is and what he's up to."

"All in good time," Myler said. "But for now, I think we need to find the two witnesses and take care of them."

CHAPTER 18

BROCK WAS EXHAUSTED. HE'D HAD a long first day at work, but it had been a good one. The guests at the lodge were, for the most part, pleasant people. Unfortunately, almost none of them had ever straddled a horse before, so he and the fellow he was replacing spent a lot of their time teaching folks how to mount and dismount, how to stay in the saddle when the horse was moving, and how to keep a horse walking up the trail.

The horses, gentle and clearly used to their roles, sensed that the riders were greenhorns and did nothing to upset them. And Brock was in his element. He loved working with horses, but he also enjoyed helping people. To him, even though it was tiring, he felt that he'd found an ideal job, and he was determined to enjoy every day to the fullest.

Finally, after taking care of the horses for the night and making sure all the tack was properly stored and secured, Brock went to his room. It was small but comfortable. It had the essentials—a microwave, small refrigerator, hot plate, some cooking gear, and an assortment of dishes and utensils. What he didn't have was food. That meant he'd have to eat at the restaurant unless he wanted to take a trip into Moab, and he was just too tired for the drive. Having been deprived of sleep for several nights, he was determined to get some. He showered, changed into clean clothes, and headed to the lodge for a leisurely meal.

He selected a table on the veranda overlooking a large bend in the Colorado River. It took him only a moment to decide what he wanted from the menu, and then his cell phone began to ring.

"Hey, how was the first day on the new job?" Dan asked when Brock answered.

Brock had been hoping Dan would call. The one blight on an otherwise good day had been his worry about Kaitlyn Glenn. He hoped Dan would have some good news about her.

"It was really good. I'm going to enjoy this job," Brock said. "Hey, tell me what's happening there."

"Kaitlyn filed a report on Jace with the police in Cheyenne and a warrant was issued, but Jace and the guy with him disappeared just before the cops got to where the men had been talking to Jordan's dad," Dan said. "Kaitlyn is safe for the time being. I talked to her on the phone. She was in Boise at the highway patrol office. But she says she's heading for Logan to pick up her horse. That worries me."

"It worries me, too," Brock said. "I'm glad that the cops can at least arrest Jace when they find him. And I'll do whatever I have to in order to make myself available to testify against him when the time comes."

"Kaitlyn doesn't want that, Brock. She wouldn't even let me tell her your name. She says that this guy will come after you if he finds out who you are," Dan told him. "And she doesn't want something to happen to you because of her."

"I think that should be my choice," Brock said. "Anyway, Jace is no danger to me if he's in jail," Brock said.

"He's a rich man, Brock—filthy rich. He'll bail out of jail if they do find him. She has reason to be concerned."

"Then that's a risk I'll have to take," Brock said. "She's got to quit being so stubborn and let others help."

"Brock, Kaitlyn is a good gal. And I think she'd put herself right back in the line of fire, so to speak, if she thought she needed to in order to protect someone else. I know that's why she's so intent on picking her horse up in Logan. Jace knows who has him, and she's afraid he and his buddy will go after that man or his family unless she gets the horse out of there."

"Who is Jace's buddy?"

Dan told him what he'd learned. "We were only guessing about his name, but it's been confirmed by the authorities now. I think he's a bad apple, all right. In fact, I know he is. He hijacked the truck of some lady truck driver who helped Kaitlyn get away from Boise. She somehow got rid of him, and because of her we now know who he is." Dan filled in more of the details for Brock about Jace and his accomplice.

"Dan," Brock began thoughtfully, "I'm more worried than ever about Kaitlyn. I wish there was something I could do."

Dan began to chuckle.

"What's so funny, Dan? I fail to see any humor in what's going on," Brock scolded.

"I'm sorry, Brock. It just strikes me that you have more than a passing interest in Kaitlyn. And I don't blame you. She'd be a real catch."

"I have a girlfriend, Dan," Brock said as he thought about Jodi.

"But it seems to me that there's nothing set in concrete with her," Dan observed slyly.

Brock didn't know what to say. His former missionary companion was absolutely right. He liked Jodi a lot, but there was just something about the two brief encounters with Kaitlyn that wouldn't leave his mind. He couldn't deny that he'd like to meet her again, this time under more favorable circumstances.

His server returned just then, giving him a way to end the uncomfortable conversation. "Let me know what else you learn, Dan" he said. "Right now I need to go. A very pretty young waitress is hovering over me."

"Eat then," Dan said with another chuckle. "And no flirting. You have enough girls on the line. I'll keep you informed."

Brock placed his order and sat thoughtfully as he waited for his salad. He gazed at the slowly moving water of the Colorado River and considered his feelings for Jodi. At least, he tried to. The captivating face of Kaitlyn Glenn and her smile, combined with the look of terror he'd seen on that face, would give him no peace.

* * *

Tony B looked healthy and happy. He seemed as pleased to see Kaitlyn as she was to see him. She barely said hello to Jim Perrett before stepping into her trailer to see her horse. He whinnied a greeting as she threw her arms around his neck and buried her face in his mane.

"Mr. Perrett, thank you so much. You've taken such good care of him," she said with a slight catch in her voice.

"And I'll continue to do so if you'll change your mind," he offered. "I'll keep him safe if you'll let me."

"Thank you, but no. You've done so much already. I just can't put you or your family at any more risk."

Fifteen minutes later, she'd hooked the trailer to her new F-250 and given Jim the little money he was willing to take for caring for Tony B the previous week. Jim said it was too much, but she knew he was just being kind, that he should have charged her much more, especially considering the trouble she had put him through. She impulsively hugged both Jim and his wife. "I'll never forget what you two have done for me."

"You be careful," the two of them said in unison as she climbed into her truck. "And keep in touch," Jim added. "We'd like to know how things go for you."

As Kaitlyn pulled out of the parking area at the Cache County Sheriff's Department, she felt a sinking sensation in her stomach. *Where to now?* she asked herself.

But she'd already decided to head toward southern Utah. She'd decide later where to go from there.

With no particular destination in mind, Kaitlyn didn't hurry. She couldn't imagine that hurrying would help her be any safer. She stopped whenever she felt like taking a break from driving. She even pulled up to a rodeo arena in Manti that afternoon. She couldn't stand it anymore. She had to get Tony B out and ride him. The two spent a relaxing hour before Kaitlyn finally loaded up her horse and drove on.

She decided she'd spend the night in the living quarters of her trailer. She turned off the highway, and a short while later pulled into a parking area at a trailhead on the Fish Lake National Forest. She put Tony B in a small corral there, threw him some hay, and prepared to spend the night. She even made up her mind that she'd go for a long ride up the trail the next morning before heading south again.

* * *

Myler insisted that Jace hole up in a hotel room when they got back to Denver on Friday. He then spent the day hanging around the rodeo arena and was lucky enough to run into Norman Thatcher. But even though Norman had some useful information about a stepbrother of Kaitlyn's, he didn't know much about the other cowboy's friend. He did suggest that he might be from the Cheyenne area, as he'd attended the rodeo there. After failing to find any sign of Kaitlyn at the rodeo that night, Myler returned to the motel and announced to Jace that he was going to Cheyenne the next morning.

Jace volunteered to fly him there.

"Don't you think that's a bit risky?" Myler said. "That's where the warrant was issued."

"I can lie low when we get there, just like I am here," he said. "Nobody will be looking for a New Yorker by the name of Roger Rodale in Cheyenne, so even leaving the plane at a hangar shouldn't present any problems."

Myler instantly regretted preparing Jace the false identity papers while they'd been back in Des Moines. He wanted to rid himself of Jace, but he couldn't be too obvious. And then there was the matter of money. He did want to collect as much from his client as he could before he cut their ties. He finally agreed.

Early Saturday morning Jace piloted the small rented Cessna northward. Myler had a feeling that before the day was over he'd learn the identity of the man who had interfered with Jace. Once he knew who he was after, he'd begin the hunt. He might, Myler decided, be the best clue to finding Kaitlyn again. It was certainly worth a try.

* * *

Kaitlyn packed herself a lunch, filled a canteen with water, and rode Tony B into the forest at about eight on Saturday morning, feeling safe. She hoped it wasn't a false sense of security, considering her circumstances. She had decided that riding in the open air might be the best thing to free her mind of the constant worry and stress she'd been living with. She could drive later. There was no hurry. She had no destination.

The day was warm but not oppressively hot. The ride soon did what she hoped it would. For the first time in days, Kaitlyn began to relax. She left the trail and rode through the trees to the edge of a small lake, where she dismounted and ate her lunch. Feeling comfortable and a little sleepy, she took a short nap in the shade of a bushy pine while Tony B, hobbled nearby, grazed contentedly on the lush green feed.

It was nearly one thirty when Kaitlyn awoke. She thought she'd start back for the trailhead and her truck. But after she caught her horse and put the saddle back on him, she began thinking about Celia. She decided it might be a good time to call her to make sure she was all right. To Kaitlyn's dismay, her cell phone had no signal.

* * *

Myler was having some success. With Jace confined to the motel room, he worked without interference. It felt great—liberating, in fact. After several hours of work, he'd learned that the young man he was looking for was most likely Brock Hankins. He also learned that Brock had a girlfriend named Jodi Henry. His source knew that Brock had been offered a new job out of state, but he didn't know exactly where. However, with a little more effort, Myler learned where Jodi lived and where she worked. That would do for now, he decided. Maybe he had enough leverage to find Kaitlyn Glenn. It wasn't a perfect idea—the one that he had recently hatched—but it was worth a try.

First, he decided not to say anything to Jace about his new information. He needed the girl—Jodi—alive, and he wasn't too sure about her chances if Jace got to her first. Jace had a notorious temper. Second, he rented a room at a seedy motel, paid for a couple of days in advance, and then drove toward Jodi's home. Early that evening, he pulled to the side of a residential street a short distance from Jodi's Cheyenne address and sat back to wait.

* * *

Brock felt like a fool. He'd completely forgotten to e-mail Jodi the night before, but she'd called to remind him of it before he went to bed. On Saturday afternoon, after finishing his work, he sat down at his computer and typed a short message. He waited to see if she might happen to access her e-mail, but when she didn't, he got into his truck and drove to Moab to buy some groceries. He looked forward to receiving a message from her when he returned.

But he was mistaken. There was no message. It bothered him a little. Perhaps Jodi was angry with him and had decided to give him a dose of his own medicine by ignoring him. Or maybe something had come up that prevented her from getting to her computer. Perhaps she'd gone somewhere with her family. He thought about calling her cell phone as she'd done with him the night before, but he didn't want to appear too pushy. She probably needed her space just as he needed his. Besides, he had e-mailed her. Hoping he was doing the right thing, he simply picked up a book and began to read instead of calling Jodi.

As he tried to read, his mind kept drifting from the sentences in the book to the young woman who was somewhere out there, trying to keep away from Jace Landry, probably afraid and hiding much of the time. He just couldn't keep his mind off Kaitlyn Glenn. Finally, he closed the book and stepped outside. He walked down to the river and watched the water as it flowed past.

Brock felt unsettled. He wished there was something he could do to help Kaitlyn. He knew he was being unreasonable. As he'd told himself a thousand times, he didn't even know her. And yet he felt like he did, and her well-being was rapidly becoming a pressing issue in his life.

He forced himself to think of Jodi. He wondered what she'd think if she knew that he was thinking about Kaitlyn so much. But then, she thought Kaitlyn was dead. He hadn't mentioned to her that he'd discovered she was alive. For that matter, Brock doubted that Jodi even remembered Kaitlyn's name. He felt a bit guilty for the feelings he had developed for Kaitlyn, almost as if they were a betrayal of Jodi.

Despondent, he turned and walked back toward his room.

* * *

Jodi read Brock's e-mail within minutes of returning home with her family after visiting her grandparents. The message from Brock was brief. He was obviously enjoying himself while she was lonely and depressed. It made her angry that he seemed so happy while she was so sad. She didn't want to be angry with Brock, and she certainly didn't want him to know how she was feeling. She finally decided to take a walk instead of responding to his message right away, hoping that when she returned she'd be in a better frame of mind.

The sun had almost gone down, and the little light that remained was disappearing quickly. The streetlight on the corner had come on, and that was reassuring. And yet Jodi began to feel uneasy.

Maybe it was the car that had started up shortly after she'd passed it. Or maybe it was the one that she now saw parked up ahead, on the darkest part of the street, similar to the one she'd seen on her street. Jodi told herself she was being silly, that she was overreacting because she was lonely and sad. She walked briskly, hoping the warm night air would clear her head and erase her jitters.

When trouble struck, it was without warning. As she passed the darkened car she'd seen from down the street, a large, heavyset man with something covering his face suddenly lunged out of the vehicle. The attacker grabbed her around the neck and clamped a huge hand over her mouth. Within seconds he had tied her hands behind her back, dragged her into his car, and roared off. He covered a full block before he turned his lights on.

"You scream, and I'll break your pretty neck," he said in a no-nonsense voice as he removed his hand from her mouth. For a moment Jodi felt as though she might faint.

A series of disconnected thoughts flashed through her mind. She regretted not having answered Brock's e-mail right after she'd read it. She knew she had received and ignored a prompting from the Spirit in her previous feelings of unease. And she feared she would never again see her family or her boyfriend.

Jodi refused to look over at her abductor. She had no idea how much time had passed since she'd been yanked into the car, but she slowly began to consider how she might get herself out of the situation.

"Why are you doing this to me?" she asked, still keeping her eyes away from the man.

The man grunted and cleared his throat, but he didn't answer her question. She waited a few minutes before trying again. "Who are you and what do you want from me?" She felt her voice break as she spoke. Surely he had taken the wrong person. He must have made a mistake. He'd figure it out soon and let her go.

But when he finally spoke, all hopes of mistaken identity vanished. "Jodi, if I wanted you to know who I was, I wouldn't bother wearing this hideous nylon stocking."

Jodi looked toward him for the first time. Lights from an oncoming car lit up his masked face. It was a hideous sight, just as he had said. She choked back a sob and turned her head away.

"You don't need to know who I am," he said. "But I need a little help, and I believe you can give me that help."

It took a moment before she was able to speak again. "What can I do?" she finally asked, unable to imagine what he could possibly want from her.

"You can tell me where to find Brock. He and I need to talk," the man said.

Jodi felt like she'd just touched a live electric wire. What in the world could this man have to do with Brock? And what would he do to Brock if he found him? She said nothing, stunned into silence.

"Maybe I should rephrase that," the man said. "You will tell me where to find Brock."

"Wh . . . what . . . why do you need to see Brock?" she finally managed to stutter.

"That's none of your business, young lady. Where is he?"

"Don't hurt Brock," she pleaded, turning her face toward the man. "He's the best thing that ever happened to me. Please . . ."

"He's an interfering fool," the masked driver said angrily. "I'm searching for a girl named Kaitlyn Glenn. He can help me find her."

"Who's Kaitlyn Glenn?" Jodi asked. Although the name had a familiar ring to it, she couldn't imagine where she might have heard it before.

"Maybe you don't know her by name, but you know her," he said. "But it's Brock that I need to talk to."

"What are you going to do to me?" she asked, forcing the words through her tight throat.

"Turn you loose as soon as you tell me what I need to know," he said.

"How do I know you'll really do that?" She didn't know where she found the courage to ask the question.

"Do you really think that I'd be wearing this uncomfortable getup if I intended to harm you?" he asked, disgust in his voice.

As terrified as she was, Jodi felt some relief. It could be true. But she couldn't tell him where Brock was. She just couldn't put him in danger.

"Okay, girl, where is he?" Myler asked.

"I don't know. I only talk to him on his cell phone and send messages to him over the Internet," she said. "I can call him if you want to talk to him."

"I'll have to think about that, but while I do, you'll be thinking about what you aren't telling me. And I expect you to think hard," he growled.

"My phone's in my pocket. Please, let's call him now," she pleaded. Jodi was confident that Brock would know what to do and what to say. She was also sure that he didn't know anything about where Kaitlyn Glenn was, whoever she might be.

Or did he?

That thought brought doubts to her mind. How well did she really know Brock? Did he have secrets he didn't want her to know about? The fact that she was riding in this car with this evil man suggested something disreputable about Brock and his past.

The car pulled up a few minutes later at a rundown motel. "You'll be staying here until I learn what I need to know. And don't even think about not cooperating. If you give me any trouble, I know someone else who would like to get his hands on you. And he won't be nearly as gentle. He's livid about what your boyfriend did to him last week after the rodeo."

At that moment, it all became clear to Jodi. Kaitlyn Glenn was the girl from the rodeo, the girl Brock had saved from some guy. And that guy was probably the one her abductor was talking about. She remembered the warning the girl had given Brock. She'd said the guy would come after him, and because of that she'd refused to let him tell her his name. Somehow, her best-laid plans had gone awry, and he'd obviously figured it out anyway. He was after Brock. And Jodi was caught in the middle.

CHAPTER 19

THE MOMENT HE ANSWERED THE phone, Brock knew something was terribly wrong.

"Brock, a man wants to talk to you," Jodi said, but from her strained voice he knew she was not okay.

"Jodi, what's wrong?" he asked fearfully.

She didn't respond, but a voice he'd never heard before did. "Your girlfriend is in good hands. But understand this, and understand it well. I'm not calling to have an argument, Mr. Hankins. I'm simply calling to make a request. Consider carefully the answer you give. Your girl's circumstances could change drastically if you give the wrong answer."

"Who is this?" Brock asked urgently.

"I'm asking the questions," the man replied curtly. "I'm searching for someone, and I believe you can help me find her."

Brock hadn't thought things could get any worse, but they just had. This call was about Kaitlyn Glenn. He knew it, and he dreaded the next question from the man on Jodi's cell phone.

"Brock, all you need to do is tell me where to find her. I'll take it from there, and your girlfriend can go home," the voice said.

There was no way Brock believed the man, and even worse, he knew there was no way he could tell the man what he wanted to know. "Who are you talking about?" he asked, stalling for time and not wanting to hear the answer.

"Kaitlyn Glenn. Where is she?" the caller asked. "And remember, I have your precious Jodi here with me. I'd advise you to answer wisely."

Wise or not, Brock answered the only way he could. "I have no idea where she is. I barely even know her."

"You defended her, my young friend. Now where is she?"

"Yes, I defended her, but I don't know her. I'd never seen her before that night in Cheyenne, and I haven't seen her since. I could sit here and guess all night about where she might be, but I honestly don't know any more than you do," Brock said, feeling both desperate and helpless.

"That isn't the answer I called for," the man said coldly. "You know Jodi's cell number. If you reconsider your willingness to help her out, call that number. Otherwise . . . well, what can I say?" At that moment, the phone went dead. Brock thought his heart might explode it was pounding so fiercely.

Where could Jodi be? Who was holding her? What could he do to help her? He fell on his knees and prayed fervently. Then, still on his knees, he called the police in Cheyenne. Within minutes, he was telling everything to a detective. "We'll start by checking at her home," the officer promised. "Keep your phone on so we can call back if we need to."

* * *

Myler paced back and forth, running his hands through his hair and alternately scratching his eyebrows. He'd honestly thought that Brock Hankins was the answer to finding Kaitlyn Glenn. As much as he hated to admit it, however, he believed the man was telling him the truth. Brock didn't know any more about where she was than he did. And here he was, stuck with a girl he really didn't want to have to hurt, a girl who would be of no help in finding the one he was determined to claim.

"Please, let me go," Jodi begged. "I won't tell anyone what has happened. I told you that Brock couldn't help you. We don't even know Kaitlyn, except for her name."

"Just shut up," he said. The stocking mask on his face was driving him crazy, and he wanted to be rid of it. It particularly hurt his nose, which still smarted from where it had smashed into the dash as Celia had jammed on her brakes and thrown him forward in her truck. But he didn't want his captive to see his face. Killing her was an option, but it wasn't high on his list. Nor did he feel like delivering her to Jace at this point.

He peered through the stocking mask at Jodi. Then he got to his feet, retrieved a towel from the tiny bathroom, and tied it around her head, covering her eyes. Then he jerked the mask off. It was such a relief to be rid of it. He realized he should have done it sooner.

As he stuffed the stocking into his pocket, he was thinking of Celia Dulce. She was the person who was most likely to know where Kaitlyn was hiding out. An idea struck him. It was worth a try, he decided, after mulling it over for a few minutes.

"I'll need to use your phone," he said to Jodi, not that he needed her permission. With a towel tied around her head and her hands secured behind her back, she was in no position to refuse him anything.

* * *

Celia was on the road again. After delivering her load to Columbus, she'd picked up another one nearby. She had also taken her truck to a body shop to have the bullet hole in the door and the damage to the rear trailer bumper repaired. What her employer didn't know wouldn't hurt him, she decided. She was now en route to Dallas, intent on driving through the night.

Celia had tried several times to call Kaitlyn, and she was worried. Her calls were not going through. She hoped the girl was okay. She knew she was worrying like a doting mother. It seemed that her friendship with Kaitlyn was both deep and lasting.

Not far from her thoughts were the men pursuing Kaitlyn. She hoped Kaitlyn was being cautious. Anger still enveloped her whenever she pictured the one she thought of as Myler. The ridiculous nylon stocking he'd pulled over his already unsightly face had been a pathetic attempt at disguise. But she was glad she hadn't let on that she knew who he was. She just hoped he hadn't figured out that part yet.

She still had his cell phone. It hadn't rung once since he'd left it behind after his awkward exit from her truck, although she had kept it fully charged.

Startling her from her unpleasant thoughts, the phone began to ring. Celia jumped. Why would it ring just at that moment? she wondered. Surely he wasn't following her and trying to reach her on his own phone. She picked it up from the seat beside her where she'd dropped it a few hours ago after the last charge. She opened it and looked at the number display.

It wasn't familiar. She left it open but laid it back on the seat. It continued to ring, irritating and obnoxious, like its owner. Finally, anxious but also curious, she picked it up again and punched the button to accept the call. She lifted it to her mouth and ear.

"Hello," she said.

"I was hoping you'd answer my phone," a familiar voice said. "You may have just saved a life. Well, two lives—your own and the girl whose phone I'm borrowing."

"Who do you think you're talking to?" she asked.

"I know who I'm talking to," her former truck mate said. "Don't pretend you don't know. You answered the phone you stole from me when you tried to kill me."

"Oh, you again. I didn't try to kill you," Celia said. "If I'd tried to kill you, you'd be dead. What do you want?" Of course she knew what he wanted. She doubted that his intentions had changed in the past couple of days.

"There's a young lady here who needs your help," he said. "She would like to go home, but she can't until I learn where Kaitlyn Glenn is hiding. I'm running out of patience. And Jodi here is running out of time."

"You just think you can take people anytime you want to, is that it? You have no regard for anyone else's life," Celia said. She came close to pure hatred at that moment. She also felt totally helpless. She didn't know who Jodi was, but Celia had a feeling that she was an innocent person who had somehow been snagged in the vicious net cast by Jace and his partner.

"Celia, all you need to do is tell me where to find Kaitlyn Glenn, and Jodi here goes free," Myler said.

"I don't know where she is," Celia said in desperation. "I told you that I left her at the airport in Denver. That's the truth. And so help me, I don't know where she is now."

"But I believe you can find out. Why don't you try?" Myler suggested, his voice almost polite. "I'll call you back in a few hours. And remember, the life of an innocent young woman is in your hands."

"How do I know that?" Celia asked. "May I talk to her?"

"Of course," Myler said. "I'm sure she would like that."

A moment later Celia heard the frightened voice of a young woman. "This man is going to kill me if you don't help him find Kaitlyn," she said, her voice so weak and shaky that it was hard for Celia to understand her.

"Who are you?" Celia asked, trying to make her deep Southern drawl sound as friendly as she could.

"My name is Jodi Henry. My boyfriend, Brock Hankins, hit this man's friend and saved Kaitlyn from him last week. I'm so afraid," she cried. "He thinks Brock knows where she is, but Brock doesn't even know her."

"Okay, honey," Celia said as she realized who this girl was. Kaitlyn's efforts to keep the girl and her boyfriend from becoming more involved in her plight had failed. "You just be calm, Jodi. I'll see what I can do to help. And whatever you do, try not to make that man angry. By the way, is he wearing a nylon stocking?"

"He was, but he blindfolded me. I think he took it off after that," Jodi said.

"That's good. That means you can't identify him. Make sure you don't see his face, and I think he'll let you go." Celia had no idea if she was telling the truth, but she felt a need to say something to console the girl.

"All right, that's enough." It was Myler again. "You wait for my call, and while you're waiting, you'd better find out where that girl is."

Myler snapped the phone shut before Celia could answer. Celia immediately began searching for the next freeway exit. She now had two innocent young women to worry about. And she didn't want to endanger anyone else because of her emotional upheaval. She had no idea what to do.

Celia finally pulled the truck to a stop at a rest area. Then she simply leaned against her large steering wheel and did something that was quite foreign to her. She cried.

* * *

Kelvin Glenn had ignored numerous calls from Norman Thatcher. But Saturday night when his phone rang and he saw that it was Norman, he took the call. "Kelvin," Norman began, "I've been trying to get ahold of you. You haven't been answering your phone."

"It's a long story, and I won't bore you with it," Kelvin said, hoping his flimsy excuse would suffice. "But I'm glad you got through to me this time. Did my sister show up at the rodeos last night or tonight?"

"No, she didn't. I guess you've learned that she didn't die after all," Norman said.

"Yes. Quite a shock, really. Now I'm back to where I was before. I'm looking for her. And so help me, when I catch up with her, she'll give me my money."

"And your horse," Norman reminded him. "My daughter didn't do so well either night in Denver, but it wasn't her fault. It was her horse. I thought he was a good one when I bought him for her, but he's not turning out so well after all. He stumbled one night in Denver and knocked over a barrel the other. It's the worst she's done in weeks. I really need that horse of Kaitlyn's. And I guarantee that I'll make it worth your time to get him for me."

"I'm working on it, but I'm not having any luck. I've got to find Kaitlyn first."

"You're not the only one looking for her," Norman said.

"I'm not? Why would anyone else be looking?" As he asked the question, Kelvin began to worry. He couldn't imagine who else might want her money, or even know about it.

"Something about family," Norman told him. "They claim to be cousins of hers, of yours, too, I guess. They really need to find her—or so they say."

"Cousins, huh?" Kelvin said, puzzled. "What did they say their names were?"

"They didn't, actually, but I learned anyway. I overheard my daughter talking to a cowboy friend of hers after the rodeo last night. One of the guys is known as Jace Landry. He's a rich guy from Des Moines, Iowa. The other one might be a man by the name of Myler Keegan, but I can't be sure about that."

"Never heard of them," Kelvin said.

"I didn't suppose you had. Seems that the Jace fellow is Kaitlyn's boyfriend, and she's pulled a fast one on him. At any rate, she's trying to get away from them."

"Is that all you heard?" Kelvin asked, already thinking ahead.

"Not quite. It seems this man was her boss. He might have some money," Norman told him.

"Hey, listen, thanks for the information," Kelvin said, anxious to get off the phone and to start working on another angle to his plan.

"No problem. Just remember, I need that horse."

"If I get my sister, I'll give you the horse," Kelvin said.

Kelvin grabbed his laptop as soon as the call was over and accessed the Internet. He typed in the name *Jace Landry* on one of the search engines. Hundreds of hits appeared. Twenty minutes later, he'd learned a lot more than he needed to know. Jace Landry, if he'd found the right

Jace—and he was fairly confident he had—indeed had money. If he could get in touch with this guy, he might be able to team up with him and help him find Kaitlyn. He could envision a grateful Landry offering him a sizeable reward. Then when Landry got Kaitlyn out of the way, he could collect her money, too.

He looked through the phone's contacts list for a while and finally came up with a cell number for Jace Landry. Then he debated his next move. Perhaps a phone call would be in order to see if he could set up a face-to-face meeting with the guy. But at the moment, he was hungry and tired. Kelvin wasn't used to so much work. Maybe, he decided, he'd just rest and think about it for a while.

* * *

Kaitlyn was up and ready to go early Sunday morning. She planned to drive into Richfield and park her truck with the horse and trailer near a chapel so she could attend church. She knew she could easily find a ward once she got to town. It seemed like it had been a month since she'd attended the meetings in Twin Falls, and yet it had been only a week. *What a horrendous week.*

She also intended to phone Celia as soon as she could get a signal on her cell phone. She loaded Tony B into the horse trailer, apologizing to him for having to put him back in such cramped quarters. Then she had a little breakfast, cleaned up, and changed into a new dress she'd bought in Boise. Finally, she began driving her new Ford back toward civilization.

Not too much later she got a signal on the cell phone. She pulled over to the side of the road and dialed Celia's number. It rang several times, and she was about to give up when she finally heard Celia's voice.

"Kaitlyn, is that you?" Celia asked.

The tone of her voice caused Kaitlyn alarm. Celia didn't sound like the usual cheerful, optimistic woman with whom she had become such good friends. She sounded tired, for one thing, but it was more than that. She identified tension in her friend's voice and immediately wondered what was going on.

Haltingly, she said, "Yes, it's me, Celia. Are you okay?"

"I'm just really tired. It's been a long night," Celia said.

"Have you been driving all night? Did I wake you up?"

"I drove quite a bit, and I did get a little bit of sleep in my truck, but no, you didn't wake me."

"Celia, what's wrong?" Kaitlyn asked. "You don't sound like yourself."

"I'm fine."

"You don't sound fine. I hope you aren't still worrying about me. I know I've been where my cell phone wouldn't work. I spent the past two nights in the mountains. I slept in my trailer and rode Tony B up a forest trail. I was never able to get a signal, or I'd have called. I'm sorry if I worried you," Kaitlyn concluded.

"It's not that," Celia said.

"Okay, then what is it? Is it something to do with Jace or Myler?" Kaitlyn asked.

There was a long pause, long enough that Kaitlyn knew she'd hit the mark with her guess. "Please, Celia. Tell me what they've done now. Have they threatened you?"

Kaitlyn could hear her friend take a deep, ragged breath. "They haven't threatened me, but they've threatened Brock Hankins and his girlfriend, Jodi."

"Who?" Kaitlyn asked, puzzled.

"Brock Hankins is the man who saved you from Jace," Celia revealed.

"Oh, Celia, I didn't want to know his name. Jace might try to force me to tell him if he ever . . ." she stopped. Then she said, "Oh, no! They've already found out who he is, haven't they? Oh, Celia, tell me he's not hurt because of me."

"Not yet, but Myler did to his girlfriend what he did to me," Celia said. "He's holding her hostage somewhere."

Kaitlyn felt the blood drain from her face, her mind reeling. Because of her, someone else was now in the clutches of the very men from whom she was fleeing. "Celia, how do you know this?" she asked.

"I shouldn't be telling you all this," Celia said. "There's nothing more we can do. I've already called the police in Cheyenne. They're doing what they can. You need to keep moving before they find you, too."

"Celia, what exactly did they do?" Kaitlyn asked, as the only solution that she thought might work settled in her mind. It was not a cheerful thought, but as she considered it, she felt a sense of serenity settle over her. There was a way to help both Brock Hankins and his girlfriend.

"I shouldn't tell you," Celia said. "You've got to protect yourself. I'm certain that Brock already knows they have Jodi, or at least that Myler has her. I only assume that Jace is with him. But there's nothing you can do. You've got to take care of yourself. I'm sure this Brock guy is smart and will do what he can."

"Celia, I've got to go now. This is awful. I can't talk about it anymore."

Brock Hankins and his girlfriend were in trouble because they'd helped her. It wasn't fair. It all went back to her bad choice in dating Jace. It was her fault, not theirs. She knew what she had to do. First, she dialed Jim Perrett's phone number. "Hello, I'm glad I caught you," she said after hearing his friendly voice.

"Kaitlyn, we've been worried about you. We tried to call, but apparently you've had your phone off."

"I was where there was no signal," she said.

"Well, I'm glad you caught me now, although you barely did. We were just leaving for church," Jim said. "And I never take my phone to church. I'm just relieved to hear your voice. What can I do for you?"

"I feel terrible asking this," she began. "But I need to have you take care of Tony B for a little while again, if you can. I know it's asking a lot, and I'm sorry, but—"

Jim cut her off. "You know that I'd be glad to take him. Where are you?"

"I'm down by Richfield. But I'll come that way now. Something's come up, and I can't even make it to church today," she said.

"Listen, our meetings will be finished in just over three hours. Would it help you if I met you somewhere and just hooked the trailer to my truck again?" he asked.

It was as if he'd read her mind. "Yes, that would be great," she answered.

"All right, we'll head south as soon as we leave church, Kaitlyn. Do you feel like talking about what's going on?" he asked.

"I'd rather not," she said. "But I'll be driving north in just a few minutes."

"I'll call when we're ready to leave Logan," Jim told her. "We'll meet wherever it works out."

"Thank you," Kaitlyn responded. "I'll just keep driving until I meet you. Thank you so much. This means a lot to me." She closed her phone and offered a sincere prayer. She then got out of her truck and checked on Tony B in the trailer. She hugged him tightly before returning to her truck and beginning the long drive north.

* * *

"Where are we going today?" Nina asked her parents as they left the restaurant where they'd just eaten breakfast.

"We'll be going on to that place we talked about, the lodge that's beside a river where we will spend a few days and let your mum get some rest," her father said.

"You mean the Red Cliff Lodge?" she asked.

"Yes, that's the place. I hear it's really nice," Maurice said. "And there are lots of beautiful places to see nearby. And we can even float down the river on a raft."

"Okay," she responded automatically and again retreated into the quiet of her own little world where she'd been biding her time ever since they left the doctor's office days before. Her parents still didn't want to tell her what was wrong with her mother, and she had given up asking. This was no longer a fun trip for her. She just hoped the time would pass quickly and they would soon be on their way home.

* * *

Brock spent the night awake, much of it on his knees. He was desperate. He'd called the police in Cheyenne and told them what he could. They'd called back later and confirmed that Jodi had gone out for a walk and hadn't returned. Her parents were so grief-stricken they could barely provide the police with basic facts. Brock felt responsible. There had to be something he could do. The problem was that he had no idea what it might be.

He showered and dressed for church. He knew that he couldn't expect the Lord to help him and those he cared for if he didn't make an effort to do everything in his power—even if that meant just going to church. Perhaps some inspiration would come to him during his worship.

* * *

Kelvin Glenn had slept on the information he'd received from Norman Thatcher. He was sure now that he needed to team up with the man Norman called Jace Landry. Together they could probably find Kaitlyn. And Kelvin was sure he could find a way, later, to get a lot of money out of the deal. Then he wouldn't have to risk any more thefts, and maybe selling drugs on the street could be a thing of the past for him. Easy street was still out there.

CHAPTER 20

WHEN MYLER ANSWERED HIS PHONE Sunday afternoon, he knew it could only be Jace or Celia, and he suspected it was Jace. He was sure his client was irate that he hadn't contacted him. It was Jace's number, and he decided, reluctantly, to take the call. But first he turned to Jodi. "If you so much as sniffle, you could die. The man who's calling wants you dead, girl. All you have to do is keep your mouth shut, and he won't figure out that I've got you here."

He answered the phone then, holding it away from his ear as if expecting to hear a stream of profanity. To his surprise, Jace sounded uncharacteristically upbeat. Instantly Myler's defenses were up. *What's Jace up to?* he wondered. *One thing I won't let him do is manipulate me.*

Jace soon had Myler's full attention, and he listened intently. He wasn't sure his client wasn't hallucinating. Maybe he was high on drugs. Myler's responses to Jace's phone conversation consisted of muttered uh-huhs, okays, and other noncommittal grunts. He had an extra set of ears listening just a few feet away, and the less she knew, the better off she'd be.

"You've been gone a long time. What have you been doing?" Jace finally asked.

"I've been following leads. Successfully, I might add," Myler told him. He could tell him the rest, at least the part he chose to reveal, when he met Jace in a little while.

The girl on the bed squirmed, but she made no sound. Jace said, "Get moving, Myler. No time to lose."

Myler said. "I'll be there in a few minutes to pick you up. You might want to call and have them get your plane ready."

"Darn. I wish I had my Lear," Jace said, sounding more like his usual belligerent self. "But I guess we'll just have to make do with the Cessna."

"Sure," Myler said, anxious to get his client off the phone. He needed time to think, to make some decisions, before he met Jace again.

After the call was over, he spoke to his captive. "I'll be leaving. Now don't go panicking. You owe me your life."

"When will you be back?" Jodi asked, her voice quavering.

"I probably won't be, but someone will, eventually. Now, I'm going to have to put something in your mouth so you won't go screaming and stirring up the other guests here," Myler said.

"I'll be quiet. I promise," Jodi said. "Please don't put anything in my mouth. It will make me sick, and I already feel awful."

"Sorry, but it's not your choice." He ripped a pillowcase and tied a piece in her mouth and around the back of her head.

"Someone will come let you loose," he said when he finished. "It may be a few hours, or even a day or more. I know you won't be comfortable, but you'll be okay. Just be patient." And with that he lumbered out of the room, shutting off the light and locking the door as he left.

The room had been paid for in advance with instructions that it was not to be cleaned that day. He was quite certain no one would bother her until he made arrangements for her to be turned loose or he came back to get her. It would all depend on whether Jace was telling him the truth and what happened after that, if he was.

* * *

Kaitlyn had been busy on her cell phone. She'd made some calls and still had one more to make. It was to Celia. "Kaitlyn, are you okay?" Celia asked as she answered the phone on the first ring.

"Yes, I'm fine," Kaitlyn told her. "How about you?"

"I'm worried sick, girl. You know that," Celia said.

Kaitlyn felt bad about the worry in Celia's voice. It seemed like that first date with Jace had not only caused herself unspeakable grief, but many others as well. It wasn't fair to any of them. "You've got to quit worrying," Kaitlyn said, trying to sound lighthearted. "How many times do I have to tell you that?"

"I can't help it. You're like the daughter I never had, Kaitlyn."

That brought tears to Kaitlyn's eyes. How was it possible in just one week to have developed that kind of friendship? she wondered. She'd made friends wherever she went, but none had ever become as close as Celia.

"Kaitlyn, are you there? Did one of us lose a signal?" Celia asked.

"I'm still here," Kaitlyn said. "But I need to go. I'm getting in some heavy traffic, and I don't want to wreck my new truck. I just wanted to thank you for all that you've done for me."

"It's not enough," Celia said. "I want to do more if I can."

"You've been great. You drive carefully now." Kaitlyn could no longer control her emotions. Abruptly she ended the call.

* * *

Brock was full of nervous energy. No inspiration had come during church, although he had felt marginally better while he was there. He felt so helpless. Jodi, because of his actions, was in grave danger. Kaitlyn, whom he'd tried to help, was also still at risk. He felt powerless to help either one of them. He prayed for Jodi. Then he prayed for Kaitlyn, and then he prayed for Jodi again. Finally, he went for a walk that afternoon.

He wandered over to the corrals and checked on the horses. Then he went up to the highway and past the vineyards. He passed the lodge and went out to the riverbank as he'd done the previous evening. It was a hot, sunny day, and he was beginning to feel physically tired as well as mentally exhausted. He sought some shade beneath a thicket of tamarisk bushes near the slowly moving water.

Brock had never been so emotionally drained. He thought of Jodi, whom he had come to like a lot. Then he thought of Kaitlyn, who he barely knew but felt drawn to as he'd never felt drawn to anyone else in his life. He could feel his shoulders heaving from the weight of his heartfelt emotions. He wasn't sure whether to keep struggling against the tears or to just let them come. He was thoroughly miserable.

Brock didn't hear footsteps behind him, and so he was startled when a small voice with a distinct English accent spoke to him. "Are you sad like I am, sir?"

Embarrassed, he wiped his face and turned toward the sound of the voice. Standing about three feet away from him was a pretty, freckle-faced girl of about nine. She had long, beautiful deep red hair and eyes the color of the sky. She was clearly sad. Brock stood up. "Yes, I'm very sad. But I'm also sorry that you are sad. Would you like to tell me about it?"

"Only if you tell me why you're crying," she said.

"Maybe we can help each other be less sad," he suggested. "Here, come sit by me and tell me who you are."

They both sat down in the shade of the tamarisk bushes. "My name is Nina Schiller. I'm from England."

"I sort of suspected that," he said. "You talk with such a beautiful accent," he said. "I love to listen to people who speak the way you do."

"And I like to listen to people who talk like you," she said.

"Well, Nina, it's nice to meet you. My name is Brock Hankins. I work here. I take care of the horses. Have you seen the horses?" he asked.

"Yes, and my father says I can ride them if I want to," Nina told him. "But I don't know if I want to. I'm too sad."

"Maybe the horses will make you happy. They do that for me. I hope you'll ride, because I'll be the one helping you," he responded. "And I'd like to teach you to ride. It would make me feel happier."

"Really?" she said.

"Yes, really."

"You *are* nice, sir," she said. "But why are you sad?"

"I'm sad because two people I care a lot about are in terrible danger," Brock said. "And I don't know what to do to help them. I don't even know where they are right now. Why are you sad?"

"Because my mum is sick and my daddy won't tell me what's wrong with her, and she won't either, and I'm afraid she's going to die, and I think my daddy is mad at her because she's going to die, and I miss my nanny." Her depressing story had streamed out in one long sentence. "This was supposed to be a fun trip, but it's not, and I want to go home."

Brock was touched. There was too much sadness in the world. Right now he couldn't help Jodi or Kaitlyn, but maybe he could help Nina. Helping her might convince the Lord how sincere he was in his desire for Him to intervene in behalf of those he couldn't help himself.

"Listen, Nina," he said. "Why don't you and I do a little more walking. I'd like to meet your parents, if it's okay with you. Maybe I could get them to let me know what's wrong. Would you let me try that?"

"Yes," she said. "But I don't know if they'll talk to you."

"Where are they now?" Brock asked.

"They're in our flat. It's in the bunkhouse closest to the pens where your horses are," she said.

Despite himself, Brock smiled at the way she mixed her terms, old-country English with western words. He rose to his feet. "Should we go see how your mum's feeling?" he asked.

"Sure, Brock," she said, brightening up. "Then would you let me pet a horse?"

"I'd love to," he said, and together they walked away from the river. "By the way, do your mum and dad know where you are?"

"They told me to go for a walk. They wanted to be alone, and anyway, I think they are tired of having me around so much. I'm usually with Ruby," she said.

"Is Ruby your sister?" he asked as he thought how sad it was for a child to have parents who must not make enough time in their busy lives for her.

"I don't have a sister or a brother. Ruby is my nanny. She's still in London. She doesn't go with us on our vacations," Nina revealed. "She takes care of me in our home while my mum and daddy are gone."

"Are your parents gone a lot?" he asked.

"Yes. They have a lot of work to do, and it takes them away from London most of the time," she answered. "But Ruby is always there."

"You must really love Ruby," he said.

"Yes, and I miss her a lot."

"Have you talked to her on the phone while you've been over here in America?" he asked.

"No, I haven't. My parents say that our vacation each year is our time to be together as a family and Ruby's time to visit her family. They say she needs time alone—without me around."

"What if I get them to give you permission to call her and just talk to her for a few minutes?" he said. "I have a phone you could use."

"Really? I guess I can ask them," she said.

"If you want, I could ask them for you, after I get to know them a little bit," Brock said. "But maybe we need to warm up to that, don't you think, Nina?"

She nodded in agreement.

Shortly, they arrived outside her room, or her *flat,* as she called it. "You go in and see if they would be willing to meet me," he suggested. "Tell them you've found a friend you want them to meet, one who will take you to see the horses."

Nina was gone for only a minute. "They don't want to talk to anyone right now," she said. "Maybe tomorrow." Her face was long, but suddenly she smiled. "I asked them if I could call Ruby on your phone, and they said I could if it was okay with you. I think maybe they said yes just because they wanted me to leave for a while. But at least I can call her."

"Well, you know it's fine with me," he said quickly. "Do you know her number?"

Nina nodded. "She'll be surprised to hear from me. But she'll be sad to hear that Mum's sick. But I can't call her right now. I have to do it when it's daytime in London. Can we see your horses now?"

Still sick with worry, but grateful to have an opportunity to help someone else in need and for the diversion it provided, Brock led Nina to the corrals. Nina had a delightful time, and Brock found himself enjoying her company. Her little fits of childish laughter and almost constant chatter as he let her pet the horses and throw them some feed gave him a joy he didn't know was possible under the circumstances.

Finally, at her insistence, he showed her where he was living, and then he escorted her back to her room. "You be careful when you're out alone," he said. "When you want company, you can come see me."

"Thank you. I will. Are you happier now?" she asked.

"I am, and it's because you let me help you. You know, Nina, I'd forgotten that you can make yourself happy by helping other people. The more you think of how others feel and the less you worry about yourself, the easier it is to be happy."

"Really?" she said.

"Yep, really. I'll see you later. When it's time to call your nanny, you come get me."

Twenty minutes later his phone rang, and his heart collided with reality. Brock didn't recognize the number displayed on the phone, but he did recognize the voice. It was the man who had called the night before.

"Brock, I only have a minute to talk. There's something you might want to do."

"Mister," Brock said, "I'm afraid I still can't help you, because I don't know where Kaitlyn is."

"I believe you," the caller told him. "But I know where your friend Jodi is. She would like someone to go get her."

Brock couldn't believe what he was hearing. "Tell me, and I'll see that someone gets there right away."

The man gave the name of a motel, an address, and a room number. "She's fine. She wasn't any more help than you were, but she wasn't hurt.

Oh, and don't bother trying to find me or have the cops look for me. It would be a waste of time, because I'm long gone."

Before Brock could respond, the man had disconnected. Brock hastily dialed the officer in Cheyenne who had been assigned as his contact person. He told him what he had just heard. "Please, call me as soon as you know anything," he begged.

Next he called Jodi's parents and gave them the address of the motel. Her father, stiff and distant, simply said, "I hope you're right, young man. You've caused my daughter enough heartache to last a lifetime. She doesn't need any more of the kind of trouble you've brought into her life."

Brock winced as if he had been struck. The last thing he'd intended was to cause Jodi pain or danger. And he hoped the information he'd been given wasn't a cruel hoax. He also wondered if Jodi would ever speak to him again. With the attitude of her father, he doubted it. Right now he was only concerned that she be found safe and sound.

* * *

The terror had long ago subsided. Jodi had resigned herself to a long wait before anyone would come to free her. Mostly, she was just uncomfortable. Occasionally, when she tried to move, the discomfort became intense pain. It was with considerable surprise, and much relief, that she heard someone at the door late Sunday afternoon. "It's the police, and we're coming in to help you, Jodi," a voice shouted.

As soon as she was freed, one of the officers introduced himself. "Would you like to call your boyfriend?" he asked.

She'd been thinking a lot about Brock ever since the kidnapping. She knew it might not be fair to him, but she still blamed him for what had happened. If he hadn't helped that girl, Kaitlyn, none of this would have happened to her. Slowly, she shook her head. "No, you tell him I'm safe, would you? I don't think I want to talk to him right now."

"But he's the one who called to tell me where we could find you," the officer said.

"I still don't want to talk to him," she responded, and seeing her parents' car pulling up, she abruptly ran to them.

* * *

Brock answered his phone the moment it started ringing. "Is Jodi okay?" he asked without preamble.

"She's badly traumatized, but she's fine otherwise," the officer reported.

"Would it be possible for me to talk to her?" he asked.

"She says she doesn't want to talk to you, at least not right now. Her father and mother just got here, and she's with them. She'll be okay."

"Thanks, officer. I might be wrong, but I think the man who did this was Myler Keegan, a PI from Iowa. I wish I could tell you more about him, but all I know firsthand is what he sounds like. And it might not even be him."

"Jodi doesn't know much either," the officer said. "But at least we can check into this Keegan fellow. It's a start. Now for a bit of advice. If I were you, I'd give the young lady some time before I called her. She's pretty upset right now. She somehow thinks this was your fault."

"I understand," Brock said. "I guess I can't blame her. But I appreciate what you did. Thanks for getting to her so quickly."

"I'm glad we could. I'll be in touch if I need anything more," he said before hanging up.

Brock knelt beside his bed and poured out his thanks to his Heavenly Father. Jodi might be angry, but she was alive and safe. He was grateful for that blessing. Now, if he could just hear that Kaitlyn was also safe, all of his prayers would be answered.

Brock thought about what Dan had said to him as he considered the anger that Jodi and her family definitely harbored toward him right now. Dan used the words "not set in concrete" in describing his relationship with Jodi. Perhaps he was right. Brock simply had to wait and see.

* * *

Depending on one's definition of safe, Kaitlyn could possibly be considered safe at that moment. She wasn't in any immediate physical danger, as far as she could tell; she was, however, in serious trouble, and her future looked even worse. She was belted securely into the backseat of a small, single-engine Cessna. The plane was taxiing down a runway in an airport near Laramie, Wyoming. At the controls was Jace Landry. Seated next to him was the man Kaitlyn now knew as Myler Keegan, a private detective from Iowa, and a man who habitually lived and worked on the dark side of the law.

Numbness had overcome Kaitlyn. She was no longer running from Jace. He was, he told her as he helped her into the plane a few minutes earlier, taking her to Las Vegas. It was only now, as they left the ground and Jace piloted the small plane upward, that she spoke. "Why are we going to Las Vegas?" she asked.

"To be married, my dear. What else?" he said over his shoulder. "And to help Mr. Keegan here catch a plane to Des Moines."

The big man turned his head toward Jace, and Kaitlyn shuddered at the look he gave the smiling pilot, who did not see it himself. The hatred was palpable, and it surprised her. She thought the two of them were buddies—or at least united in their unscrupulous plans.

"Before you marry her, Jace, you and I have a bill to settle," Myler said, his voice charming but his expression forced.

"You have a job to finish," Jace said, not so charmingly. "You agreed to find the two who caused me so much trouble in Cheyenne."

Kaitlyn's stomach knotted, and she folded her arms across it protectively. It was for the safety of Brock and his girlfriend that she had surrendered herself to Jace. She'd fight him, she vowed, and force him to either let her go again or to kill her if he pursued the man who had risked his own life to save her.

Her throat began to burn as she attempted to keep herself from vomiting. The hand on her stomach instinctively flew up and covered her mouth.

"I already did that, Jace," Myler responded condescendingly. "How do you think Kaitlyn was convinced to come back to you? I applied some pressure in just the right places."

Jace's head twisted hard, and he stared at the man he'd hired to hunt down Kaitlyn. "Where are they now?" he demanded.

"They are wherever they choose to be," Myler said.

"Then you get nothing for finding them," Jace barked angrily.

"Actually, I do get something for that," Myler corrected him as his ugly face again twisted in hatred. "After I get my money, then I'll consider telling you where you can find them."

For a moment, Jace said nothing. Then he roared, "Half when we get to Vegas. The rest when they are in my hands."

Convinced that she wouldn't throw up, Kaitlyn spoke up. "Jace, I am not marrying you because I want to, and so help me, I will never marry you unless you agree right now to leave Brock and his girlfriend out of this."

Jace twisted in the seat and looked at her with a smirk on his face. "Oh, baby, you will marry me no matter what. I promised your brother that you would, and I don't intend to disappoint him."

Kaitlyn recoiled. "My brother?" she said shakily.

"Yep. Kelvin Glenn. Remember him? He promised to help me find you. But you—with Myler's help, I guess—found me instead. But I did tell him we were going to get married. He seemed very pleased about that."

"I have no brother, only a stepbrother, and believe me, he lied to you. Kelvin wants only one thing, and that's my money. If you marry me, he'll lose what he keeps thinking he'll get," she said.

"And what kind of money do you have?" Jace asked.

"My trust fund—money that was left to me by my father."

Both Jace and Myler turned and looked at her when she said that. "You have money?" Myler asked.

"Yes, lots of it. But there is no way Kelvin will ever get a dime of it," she said.

"That's right, because it will be ours—yours and mine together—after we're married," Jace said.

"Listen, Jace. There will be no wedding unless you promise to leave Brock and his girlfriend alone. And besides that, you also have to pay whatever Mr. Keegan says you owe him," Kaitlyn said.

To her surprise, Jace shrugged his shoulders. "You drive a hard bargain, Kaitlyn," he said, "but I already have the real prize. I have you. Fine, I agree to your terms. I would rather have you willing and legal than have to hide you away somewhere and keep you as my unwilling common-law wife."

Kaitlyn shuddered. "And you, Mr. Keegan," she said. "You have to promise that once you have your money from Jace, you will never bother Brock or his girlfriend again, or tell Jace where they are."

Myler turned toward her. He smiled, and his ludicrous mustache began to twitch. "Sounds like a deal to me. Now, how much money does my friend here get when he marries you?"

"That's none of your business," she said.

Myler turned to Jace. At that moment the smile was replaced by that same look of intense hatred she'd seen moments before. Jace, looking forward as he piloted the plane, was oblivious to the change.

Conversation in the small plane ended then. And Kaitlyn returned to her own thoughts once more. All she'd wanted in life from the moment she'd joined the Church was now unattainable. Living a life of luxury with a man she despised and feared had now become her unwelcome lot.

* * *

Myler Keegan was absorbed in thoughts of his own. Kaitlyn was a better prize than he had imagined. Not only was she unbelievably beautiful, but it seemed she also had wealth. Both she and her money would be his. Neither Jace nor Kaitlyn's dim-witted brother would ever see a dime of it. Jace Landry could start counting his days—possibly even his hours. As soon as he was paid what Jace owed him, Myler could begin implementing his new plan for Kaitlyn—one that did not include Jace.

As the plane headed southwest toward Las Vegas, Myler schemed. He was the hunter, and this time he would possess the quarry as well as the fee for finding her.

CHAPTER 21

THE CONSTANT DRONE OF THE plane's engine induced drowsiness. Kaitlyn wasn't sure how long they'd been flying when she was suddenly jolted into complete wakefulness as the plane's engine issued a strange sound and the plane jumped hard in response.

Jace cursed and began flipping switches. "I should have known this would be a piece of junk," he muttered.

Kaitlyn anxiously looked out the window as the plane began losing altitude. The sun was now gone, and the light of a full moon illuminated the eerie landscape below. Myler began to shout at Jace to get control of the plane while Jace wrestled with the controls. Kaitlyn gritted her teeth and clung to the arms of her seat.

"Get this thing under control!" Myler ordered once more, his voice high-pitched with panic.

Kaitlyn was afraid. But plunging to her death in this small plane was less terrifying than being forced to marry Jace. She didn't want to die, but if that happened, she knew she could accept it. With amazing calmness, Kaitlyn sat back in her seat and released her death grip on the seat arms while the two men ranted in terror. She prayed that the Lord would watch over her in whatever way was in her best interest. Praying was something she doubted either Jace or Myler knew anything about. She just hoped the Lord could hear her prayers over their disgusting profanity.

"Make it go up!" Myler screamed.

"I can't! The engine's quit!" Jace screamed in return.

"Start it again, you idiot!"

"I'm trying!"

Kaitlyn could pick out details in the rapidly approaching ground. She closed her eyes.

Suddenly the engine coughed and came to life. "It's going!" Jace shouted.

"Let's find an airport and get another plane," Myler croaked, his voice still shaking from the terror of the near-crash.

The words had barely left his mouth when the engine began to sputter again. "Still something wrong," Jace said. "I've hardly got any power."

That was obvious as they again began losing altitude. It wasn't as rapid as it had been moments before, but the dark landscape beneath them was dangerously close.

"Do something!" Myler ordered.

"I'm going to try to set it down as gently as I can," Jace said, obviously trying to sound confident.

For once, Kaitlyn actually found something admirable in Jace. He had quit cursing and was acting like a pilot in command.

When a collision between the rolling rock dunes below them and the single-engine Cessna appeared unavoidable, Kaitlyn checked her seat belt, leaned forward, and put her head down on her knees. She closed her eyes and again began to pray. She could feel the rapid decrease in the forward speed of the plane, and her popping ears and disequilibrium told her they were continuing to lose altitude.

"This is it!" Jace shouted a few seconds later.

The wheels smashed against something solid, bouncing the plane forward but also decelerating it even more. For a millisecond Kaitlyn thought that Jace must have found a safe place to land the crippled plane. When she felt the tail of the plane lift into the air and the nose hit the ground, she realized her error. A terrible, grinding crash followed by a gigantic flash of light overloaded Kaitlyn's senses. Myler's high-pitched screams filled the air of the cabin, accompanied by Jace's shrill calls for help. Then blackness enveloped her.

* * *

Seated at a table near the windows, Nina and her parents were having a late-evening dinner in the lodge. Nina had asked them if they could sit out on the deck, but her parents preferred to eat inside. As a compromise, her father had asked to be seated by the windows. Recalling the advice of her new friend, Brock, Nina agreed that it would be fine. And it actually cheered her up, knowing that she was thinking more of her parents at that moment than of herself.

However, it was so boring inside that Nina finally asked her parents if she could go outside while they waited for their food to be prepared. With their permission she walked out onto the deck and stood against the railing, watching the river flow around the big bend just beyond where she was standing. Her eyes lifted to the gigantic moonlit cliffs that towered above the far side of the river. A slight skyward movement caught her attention, and she peered into the sky just above the rim of the canyon.

She gaped in amazement as she saw something gliding earthward beyond the rim of the canyon. She was certain it was a small airplane. She watched it for only three or four seconds before it disappeared, hidden by the towering cliffs. Just a few seconds later, a cloud of dust arose, and then it slowly settled. With a sick feeling in her stomach, Nina continued to stare. When the cloud of dust cleared away, she stood thinking about what had just happened. It seemed clear to her that she had just seen a small airplane crash on the plateau beyond the canyon's rim. She knew from studying maps of the area in her flat that the crash had occurred somewhere in Arches National Park, a place they were still planning to visit before the end of their vacation.

She ran back inside. "Mum, Daddy," she said dramatically, "I just saw an airplane crash!"

"Shh!" her dad warned, putting his finger to his mouth. "Use your polite voice. And remember what we said about telling lies."

"But I really did!" she insisted loudly.

"You're imagining things," her mum said. "Now sit down, Nina. Here comes our dinner."

"No, Mum, Daddy. Someone might need help. I really did see a plane crash. It was somewhere past the top of those cliffs on the other side of the river."

The waitress had arrived, and she placed Nina's order of chicken nuggets in front of her. "What did you see?" she asked.

"I saw a plane crash!"

The waitress gasped. "Where? Are you sure?" she asked, clearly alarmed.

"We're sorry," her father broke in quickly. "Nina has a tendency to make things up when she gets bored, and I'm afraid she's bored tonight."

"Dad, I'm not bored now. I did see a plane crash."

People at nearby tables paused in their eating and visiting as all ears tuned in to Nina's table. Her mother's face turned scarlet, while dark thunderclouds hovered over her father's face. Clearly uncomfortable, the waitress went back to her work, placing a steaming hot steak in front of Nina's mother.

An elderly fellow from a nearby table got to his feet and stepped over. "Where did you see the plane crash, little lady?" he asked.

"She's making it up," her father insisted.

But Nina got to her feet. "It was up there on Arches National Park," she said. "Come here and I'll show you."

Despite her father's embarrassed protests, Nina led the old gentleman onto the deck where other late diners were busy with their meals. None of them looked up. No one else had seen a plane crash. But Nina knew what she'd seen, and she led the man over to the railing and pointed up and across the bend of the river. "It crashed right over there, above those cliffs," Nina insisted. "I saw a plane in the moonlight for just a few seconds. Then it disappeared."

"Was that all you saw?" he asked as Nina's father joined them.

"Nina, that's enough now," Maurice said angrily. "You are disturbing people's dinner."

"No, Dad, it was right up there. It disappeared, and then there was a big bunch of dust. I know it crashed," she insisted.

"Was there a flame or fire?" the elderly gentleman asked.

"No, just dust . . . or maybe it was smoke."

"Did you hear anything?"

"No, but I saw it," she said as tears filled her eyes. She knew that no one believed her. The old man turned and walked back inside. "Daddy, I really saw it," Nina said again through her tears. "Why doesn't anyone believe me?"

"Not another word about it," Maurice said. "Come inside and eat now. Your dinner is getting cold."

"But Dad—" she began again.

"Not another word! You say anything else about a plane wreck, and you will not be eating dinner. You are upsetting your mum with your little story, and I won't stand for it," he said.

"Fine. I don't want to eat. I'm not hungry anymore. I want to go back to our room," she said.

"Then go. You have your key, don't you?"

"Yes."

"Your mum and I will see you back there when we finish," Maurice said sternly. "And don't you say another word about your little plane crash, not to anyone. You've caused enough trouble already. Do you understand me?"

"Yes, Daddy," she said meekly and walked rapidly from the restaurant. Yes, she understood what he'd said, but she had no intention of keeping the story to herself. As soon as she was outside, she began to run. Her new friend Brock would believe her. And he would know what to do so that help could be sent to whoever was in that plane—if they were still alive.

* * *

She was still alive! That was Kaitlyn's amazing conclusion when she opened her eyes. The plane was sitting at an angle, and she could see that the left wing had been sheered off. The windows were shattered, and the body of the plane was crumpled. But she was alive! She began looking for a way to get out. In the front, Myler was also stirring. "Jace? You okay, Jace?" he asked.

Jace moaned but didn't speak.

"Kaitlyn, are you okay?" Myler called out.

"Yes, but we need to get out. I can smell fuel," she said.

Myler began frantically pushing on the mangled door to his right. When it eventually gave way, he clambered out. Then he reached back in, shoved the seat forward, and cleared a path for Kaitlyn. She had no desire to linger near the plane once her feet hit the ground. But in her haste, she stumbled and fell to her knees. Ignoring the pain, she forced herself to get up and move on. Finally, after stumbling along for what she felt was a safe distance, she stopped and looked back at the plane.

Myler had followed her, and the two of them watched for a minute. There was no explosion. Finally, Myler said, "I'm going back. You stay here."

She watched Myler return to the mangled hulk of metal. *Noble* was the word that crossed Kaitlyn's mind as Myler walked toward the wreckage. She knew from the looks that had crossed his face earlier that he hated Jace. But here he was, going back to help Jace exit the plane just as he had helped her.

Myler's head and part of his body disappeared inside the crushed cabin. He worked feverishly, probably trying to release Jace's seat belt, Kaitlyn thought. When he emerged a moment later, however, what she saw in Myler's hand was a wallet. Jace's, she presumed.

Kaitlyn knew she should be distancing herself from the crash site. But she was puzzled by Myler's actions. He looked around quickly, opened the wallet, and pulled out a stack of bills. Jace always carried a huge amount of cash, some in his wallet and some in a money clip in his right front pocket. Myler also removed what she thought might be a number of credit cards. It was hard to be sure with only the light of the moon to see by. Finally, he stuffed the money and cards into the front pocket of his pants and then partially reentered the plane. *Now he'll finally help Jace get out,* she thought.

But the next time he emerged, Myler had what looked like more money, folded into a money clip, the one she had remembered. All Myler was after was money, she realized. He stuffed it into his other front pocket, then reached inside again. This time he held a gun in his hand. He turned and started walking toward Kaitlyn.

"Get farther away," he yelled. "The plane's going to blow."

"It hasn't so far," she said.

"But it's going to now. Believe me, I know what I'm talking about," Myler insisted.

"But we've got to help Jace," she protested. "We can't just leave him in there. Please, help me get him out."

"Kaitlyn, you've got to understand. He's dead. I was just in there. I saw him. There's nothing more we can do for him," Myler said.

The lie had no sooner been uttered than they heard Jace's voice. "Help me!" he called. "I can't move. I'm pinned. Myler, you've got to get me out of here."

"Get moving, Kaitlyn," Myler ordered. "You're mine now. To the victor go the spoils, you know."

Kaitlyn couldn't believe what she had just heard. She stubbornly stood there. She detested Jace, but she couldn't be an accomplice to murder by just leaving him to die in the wreckage. She started back toward the plane.

Myler jumped ahead of her, waving his pistol in her face. "Stop right now," he demanded.

She stopped, her body trembling as she watched the plane.

"Turn around," Myler ordered.

She slowly turned away from the plane.

"Get marching. I'm not going to let you risk your life for him. He's not worth it."

"And if I try to go back?" she asked.

"I'll shoot you. Believe me, I don't want to, but I will if you force me to."

Tears flooded her eyes, but Kaitlyn followed Myler's orders. He had the gun. He was calling the shots. She turned and began to run as fast as her legs, the moonlight, and the rough terrain would allow. If she couldn't help Jace, then she would at least try to get away from Myler. She could hear his heavy footsteps following her. Jace's screams and cries for help continued to fill the night.

Finally, Myler came to a stop and turned back. Kaitlyn stopped her flight for a moment and looked back at him. She gasped as he lifted the gun and pointed it toward the crashed airplane.

* * *

Brock answered the knock on his door and was surprised to find Nina standing there. "Brock," she cried, "you've got to help. A plane has crashed on that mountain over there."

She rushed out of his room and began running. He followed, and after a few steps she stopped, breathing hard. Pointing and gasping for breath, she said, "It crashed over there. I saw it, but no one believes me."

He looked up at the towering red rock cliffs on the far side of the river. Then he looked higher, to their very tops. She continued to point. At that moment a huge ball of flame exploded into the darkness, followed a few seconds later by a loud concussion. "Nina, you're right," he said. "It just blew up. Let me get my phone. It's in my room. We need to call for help."

* * *

Kaitlyn froze at the almost simultaneous discharge of Myler's weapon and the fiery eruption as the wrecked plane exploded. She watched in horror as flames engulfed the plane and then burst high into the air. Laughing, Myler slowly lowered his pistol. "That'll teach you, you miserable, greedy lowlife!" he shouted back at the plane. "Now who's got the girl?"

Kaitlyn fled again. She had detested Jace, but this man, this murderer, was even worse. She had to get away from him. Paying no attention to direction or to her surroundings, she ran as fast as she could. She stumbled several times. Soon her knees were sore, and blood seeped through her torn pants. Her hands were scratched and also bleeding. But she kept going, ignoring the pain.

"Stop! You come back here or, so help me, I'll shoot your shapely legs right out from under you," Myler threatened.

She looked back. He had gained ground on her and was pointing his gun toward her. A sheet of flame exploded from the barrel, the sound of the shot punctuating the silence of the night. She both heard and saw the bullet as it struck the ground barely a foot away. She dropped down, making herself into a smaller target, and began to crawl. Looking left and right, Kaitlyn saw a large boulder and scrambled behind it. Then, as her heart thumped in her chest, she tried to listen. Myler was coming. She could hear his feet as they kicked rocks and smashed small branches. She was tempted to flee again, but she was afraid that if she got up to run, he would shoot. This time he might not miss, and then not only would she be crippled, but he would get his horrid hands on her.

She remained stationary, crouched behind the rock. She could tell Myler was moving slowly now and more carefully. She wasn't sure if he knew where she was or not.

"Come out, Kaitlyn, wherever you are. You can't get away from me. I always find what I search for. I'll find you. And when I do, I'll make sure you don't get away from me again."

She tried to slow her breathing as she felt around with one hand, glancing only briefly at the ground. She found a loose rock about the size of a softball. She picked it up with her right hand. It was not a great weapon, but it was her only chance if Myler found her. She had to wait, to strike him if he came too close, and then flee again.

Once more he called out. "Kaitlyn, you would never have been Jace's. Don't you see that? I'm the one who searched for you. I'm the one who forced you to come back to him. But I did it for the two of us, Kaitlyn, not for Jace. You and I are meant to be together. I don't want to have to hurt you to make that happen. Stand up now, and we can go together to find help." He lowered his voice slightly. "With your money and what I can get of Jace's, we can live in luxury on some island in the Caribbean," he said. His last words were almost unintelligible. "Wouldn't that be lovely, just you and me?"

Being with him would not be lovely. It would scarcely be living. She had been willing to sacrifice herself to Jace for the sake of the man who had saved her, for Brock Hankins and his girlfriend, but this was a different matter. She hadn't thought anything could be more horrible than being forced to marry Jace, but she now knew that living with Myler would be infinitely worse. She would die first. Jace was no longer a threat to Brock. Myler had taken care of that. He and his girlfriend were safe now. There was no longer a reason to sacrifice herself for anyone.

The footsteps continued to approach. They were too close. She began to wonder if Myler had been trying to fool her into thinking that he didn't know where she was hiding. He stepped forward again, just past her hiding place, only a couple of feet to her right. If he turned, he'd be able to see her.

Kaitlyn gripped the rock as Myler took another step. She drew in a deep breath and slowly, silently rose to her feet. Before Myler moved again, she lunged, smashing the back of his head with her primitive weapon. He stumbled forward and then fell face-first to the rocky ground. She was aware of the gun as it fell from his hands, but she didn't see where it landed. She didn't dare take the time to search for it. She had no idea how badly she'd injured him. She only knew that she had to get away before he could pursue her again.

Kaitlyn kept looking back as she raced away from Myler. She judged herself to be at least a hundred feet from him now. It wasn't nearly far enough, even though he hadn't yet moved. She took courage and pressed on, continually looking back as his shape became harder to decipher. If he was hard to see, she reasoned, so was she.

Five more minutes passed before she thought she saw him move. She was too far away now to be sure, so she watched for a moment. Then she was certain. His shadowy figure rose to its full height. She hunched down and moved on. Shortly, she came to a deep ravine. She carefully entered it and slowly made her way along its rocky floor. The going was rough, but at least she was concealed for the moment.

A voice pierced the night. "I'll get you. You can't escape from me."

Kaitlyn shuddered. Surely she would find help somewhere, somehow—wouldn't she?

* * *

No one doubted Nina now. She and Brock were not the only ones who had seen the flash of fire on the far horizon and heard the explosion a few seconds later. The old gentleman in the lodge who had followed her to the deck had seen it. Several people eating on the deck had also witnessed the explosion. Even one of the waitresses had seen it. Brock's was only the first 911 call. A search was soon underway.

Brock led Nina back inside to find her parents, both of whom apologized for not believing her story. The old gentlemen told her that she was a good girl and complimented her on how observant she was. The management of the restaurant insisted that she receive another plate of chicken nuggets to replace the ones that had become cold when her father had sent her away from the table. Brock sat with the family, getting acquainted as they ate. They seemed like nice folks, he thought, and he wondered why they neglected Nina so much.

Later, as he made his way back to his room to try to sleep, Brock could think only of Kaitlyn Glenn. He prayed that she was safe, wherever she was. He didn't think about Jodi until his phone rang around ten thirty. He wasn't sure what was going on when he saw that it was Jodi's number. *Has she decided to forgive me? If she has, what's next?*

CHAPTER 22

"HI, BROCK," SHE SAID.

"Hi, Jodi, how are you?"

"I'm fine, I guess. But it was terrible," she told him. "You can't even imagine what I've been through."

"I'm so sorry. I can't believe what happened. It makes me sick," Brock said awkwardly.

"Yeah, me too. Are you okay, Brock?"

"Yes, I'm fine."

"I'm glad."

She clammed up then, and Brock felt clumsy in the ensuing silence. Finally, he said, "A strange thing happened here tonight."

"Oh, what's that?" Jodi asked.

"A little English girl who's a guest here saw what she thought was a plane crashing above the red cliffs, the ones this place was named after," Brock explained to Jodi. "Nobody believed her at first, not even her parents. That's when she came and told me. Just after she got to my room, we looked up at where she thought she saw the plane go down, and there was a big explosion. We think it was the plane blowing up. They have searchers out there now. It's somewhere in Arches National Park."

"That's too bad," Jodi said, clearly unimpressed. "Brock, we need to talk."

"We're talking," he said.

"I mean about us," she said.

"What about us?" he asked.

"I'm really mad at you, Brock," she said. "If you hadn't helped Kaitlyn that night, I wouldn't have been embarrassed, hurt, threatened, or kidnapped."

"I'm sorry, Jodi. I certainly didn't mean for this to happen to you. But I still did what I had to do. I'd have done it for you if you'd been in her place," he said.

"I suppose you would. But I don't think you'd have gone looking to see if I was in trouble," she told him.

Brock felt a chill. "What do you mean?" he asked.

"I think you know what I mean," Jodi said. "I've been thinking about that night. I had a lot of time to think while I was lying on that horrible bed in that smelly motel room wondering if I was going to be killed or raped or something else."

"I'm so sorry," Brock said again.

"While I was lying there thinking all that time, I got to wondering about why you really walked that direction that night. I saw that girl smile at you when she went by," she revealed to him. "At least, after thinking about it, I figured it was you she was smiling at. And then I saw her frown. You went around that way to find her to see if she was okay."

"Yes, Jodi, I admit she looked really frightened. I didn't know if anyone else saw it, but I did, and I thought that since it would actually be easier to walk that way and keep out of the crowds, I could just see if, well, if something was happening. I feel like I was prompted to do that, Jodi. And I know I felt that way because she was actually in trouble. And as you recall, we did help her out of a dangerous situation," he said.

"You helped her. I was just there, Brock, because you took me there. But by being there, it put me in a dangerous situation. And I don't think it was fair to me for you to do that. Surely you can see how I feel," she said with a bitterness in her voice that hurt Brock.

"Jodi, I'm sorry you feel this way," he said. "But you've got to believe me—I didn't do it to hurt you. I did it because it was the right thing to do. And if that makes you angry, then I guess that's the way it is. And you've got to admit that at the time, you and I really didn't know each other very well. But even then, if I was put back in the same circumstances, I'd probably do the same thing."

"That's what I was afraid of," Jodi said. "And since I can't live with that, I guess you and I will just have to go our separate ways."

"Jodi—I'm not sure what to say," he said.

"Don't worry about it," she countered. "Thanks for the fun times, and no thanks for the hurt. Good-bye, Brock. I wish you the best."

"And I wish the same for you," he said. "I'm sorry it had to end this way. But I'm so grateful you're okay."

"I'm sorry, too, but that's the way it has to be. Good-bye, Brock."

Before he could slip in his own good-bye, Jodi abruptly ended the call.

For a long time that night, Brock thought about Jodi and all that had happened. Maybe he would never find the girl that he hoped to, the girl he had thought Jodi might turn out to be. He finally fell asleep thinking it was probably best that she'd called off their relationship.

He woke up early the next morning thinking about Kaitlyn Glenn, wondering where she was and whether she was okay.

* * *

Kaitlyn was not okay. She'd fallen asleep after spending several hours running from Myler. When the moon had gone down and it had become too dark to keep going, she'd hidden herself in another ravine, the seventh or eighth she'd come to. There, huddled against the rocky edge in an attempt to keep warm, she finally fell asleep. The sun was up now, and she painfully crawled to the top of the ravine and surveyed the surrounding area. She couldn't believe what a wild but beautiful place it was. In the distance stood huge stone arches. She suspected that she was in Utah and that the plane had crashed in Arches National Park. Although she had never been there before, she had seen pictures of the place. *This definitely could be Arches,* she told herself.

As enthralled as she was by the rugged beauty of the area, Kaitlyn recognized the peril of her situation. She wasn't exactly camping out as part of a well-earned vacation. She scoured the countryside searching for Myler. Although she couldn't see him, she was sure he was still after her. Thirsty and hungry, she simply needed to go on and hope she would eventually run into someone in the park who could help her.

She moved back down into the ravine and took a minute to examine herself. Through her torn pant legs she could see that her knees were covered with blood. Her hands were like raw meat. She could feel numerous other bruises, some of them extremely painful. She recognized that the more painful ones were probably from the plane wreck. As she thought of the crash, she knew that her surviving it was a miracle. She had to admit that Jace's skill as a pilot was probably part of the reason the crash hadn't been worse than it was.

We all would have survived if it hadn't been for Myler, Kaitlyn thought. *He intentionally shot the fuel-soaked plane, knowing Jace was alive.* That thought was enough to get her moving. The man who was now hunting her was a cold-blooded killer.

* * *

Myler was also on the move again. He knew that Kaitlyn had neither food nor water with her. He, on the other hand, had a couple of bottles of water and a jacket pocket full of candy bars. He clearly had the advantage. Furthermore, he knew approximately where she was, because he'd been tracking her since first light. He was fairly sure she had no idea where he was. Another advantage to him. She was frightened; he was determined. His advantage again. Not for one moment did Myler Keegan doubt that he would win this lopsided game. Kaitlyn and all her money would soon be his.

* * *

Brock ate a quick breakfast and headed for the stables and corrals early. He expected a group of guests to show up at about ten. Since he already knew how many were coming, he was busy getting their horses ready when he heard a sweet English voice. "Hi, Brock. Can I go riding this morning?"

He looked around and saw Nina's bright red hair framing her smiling, freckled face. Nina's father was with her. "I hope she won't be any bother, Mr. Hankins," he said.

"Of course not," Brock responded as the two of them walked over to where he was saddling a tall bay mare. "I know just the horse for you, Nina." She grinned up at him. "You can both help me catch him if you like. And I also have one that would be perfect for you, Mr. Schiller."

"No thanks. I think I'll check on my wife while Nina rides, if that's okay," Maurice said.

"Sure, that's fine," Brock said. "I'll personally look after Nina."

"Thanks," he said. Then he turned to his daughter. "You'll do exactly what Mr. Hankins says, won't you, Nina?"

"Of course. And you take good care of Mum."

After her father had left, Nina asked, "Brock, would it be okay if I call my nanny now? My dad said it would be a good time. He says it's about four in the afternoon in London."

"Sure, my phone is right here in my pocket," he said. "Maybe we can make the call as soon as I catch that horse for you. Then you can talk while I saddle him."

He couldn't help smiling a few minutes later as he overheard Nina talking to Ruby while he first curried and then saddled the horse he'd picked out for her. She was bubbling over with excitement as she told Ruby about the plane wreck she'd seen, about the tall red cliffs, about the flat they had in a bunkhouse, and on and on. Only when she drew to the end of her conversation did she grow sad again.

"Mum's very sick, Ruby," she finally confessed. "I think she's going to die. Daddy and Mum won't tell me anything about what's wrong. It makes Daddy mad if I ask about it. I just wanted to go home until I met Brock. He's a really nice man. He's going to take me for a ride on a horse now."

Nina was tired by the time they returned that afternoon. But she stayed around while Brock took care of the horses, unsaddling and rubbing down each of them before returning them, one at a time, to the corral. It was time-consuming work, but as tired as she was, Nina was still with him when he finished.

"What do you have to do now?" she asked.

"I'm going back to my room to take a break," he said. "Later I'll come back and feed the horses. Would you like me to walk you to your—uh, your flat?" he asked.

"That would be cool," she said.

* * *

The day was hot, and Kaitlyn stopped for a few moments' rest. Her mouth was so dry it felt like it had been stuffed with sand. She was hungry, too, but her thirst was worse. Her flight from Myler had been extremely difficult, taxing what few reserves she had left. As she leaned against a small shrub, a new sound reverberated across the wide expanse. When she finally identified the sound as the engine brakes on a distant truck, she thought her luck had changed.

What she discovered next was totally unexpected. Intent on getting closer to the faraway truck, she quickly walked straight ahead—right to the edge of a cliff. She had to lie on her stomach and inch her way forward to see how far down it was to the base of the cliff. She moaned helplessly upon discovering that she was hundreds of feet above the river valley below. She looked both ways and realized that the cliffs extended pretty much the same distance in either direction. After considering her options and venting her frustration, Kaitlyn decided to go east.

As she began her trek east, she spotted a figure in the distance to the north. *Myler Keegan.* Her thirst forgotten, she hurried on. If she could find a way down to the valley, she might be able to find safety.

* * *

As evening approached, Brock thought how lonely his life would be when Nina and her family left. He'd grown fond of the child in such a short time. Even as he was thinking about her, she tapped on his door. "Mum says there really was a plane crash," she announced proudly. "She saw it on the telly."

Brock hadn't heard anything further, but then he hadn't had either a radio or television on. Even now, he didn't access either but turned on his computer and began a search for the story. He soon found ample coverage of the crash.

With Nina looking over his shoulder, he read the account. The plane had indeed crashed and burned. Only one person had been found onboard, and that was the pilot. A check of the plane's serial number, which was still readable in the wreckage, revealed that it had been rented in the Denver area by a man identified as Roger Rodale from New York.

It was noted that the plane's latest flight plan had been filed from Cheyenne, Wyoming, to Las Vegas, Nevada, which would have taken it across the general area in which it had crashed. Brock wondered if the pilot had family, because that wasn't mentioned. As he continued to read through the article, he suddenly took a sharp breath. The previous flight plan of the plane had been from Denver to Cheyenne; the one prior to that had been from Des Moines to Denver; and the first plan filed by the pilot who had rented the plane had been from Denver to Des Moines.

Brock reread that portion of the article. It seemed like a huge coincidence that those particular cities had been stops for Roger Rodale, whoever he was. Then, near the end of the article, he read something that seemed the most peculiar of all. A witness in Cheyenne, where the plane had left Sunday evening, was adamant that he'd seen three people get onboard, not just the pilot. The others had been a large man and an attractive young woman. Authorities were puzzled since the remains of only one body had been found at the scene. They were assuming that the plane had made an unscheduled stop somewhere, and that was being checked out further.

Another puzzling aspect of the accident was the fact that a witness had seen the plane go down but that it had been several minutes later before several witnesses saw the explosion. Nina was not mentioned by name, but she grinned at Brock when he read that part of the account to her. Finally, the article indicated that both the Federal Aviation Administration and the National Transportation Safety Board would be further investigating the case. In the meantime, it was thought the small Cessna had experienced engine problems.

Brock searched for a few minutes for other accounts of the plane crash, but he found nothing that added significantly to the story. Nina left shortly after that, anxious to share with her parents the additional information she'd just learned.

After she was gone, Brock went to his computer again, thinking about Jodi and how she had been so insistent that they exchange e-mail messages each day. Hoping that maybe she'd forgiven him and sent him a message, he accessed his e-mail account. There was no message from her.

It's over, he thought as he exited the Internet. He felt sad that it was over, and yet, as Kaitlyn Glenn again came to his mind, Brock guessed it was okay. Not that he'd ever see Kaitlyn again. That seemed most unlikely, but maybe someone like her would come along someday.

Also most unlikely, he admitted to himself.

* * *

Kelvin had never worked so hard in his life. Trying to figure out where Kaitlyn had gone was mentally tiring. What kept him at it was greed—that, and his anger at Kaitlyn for not just handing over the money.

He was heading for Moab, Utah. His decision to drive there had been finalized after he'd figured out that the plane he was convinced was carrying his sister had crashed near there. He was almost certain that the pilot, a man identified as Roger Rodale, was in fact Jace Landry. Jace had made him some promises. Then, according to witnesses at the small airport where the plane had taken off, he'd loaded a young woman who looked like Kaitlyn and a man who fit the description of the one who had talked to Norman Thatcher in Denver. That was not what Jace had told Kelvin he would do when he caught up with Kaitlyn.

Kelvin had every reason to believe that only Jace had died in the crash. If so, that essentially concluded their business agreement. But he wasn't about to let the other man get away with his money, if that's what was happening. With Norman's help, he'd also learned that someone who had somehow interfered in Kaitlyn's affairs, a man by the name of Brock Hankins, was living and working at a place called the Red Cliff Lodge near Moab. Perhaps this Mr. Hankins would know something about what was going on with Kaitlyn. He intended to find out.

CHAPTER 23

SICK WITH FATIGUE, HUNGER, AND THIRST, Kaitlyn struggled on. It seemed like miles before she finally reached a canyon that led her down from the plateau. She thought for a while that the giant cliffs would go on forever, and it was a great relief to find the canyon. But it was steep, rugged, and not easy to climb down. When she finally descended, she found the mighty Colorado River. *And it was full of water.*

The water was wet! It was also dirty, but that didn't stop her from drinking. She policed herself however. Familiar with water's effect on horses that had suffered dehydration, she took only small sips at a time, allowing that to begin to refresh her parched body before taking more. Despite her ever-gnawing hunger, the water refreshed Kaitlyn. With renewed energy, she was ready to move on and confront a new challenge. Civilization!

Unfortunately, the yearned-for civilization that might yield help for her lay across the broad river. And for as far as she could see, there were no bridges. The thought of swimming the river, though not impossible, was daunting.

Kaitlyn had seen no signs of her pursuer for hours, although she had to assume he was still behind her somewhere. She could only hope he was way back there. Her confidence received a generous boost when her careful scrutiny of the landscape still turned up no sign of Myler.

From the cliffs, several hours earlier, she'd seen what looked like a lodge with a number of long, low outbuildings around it. Numerous cars were parked near each building. The entire complex was positioned a short distance from the water on the opposite bank of the river. Kaitlyn decided to work her way up the bank of the river until she was directly across from the buildings. At that point, she hoped she could attract someone's attention.

* * *

Myler had made good time. Despite the extra weight he carried around his midsection, he was a strong man. Although his ankle was still sore from his unplanned exit from the semi, he surprised himself with his ability to traverse the rough terrain. He knew that Kaitlyn was becoming increasingly weaker. As he had assessed earlier, most of the advantages were his. Kaitlyn was the trailblazer, and he was the follower. Many times he was able to take shortcuts, once he knew where she was heading. And he still had food and water while she had none.

He had a feeling there was something else working in his favor. He was certain that the girl seriously underestimated him. As the day and evening wore on, she'd looked behind her less often. He managed to keep out of sight enough that, even though he was closing the distance between them, he felt she was probably convinced that he was losing ground rather than gaining.

As they approached a large bend in the river—both the hunted and the hunter—Kaitlyn slowed down. Instinctively, Myler sped up. The sound of water lapping against the bank to their left was just loud enough to cover any errant noise he might inadvertently make as he steadily closed the gap between them.

* * *

Darkness had set in by the time Kaitlyn reached the large bend in the river. Across the river and slightly downstream, she could see the buildings she'd observed earlier. Fortunately, the moon was up and almost full. She stood on an exposed area of the riverbank and began to call for help. It soon became apparent that her pleas were fruitless. The people on the other side of the river, though visible to her as shadowy moving figures, simply could not hear her. The water, though flowing very slowly at this point in the river, still made noise, especially where it lapped against the bank beneath her.

For several minutes she stood there, wondering what to do. The thought of jumping into the water and fighting the current as she swam to the other side seemed impossible to her, even though she was a strong swimmer. Her ordeal of the past twenty-four hours had seriously weakened her. Although she had been willing, earlier that afternoon, to try to swim the width of the river, Kaitlyn now feared drowning almost more than she feared Myler. *She was so close and yet so very far away.*

Kaitlyn entertained several ideas as she stood watching the restless water. She remembered seeing, from the cliffs above, several rafts full of people going down the river. If she could make it through the night, surely she could attract the attention of someone in a raft the next morning, and then they could ferry her across. But did she have that much time? She simply didn't know.

She also considered going back upriver a short distance to find a large piece of driftwood that she could launch into the water and hold onto as she paddled her way across. At least that way she wouldn't be in as much danger of sinking, and the current would work to her advantage. Or she could also simply swim from farther upstream and not have to fight the current as much.

The only other option she could think of was to start hiking back along the river the way she'd already come, pass the canyon she had descended, and go on until she found a bridge. Surely these people occasionally crossed the river. There had to be a bridge out there somewhere. But would she run into Myler if she did that? She continued to rack her brain for other options.

At that moment Kaitlyn heard the distinct sound of a stick snapping, and when she turned, she knew her options had run out. Out of the tamarisk bushes directly behind her strolled Myler Keegan, his pistol in front of him and a grin on his ugly face. *How did he do it?* Panic swept over her. She'd thought she was far ahead of him, and yet here he was.

"Well, well, well, my pretty, what do we have here?" Myler taunted. "You underestimated me, didn't you?"

In despair, Kaitlyn admitted to herself that she had in fact done just that. She was trapped. She couldn't go right or left because of the tamarisk that grew there. This had been the only clear spot for some distance. She couldn't just charge through him. He not only had the weapon but also the greater size.

"Come on, Kaitlyn. It's just you and me now," he said. "Why fight it?"

"I would rather die first."

"No, you don't want to die," he said. "And I don't want to kill you. But I will scar that beautiful body of yours if I have to. Now, please, don't make me shoot you in the leg. That would be such a tragedy."

With his free hand, he reached into a pocket of his torn, soiled jacket. "Look," he said, withdrawing his hand, which clutched a Snickers bar. "I have more of these left." He laughed then. "You see, I had food while you had none. But I'll share it with you, Kaitlyn. Then we can find a place to cozy up for the night, and tomorrow we'll hail a raft. Someone will help us, *if you cooperate.*"

"Myler, I won't go with you."

"Oh, but you will," he said, waving the candy bar. He lowered the gun and grinned, his offensive mustache twitching. "Really, Kaitlyn, make it easy on yourself. You have no choice."

But Myler was wrong. Kaitlyn did have a choice. In one swift move she spun around and launched herself off the embankment and into the river.

* * *

Nina was standing at the same point where she'd been the night before when she'd seen the plane go down. Her parents were inside eating. After she'd finished her dinner, she'd asked permission to go out on the deck again. "Don't go getting into any trouble," her father had warned her. "We'd like a quiet night."

"I won't," she promised as she skipped outside.

For the past minute or so, she'd been watching the far bank of the river. She could see a figure there in the moonlight. She wondered if it was a deer, but it was hard to tell from this angle. Suddenly, it leaped into the river and disappeared beneath the surface. She heard a pop and saw a bright light immediately in front of a second figure, one she hadn't seen before. Mesmerized, she watched the river, wondering if she had just seen a hunter trying to shoot a deer. She hoped not, because she liked wildlife.

She kept her eyes on the water. After a few moments something bobbed to the surface. The pop and flash of light came again from the figure on the bank, and the figure disappeared beneath the water once more. She started hopping up and down on the deck as she clutched the rail, silently cheering the hunted on.

"Nina, we're done now. Let's go back to our flat," her father said from over her shoulder. "There won't be any more planes crashing tonight."

"I know," she said, "but I've been watching a deer." She almost mentioned the hunter, but remembering her father's warning earlier about not stirring trouble, she decided to keep it to herself.

"Where is the deer?" he asked, smiling.

"Over there," she said, waving toward the far side of the river. "Is it okay if I watch for a little while longer? I'll come back to the flat in a few minutes."

"Okay, but don't be too long," he said and went back inside.

Wishing she hadn't been distracted, Nina turned back toward the river. She looked first for the deer but couldn't see it. Then she looked beyond it at the hunter. To her amazement, the hunter also jumped into the river. She leaned more heavily against the wooden rail, fascinated and still silently cheering for the deer.

* * *

The current was stronger than Kaitlyn had guessed, and she was very literally swimming against it. Angling slightly upriver, she hoped to somehow reach the far bank somewhere near the lodge. Her muscles were screaming, and her leg, though burning, was still functioning. When she came up for air the first time after diving into the river, she had heard Myler fire his pistol. She'd felt a sting just above her right knee. She could hardly believe his bullet had struck her, but she fought off panic. She didn't think it would mean the difference between whether she made it or not. *It's just a little nick,* she told herself. Endurance, at this point, was the key.

Determined not to let Myler win, she offered a short prayer and dug deeper into her reserve of strength, willing her body to go beyond its normal bounds.

One stroke at a time, she swam on. Gradually, she could see the south bank drawing closer. *I can do it,* she told herself. *I can make it.*

* * *

Myler was fuming. He had underestimated the girl, just as she had underestimated him. But once again, he knew he had the advantage.

It's all about fuel for the body, he reminded himself. *I've had fuel; she hasn't.* He actually chuckled when he thought about the other ace up his sleeve—the trophies he'd won as high school swimming champ that once lined the mantel of his parents' living room.

* * *

Kaitlyn instinctively looked over her shoulder as she slowed for a moment to catch her breath. She couldn't believe it. Myler was also in the river, and he was closing the distance between them.

Trying to remain calm, she began stroking faster and with more power. She felt an adrenaline rush, her body suddenly seeming to glide effortlessly through the water.

* * *

Nina was breathless as she watched the action in the river. The moon was bright, reflecting off the water. Both the deer and the hunter were easier to see as they passed the midpoint of the river. For a short while she watched, almost breathlessly. The hunter was catching up. "No," she cried softly, so that no one would overhear her. "Swim faster, please. Don't let him catch you."

The race continued. Suddenly, as Nina watched the deer, three-fourths of the way across the river now, she was shocked to discover that the deer was not a deer but a person. She squinted to see more clearly to be sure of what she was really seeing. It took another couple of minutes before she concluded that it was a woman with long hair that was in the lead. It definitely was not a deer. Her sharp young mind digested what she was seeing and compared it with what she'd seen earlier. The conclusion she came to was very simple—childishly simple. *The hunter was trying to kill the woman.*

They were approaching the shore now. The hunter had almost caught up with the woman. Nina's body was taut as she watched the drama unfolding below. "Hurry! Swim faster!" she cried out.

Realizing that she'd spoken out loud, she quickly looked behind her. The rest of the guests had left the deck. She was alone. When she turned back, she spotted something else in the water. It looked like a log, and it was about to crash into the woman. "Look out!" she screamed at the very top of her lungs.

* * *

Kaitlyn could have sworn she heard a voice—a shrill, high-pitched voice. It was that voice that saved her. When she heard it, she looked up just in time to see a large log drifting straight toward her. She dived, going deep into the water just in time to avoid being hit. She surged forward and then resurfaced, shaking at the near hit but grateful that it had missed her. She looked back again, just in time to see the log strike Myler. She was flabbergasted that he'd been so close. He'd almost caught her. As adrenaline surged through her again, she spurted ahead, briefly eyeing a bushy tamarisk extending over the water only a short distance in front of her. *She had to make it to that shrub.*

* * *

Nina cheered when the log missed the woman but hit the man who was just behind her. For a minute he disappeared under the water. Then he came to the surface again. He was drifting downstream, but he was still trying to swim. The woman wasn't out of danger yet.

Nina's eyes again flickered to the swimming woman. Nina cheered as she reached a large thicket that was hanging over and touching the water. Then the woman disappeared beneath it. Impulsively, Nina turned and scrambled from the deck. She'd been to the edge of the river below the lodge several times since her family had arrived at the Red Cliff Lodge. She knew exactly where the stairway was, and she flew down it as fast as her legs would carry her. She raced across the grass, heading straight for the large bush where the woman had disappeared.

CHAPTER 24

NINA SCRAMBLED BENEATH THE HUGE bush, scratching her arms and face and getting covered with mud.

"Ma'am, are you there?" she called out as soon as she was at the water's edge. "Can I help you?"

Nina heard a muffled cry and saw a hand reach from the water. "Help me," a voice called from deep within the inky blackness beneath the foliage. Nina reached out, took the shadowy hand, and began to tug. Slowly, the woman came toward her. Then she gently shook free of Nina's hand and pulled herself from the water by grabbing onto the thick lower branches of the bush. Once out of the water, she flopped down beside Nina, her breath coming in great heaving gasps.

Nina tenderly patted the woman's face and waited while she caught her breath. "We better get you somewhere safe," she finally said. "That man is after you."

The woman slowly pulled herself upright. "Thank you for helping me," she said.

Nina worried about the man who had been trying, at least in her mind, to kill this woman. "We've got to hurry. Come with me. I'll take you to someone who will keep you safe."

The two of them worked their way from beneath the tamarisk and started up the steep embankment that led to the edge of the lawn. They hadn't quite made it to the lawn when someone very large and very angry stepped in front of them. It was the hunter.

"Kaitlyn, this is it, now. I've had enough of your nonsense. You're coming with me," he said, grabbing Kaitlyn roughly by the arm.

But Nina had different ideas. She launched herself at him, biting his hand so hard that he cursed and let the woman he called Kaitlyn loose. At the same time, he flung his arm, tossing Nina onto the ground, where she began to roll back down the embankment toward the river. By the time she'd stopped rolling and gotten to her feet, Kaitlyn was at her side, and the big man was coming toward them.

Nina reached down, grabbed a handful of sand, and threw it furiously into the man's face. The hunter grabbed at his eyes, rubbing them and swearing profusely. Kaitlyn grabbed Nina's hand, and the two of them ran up the embankment and across the lawn. Nina looked back as they rounded the edge of the lodge and started up the long stairway. The man was coming, but not very rapidly, and he was still rubbing his eyes.

"Where to now?" Kaitlyn asked breathlessly when they reached the top of the stairs.

"Follow me!" Nina shouted as she darted across the parking area. Twice Kaitlyn stumbled, and twice Nina helped her back to her feet. "Don't give up now. We're almost there," Nina encouraged her.

* * *

Kaitlyn had no idea why this little girl with the fetching English accent was helping her or where she had come from, but she was grateful. For one so young, she seemed quite clever, and so Kaitlyn, weak and running out of ideas of her own, followed without questioning. Soon they arrived at the front door of a small apartment near a corral full of horses. There Nina knocked loudly as Kaitlyn doubled over, her hands on her knees, her lungs still seeking air.

A light suddenly flooded the doorway, and Kaitlyn looked up. She couldn't believe what her eyes told her brain they were seeing. She shut them and opened them again. The picture was still the same. Standing before her, framed in the doorway, was the cowboy from Cheyenne. But this time he was without the identifying black hat.

"You've got to help her, Brock!" Nina was saying urgently. "There's a man trying to kill her."

For the second time, Kaitlyn was grateful for the quickness of Brock's decision-making in the face of danger. He grabbed Kaitlyn and pulled her into the room behind Nina. Then, in almost a single motion, he shut and locked the door. He turned to Kaitlyn and helped her to a bed in the far corner of the room beneath a window.

"Kaitlyn, is that you? Is it really you?" he asked.

"Yes, it's me. Myler is after me. I think I'm going to pass out," she said, and a warm, welcome darkness settled over her.

* * *

"You know her?" Nina asked as Brock tenderly placed a blanket over Kaitlyn's wet, shivering body.

"Yes, I know her. She's the reason I've been sad and worried. I didn't know how to find her or how to help her. Where did you find her?" he asked his little friend.

Nina began to recite her amazing tale while Brock dialed 911 on his cell phone. "We need officers and an ambulance," he said. "Did you say the man had a gun?" he asked Nina, causing her to pause in her recitation.

"Yes, he had a gun," Nina said. "He was shooting at her."

Brock relayed the information to the dispatcher and then gave her his address. After hanging up, he looked at Nina, who was finally concluding her narrative.

"This man, Nina," he interrupted, "where did you last see him?"

"On the grass behind the lodge. I threw sand in his face, and he was rubbing his eyes, but he was still trying to follow Kaitlyn," Nina answered, her bright eyes shining.

A loud thump on the door caused them both to jump. "He's here!" Nina cried in alarm.

"Quick! In there," Brock said, pointing to the bathroom. "Get down on the floor and stay there 'til I tell you to come out."

There was another thump. "I know you're in there, Kaitlyn. Let me in or I'll shoot the lock out."

Brock hadn't even brought a gun with him from Wyoming. The best weapon he had was a kitchen knife. He grabbed one and faced the door. Then, realizing that a bullet through the door would likely strike him, he scurried onto the bed, stepped across Kaitlyn, and shoved open the window that was above the bed. Impulsively, he scrambled back off the bed, trying not to bounce Kaitlyn too much. On the far side of the room, a lariat hung from a hook on the wall. He grabbed the rope and returned to the window.

He wiggled his way out of the window even as the man at the door continued to scream threats. Brock slipped around to the front and peered past the corner. He didn't know the man at the door. He wasn't wet. That didn't make sense. But it had to be the same guy. The man was holding a pistol and staring angrily at the door.

Brock wasn't the expert roper his friend and former missionary companion Dan was, but, having grown up on a ranch, he was still pretty good. He silently shook out a loop. Then, as the man at the door raised his gun and aimed at the lock, Brock stepped into the open and threw a hard, fast loop. It caught the intruder off guard, dropping over his head and shoulders and settling around his stomach. Brock jerked the rope hard, the gun fell from the man's hand, and then, when Brock jerked again, the man dropped awkwardly to the ground.

Moving like a mountain lion after its prey, Brock soon had him bound tightly. Then he opened the door with his key and stepped inside. "It's okay now, Nina," he called. "You can come out."

The little redhead bounced from the bathroom and ran to the door. She looked at the squirming, cursing man on the ground in puzzlement. "That's not him," she said.

"It's not?" Brock asked in surprise. "Then who is he?"

But he wasted no more time on words. Obviously, if this wasn't Myler, then Myler was still out there. He put the man's pistol in his own belt, pulled the intruder into the room, and once again shut and locked the door. To cut off the stream of profanity, he grabbed a bandana from a drawer and shoved it into the man's foul mouth. Then he tied him up tighter, making sure that he would not be a further threat to them until the police arrived.

Now I have a gun, Brock thought grimly as he straightened up from his task and felt the pistol where he'd shoved it between his belt and his jeans. *And I have a prisoner whose identity I don't even know.*

A groan from the bed drew Brock's attention. Kaitlyn was struggling to sit up. Tenderly, he touched her arm. "Lie back down," he instructed. "An ambulance is on its way. And until it comes, maybe I can take care of some of your cuts a little bit."

She shook her head. "Brock, I heard Kelvin," she said. "I swear I heard Kelvin."

"Who?" he asked.

"Kelvin. My stepbrother. He's also been after me. He's been trying to steal the inheritance my father left me."

"I see. Well, take a look over by the door," he said.

"Kelvin! What are you doing here?" she gasped weakly.

"He can't talk right now," Brock said mildly. "And until he is ready to behave himself and quit swearing and threatening people, he isn't going to be able to talk. I don't allow that kind of language in my modest apartment."

Brock was making an effort to appear relaxed and at ease, but he was worried. The man called Myler was still out there, and he posed a huge threat. Kaitlyn and Nina were both here, and they were in danger until Myler was arrested. He stepped over to the phone on the little table in the center of the room and picked it up. "We better call your folks, Nina. They must be worried sick about you."

"Oh, yes. I've been gone longer than I was supposed to be," she agreed.

"But tell them to wait to come get you until the police arrive and Myler has been arrested," he warned, handing the phone to the little girl.

Then Brock turned his attention to Kaitlyn.

"I must look awful," she said.

"Actually, I was thinking how pretty you are," Brock said.

"But I'm making a terrible mess of your bed. I'm sorry," she added.

"Forget it. I'm just relieved to have you here safe and in one piece," he told her as he began to inspect the cuts and bruises on her arms.

"I'm sorry about my stepbrother," she added, shaking her head in disgust as she glanced at Kelvin. "All he's ever wanted to do is take from others."

The man on the floor squirmed and grunted angrily. Brock ignored him, intent on tending to Kaitlyn's injuries.

Nina finished her conversation with her parents. "They wondered what was going on. I told them I'd tell them in a little while, that there was a bad man out there. I don't think they believed me," she said.

"They aren't going to try to come over now, are they?" Brock asked in alarm.

"I think so. At least my father is. Mum says he's stubborn."

"Excuse me, Kaitlyn," Brock said, gently squeezing her arm and smiling at her. "I'm afraid I'm not a very good host. But I'd better make another call."

He dialed the Schillers' room again, and Nina's mother answered. "This is Brock Hankins. May I speak with your husband?"

"I'm sorry, he just left. He's coming over to your flat to get Nina," she said.

There was no point in alarming her, so Brock simply said, "Thank you, I'll talk to him when he gets here."

Now he was extremely worried. He wished the police would show up. With a violent, angry man out there, everyone was in danger. He thought about slipping out his window as he had before, but he didn't feel right leaving Kaitlyn and Nina with Kelvin. He checked the gun he'd taken from Kaitlyn's brother. It was a 9 millimeter semiautomatic, and the clip was full. There was also a round in the chamber. He checked the safety, and when he discovered that it was off, he flipped it on. He didn't want the weapon accidentally firing. Then he stuck it back in his belt and again joined Kaitlyn at the bed.

She was sitting up now with her legs over the side. Nina was beside her, chattering like an angry chipmunk, her delightful English accent filling the room.

"Someone ought to be getting here pretty soon," Brock said. "Even if they had to come all the way from Moab, it shouldn't take much longer."

"I'm feeling stronger now," Kaitlyn said. "I'm just hungry and thirsty."

"I'm sorry. Let me get you something," he said. "Let's see what I have in my little fridge."

"Just a few bites of cereal or a piece of buttered bread would be fine for now," she said. "I think my stomach's shrunk."

"Brock, do you have a comb?" Nina asked.

"Sure," he said, fishing into his pocket. "What do you need a comb for?"

She rolled her eyes at him and then looked toward Kaitlyn. "I want to help her with her hair. Can't you see how bad she feels being so dirty and messy in front of her boyfriend?"

"Oh, Nina—" Kaitlyn began, blushing.

Brock cut her off. "You're right. You pretty her up while I fix her a bite to eat."

When Brock handed her a slice of bread a minute later, Kaitlyn said, "I'm sorry about Jodi getting hurt."

"Jodi?" Brock said, raising his eyebrows. "She's fine. She's home with her family. She doesn't have anything to say to me, but that's okay. She really isn't my type."

"Brock, I'm sorry. I didn't mean to interfere."

He touched her lips gently. "Shh. You didn't interfere. Everything's okay. You're here, and that's all I care about."

"Really?" she said, her blue eyes showing signs of life.

"Yes, really. You have no idea how glad I am."

He then found a washcloth and began to clean the cuts on her arms and knees as Nina ran the comb through her long hair.

"This is a strange cut here," Brock said. Her pants were torn, and he tore them a little more, exposing the wound that was just above her knee.

"It was a bullet," she said. "Myler shot at me when I dived into the river. I'm lucky it's not worse than it is or I couldn't have made it across the river."

"Myler. I wonder where he is. And I wonder where the cops are," he said, suddenly pulling his phone from his pocket. He dialed 911 again. When his call was answered, he said, "This is Brock Hankins again, at the Red Cliffs Lodge. We're in serious danger here and this young woman has been shot. When will someone be arriving?"

There was an uncomfortable pause. Finally the dispatcher responded. "There's been a bad truck wreck on a narrow spot in the canyon. It has the road completely blocked and there's no way around. They're trying to move it so they can get through. But it's going to be a while. There's nothing more they can do right now. The ambulance is stuck there, too."

"Isn't there another way to get here?" he asked urgently. "We need help."

"Yes, there's a road over the mountain, past Castle Valley, and another one that connects with I-70. There are officers coming toward you from both roads, but it will take them some time. It's a long way around. I'm sorry. There's nothing we can do beyond what we're doing. Does the injured woman need immediate attention?"

"Nothing that I can't provide," he said. "It's the armed killer outside that I'm worried about. Thank you for all you're doing. I guess we'll just have to wait, but if there's any way you can speed things up, we'd sure appreciate it." He was about to mention Kelvin Glenn, who was lying bound on his floor, but he decided against it. Kelvin was no danger to them now. *But Myler Keegan was.*

* * *

Myler had finally figured out where the redheaded brat and Kaitlyn had gone. This was it. He was going to take Kaitlyn, and he didn't care who got hurt in the process.

He stood back for a moment, eyeing the small apartment. His eyes still stung from the sand the brat had thrown, but at least he could see again. He'd lost a lot of time when he had to go back to the river and wash his eyes. He had his pistol in his hand. It had stayed safely in the holster on his belt as he swam across the river. It was time to use it now. He looked around and then moved stealthily toward the door of the apartment. He was quite certain Kaitlyn was in there.

A large cottonwood tree stood near the apartment. He hesitated beside it. Then he heard a sound, something soft but directly behind him. He began to turn, but he was too late to stop the descending blow. He crumpled and fell to the ground.

* * *

A loud pounding on the door began again. Brock once more sent Nina scrambling for the bathroom and directed Kaitlyn to lie on the floor. "Let me in, please," a strongly accented male voice called out.

Relief flooded over Brock as he dashed to the door and flung it open. "Get in here, quick, there's a killer out there."

"I think he's unconscious," Nina's father said. "And here's his gun."

Thoroughly surprised, Brock nonetheless moved quickly. "Show me where he is," he ordered.

Maurice simply turned and pointed. "He's right there. I jumped behind that tree when I heard him coming. I was carrying a heavy walking stick. He stopped beside the tree, and I saw his gun. That's when I hit him and took his gun," he said as he followed Brock to the fallen man.

"That's him. That's Myler," Kaitlyn said.

She'd followed Brock out of the apartment and was standing on unsteady feet beside him. He turned toward her. "Good. It looks like he's out cold," he said.

"Where is Nina?" Maurice asked urgently.

"She's in the bathroom. Why don't you go get her? She's a gem, that girl is," Brock said without taking his eyes from Kaitlyn's. *You're a gem, too*, he was thinking.

Maurice hurried into the apartment, and Brock reached out and took Kaitlyn into his arms. "I know this probably seems crazy because I don't really even know you, but I've never been so glad to see anyone in my life. I've been worried sick about you."

She smiled as she gently leaned into him. "I've thought about you a million times the past few days. Thank you for being here for me," she said.

EPILOGUE

Seven months later

"WHO IS IT, DEAR?" KAITLYN asked after Brock answered the phone.

"It's Nina, calling from London," he said. "She says she has news she wants both of us to hear." Then into the phone he told Nina that Kaitlyn was going to get the other phone so they could all talk.

Nina was excited, and once both Brock and Kaitlyn were on the line, she made her announcement. "I have a new little baby brother," she gushed.

The newly married couple had been expecting the call. The day after all the terror had come to an end, Brock had spoken with Maurice, and he'd told Brock that the mysterious illness his wife had been experiencing was a most unexpected pregnancy. It was not some dreaded disease that made her so ill; it was morning sickness, and she'd had a very bad case of it.

Maurice had been angry at first. He didn't figure he had time for more children. But he explained that the experience Nina, Brock, and Kaitlyn had been through was a wake-up call to him. He and his wife had talked a long time after Nina had gone to sleep following the arrest of Kelvin and Myler, and they had decided to be parents first. Whatever else they wanted to do or to be would have to take second place.

A few months later, after Brock and Kaitlyn announced their plans to marry, Maurice offered to pay for their honeymoon if they would travel to London and visit them. Brock had argued that they shouldn't have to pay for what was his expense, but Maurice insisted. "You were the influence that changed our lives, that helped us focus on what's really important. It's the least we can do," he said.

Brock, after discussing it with Kaitlyn, ultimately accepted the offer. And they enjoyed a wonderful time in England. After returning home, they'd rented an apartment, and Brock went back to school. Tony B was kept in a rented pasture nearby, and Kaitlyn seldom went a day without seeing him. But she didn't race anymore. Barrel racing no longer held the appeal it had earlier. Her life was full enough being the wife of the man she'd fallen in love with as she rode her horse in a rodeo arena and saw his smiling face in the stands.

ABOUT THE AUTHOR

CLAIR M. POULSON RETIRED after twenty years in law enforcement. During his career he served in the U.S. Military Police Corps, the Utah Highway Patrol, and the Duchesne County Sheriff's Department, where he was first a deputy and then the county sheriff. He currently serves as a justice court judge for Duchesne County, a position he has held for eighteen years. His nearly forty-year career working in the criminal justice system has provided a wealth of material from which he draws in writing his books.

Clair has served on numerous boards and committees over the years. Among them are the Utah Judicial Council, an FBI advisory board, the Peace Officer Standards and Training Council, the Utah Justice Court Board of Directors, and the Utah Commission on Criminal and Juvenile Justice.

Other interests include activity in the LDS Church, assisting his oldest son in operating their grocery store, ranching with his oldest son and other family members, and raising registered Missouri Fox Trotter horses.

With this latest book, Clair has published sixteen novels, many of them bestsellers.

Clair and his wife, Ruth, live in Duchesne and are the parents of five married children. They have eighteen grandchildren.